Fifty Favourite
Fairy Tales

FIFTY FAVOURITE
FAIRY TALES

Chosen from the Colour Fairy Books of
ANDREW LANG by KATHLEEN LINES
With illustrations by MARGERY GILL

LEOPARD

This edition published in 1995 by Leopard Books,
a division of Random House UK Ltd,
20 Vauxhall Bridge Road, London SW1V 2SA

The Colour Fairy Books of Andrew Lang
were first published between
1889 and 1910.
This selection was first published as a
Nonesuch Cygnet in 1963, and reissued
under the Bodley Head imprint in 1973.

ISBN 0 7529 0165 6

Printed in Great Britain

The Fifty Tales

The Fifty Tales

Blockhead-Hans

FAR AWAY in the country, in an old manor-house, lived an old squire. He had two sons who thought themselves so clever, that if they had known only half of what they did know, it would have been quite enough. They both wanted to marry the King's daughter, for she had proclaimed that she would take for her husband the man who knew best how to give a good account of himself.

The two sons spent a week in preparation. This was all the time allowed them; but, indeed, it was quite long enough, for they both had had a good education, and everyone knows how useful that is. One of them knew the whole Latin dictionary off by heart, and also the daily paper for the last three years, so that he could repeat it all backwards or forwards as you pleased. The other had worked on municipal law and knew by heart what every member of the corporation ought to know, so that he thought he could quite well give his opinion on matters of state. He knew, besides this, how to embroider braces with scrolls and roses and other flowers, for he was very ready with his fingers.

'I shall win the King's daughter!' they both cried.

Their old father gave them each a fine horse. The one who knew the dictionary and the daily paper by heart had a black horse; while the other who was so clever at corporation law had a milk-white one. Then they oiled the corners of their mouths so that they might be able to speak more fluently. All the servants stood in the courtyard to see them mount their steeds, and here by chance came the youngest brother; for the squire had three sons, but the third did not count for much, as he was not nearly so learned as his brothers, and he was generally called 'Blockhead-Hans'.

'Oh, oh!' said Blockhead-Hans. 'Where are you off to, all in your Sunday-best clothes?'

'We are going to Court, to woo the Princess with our fine words. Don't you know what is known throughout all the countryside?' And they told him all about it.

'Hurrah! I'll go too!' cried Blockhead-Hans; but his brothers laughed at him and rode off.

'Dear father!' cried Blockhead-Hans, 'I must have a horse too. A great desire for marriage has seized me! If she will have me, she *will* have me, and if she won't have me, then I'll marry her all the same.'

'What nonsense!' said the old man. 'I will not give you a horse. *You* can't speak; *you* don't know how to choose your words. Your brothers! Ah! they are very clever lads!'

'Well,' said Blockhead-Hans, 'if I can't have a horse, I'll ride the billy-goat. He is my own, and he can carry me, I know.'

So he sat astride the goat, struck his heels into its side, and went rattling down the high-road like a hurricane.

Cloppetty clop! What a ride! 'Here I come!' bawled Blockhead-Hans, so loudly that the echoes were roused far and near. But his brothers rode silently on ahead. They were not talking because they were thinking over all the clever things they were going to say, for everything had to be thought out.

'Hullo, hullo!' shouted Blockhead-Hans, 'here I am! Just look what I found on the road!' – and he showed them a dead crow which he had picked up.

'Blockhead!' said his brothers, 'what are you going to do with that?'

'With the crow? I shall give it to the Princess!'

'Do so, certainly!' they said, laughing loudly and riding on.

'Slap! bang! here I am again! Look what I have just found! You don't find such things every day on the road!'

And the brothers turned round to see what in the world he could have found.

'Blockhead!' said they, 'that is an old wooden shoe! Are you going to send that, too, to the Princess?'

'Of course I shall!' returned Blockhead-Hans; and the brothers laughed and rode on a good way.

'Slap! bang! here I am!' cried Blockhead-Hans; 'better and better – it is really famous!'

'What have you found now?' asked the brothers.

'Oh,' said Blockhead-Hans, 'it is really too good! How pleased the Princess will be!'

'Why!' said the brothers, 'this is pure mud, and straight from the ditch.'

'Of course it is!' said Blockhead-Hans, 'and it is the best kind! Look how it runs through one's fingers!' and, so saying, he filled his pocket with mud.

But the brothers now rode on so fast that dust and sparks flew all around, and they reached the gate of the town a good hour before Blockhead-Hans. Here the suitors were numbered according to their arrival, and they were ranged in rows, six in each row, and they were so tightly packed that they could not move their arms. This was a very good thing, for otherwise they would have torn each other in pieces, merely because the one was in front of the other.

All the country people were standing round the King's castle, and were crowded together in thick masses against the windows to watch the Princess receive the suitors; but as each one came into the room all his fine phrases went out like a candle!

'No good!' the Princess would say. 'Away with him!'

At last it was the turn of the brother who knew the dictionary by heart. But he did not know it any longer; he had quite forgotten it while waiting in the queue. And the floor creaked, and the ceiling was all made of glass mirrors, so that he saw himself standing on his head. And by the windows stood three reporters and an editor, who wrote down everything that was said, so that it could all go into the newspaper and be sold at the street corners for a penny. It was dreadful, and they had made up such a fire that the heat was stifling.

'It is hot in here, isn't it?' said the first brother.

'Of course it is! My father is roasting young chickens to-day!' said the Princess.

'Oh . . . ah . . .' There he stood like an idiot. He was not prepared for such a remark; he did not know what to answer, although he wanted to say something witty. 'Er . . . ah . . .'

'No good!' said the Princess. 'Take him out!' And out he had to go. Now the other brother entered.

'How hot it is!' he said.

'Of course! We are roasting young chickens to-day!' said the Princess.

'How do you – um!' he said, and the reporters wrote down 'How do you – um.'

'No good!' said the Princess. 'Take him out!'

Then Blockhead-Hans came in; he rode his billy-goat right into the hall.

'I say! How roasting hot it is here!' said he.

'Of course! I am roasting young chickens to-day!' said the Princess.

'That's good!' replied Blockhead-Hans; 'then can I roast a crow with them?'

'With the greatest of pleasure!' said the Princess; 'but have you anything you can roast it in? for I have neither pot nor pan.'

'Oh, rather!' said Blockhead-Hans. 'Here is a cooking implement with tin rings,' and he drew out the old wooden shoe, and laid the crow in it.

'That will be quite a meal!' said the Princess; 'but what shall we do for gravy?'

'I've got that in my pocket!' said Blockhead-Hans. 'I have more than enough!' and he poured some mud out of his pocket.

'I like you!' said the Princess. 'You have a ready answer, and you can speak up for yourself. I will marry you. But do you realise that every word we are saying and have said has been taken down and will be in the newspaper to-morrow? Look, there by the windows, do you see, there are three reporters and an editor, and the old editor is the worst, for he doesn't understand a thing!' But she only said this to frighten Blockhead-Hans. And the reporters giggled, and each dropped a blot of ink on the floor.

'Ah! are those the great people?' said Blockhead-Hans. 'Then I will give the editor the best!' So saying, he turned his pockets inside out, and threw the mud right in his face.

'That was neatly done!' said the Princess. 'I couldn't have done it; but I'll soon learn!'

So Blockhead-Hans became king; he got a wife and a crown, and sat on the throne. All this we have still damp from the editor's newspaper, so it may not be perfectly true.

The Boy who found Fear at last

ONCE UPON a time there lived a woman who had one son whom she loved dearly. The little cottage in which they dwelt was built on the outskirts of a forest, and as they had no neighbours, the place was very lonely, and the boy was kept at home by his mother to bear her company.

They were sitting together on a winter's evening, when a storm suddenly sprang up, and the wind blew the door open. The woman started and shivered, and glanced over her shoulder as if she half expected to see some horrible thing behind her. 'Go and shut the door,' she said hastily to her son, 'I feel frightened.'

'Frightened?' repeated the boy. 'What does it feel like to be frightened?'

'Well – just frightened,' answered the mother. 'A fear of something, you hardly know what, takes hold of you.'

'It must be very odd to feel like that,' replied the boy. 'I will go through the world and seek fear till I find it.' And the next morning, before his mother was out of bed, he had left the forest behind him.

After walking for some hours he reached a mountain, which he began to climb. Near the top, in a wild and rocky spot, he came upon a band of fierce robbers, sitting round a fire. The boy, who was cold and tired, was delighted to see the bright flames, so he went up to them and said, 'Good greeting to you, sirs,' and wriggled himself in between the men, till his feet almost touched the burning logs.

The robbers stopped drinking and eyed him curiously, and at last the captain spoke.

'No caravan of armed men would dare to come here, even the very birds shun our camp, and who are you to venture in so boldly?'

'Oh, I have left my mother's house in search of fear. Perhaps you can show it to me?'

'Fear is wherever *we* are,' answered the captain.

'But *where*?' asked the boy, looking round. 'I see nothing.'

'Take this pot and some flour and butter and sugar over to the churchyard which lies down there, and bake us a cake for supper,' replied the robber. And the boy, who was by this time quite warm, jumped up cheerfully, and slinging the pot over his arm, ran down the hill.

When he got to the churchyard he collected some sticks and made a fire; then he filled the pot with water from a little stream close by, and mixing the flour and butter and sugar together, he set the cake on to cook. It was not long before it grew crisp and brown, and then the boy lifted it from the pot and placed it on a stone, while he put out the fire. At that moment a hand stretched from a grave, and a voice said:

'Is that cake for me?'

'Do you think I am going to give to the dead the food of the living?' replied the boy, with a laugh. And giving the hand a tap with his spoon, and picking up the cake, he went up the mountain side, whistling merrily.

'Well, have you found fear?' asked the robbers when he held out the cake to the captain.

'No; was it there?' answered the boy. 'I saw nothing but a hand which came from a grave, and belonged to someone who wanted my cake, but I just rapped the fingers with my spoon, and said it was not for him, and then the hand vanished. Oh, how nice the fire is!' And he flung himself on his knees before it, and so did not notice the glances of surprise cast by the robbers at each other.

'There is another chance for you,' said one of the robbers at length. 'On the other side of the mountain lies a deep pool; go to that, and perhaps you may meet fear on the way.'

'I hope so, indeed,' answered the boy. And he set out at once.

He soon beheld the waters of the pool gleaming in the moonlight, and as he drew near he saw a tall swing standing just over it, and in the swing a child was seated, weeping bitterly.

'That is a strange place for a swing,' thought the boy; 'but I wonder what he is crying about.' And he was hurrying on towards the child, when a maiden ran up and spoke to him.

'I want to lift my little brother from the swing,' cried she, 'but it is so high above me, that I cannot reach. If you will get closer to the edge of the pool, and let me mount on your shoulder, I think I can reach him.'

'Willingly,' replied the boy, and in an instant the girl had climbed to his shoulders. But instead of lifting the child from the swing, as she could easily have done, she pressed her feet so firmly on each side of the youth's neck, that he felt that in another minute he would be choked, or else fall into the water beneath him. So, gathering up all his strength, he gave a mighty heave, and threw the girl backwards. As she touched the ground a bracelet fell from her arm, and this the youth picked up.

'I may as well keep it as a remembrance of all the queer things that have happened to me since I left home,' he said to himself, and turning to look for the child, he saw that both it and the swing had vanished, and that the first streaks of dawn were in the sky.

With the bracelet on his arm, the youth started for a little town which was situated in the plain on the farther side of the mountain, and as, hungry and thirsty, he entered its principal street, a merchant stopped him, and said, 'Where did you get that bracelet? It belongs to me.'

'No, it is mine,' replied the boy.

'It is not. Give it to me at once, or it will be the worse for you!' cried the merchant.

'Let us go before a judge, and tell him our stories,' said the boy. 'If he decides in your favour, you shall have it; if in mine, I will keep it!'

To this the merchant agreed, and the two went together to the great hall, in which the kadi was administering justice. He listened very carefully to what each had to say, and then pronounced his verdict. Neither of the two claimants had proved his right to the bracelet, therefore it must remain in the possession of the judge till its fellow was brought before him.

When they heard this, the merchant and the boy looked at each other, and their eyes said, 'Where are we to go to find the other one?' But as they knew there was no use in disputing the decision, they bowed low and left the hall of audience.

Wandering he knew not whither, the youth found himself on the sea-shore. At a little distance was a ship which had struck on a hidden rock, and was rapidly sinking, while on deck the crew were gathered, with faces as white as death, shrieking and wringing their hands.

'Have you met with fear?' shouted the boy. And the answer came above the noise of the waves.

'Oh, help! help! We are drowning!'

Then the boy flung off his clothes, and swam to the ship, where many hands were held out to draw him on board.

'The ship is tossed hither and thither, and will soon be sucked down,' cried the crew. 'Death is very near, and we are frightened!'

'Give me a rope,' said the boy in reply, and he took it and made it safe round his body at one end, and to the mast at the other, and sprang into the sea. Down he went, down, down, down, till at last his feet touched the bottom, and he stood up and looked about him. There, sure enough, a sea-maiden with a wicked expression was tugging hard at a chain which she had fastened to the ship with a grappling iron, and was dragging it bit by bit beneath the waves. Seizing her arms in both his hands, he forced her to drop the chain, and the ship above remaining steady, the sailors were able gently to float her off the rock. Then taking a rusty knife from a heap of sea-weed at his feet, he cut the rope round his waist and fastened the sea-maiden firmly to a stone, so that she could do no more mischief, and bidding her farewell, he swam back to the beach, where his clothes were still lying.

The youth dressed himself quickly and walked on till he came to a beautiful shady garden filled with flowers, and with a clear little stream running through it. The day was hot, and he was tired, so he entered the gate, and seated himself under a clump of bushes covered with sweet-smelling red blossoms, and it was not long before he fell asleep. Suddenly a rush of wings and a cool breeze awakened him, and raising his head cautiously, he saw three doves plunging into the stream. They splashed joyfully about, and shook themselves, and then dived to the bottom of a deep pool. When they appeared again they were no longer three doves, but three beautiful damsels, bearing between them a table made of mother-of-pearl. On this they placed drinking cups fashioned from pink and green shells, and one of the maidens filled a cup from a crystal flagon, and was raising it to her mouth, when her sister stopped her.

'To whose health do you drink?' asked she.

'To the youth who prepared the cake, and rapped my hand with the spoon when I stretched it out of the earth,' answered the maiden, 'and was never afraid as other men were! But to whose health do you drink?'

'To the youth on whose shoulders I climbed at the edge of the pool, and who threw me off with such a jerk, that I lay unconscious on the ground for hours,' replied the second. 'But you, my sister,' added she, turning to the third girl, 'to whom do you drink?'

'Down in the sea I took hold of a ship and shook it and pulled it till it would soon have been lost,' said she. And as she spoke she looked quite different from what she had done with the chain in her hands, seeking to work mischief. 'But a youth came, and freed the ship and bound me to a rock. To his health I drink,' and they all three lifted their cups and drank silently.

As they put their cups down, the youth appeared before them.

'Here am I, the youth whose health you have drunk; and now give me the bracelet that matches a jewelled band which of a surety fell from the arm of one of you. A merchant tried to take it from me, but I would not let him have it, and when I appealed to the kadi, he kept my bracelet till I could show him its fellow. And I have been wandering hither and thither in search of it, and that is how I have found myself in such strange places.'

'Come with us, then,' said the maidens, and they led him down a passage into a hall, out of which opened many chambers, each one of greater splendour than the last. From a shelf heaped up with gold and jewels the eldest sister took a bracelet, which in every way was exactly like the one which was in the judge's keeping, and fastened it to the youth's arm.

'Go at once and show this to the kadi,' said she, 'and he will give you the fellow to it.'

'I shall never forget you,' answered the youth, 'but it may be long before we meet again, for I shall never rest till I have found fear.' Then he went his way, and won the bracelet from the kadi. After this, he again set forth in his quest of fear.

On and on walked the youth, but fear never crossed his path, and one day he entered a large town, where all the streets and squares were so full of people, he could hardly pass between them.

'Why are all these crowds gathered together?' he asked of a man who stood next him.

'The King of this country is dead,' was the reply, 'and as he had no children, it is needful to choose a successor. Therefore each morning one of the sacred pigeons is let loose from the tower yonder, and on whomsoever the bird shall perch, that man is our king. In a few minutes the pigeon will fly. Wait and see what happens.'

Every eye was fixed on the tall tower which stood in the centre of the chief square, and the moment that the sun was seen to stand straight over it, a door was opened, and a beautiful pigeon, gleaming with pink and grey, blue and green, came rushing through the air. Onward it flew, onward, onward, till at length it rested on the head of the boy. Then a great shout arose:

'The King! the King!' but as he listened to the cries, a vision, swifter than lightning, flashed across his brain. He saw himself seated on a throne, spending his life trying, and never succeeding, to make poor people rich; miserable people happy; bad people good; never doing anything he wished to do, not able even to marry the girl that he loved.

'No! no!' he cried, hiding his face in his hands; but the crowds who heard him thought he was overcome by the grandeur that awaited him, and paid no heed.

'Well, to make quite sure, let fly more pigeons,' said they, but each pigeon followed where the first had led, and the cries arose louder than ever:

'The King! the King!' And as the young man heard, a cold shiver, that he knew not the meaning of, ran through him.

'This is fear whom you have so long sought,' whispered a voice, which seemed to reach his ears alone. And the youth bowed his head as the vision once more flashed before his eyes, and he accepted his destiny, and made ready to pass his life with fear beside him.

The Brave Little Tailor

ONE SUMMER'S day a little tailor sat on his table by the window in the best of spirits, and sewed for dear life. As he was sitting thus a peasant woman came down the street, calling out, 'Good jam to sell, good jam to sell.' This sounded sweetly in the tailor's ears; he put his frail little head out of the window, and shouted, 'Up here, my good woman, and you'll find a willing customer.'

The woman climbed up the three flights of stairs with her heavy basket to the tailor's room, and he made her spread out all the pots in a row before him. He examined them all, lifted them up and smelt them, and said at last, 'This jam seems good, weigh me four ounces of it, my good woman; and even if it's a quarter of a pound I won't stick at it.' The woman, who had hoped to make a good sale, gave him what he wanted, but went away grumbling wrathfully.

'Now heaven bless this jam for my use,' cried the little tailor, 'and it shall sustain and strengthen me.' He fetched some bread out of a cupboard, cut a round off the loaf, and spread the jam on it. 'That won't taste amiss,' he said; 'but I'll finish that waistcoat first before I take a bite.' He placed the bread beside him, went on sewing, and in the lightness of his heart kept on making his stitches bigger and bigger.

In the meantime the smell of the sweet jam rose to the ceiling, where many flies had collected, and attracted them to such an extent that they swarmed down on to it. 'Ha! who invited you?' said the tailor, and chased the unwelcome guests away. But the flies, who didn't understand his words, refused to let themselves be warned off, and returned again in even greater numbers. At last the little tailor, losing all patience, reached for a duster, and exclaiming, 'Wait, and I'll give it to you,' he beat them mercilessly with it. When he left off he counted the slain, and no fewer than seven lay dead before him with outstretched legs.

'What a desperate fellow I am!' said he, and he was filled with admiration at his own valour. 'The whole town must know about this;' and in great haste the little tailor cut out a girdle, hemmed it, and embroidered on it in big letters, 'SEVEN AT A BLOW'. 'What did I say, the town? No, the whole world shall hear of it,' he said; and his heart quivered with joy, like a lamb's tail.

The tailor strapped the girdle round his waist and resolved to go out into the wide world, for he considered his workroom too small a field for his prowess. Before he set out he looked round about him, to see if there was anything in the house he could take with him on his journey; but he found nothing except an old cheese, which he put in his pocket. In front of the house he observed a bird that had been caught in the thicket, and this he put into his pocket beside the cheese. Then he went on his way merrily, and being light and agile he did not quickly tire.

His way led up over a mountain on top of which sat a powerful giant, who was calmly surveying the landscape. The little tailor went up to him, and greeting him cheerfully said, 'Good-day, friend; here you sit at your ease viewing the whole wide world. I'm just on my way there. What do you say to accompanying me?' The giant looked contemptuously at the tailor, and said, 'What a poor wretched little creature you are!' 'That's a good joke,' answered the little tailor, and unbuttoning his coat he showed the giant the girdle. 'There now, you can read what sort of a fellow I am.'

The giant read, 'SEVEN AT A BLOW'; and thinking they were human beings the tailor had slain, he conceived a certain respect for the little man. But first he thought he'd test him, so taking up a stone in his hand, he squeezed it till some drops of water ran out. 'Now you do the same,' said the giant, 'if you really wish to be thought strong.' 'Is that all?' said the little tailor; 'that's child's play to me.' So he put his hand in his pocket, brought out the cheese, and pressed it till the whey ran out. 'My squeeze was in sooth better than yours,' said he. The giant didn't know what to say, for he couldn't have believed it of the little fellow.

To prove him again, the giant lifted a stone and threw it so high that the eye could hardly follow it. 'Now, my little pigmy, let me see you do that.' 'Well thrown,' said the tailor; 'but, after all, your stone fell to the ground; I'll throw one that won't come down at all.' He put his hand in his pocket again, and grasping the bird, he threw it up into the air. The bird, enchanted to be free, soared up into the sky, and flew away never to return. 'Well, what do you think of that little piece of business, friend?' asked the tailor. 'You can certainly throw,' said the giant; 'but now let's see if you can carry a proper weight.'

With these words he led the tailor to a huge oak tree which had been felled to the ground, and said, 'If you are strong enough, help me to carry the tree out of the wood.' 'Most certainly,' said the little tailor; 'just you take the trunk on your shoulder; I'll bear the top and branches, which is certainly the heaviest part.' The giant laid the trunk on his shoulder, but the tailor sat at his ease among the branches; and the giant who couldn't see what was going on behind him, had to carry the whole tree, and the little tailor into the bargain. There he sat behind in the best of spirits, lustily whistling a tune, as if carrying the tree were mere sport. The giant, after dragging the heavy weight for some time, could get on no further, and shouted out, 'Hi! I must let

the tree fall.' The tailor sprang nimbly down, seized the tree with
both hands as if he had carried it the whole way, and said to the giant,
'Fancy a big lout like you not being able to carry a tree!'

They continued to go on their way together, and as they passed by
a cherry tree the giant grasped the top of it, where the ripest fruit
hung, gave the branches into the tailor's hand, and bade him eat. But

the little tailor was far too weak to hold the tree down, and when the giant let go the tree swung back into the air, bearing the little tailor with it. When he had fallen to the ground again without hurting himself, the giant said, 'What! do you mean to tell me you haven't the strength to hold down a feeble twig?' 'It wasn't strength that was wanting,' replied the tailor; 'do you think that would have been anything for a man who has killed seven at a blow? I jumped over the tree because the huntsmen are shooting among the branches near us. Do you do the like if you dare.' The giant made an attempt, but couldn't get over the tree, and stuck fast in the branches, so that here too the little tailor had the better of him.

'Well, you're a fine fellow, after all,' said the giant; 'come and spend the night with us in our cave.' The little tailor willingly consented to do this, and following his friend they went on till they reached a cave where several other giants were sitting round a fire, each holding a roast sheep in his hand, of which he was eating. The little tailor looked about him, and thought, 'Yes, there's certainly more room to turn round in here than in my workshop.' The giant showed him a bed, and bade him lie down and have a good sleep. But the bed was too big for the little tailor, so he didn't get into it, but crept away into the corner. At midnight, when the giant thought the little tailor was fast asleep, he rose up, and taking his big iron club, he broke the bed in two with a blow, and said to himself, 'That's made an end of the little grasshopper.'

At early dawn the giants went off to the wood, and quite forgot about the little tailor, till all of a sudden they met him trudging along in the most cheerful manner. The giants were terrified at the apparition, and, fearful lest he should slay them, they all took to their heels as fast as they could.

The little tailor continued to follow his nose, and after he had wandered about for a long time he came to the courtyard of a royal palace, and feeling tired he lay down on the grass and fell asleep. While he lay there the people came, and looking him all over read on his girdle, 'SEVEN AT A BLOW'. 'Oh!' they said, 'what can this great hero of a hundred fights want in our peaceful land? He must indeed be a mighty man of valour.' They went and told the King about him, and said what a weighty and useful man he'd be in time of war, and that it would be well to secure him at any price. This counsel pleased the King, and he sent one of his courtiers down to the little tailor, to offer him, when he awoke, a commission in their army. The messenger remained standing by the sleeper, and waited till he stretched his limbs and opened his eyes, when he tendered his proposal. 'That's the very thing I came here for,' answered the little tailor. 'I am quite ready to enter the King's service.' So he was received with all honour, and given a special house of his own to live in.

But the other soldiers resented the success of the little tailor, and wished him a thousand miles away. 'What's to come of it all?' they asked each other. 'If we quarrel with him, he'll strike at us, and at every blow seven will fall. There'll soon be an end of us.' So they resolved to go in a body to the King, and all to send in their papers. 'We are not made,' they said, 'to hold out against a man who kills seven at a blow.'

The King was grieved at the thought of losing all his faithful soldiers for the sake of one man, and he wished heartily that he had never set eyes on him, or that he could get rid of him. But he didn't dare to send him away, for he feared the tailor might kill him along with his people, and place himself on the throne. He pondered long and deeply over the matter, and finally came to a conclusion. He sent for the tailor and told him that, seeing what a great and war-like hero he was, he was about to make him an offer. In a certain wood of his kingdom there dwelt two giants who did much harm. Because of the way they robbed, murdered, burnt, and plundered everything about them, no one could approach them without endangering his life. But if the tailor could overcome and kill these two giants, he should have the King's only daughter for wife, and half the kingdom into the bargain; he might have a hundred horsemen, too, to back him up.

'That's the very thing for a man like me,' thought the little tailor; 'one doesn't get the offer of a beautiful princess and half a kingdom every day.' 'Done with you,' he answered; 'I'll soon put an end to the giants. But I haven't the smallest need of your hundred horsemen; a fellow who can slay seven at a blow need not be afraid of two.'

The little tailor set out, and the hundred horsemen followed him. When he came to the outskirts of the wood he said to his followers,

'You wait here, I'll manage the giants by myself;' and he went on into the wood, casting his sharp little eyes right and left about him. After a while he spied the two giants lying asleep under a tree, and snoring till the very boughs bent with the breeze.

The little tailor lost no time in filling his pocket with stones, and then climbed up the tree under which they lay. When he got to about the middle of it he slipped along a branch till he sat just above the sleepers, when he threw down one stone after the other on the nearest giant. The giant felt nothing for a long time, but at last he woke up, and pinching his companion said, 'What did you strike me for?' 'I didn't strike you,' said the other, 'you must be dreaming.' They both lay down to sleep again, and the tailor threw down a stone on the second giant, who sprang up and cried, 'What's that for? Why did you throw something at me?' 'I didn't throw anything,' growled the first one. They wrangled on for a time, till, as both were tired, they made up the matter and fell asleep again.

The little tailor began his game once more, and flung the largest stone he could find with all his force, and hit the first giant on the chest. 'This is too much of a good thing!' yelled the giant, and springing up like a madman, he knocked his companion against the tree till he trembled. The second giant, however, gave as good as he got, and both became so enraged that they tore up trees and beat each other with them, till they both fell dead at once on the ground.

Then the little tailor jumped down. 'It's a mercy,' he said, 'that they didn't root up the tree on which I was perched, or I should have had to jump like a squirrel on to another, which, nimble though I am, would have been no easy job.' He drew his sword and gave each of the giants two or three deep wounds in the chest, and then went to the horsemen and said, 'The deed is done, I've put an end to the two of them; but I assure you it has been no easy matter, for they even tore up trees in their struggle to defend themselves. But they stood no chance against one who slays seven at a blow.' 'Weren't you wounded?' asked the horsemen. 'No fear,' answered the tailor; 'they haven't touched a hair of my head.' But the horsemen wouldn't believe him till they rode into the wood and found the giants weltering in their blood, and the trees lying around, torn up by the roots.

The little tailor now demanded his reward. But the King repented his promise, and pondered once more how he could rid himself of the hero. 'Before you obtain the hand of my daughter and half my kingdom,' he said to him, 'you must do another deed of valour. A unicorn is running about loose in the wood, and doing much mischief; you must catch it alive for me.'

'I'm even less afraid of one unicorn than of two giants,' answered the tailor. 'Seven at a blow, that's my motto.' He took a piece of cord and an axe with him and set out. On the outskirts of the wood he told the men who had been sent with him to wait for his return. He hadn't to search long, for the unicorn soon appeared and, on perceiving the tailor, dashed straight at him as though it were going to run him through on the spot.

'Gently, gently,' said he, 'not so fast, my friend,' and standing still he waited till the beast was quite near, when he sprang lightly behind a tree. The unicorn ran with all its force against the tree, and rammed its horn so firmly into the trunk that it had no strength left to pull it out again, and was thus successfully captured. 'Now I've caught my bird,' said the tailor, and he came out from behind the tree, placed the cord round its neck first, cut the horn out of the tree with his axe, and then led the beast before the King.

Still the King didn't want to give him the promised reward, and made a third demand. The tailor was to catch a wild boar that did a great deal of harm in the wood; and again he might have the huntsmen to help him. 'Willingly,' said the tailor; 'that's mere child's play.' But he didn't take the huntsmen into the wood with him, and they were well enough pleased to remain behind, for the wild boar had often received them in a manner which did not make them desire its further acquaintance.

As soon as the boar perceived the tailor it ran at him with foaming mouth and gleaming teeth, and tried to knock him down; but the nimble little tailor ran into a chapel that stood near, and got out of the window again with a jump. The boar pursued him into the church, but the tailor skipped round to the door, and closed it securely. So the raging beast was caught, for it was far too heavy and unwieldy to spring out of the window. The little tailor summoned the huntsmen together, that they might see the prisoner with their own eyes. Then he betook himself to the King, who was obliged now, whether he liked it or not, to keep his promise, and hand over his daughter and half his kingdom. Had he known that no hero-warrior, but only a little tailor stood before him, it would have gone even more to his heart. So the wedding was celebrated with much splendour and little joy, and the tailor became a king.

After a time the young Queen heard her husband saying one night in his sleep, 'My lad, make that waistcoat and patch these trousers, or I'll box your ears.' Thus she learnt in what rank her lord had been born, and next day she poured forth her woes to her father, and begged him to help her to get rid of a husband who was nothing more nor less than a tailor. The King comforted her, and said, 'Leave your bedroom door open to-night; my servants shall stand outside, and when your husband is fast asleep they shall enter, bind him fast, and carry him on to a ship, which shall sail away out into the wide ocean.'

The Queen was well satisfied with the idea, but the armour-bearer, who had overheard everything, being much attached to his young master, went straight to him and revealed the whole plot. 'I'll soon put a stop to that business,' said the tailor. That night he and his wife went to bed at the usual time, and when she thought he had fallen asleep she got up, opened the door, and then lay down again. The little tailor, who had only pretended to be asleep, began to call out in a clear voice, 'My lad, make that waistcoat and patch those trousers, or I'll box your ears. I have killed seven at a blow, slain two giants, led a unicorn captive, and caught a wild boar, and why should I be afraid of those men standing outside my door?' The men, when they heard the tailor saying these words, were so terrified that they fled as if pursued by a whole army, and didn't dare go near him again. So the little tailor was a king and remained one all the days of his life.

Brother and Sister

BROTHER TOOK Sister by the hand and said, 'We haven't had one single happy hour since our mother died. That step-mother of ours beats us regularly every day, and if we dare go near her she kicks us away. We never get anything but hard dry crusts to eat – why, the dog under the table is better off than we are, she does throw him a good morsel or two now and then. Alas, if our own dear mother only knew! Come, let us leave and go forth into the wide world together.'

They walked the whole day long through fields and meadows, over hedges and ditches; and when it rained Sister said, 'Heaven and our hearts are weeping together.' Towards evening they came to a large forest, and they were so tired out with sorrow and hunger and their long walk that they crept into a hollow tree and soon fell asleep.

Next morning, when they woke up, the sun, already high in the heavens, was shining down bright and warm into the tree. Then said Brother, 'I'm so thirsty, Sister; if I did but know where to find a little stream, I'd go and have a drink. I do believe I hear one.' He jumped up, took Sister by the hand, and set off to hunt for the brook.

Now their cruel step-mother was in reality a witch, and she knew perfectly well that the two children had run away. She had crept secretly after them, and had cast her spells over all the streams in the forest.

Presently the children found a little brook dancing and glittering over the stones, and Brother was eager to drink of it, but as it rushed past Sister heard it murmuring:

'Who drinks of me will be a tiger! who drinks of me will be a tiger!'

So she cried out, 'Oh! dear Brother, pray don't drink, or you'll be turned into a wild beast and tear me to pieces.'

Brother was dreadfully thirsty, but he did not drink.

'Very well,' said he, 'I'll wait till we come to the next spring.'

When they came to the second brook, Sister heard it say:

'Who drinks of me will be a wolf! who drinks of me will be a wolf!'

And she cried, 'Oh! Brother, pray don't drink here either, or you'll be turned into a wolf and eat me up.'

Again Brother did not drink, but he said, 'Well, I'll wait a little longer till we reach the next stream, but then, whatever you may say, I really must drink, for I can bear this thirst no longer.'

And when they got to the third brook, Sister heard it say as it rushed past:

'Who drinks of me will be a fawn! who drinks of me will be a fawn!'

And she begged, 'Ah! Brother, don't drink yet, or you'll become a fawn and run away from me.'

But her brother was already kneeling by the brook and bending over it to drink, and, sure enough, no sooner had his lips touched the water than he fell on the grass transformed into a little roebuck.

Sister cried bitterly over her poor bewitched brother, and the little fawn wept too, and sat sadly by her side. At last the girl said, 'Never mind, dear little fawn, I will never forsake you,' and she took off her golden garter and tied it round the fawn's neck.

Then she plucked rushes and plaited a soft cord of them, which she fastened to the collar. When she had done this she led the fawn farther and farther into the depths of the forest.

After they had gone a long, long way they came to a little house, and when the girl looked into it and found it was quite empty, she thought, 'Perhaps we might stay and live here.'

So she gathered leaves and moss to make a soft bed for the little fawn. And every morning and evening she went out and gathered roots, nuts, and berries for herself, and tender young grass for the fawn, who fed from her hand, and played round her and seemed quite happy. In the evening, when Sister was tired, she said her prayers and then laid her head on the fawn's back and fell sound asleep with it as a pillow. And if her brother had but kept his natural form, it would indeed have been a delightful life.

They had been living there alone for some time when it came to pass that the King of that country had a great hunt through the woods. Then the whole forest rang with such a blowing of horns, baying of dogs, and joyful cries of huntsmen, that the little roebuck heard it and longed to join in too.

'Ah!' said he to Sister, 'do let me go off to the hunt! I can't keep still any longer.' And he begged and prayed till at last she consented.

'But,' said she, 'mind you come back in the evening. I shall shut the door fast for fear of those rough huntsmen; so, to make sure of my knowing you, knock at the door and say, "My sister dear, open; I'm here." If you don't say this I shan't open the door.'

So away sprang the little fawn, free and happy in the open air.

The King and his huntsmen soon saw the beautiful creature and started in pursuit, but they could not come up with it, and whenever they thought they almost had it, it bounded off into the bushes and disappeared. When night came it ran home, and knocking at the door of the little house cried, 'My sister dear, open; I'm here.' The door opened, and he ran in and rested all night on his soft mossy bed.

Next morning the hunt began again, and as soon as the little fawn heard the horns and the 'Ho! ho!' of the huntsmen, he could not rest another moment, and said, 'Sister, let me out, I must be off.'

So Sister opened the door and said, 'Now mind, you must be back by nightfall, and say your little rhyme.'

When the King and his huntsmen saw the fawn with the golden collar they all chased it, but it was far too quick and nimble for them. This went on all day, but by evening the huntsmen had gradually encircled the fawn, and one of them wounded it slightly in the foot, so that it limped and ran slowly.

Then a huntsman followed quietly after it as far as the little house, and heard it call out, 'My sister dear, open; I'm here', and he saw the door open and close immediately the fawn had run in.

The huntsman went off straight to the King and told him all he had seen and heard.

'To-morrow we will hunt again,' said the King.

Poor Sister was terribly frightened when she saw how her little fawn had been wounded. She washed off the blood, bound up the injured foot with herbs, and said, 'Now, dear fawn, go and lie down and rest, so that your wound may heal.'

The wound was really so slight that it was quite well next day, and no sooner did he hear the sounds of hunting in the forest than the fawn cried out, 'I can't bear it, I must be there too; I'll take care they shan't catch me.'

Sister began to cry, and said, 'They are certain to kill you, and then I shall be left all alone in the forest and forsaken by everyone. I can't and won't let you out.'

'Then I shall die of grief,' replied the little roebuck, 'for when I hear the horns I feel as if I must jump right out of my skin.'

So at last, when Sister found there was nothing else to be done, she opened the door with a heavy heart, and the roebuck darted forth full of glee and health into the forest.

As soon as the King saw the little creature, he said to his huntsman, 'Now, give chase to it all day till evening, but be careful that it comes to no harm.'

When the sun had set the King said to his huntsman, 'Come now and show me the little house in the wood.'

And when he got to the house he knocked at the door and said, 'My sister dear, open; I'm here.' Then the door opened and the King walked in, and there stood the loveliest maiden he had ever seen.

The girl was much startled when instead of her little fawn a man with a golden crown on his head came in. But the King looked kindly at her, held out his hand, and said, 'Will you come with me to my castle and be my dear wife?'

'Oh yes!' replied the maiden, 'but you must let my fawn come too. I could not possibly forsake it.' And the King said, 'It shall stay with you as long as you live, and shall want for nothing.'

Just then the fawn came bounding in, and Sister tied the rush cord once more to its collar, took the end in her hand, and so they all left the little house in the forest together.

The King lifted the lovely maiden on to his horse, and led her to his castle, where the wedding was celebrated with the greatest splendour. The fawn was petted and caressed, and ran about at will in the palace gardens.

Now all this time the wicked step-mother, who had been the cause of the poor children's misfortunes, was feeling fully persuaded that Sister had been torn to pieces by wild beasts, and Brother shot to death in the shape of a fawn. When she heard how happy and prosperous they were, her heart was filled with envy and hatred, and she could think of nothing but how to bring more misfortune on them. Her own daughter, who was as hideous as night and had only one eye, reproached her by saying, 'It is I who ought to have had this good luck and been queen.'

'Hold your peace,' said the old woman; 'when the time comes I shall be ready.'

Now after some time it had happened one day when the King was out hunting that the Queen gave birth to a beautiful little boy. The old witch thought here was a good chance for her; so she took the form of the lady-in-waiting, and, hurrying into the room where the Queen lay in her bed, called out, 'The bath is quite ready; it will help to make you strong again. Come, let us be quick, for fear the water should get cold.' Her daughter was at hand, too, and between them they carried the Queen, who was still very weak, into the bathroom and laid her in the bath; then they locked the door and ran away. But they had made a blazing hot fire under the bath, so that the lovely young Queen was soon suffocated.

Then the old witch tied a cap on her daughter's head and laid her in the Queen's bed. She managed, too, to make her figure and general appearance look like the Queen's, but even her power could not restore the eye she had lost; so she made her lie on the side of the missing eye, in order to prevent the King's noticing anything.

In the evening, when the King came home and heard the news of his son's birth, he was full of delight, and insisted on going at once to his dear wife's bedside to see how she was getting on. But the old witch cried out, 'Take care and keep the curtains drawn; don't let the light get into the Queen's eyes; she must be kept perfectly quiet.' So the King went away and never knew that it was a false queen who lay in the bed.

When midnight came and everyone in the palace was sound asleep, the nurse who alone watched by the baby's cradle in the nursery, saw the door gently open, and the real Queen come in. She lifted the child from its cradle, laid it on her arm, and nursed it for some time. Then she carefully shook up the pillows of the little bed, laid the baby down and tucked the coverlet in all round him. She did not forget the little fawn either, but went to the corner where it lay, and gently stroked its back. Then she silently left the room. Next morning when the nurse asked the sentries if they had seen anyone go into the castle that night, they all said, 'No, we saw no one at all.'

For many nights the Queen came in the same way, but she never spoke a word, and the nurse was too frightened to say anything about her visits.

After some little time had elapsed the Queen spoke one night, and said:

> 'Is my child well? Is my fawn well?
> I'll come back twice and then farewell.'

The nurse made no answer, but as soon as the Queen had disappeared she went to the King and told him all. The King exclaimed, 'Good heavens! what do you say? I will watch myself tonight by the child's bed.'

When the evening came he went to the nursery, and at midnight the Queen appeared and said:

> 'Is my child well? Is my fawn well?
> I'll come back once and then farewell.'

And she nursed and petted the child as usual before she disappeared. The King dared not trust himself to speak to her, but the following night he kept watch again.

That night when the Queen came she said:

> 'Is my child well? Is my fawn well?
> I've come this once, and now farewell.'

Then the King could restrain himself no longer, but sprang to her side and cried, 'You can be no one but my dear wife!'

'Yes,' she said, 'I am your dear wife!' and in the same moment she was restored to life, and was as fresh and well and rosy as ever. Then she told the King all the cruel things the wicked witch and her daughter had done. The King had them both arrested at once and brought to trial, and they were condemned to death. The daughter was led into the forest, where the wild beasts tore her to pieces, and the old witch perished miserably in the fire.

As soon as she was reduced to ashes the spell was taken off the little fawn, and he was restored to his natural shape once more, and so Brother and Sister lived happily ever after.

The Brown Bear of Norway

THERE WAS once a king in Ireland, and he had three daughters, and very nice princesses they were. And one day, when they and their father were walking on the lawn, the King began to joke with them, and to ask them whom they would like to be married to.

'I'll have the King of Ulster for a husband,' says one; 'and I'll have the King of Munster,' says the second; 'and,' says the youngest, 'I'll have no husband but the Brown Bear of Norway.' For her nurse used to be telling her of an enchanted prince that she called by that name, and she had fallen in love with him, and his name was the first name on her tongue, for the very night before she was dreaming of him. Well, one laughed, and another laughed, and they joked with the Princess all the rest of the evening.

But that very night she woke up out of her sleep to find herself in a great hall that was lighted up with a thousand lamps; the richest carpets were on the floor, and the walls were covered with cloth of gold and silver, and the place was full of grand company, and the very beautiful prince she had seen in her dreams was there, and it wasn't a moment till he was on one knee before her, and telling her how much he loved her, and asking wouldn't she be his queen. Well, she hadn't the heart to refuse him, and married they were the same evening.

'Now, my darling,' says he, when they were left by themselves, 'you must know that I am under enchantment. A sorceress, that had a beautiful daughter, wished me for her son-in-law and she got power over me, and when I refused to wed her daughter she made me take the form of a bear by day, and I was to continue so till a lady would marry me of her own free will, and endure five years of great trials after.'

Well, when the Princess woke in the morning, she missed her husband from her side, and spent the day very sadly. But as soon as the lamps were lighted in the grand hall, where she was sitting on a sofa covered with silk, the folding doors flew open, and the Prince was by her side the next minute. So they spent another happy evening, but he warned her that whenever she began to tire of him, or ceased to have faith in him, they would be parted for ever, and he'd be obliged to marry the witch's daughter.

She got used to finding him absent by day, and they spent a happy twelvemonth together, and at last a beautiful little boy was born; and happy as she was before, she was twice as happy now, for she had her child to keep her company in the day-time when she couldn't see her husband.

At last, one evening, when herself, and himself, and her child were sitting with a window open because it was a sultry night, in flew an eagle, took the infant's sash in his beak, and flew up in the air with him. The Princess screamed, and was going to throw herself out through the window after him, but the Prince caught her, and looked at her very seriously. She bethought of what he said soon after their marriage, and she stopped the cries and complaints that were on her tongue. She spent her days very lonely for another twelvemonth, when a beautiful little girl was born to her. Then she thought to herself she'd have a sharp eye about her this time; so she never would allow a window to be more than a few inches open.

But all her care was in vain. One evening, when they were all so happy, and the Prince dandling the baby, a beautiful greyhound stood before them, took the child out of the father's hand, and was out of the door before you could wink. This time the Princess shouted and ran after the greyhound, but there were servants in the next room, and all declared that neither child nor dog had passed out. She felt, somehow, as if it was her husband's fault, but still she kept command over herself, and didn't once reproach him.

When a third child was born she would hardly allow a window or a door to be left open for a moment; but she wasn't the nearer to keep the child to herself. They were sitting one evening by the fire, when a lady appeared standing by them. The Princess opened her eyes in a great fright and stared at her, and while she was doing so, the lady wrapped a shawl round the baby that was sitting in its father's lap, and either sank through the ground with it or went up through the wide chimney. This time the mother kept her bed for a month.

'My dear,' said she to her husband, when she was beginning to recover. 'I think I'd feel better if I was to see my father and mother

and sisters once more. If you give me leave to go home for a few days I'd be glad.' 'Very well,' said he, 'I will do that, and whenever you feel inclined to return, only mention your wish when you lie down at night.' The next morning when she awoke she found herself in her own old chamber in her father's palace. She rang the bell, and in a short time she had her mother and father and married sisters about her, and they laughed till they cried for joy at finding her safe back again.

In time she told them all that had happened to her, and they didn't know what to advise her to do. She was as fond of her husband

39

as ever, and said she was sure that he couldn't help letting the children go; but still she was afraid beyond the world to have another child torn from her. Well, the mother and sisters consulted a wise woman that used to bring eggs to the castle, for they had great faith in her wisdom. She said the only plan was to secure the bear's skin that the Prince was obliged to put on every morning, and get it burnt, and then he couldn't help being a man night and day, and the enchantment would be at an end.

So they all persuaded her to do that, and she promised she would; and after eight days she felt so great a longing to see her husband again that she made the wish the same night, and when she woke three hours after, she was in her husband's palace, and he himself was watching over her. There was great joy on both sides, and they were happy for many days.

Now she began to think how she never saw her husband leaving her in the morning, and how she never found him neglecting to give her a sweet drink out of a gold cup just as she was going to bed.

One night she contrived not to drink any of it, though she pretended to do so; and she was wakeful enough in the morning, and saw her husband passing out through a panel in the wainscot, though she kept her eyelids nearly closed. The next night she put a few drops of the sleepy posset that she saved the evening before into her husband's night drink, and that made him sleep sound enough. She got up after midnight, passed through the panel, and found a beautiful brown bear's skin hanging in the corner. Then she stole back, and went down to the parlour fire, and put the hide into the middle of it till it was all fine ashes. She then lay down by her husband, gave him a kiss on the cheek, and fell asleep.

If she was to live a hundred years she'd never forget how she wakened next morning, and found her husband looking down on her with misery and anger in his face. 'Unhappy woman,' said he, 'you have separated us for ever! Why hadn't you patience for full five years? I am now obliged, whether I like or no, to go a three days' journey to the witch's castle, and marry her daughter. The skin that was my guard you have burnt it, and the egg-wife that gave you the counsel was the witch herself. I won't reproach you: your punishment will be severe enough without it. Farewell for ever!'

He kissed her for the last time, and was off the next minute, walking as fast as he could. She shouted after him, and then seeing there was no use, she dressed herself and pursued him. He never stopped, nor stayed, nor looked back, and still she kept him in sight; and when he was on the hill she was in the hollow, and when he was in the hollow she was on the hill. Her life was almost leaving her, when, just as the sun was setting, he turned up a lane, and went into a little house. She crawled up after him, and when she got inside there was a beautiful little boy on his knees, and he kissing and hugging him.

'Here, my poor darling,' says he, 'is your eldest child, and there,' says he, pointing to a woman that was looking on with a smile on her face, 'is the eagle that carried him away.' She forgot all her sorrows in a moment, hugging her child, and laughing and crying over him. The woman washed their feet, and rubbed them with an ointment that took all the soreness out of their bones, and made them both as fresh as a daisy. Next morning, just before sunrise, the Prince was up, and prepared to be off. 'Here,' said he to her, 'is a thing which may be of use to you. It's a pair of scissors, and whatever stuff you cut with them will be turned into silk. The moment the sun rises, I'll lose all memory of yourself and the children, but I'll get it at sunset again. Farewell!' But he wasn't far gone till she was in sight of him again, leaving her boy behind. It was the same to-day as yesterday: their shadows went before them in the morning and followed them in the evening. He never stopped, and she never stopped, and as the sun was setting he turned up another lane, and there they found their little daughter. It was all joy and comfort again till morning, and then the third day's journey began.

But before he started he gave her a comb, and told her that whenever she used it, pearls and diamonds would fall from her hair. Still he had his memory from sunset to sunrise; but from sunrise to sunset he travelled on under enchantment, and never threw his eye behind. This night they came to where the youngest baby was, and the next morning, just before sunrise, the Prince spoke to her for the last time. 'Here, my poor wife,' said he, 'is a little hand-reel, with gold thread that has no end, and the half of our marriage ring. If you ever find me and put your half-ring to mine, I shall remember you. But the moment I enter yonder wood I shall forget everything that ever happened between us, just as if I was born yesterday. Farewell, dear wife and child, for ever!'

Just then the sun rose, and away he walked towards the wood. She saw it open before him and close after him, and when she came up, she could no more get in than she could break through a stone wall. She wrung her hands and shed tears, but then she recollected herself, and cried out, 'Wood, I charge you by my three magic gifts, the scissors, the comb, and the reel, to let me through;' and it opened, and she went along a path till she came in sight of a palace, and there was a woodman's cottage on the edge of the wood where it came nearest the palace grounds.

She went into this lodge, and asked the woodman and his wife to take her into their service. They were not willing at first; but she told them she would ask no wages, and would give them diamonds, and pearls, and silk stuffs, and gold thread whenever they wished for them, and then they agreed to let her stay.

It wasn't long till she heard how a young prince, that was just arrived, was living in the palace of the young mistress, who was the witch's daughter. He seldom stirred abroad, and everyone that saw him remarked how silent and sorrowful he went about, like a person that was searching for some lost thing.

The servants and folk at the big house began to take notice of the beautiful young woman at the lodge, and to annoy her with their impudence. The head footman was the most troublesome, and at last she invited him to come and take tea with her. Oh, how rejoiced he was, and how he bragged of it in the servants' hall! Well, the evening came, and the footman walked into the lodge, and was shown to her sitting-room; for the lodge-keeper and his wife stood in great awe of her, and gave her two nice rooms for herself. Well, he sat down as stiff as a ramrod, and was talking in a grand style about the great doings at the castle, while she was getting the tea and toast ready.

'Oh,' says she to him, 'would you put your hand out at the window and cut me off a sprig or two of honeysuckle?' He got up in great glee, and put out his hand and head; and said she, 'By virtue of my magic gifts, let a pair of horns spring out of your head!' Just as she wished, so it was. Great horns sprang from the front of each ear, and met at the back. Oh, the poor wretch! And how he bawled and roared! And the servants that he had boasted to were soon flocking from the castle, and grinning, and huzzaing and beating tunes on tongs and shovels and pans; and he cursing and swearing, and the eyes ready to start out of his head, and he so black in the face, and kicking out his legs behind like mad.

At last she pitied him, and removed the charm, and the horns dropped down on the ground, and he would have killed her on the spot, only he was as weak as water, and his fellow-servants came in and carried him up to the big house.

Well, some way or other the story came to the ears of the Prince, and he strolled down that way. She had only the dress of a country-woman on her as she sat sewing at the window, but that did not hide her beauty, and he was greatly puzzled after he had a good look, just as a body is puzzled to know whether something happened to him when he was young or if he only dreamed it. Well, the witch's daughter heard about it too, and she came to see the strange girl; and what did she find her doing but cutting out the pattern of a gown from brown paper; and as she cut away, the paper became the richest silk she ever saw.

The witch's daughter looked on with greedy eyes, and, says she, 'What would you be satisfied to take for those scissors?' 'I'll take nothing,' says she, 'but leave to spend one night outside the Prince's chamber.' Well, the proud lady fired up, and was going to say something dreadful; but the scissors kept on cutting, and the silk growing richer and richer every inch. So she promised what the girl had asked her.

When night came on she was let into the palace and the Prince was in such a dead sleep that all she did couldn't awake him. She sang this verse to him, sighing and sobbing, and kept singing it the night long, and it was all in vain:

> 'Four long years I was married to thee;
> Three sweet babes I bore to thee;
> Brown Bear of Norway, turn to me.'

At the first dawn the witch's daughter was in the chamber, and led her away, and the footman of the horns put out his tongue at her as she was leaving the palace.

So there was no luck so far; but the next day the Prince passed by again and looked at her, and saluted her kindly, as a prince might a farmer's daughter, and passed on; and soon the witch's daughter passed by, and found her combing her hair, and pearls and diamonds dropping from it.

Well, another bargain was made, and the Princess spent another night of sorrow, and she left the castle at daybreak, and the footman was at his post and enjoyed his revenge.

The third day the Prince came by, and stopped to talk. He asked her could he do anything to serve her, and she said he might. She asked him did he ever wake at night. He said that he often did, but that during the last two nights he was listening to a sweet song in his dreams, and could not wake, and that the voice was one he must have known and loved in some other world long ago. Says she, 'Did you drink any sleepy posset either of these evenings before you went to bed?' 'I did,' said he. 'Those two evenings my wife gave me something to drink, but I don't know whether it was a sleepy posset or not.' 'Well, Prince,' said she, 'as you say you would wish to oblige me, you can do it by not tasting any drink to-night.' 'I will not,' says he, and then he went on his walk.

Well, the witch's daughter came soon after the Prince, and found the stranger using her hand-reel and winding threads of gold off it, and the third bargain was made.

That evening the Prince was lying on his bed at twilight, and his mind much disturbed; and the door opened, and in his Princess came, and down she sat by his bedside and sang:

'Four long years I was married to thee;
Three sweet babes I bore to thee;
Brown Bear of Norway, turn to me.'

'Brown Bear of Norway!' said he. 'I don't understand you.' 'Don't you remember, Prince, that I was your wedded wife for four years?' 'I do not,' said he, 'but I'm sure I wish it was so.' 'Don't you remember our three babes, that are still alive?' 'Show me them. My mind is all a heap of confusion.' 'Look for the half of our marriage ring, that hangs at your neck, and fit it to this.' He did so, and the same moment the charm was broken. His full memory came back on him, and he flung his arms round his wife's neck, and both burst into tears.

Well, there was a great cry outside, and the castle walls were heard splitting and cracking. Everyone in the castle was alarmed, and made their way out. The Prince and Princess went with the rest, and by the time all were safe on the lawn, down came the building, and made the ground tremble for miles around. No one ever saw the witch and her daughter afterwards. It was not long till the Prince and Princess had their children with them, and they set out for their own palace. The Kings of Ireland and of Munster and Ulster, and their wives, soon came to visit them, and may everyone that deserves it be as happy as the Brown Bear of Norway and his family.

The Donkey Cabbage

THERE WAS once a young hunter who went boldly into the forest. He had a merry and light heart, and as he went whistling along there came an ugly old woman, who said to him, 'Good-day, dear hunter! You are very merry and contented, but I suffer hunger and thirst, so give me a trifle.'

The hunter was sorry for the poor old woman, and he felt in his pocket and gave her all he could spare. He was going on then, but the old woman stopped him and said, 'Listen, dear hunter, to what I say. Because of your kind heart I will make you a present. Go on your way, and in a short time you will come to a tree on which sit nine birds who have a cloak in their claws and are quarrelling over it. Take aim with your gun and shoot in the middle of them; they will let the cloak fall, but one of the birds will be hit and will drop down dead. Take the cloak with you; it is a wishing-cloak, and when you throw it on your shoulders you have only to wish yourself at a certain place, and in the twinkling of an eye you are there. Take the heart out of the dead bird and swallow it whole, and every morning when you get up you will find a gold piece under your pillow.'

The hunter thanked the wise woman, and thought to himself, 'These are splendid things she has promised me, if only they come to pass!' So he walked on about a hundred yards, and then he heard above him in the branches such a screaming and clamour that he looked up, and there he saw a crowd of birds tearing a cloth with their beaks and feet, shrieking, tugging, and fighting, as if each wanted it for himself.

'Well,' said the hunter, 'this is wonderful! It is just as the old woman said;' and he took his gun on his shoulder, pulled the trigger, and shot into the midst of them, so that their feathers flew about. Then the flock took flight with much screaming, but one fell dead, and the cloak fluttered down. Then the hunter did as the old woman had told him: he cut open the bird, found its heart, swallowed it, and took the cloak home with him. The next morning when he awoke he remembered the promise, and wanted to see if it had come

46

true. And when he lifted up his pillow, there sparkled the gold piece, and the next morning he found another, and so on every time he got up. He collected a heap of gold, but at last he thought to himself, 'What good is all my gold to me if I stay at home? I will travel and look a bit about me in the world.' So he took leave of his parents, put on his cloak, slung his hunting knapsack and his gun round him, and journeyed into the world.

It happened that one day he went through a thick wood, and when he came to the end of it there lay in the plain before him a large castle. At one of the windows stood an old woman with a most beautiful maiden by her side, looking out. But the old woman was a witch, and she said to the girl, 'There comes one out of the wood who has a wonderful treasure in his body which we must manage to possess ourselves of, darling daughter; we have more right to it than he. He has a bird's heart in him, and so every morning there lies a gold piece under his pillow.'

The witch told her how they could get hold of it, and how she was to coax it from him, and at last threatened her angrily, saying, 'And if you do not obey me, you shall repent it!'

When the hunter came nearer he saw the maiden, and said to himself, 'I have travelled so far now that I will rest, and turn into this beautiful castle; money I have in plenty.' But the real reason was that he had caught sight of the lovely face.

He went into the house, and was kindly received and hospitably entertained. It was not long before he was so much in love with the witch-maiden that he thought of nothing else, and only looked in her eyes, and whatever she wanted, that he gladly did. Then the old witch said, 'Now we must have the bird-heart; he will not feel when it is gone.' She prepared a drink, and when it was ready she poured it in a goblet and gave it to the maiden, who had to hand it to the hunter.

'Drink to me now, my dearest,' she said. Then he took the goblet, and when he had swallowed the drink the bird-heart came out of his mouth. The maiden had to get hold of it secretly and then swallow it herself, for the old witch wanted to have it. Thenceforward the hunter found no more gold under his pillow, and it lay under the maiden's; but he was so much in love and so much bewitched that he thought of nothing except spending all his time with the maiden.

Then the old witch said, 'We have the bird-heart, but we must also get the wishing-cloak from him.'

The maiden answered, 'We will leave him that; he has already lost his wealth!'

The old witch grew angry, and said, 'Such a cloak is a wonderful thing, it is seldom to be had in the world, and have it I must and will.' She beat the maiden, and said that if she did not obey it would go ill with her.

So she did her mother's bidding, and, standing one day by the window, she looked away into the far distance as if she were very sad.

'Why are you standing there looking so sad?' asked the hunter.

'Alas, my love,' she replied, 'over there lies the granite mountain where the costly precious stones grow. I have a great longing to go there, so that when I think of it I am very sad. For who can fetch them? Only the birds who fly; a man, never.'

'If you have no other trouble,' said the hunter, 'that one I can easily remove from your heart.'

So he wrapped her round in his cloak and wished themselves to the granite mountain, and in an instant there they were, sitting on it! The precious stones sparkled so brightly on all sides that it was a pleasure to see them, and they collected the most beautiful and costly together. But now the old witch, through her witchcraft, caused the hunter's eyes to become heavy.

He said to the maiden, 'We will sit down for a little while and rest; I am so tired that I can hardly stand on my feet.'

So they sat down, and he laid his head on her lap and fell asleep. As soon as he was sound asleep she unfastened the cloak from his shoulders, threw it on her own, left the granite and stones, and wished herself home again.

And when the hunter had finished his sleep and awoke, he found that his love had betrayed him and left him alone on the wild mountain. 'Oh,' said he, 'why is faithlessness so great in the world?' and he sat down in sorrow and trouble, not knowing what to do.

But the mountain belonged to fierce and huge giants, who lived on it and traded there, and he had not sat long before he saw three of them striding towards him. So he lay down as if he had fallen into a deep sleep.

The first giant pushed him with his foot, and said, 'What sort of an earthworm is that?' The second said, 'Crush him dead.' But the third said contemptuously, 'It is not worth the trouble! Let him be; he cannot live here, and if he goes higher up the mountain the clouds will take him and carry him off.'

Having spoken thus they went away. But the hunter had listened to their talk, and as soon as they had gone he rose and climbed to the summit. When he had sat there a little while a cloud swept by, and, seizing him, carried him away. It travelled for a time in the sky, and then it sank down and hovered over a large vegetable garden surrounded by walls, so that he came safely to the ground amidst cabbages and other vegetables. The hunter then looked about him, saying, 'If only I had something to eat! I am so hungry, and it will go badly with me in the future, for I see here not an apple or pear or fruit of any kind – nothing but vegetables everywhere.'

At last he thought, 'At a pinch I can eat a cabbage; it may not taste particularly nice, but it will refresh me.' So he looked about for a good cabbage-head and ate it, but no sooner had he swallowed a couple of mouthfuls than he felt very strange, and found himself wonderfully changed. Four legs began to grow on him, a thick head, and two long ears, and he saw with horror that he had changed into a donkey. But as he was still very hungry and the juicy salad tasted very good to his present nature, he went on eating with a still greater appetite. At last he got hold of another kind of cabbage, but scarcely had swallowed it when he felt another change, and he once more regained his human form.

The hunter now lay down and slept off his weariness. When he awoke the next morning he broke off a head of the bad and a head of the good cabbage, thinking, 'This will help me to regain my own, and to punish faithlessness.'

Then he put the cabbages in his knapsack, climbed the wall, and started off to seek the castle of his love. When he had wandered about for a couple of days he found it quite easily. He then browned his face, so that his own mother would not have known him, and went into the castle, where he begged for a lodging.

'I am so tired,' he said. 'I can go no farther.'

The witch asked, 'Countryman, who are you, and what is your business?'

He answered, 'I am a messenger of the King, and have been sent to seek the finest salad that grows under the sun. I have been so lucky as to find it, and am bringing it with me; but the heat of the sun is so great that the tender cabbage threatens to grow soft, and I do not know if I shall be able to bring it any farther.'

When the old witch heard of the fine salad she wanted to eat it, and said, 'Dear countryman, just let me taste the wonderful salad.'

'Why not?' he answered; 'I have brought two heads with me, and will give you one.'

So saying, he opened his sack and gave her the bad one. The witch suspected no evil, and her mouth watered to taste the new dish, so that she went into the kitchen to prepare it herself. When it was ready she could not wait till it was served at the table, but immediately tasted it. No sooner, however, had she swallowed a morsel than she lost human form, and ran into the courtyard in the shape of a donkey.

Now the servant came into the kitchen, and when she saw the salad standing there ready for the table she was about to carry it up, but on the way, according to her old habit, she tasted it and ate a couple of leaves. Immediately the charm worked, and she became a donkey, and ran out to join the old witch, and the dish with the salad in it fell to the ground. In the meantime, the hunter was sitting with the lovely maiden, and as no one came with the salad, and she wanted very much to taste it, she said, 'I don't know where the salad is.'

Then thought the hunter, 'The cabbage must have already begun to work.' And he said, 'I will go to the kitchen and fetch it myself.'

When he came there he saw the two donkeys running about in the courtyard, but the salad was lying on the ground.

'That's all right,' said he; 'two have had their share!' And lifting the remaining leaves up, he laid them on the dish and brought them to the maiden.

'I am bringing you the delicious food my own self,' he said, 'so that you need not wait any longer.'

Then she ate, and, as the others had done, she at once lost her human form, and ran as a donkey into the yard.

When the hunter had washed his face, so that the changed ones might know him, he went into the yard, saying, 'Now you shall receive a reward for your faithlessness.'

He tied them all three with a rope and drove them away till he came to a mill. He knocked at the window, and the miller put his head out and asked what he wanted.

'I have three tiresome animals,' he answered, 'which I don't want to keep any longer. If you will take them, give them food and stabling, and do as I tell you with them, I will pay you as much as you want.'

The miller replied, 'Why not? What shall I do with them?'

Then the hunter said that to the old donkey, which was the witch, he must give three beatings and one meal; to the younger one, which was the servant, one beating and three meals; and to the youngest one, which was the maiden, no beating and three meals, for he could not find it in his heart to let the maiden be beaten.

Then he went back into the castle, and found there all that he wanted. After a couple of days the miller came and said that he must tell him that the old donkey which was to have three beatings and only one meal had died. 'The other two,' he added, 'are certainly not dead, and get their three meals every day, but they are so sad that they cannot last much longer.'

Then the hunter took pity on them, laid aside his anger, and told the miller to drive them back again. And when they came he gave them some of the good cabbage to eat, so that they became human again. Then the beautiful maiden fell on her knees before him, saying, 'Oh, my dearest, forgive me the ill I have done you! My mother compelled me to do it; it was against my will, for I love you dearly. Your wishing-cloak is hanging in a cupboard, and as for the bird-heart I will make a drink and give it back to you.'

But he changed his mind, and said, 'Keep it; it makes no difference, for I will take you to be my own dear true wife.'

And the wedding was celebrated, and they lived happy together till death.

The Dragon and his Grandmother

THERE WAS once a great war, and the King had a great many soldiers, but he gave them so little pay that they could not live on it. Then three of them took counsel together and determined to desert.

One of them said to the others, 'If we are caught, we shall be hanged on the gallows; how shall we set about it?' Another said, 'Do you see that large cornfield there? If we were to hide ourselves in that, no one could find us. The army cannot get into it, and to-morrow it is to march on.'

So they crept into the cornfield, but the army did not march on, but remained encamped close around them. The three sat for two days and two nights in the corn, and grew so hungry that they nearly died; but if they had ventured out, it would have been certain death.

They said at last, 'What use was it our deserting if we must perish miserably here?'

Whilst they were speaking a fiery dragon came flying through the air. It hovered near them, and asked why they were hidden there. They answered, 'We are three soldiers, and have deserted because our pay was so small. Now if we remain here we shall die of hunger, and if we move out we shall be strung up on the gallows.'

'If you will serve me for seven years,' said the dragon, who was none other than the Devil, 'I will lead you through the midst of the army so that no one shall catch you.'

'We have no choice, and must take your offer,' said they. Then the dragon seized them in his claws, took them through the air over the army, and set them down on the ground a long way off.

He gave them a little whip, saying, 'Whip and slash with this, and as much money as you want will jump up before you. You can then live as great lords, keep horses, and drive about in carriages. But after seven years you are mine.' Then he put a book before them, which he made all three of them sign. 'When the time comes, I will first ask you a riddle,' he said, 'and if you guess it, you shall be free and out of my power.' The dragon then flew away, and the soldiers journeyed on with their little whip, and had as much money as they wanted. They wore grand clothes, and travelled about the world; and wherever they went they lived in merrymaking and splendour, drove about in fine carriages, ate and drank, but did nothing wrong.

The time passed quickly away, and when the seven years were nearly ended two of them grew terribly anxious and frightened, but the third made light of it, saying, 'Don't be afraid, brothers; I have my wits about me; I will guess the riddle.'

As they sat talking in a field, and the two were disconsolate, an old woman passed by, and asked them why they were so sad. 'Alas! what is that to you? You cannot help us.' 'Who knows?' she answered. 'Just confide your trouble in me.'

Then they told her how they had become the dragon's servants for seven long years, and how he had given them money as plentifully as blackberries; but as they had signed their names they were his, unless when the seven years had passed they could guess a riddle. The old woman said, 'If you would save yourselves, one of you must go into the wood, and there he will come upon a mass of fallen rock which looks like a little house. He must go in, and there he will find help.'

The two melancholy ones thought, 'That won't save us!' and they remained where they were. But the third and merry one jumped up and searched in the wood till he found the rock hut. In the hut sat a very old woman, who was the dragon's grandmother. She asked him how he came, and what was his business there. He told her all that happened, and because she was pleased with him she took compassion on him, and said she would help him.

She lifted up a large stone which lay over the cellar, saying, 'Hide yourself there; you can hear all that is spoken in this room. Only sit still and don't stir. When the dragon comes, I will ask him what the riddle is, for he tells me everything; then listen carefully to what he answers.'

At midnight the dragon flew in, and asked for his supper. His grandmother laid the table, brought out food and drink, and they ate and drank together. Then in the course of the conversation she asked him what he had done in the day, and how many souls he had won.

'I haven't had much luck to-day,' he said, 'but I have a tight hold on three soldiers.'

'Indeed! three soldiers!' said she. 'And cannot they escape you?'

'They are mine,' answered the dragon scornfully, 'for I shall ask them just one riddle which they will never be able to guess.'

'What riddle is it?' she asked.

'I will tell you. In the North Sea lies a dead sea-cat – that shall be their roast meat; and the rib of a whale – that shall be their silver spoon; and the hollow foot of a dead horse – that shall be their wineglass.'

When the dragon had gone to bed, his old grandmother pulled up the stone and let out the soldier.

'Did you pay attention to everything?'

'Yes,' he replied, 'I know enough, and can help myself splendidly.'

Then he went out by the window secretly, and in all haste back to his comrades. He told them how the dragon had been outwitted by his grandmother, and how he had heard from his own lips the answer to the riddle.

Then they were all delighted and in high spirits, took out their whip, and cracked so much money that it came jumping up from the ground. When the seven years had quite gone, the Devil came with his book, and, pointing at the signatures, said, 'I will take you underground with me; you shall have a meal there. If you can tell me what you will get for your roast meat, you shall be free, and shall also keep the whip.'

Then said the first soldier, 'In the North Sea lies a dead sea-cat; that shall be our roast meat.'

The dragon was much annoyed, but only muttered, 'Hm ... hm ... hm ...' to himself. Then he asked the second, 'But what shall be your spoon?'

'The rib of a whale shall be our silver spoon.'

The dragon made a face, and growled again three times, 'Hm ... hm ... hm ...' and said to the third, 'Do you know what your wineglass shall be?'

'An old horse's hoof shall be our wineglass.'

Then the Devil flew away with a loud shriek, and had no more power over them. But the three soldiers took the little whip, whipped as much money as they wanted, and lived happily to their lives' end.

Drakestail

DRAKESTAIL WAS very little, that is why he was called Drakestail; but tiny as he was he had brains, and he knew what he was about, for having begun with nothing he ended by amassing a hundred crowns. Now the King of the country, who was very extravagant and could never keep any money, having heard that Drakestail had some, went one day in his own person to borrow Drakestail's hoard. And, my word, in those days Drakestail was not a little proud of having lent money to the King. But after the first and second year, seeing that no interest was paid to him, he became uneasy, and at last he resolved to go to His Majesty himself, and ask to be repaid. So one fine morning Drakestail, very spruce and fresh, takes the road, singing:

> 'Quack, quack, quack,
> When shall I get my money back?'

He had not gone far when he met friend Fox, on his rounds that way.

'Good-morning, neighbour,' says friend Fox, 'where are you off to so early?'

'I am going to the King for what he owes me.'

'Oh! take me with you!'

Drakestail said to himself, 'One can't have too many friends.' ... 'I will,' says he, 'but going on all-fours you will soon be tired. Make yourself quite small, get into my throat – go into my gizzard and I will carry you.'

'Happy thought!' says friend Fox. He takes bag and baggage, and, presto! is gone like a letter into the post.

And Drakestail is off again, all spruce and fresh, still singing:

'Quack, quack, quack,
    When shall I get my money back?'

He had not gone far when he met his lady-friend Ladder, leaning on her wall.

'Good-morning, my duckling,' says lady-friend Ladder, 'whither away so bold?'

'I am going to the King for what he owes me.'

'Oh! take me with you!'

Drakestail said to himself, 'One can't have too many friends.' ... 'I will,' says he, 'but with your wooden legs you will soon be tired. Make yourself quite small, get into my throat – go into my gizzard and I will carry you.'

'Happy thought!' says lady-friend Ladder, and nimble, bag and baggage, goes to keep company with friend Fox.

And 'Quack, quack, quack.' Drakestail is off again, singing and spruce as before. A little farther he meets his sweetheart, friend River, wandering quietly in the sunshine.

'Well, my cherub,' says she, 'whither so lonesome, with arching tail, on this muddy road?'

'I am going to the King for what he owes me.'

'Oh! take me with you!'

Drakestail said to himself, 'One can't have too many friends.' ... 'I will,' says he, 'but you who sleep while you walk will soon be tired. Make yourself quite small, get into my throat – go into my gizzard and I will carry you.'

'Happy thought!' says friend River. She takes bag and baggage, and glou, glou, glou, she takes her place between friend Fox and lady-friend Ladder.

And 'Quack, quack, quack.' Drakestail is off again singing. A little farther on he meets General Wasp, manoeuvring his army.

'Well, good-morning, friend Drakestail,' says General Wasp, 'where are we bound for so spruce and fresh?'

'I am going to the King for what he owes me.'

'Oh! take me with you!'

Drakestail said to himself, 'One can't have too many friends.' ...
'I will,' says he, 'but with your battalion to drag along, you will soon
be tired. Make yourself quite small, go into my throat – get into my
gizzard and I will carry you.'

'By Jove! that's a good idea!' says General Wasp.

And left turn! He takes the same road to join the others with all
his party. There was not much more room, but by closing up a bit
they managed. .... And Drakestail is off again singing.

He arrived thus at the capital, and threaded his way straight up the
High Street, still running and singing:

> 'Quack, quack, quack,
>   When shall I get my money back?'

to the great astonishment of the good folk, till he came to the King's
palace.

He strikes with the knocker, 'Toc! toc!'

'Who is there?' asks the porter, putting his head out of the wicket-
door.

''Tis I, Drakestail. I wish to speak to the King.'

'Speak to the King! ... That's easily said. The King is dining,
and will not be disturbed.'

> 'Tell him that it is I,
>   And I have come, he well knows why.'

The porter shuts his wicket and goes up to say it to the King, who
was just sitting down to dinner with a napkin round his neck, in the
company of all his ministers.

'Good, good!' said the King laughing. 'I know what it is! Make
him come in, and put him with the turkeys and chickens.'

The porter descends.

'Have the goodness to enter.'

'Good!' says Drakestail to himself, 'I shall now see how they eat
at Court.'

'This way, this way,' says the porter. 'One step further. ... There,
there you are.'

'How? What? In the poultry yard?'

Fancy how vexed Drakestail was!

'Ah! so that's it,' says he. 'Wait! I will compel you to receive me.

> 'Quack, quack, quack,
> When shall I get my money back?'

But turkeys and chickens are creatures who don't like people that are not as themselves. When they saw the new-comer and how he was made, and when they heard him crying too, they gave him black looks.

'What is it? What does he want?'

Finally they rushed at him all together, to peck him to death.

'I am lost!' said Drakestail to himself, when by good luck he remembers friend Fox, and he cries:

> 'Reynard, Reynard, come out of your earth,
> Or Drakestail's life is of little worth.'

Then friend Fox, who was only waiting for these words, hastens out, throws himself on the wicked fowls, and quick! quack! he tears them to pieces; so much so that at the end of five minutes there was not one left alive. And Drakestail, quite content, began to sing again:

> 'Quack, quack, quack,
> When shall I get my money back?'

When the King who was still at table heard this refrain, and the poultry woman came to tell him what had been going on in the yard, he was terribly annoyed.

He ordered them to throw this tail of a drake into the well, to make an end of him.

And it was done as he commanded. Drakestail was in despair of getting himself out of such a deep hole, when he remembered his lady-friend Ladder.

> 'Ladder, Ladder, come out of your hold,
> Or Drakestail's days will soon be told.'

And friend Ladder, who was only waiting for these words, hastens out, leans her two arms on the edge of the well, then Drakestail climbs nimbly on her back, and hop! he is in the yard, where he begins to sing louder than ever.

> 'Quack, quack, quack,
> When shall I get my money back?'

When the King, who was still at table and laughing at the good trick he had played his creditor, heard Drakestail again, he became livid with rage.

He commanded that the furnace should be heated, and this tail of a drake thrown into it, because he must be a sorcerer.

The furnace was soon hot, but this time Drakestail was not so afraid; he counted on his sweetheart, friend River.

> 'River, River, outward flow,
> Or to death Drakestail must go.'

Then friend River hastens out, and errouf! throws herself into the furnace, which she floods, with all the people who had lighted it; after which she flowed growling into the hall of the palace to the height of more than four feet.

And Drakestail, quite content, begins to swim, singing deafeningly:

> 'Quack, quack, quack,
> When shall I get my money back?'

The King was still at table, and thought himself quite sure of his game; but when he heard Drakestail singing again, and when they told him all that had passed, he became furious and got up from table brandishing his fists.

'Bring him here, and I'll cut his throat! Bring him here quick!' cried he.

And quickly two footmen ran to fetch Drakestail.

'At last,' said the poor little fellow, going up the great stairs, 'they have decided to receive me.'

Imagine his terror when on entering he sees the King as red as a turkey cock, with all his ministers attending him standing sword in hand. He thought this time it was all up with him. Happily, he remembered that there was still one remaining friend, and he cried with dying accents:

> 'General Wasp, now make a sally,
> Or Drakestail never more may rally.'

Hereupon the scene changes.

'Bz, bz, bayonet them!' The brave General Wasp rushes out with all his troops. They threw themselves on the infuriated King and his ministers, and stung them so fiercely in the face that they lost their heads, and not knowing where to hide themselves they all jumped pell-mell from the window and broke their necks on the pavement.

Behold Drakestail much astonished, all alone in the big saloon and master of the field. He could not get over it.

Nevertheless, he soon remembered what he had come for to the palace, and improving the occasion, he set to work to hunt for his precious money. But in vain he rummaged in all the drawers; he found nothing; all had been spent.

And ferreting thus from room to room he came at last to the one with the throne in it, and feeling fatigued, he sat himself down on it to think over his adventure. In the meanwhile the people had found their King and his ministers with their feet in the air on the pavement, and they had gone into the palace to discover what had occurred. On entering the throne-room, when the crowd saw that there was already someone on the royal seat, they broke out in cries of surprise and joy:

> 'The King is dead, long live the King!
> Heaven has sent us down this thing.'

Drakestail, who was no longer surprised at anything, received the acclamations of the people as if he had never done anything else all his life.

A few of them certainly murmured that a Drakestail would make a fine king; those who knew him replied that a knowing Drakestail was a more worthy king than a spendthrift like him who was lying on the pavement. In short, they ran and took the crown off the head of the deceased, and placed it on that of Drakestail, whom it fitted like wax.

Thus he became King.

'And now,' said he after the ceremony, 'ladies and gentlemen, let's go to supper. I am so hungry!'

East of the Sun
and West of the Moon

ONCE UPON a time there was a poor husbandman who had many
children and little to give them in the way either of food or clothing.
They were all handsome, but the prettiest of all was the youngest
daughter, who was so beautiful that there were no bounds to her
beauty.

So once – it was late on a Thursday evening in autumn, and wild
weather outside, terribly dark, and raining so heavily and blowing so
hard that the walls of the cottage shook again – they were all sitting
together by the fireside, each of them busy with something or other,
when suddenly someone rapped three times against the window-pane.

The man went out to see what could be the matter, and when he got outside there stood a great big white bear.

'Good-evening to you,' said the White Bear.

'Good-evening,' said the man.

'Will you give me your youngest daughter?' said the White Bear. 'If you will, you shall be as rich as you are now poor.'

Truly the man would have had no objection to be rich, but he thought to himself, 'I must first ask my daughter about this,' so he went in and told them that there was a great white bear outside who had faithfully promised to make them all rich if he might but have the youngest daughter.

She said 'no', at once, and would not hear of it; so the man went out again, and settled with the White Bear that he should come again next Thursday evening, and get an answer. Then the father set out to persuade her. He kept on telling her about the wealth that they would all have, and what a good thing it would be for herself, that at last she made up her mind to go. She washed and mended all her rags, made herself as smart as she could, and held herself in readiness to set out. Little enough had she to take away with her.

Next Thursday evening the White Bear came to fetch her. She seated herself on his back with her bundle, and thus they departed. When they had gone a bit of the way, the White Bear said, 'Are you afraid?'

'No, that I am not,' said she.

'Keep tight hold of my fur, and then there is no danger,' said he.

And thus she rode far, a long, long way, until they came to a great mountain. Then the White Bear knocked on it, and a door opened, and they came into a castle where there were many brilliantly lighted rooms which shone with gold and silver; likewise there was a well-spread table, and it was so magnificent that it would be hard to make anyone understand how splendid it was. The White Bear gave her a silver bell, and told her that when she needed anything she had but to ring this bell and what she wanted would appear. Well, when she had eaten, and night was drawing near, she grew sleepy after her journey, and thought she would like to go to bed. She rang the bell, and scarcely had she touched it before she found herself in a chamber where a bed stood ready made for her, which was as pretty as anyone could wish to sleep in. It had pillows of silk, and curtains of silk fringed with gold, and everything in the room was of gold or silver; but when she had lain down and put out the light a man came and lay down beside her, and it was the White Bear, who cast off the form of a beast during the night. She never saw him, however, for he always came after she had put out her light, and went away before daylight appeared.

So all went well and happily for a time, but then she began to be very sad and sorrowful; for all day long she had to go about alone, and she did so wish to go home to see her father and mother and brothers and sisters. Then the White Bear asked what it was that she lacked, and she told him that it was so dull and lonely there in the mountain, and that in her parents' house at home there were all her brothers and sisters, and it was because she could not go to them that she was so sorrowful.

'There might be a cure for that,' said the White Bear, 'if you would but promise me never to talk alone with your mother, but only when the others are there too; for she will take you by the hand,' he said, 'and will want to lead you into a room to talk with you alone; but that you must not do, or you will bring great misery on both of us.'

So one Sunday the White Bear came and said that now they could set out to see her father and mother. So they journeyed thither, she sitting on his back, and they went a long, long way, and it took a long, long time; but at last they came to a large white farmhouse, and her brothers and sisters were running about outside it, playing, and it was so pretty that it was a joy to see.

'Your parents dwell here now,' said the White Bear; 'but do not forget what I said to you, or you will do much harm both to yourself and me.'

'No, indeed,' said she, 'I shall not forget;' and as soon as she was at the door the White Bear turned round and went back again.

There were such rejoicings when she went in to her parents that it seemed as if they would never come to an end. None of them thought they could thank her enough for all she had done for them. Now they had everything they wished for, and all as good as it could be. They all asked her how she was getting on where she was. All was well with her too, she said, and she had everything that she could want. What other answers she gave I cannot say, but I am pretty sure that they did not learn much from her. But in the afternoon, after they had dined at mid-day, all happened just as the White Bear had said. Her mother wanted to talk with her alone in her own chamber. But she remembered what the White Bear had said, and would not go. 'What we have to say can be said at any time,' she answered. But somehow or other her mother at last persuaded her, and she was forced to tell the whole story.

So she told how every night a man came and lay down beside her when the lights were all put out, and how she never saw him, because he always went away before it grew light in the morning, and how she continually went about in sadness, thinking how happy she would be if she could but see him, and how all day long she was alone, and it was so dull and solitary. 'Oh!' cried the mother, in horror, 'you are very likely sleeping with a troll! But I will teach you a way to see him. You shall have a bit of candle, which you can carry home hidden in your bosom. Light that when he is asleep, but take care not to let any tallow drop upon him.'

So she took the candle, and hid it in her bosom, and when evening drew near the White Bear came to fetch her away. When they had gone some distance on their way, the White Bear asked her if everything had not happened just as he had foretold, and she could not but own that it had. 'Then if you have done what your mother wished,' said he, 'you have brought great misery on both of us.' 'No,' she said, 'I haven't done anything at all.' So when she reached home and went to bed it was just the same as it had been before, and a man came and lay down beside her. But at dead of night, when she could hear that he was sleeping, she got up and kindled a light, lit her candle, let the light shine on him, and saw him, and he was the handsomest prince that eyes had ever beheld, and she loved him so much that it seemed to her that she must die if she did not kiss him that very moment. So she did kiss him; but while she was doing it three drops of hot tallow fell upon his shirt and he awoke.

'What have you done?' he cried. 'Now you have brought misery on both of us. If you had but held out for the space of one year I should have been free. For I have a step-mother who is a troll, and she has bewitched me so that I am a white bear by day and a man by night. But now all is at an end between you and me, and I must leave you and go to her. She lives in a castle which lies east of the sun and west of the moon, and there too is a princess, with a nose three ells long, and she now is the one whom I must marry.'

She wept and lamented, but all in vain, for go he must. Then she asked him if she could not go with him. But no, that could not be. 'Tell me the way then, and I will seek you – that I may surely be allowed to do!'

'Yes, you may do that,' said he; 'but there is no way thither. It lies east of the sun and west of the moon, and never would you find your way there.'

When she awoke in the morning both Prince and castle were gone, and she was lying on a small green patch in the midst of a dark, thick wood. By her side lay the self-same bundle of rags which she had brought with her from her old home. So when she had rubbed the sleep out of her eyes, and wept till she was weary, she set out on her way, and thus she walked for many and many a long day, until at last she came to a lofty crag. Under it sat an aged woman, playing with a golden apple. The girl asked her if she knew the way to the Prince who lived with his step-mother in the castle which lay east of the sun and west of the moon, and was to marry a princess with a nose three ells long.

'How do you happen to know about him?' asked the old woman; 'maybe you are she who ought to have had him.' 'Yes, indeed, I am,' she said. 'So it is you, then?' said the old woman. 'I know nothing about him but that he dwells in a castle which is east of the sun and west of the moon. You will be a long time in getting to it, if ever you get to it at all; but you shall have the loan of my horse, and then you can ride to my neighbour; perhaps she can tell you more. When you have got there just strike the horse beneath the left ear and bid him go home again; and you may take this golden apple with you.'

So the girl seated herself on the horse, and rode for a long, long way, till she came to another crag, where an aged woman was sitting with a gold carding-comb. The girl asked her if she knew the way to the castle which lay east of the sun and west of the moon, and she answered like the first old woman, 'I know nothing about it, but that it is east of the sun and west of the moon, and that you will be a long time in getting to it, if ever you get there at all; but you shall have the loan of my horse to my next neighbour; perhaps she may tell you more. When you get there just strike the horse beneath the left ear and bid him go home again.' Then the old woman gave her the gold carding-comb, for it might, perhaps, be useful, she said.

So the girl seated herself on the horse, and rode a wearisome long way onwards again, and at last she came to a great crag where an aged woman sat spinning at a golden spinning-wheel. Of this woman, too, she inquired if she knew the way to the Prince, and where to find the castle which lay east of the sun and west of the moon. And it was the same thing once again. 'Maybe it was you who should have had the Prince,' said the old woman. 'Yes, indeed, I should have been the one,' said the girl. But this old crone knew the way no better than the others – it was east of the sun and west of the moon, she knew that, and 'you will be a long time in getting to it, if ever you get to it at all,' she said. 'But I'll lend you my horse, and I think you had better ride to the East Wind, and ask him: perhaps he may know where the castle is, and will blow you thither. When you have got to him just strike the horse beneath the left ear, and he will come home again.' And then she gave her the golden spinning-wheel, saying, 'Perhaps you may find that you have a use for it.'

The girl had to ride for a great many days, and for a long and wearisome time, before she got there; but at last she did arrive, and she asked the East Wind if he could tell her the way to the Prince who dwelt east of the sun and west of the moon. 'Well,' said the East Wind, 'I have heard tell of the Prince, and of his castle, but I do not know the way to it, for I have never blown so far; but, if you like, I will go with you to my brother the West Wind; he may know that, for he is much stronger than I am. You may sit on my back, and I'll carry you there.' So she seated herself on his back, and they did go swiftly! When they got there, the East Wind said that the girl was the one who ought to have had the Prince up at the castle which lay east of the sun and west of the moon, and that now she was searching to find him again, so she would like to hear if the West Wind knew whereabouts the castle was. 'No,' said the West Wind; 'so far as that have I never blown: but if you like I will go with you to the

South Wind, for he is much stronger than either of us, and he has roamed far and wide, and perhaps he can tell you what you want to know. You may seat yourself on my back, and I'll carry you to him.'

So she did this, and they journeyed to the South Wind, and were not long on the way. When they got there, the West Wind asked him if he could tell her the way to the castle that lay east of the sun and west of the moon, for she was the girl who ought to marry the Prince who lived there.

'Oh, indeed!' said the South Wind, 'is that she? Well,' said he, 'I have wandered about a great deal in my time, and in all kinds of places, but I have never blown so far as that. If you like, however, I will go with you to my brother the North Wind; he is the oldest and strongest of all of us, and if he does not know where it is no one in the whole world will be able to tell you. You may sit upon my back, and I'll carry you there.'

So she seated herself on his back, and off he went from his house in great haste, and they were not long on the way. When they came near the North Wind's dwelling, he was so wild and frantic that they felt cold gusts a long while before they got there.

'What do you want?' he roared out from afar, and they froze as they heard. Said the South Wind, 'It is I, your brother, and this is she who should have had the Prince who lives in the castle which lies east of the sun and west of the moon. And now she wishes to ask you if you have ever been there, and can tell her the way, for she would gladly find him again.'

'Yes,' said the North Wind, 'I know where it is. I once blew an aspen leaf there, but I was so tired that for many days afterwards I was not able to blow at all. However, if you really are anxious to go there, and are not afraid to go with me, I will take you on my back, and try if I can blow you there.'

'Get there I must,' said she; 'and if there is any way of going I will; and I have no fear, no matter how fast you go.'

'Very well then,' said the North Wind; 'but you must sleep here to-night, for if we are ever to get there we must have the day before us.'

The North Wind woke her betimes next morning, and puffed himself up, and made himself so big and so strong that it was frightful to see him, and away they went, high up through the air, as if they would not stop until they had reached the very end of the world. Down below there was such a storm! It blew down woods and houses, and when they were above the sea the ships were wrecked by hundreds. And thus they tore on and on, and a long time went by, and then yet more time passed, and still they were above the sea, and the North Wind grew tired, and more tired, and at last so utterly weary that he was scarcely able to blow any longer, and he sank and sank, lower and lower, until at last he went so low that the crests of the waves dashed against the heels of the poor girl he was carrying.

'Are you afraid?' said the North Wind. 'I have no fear,' said she; and it was true. But they were not very far from land, and there was just enough strength left in the North Wind to enable him to throw her up on to the shore under the walls of the castle which lay east of the sun and west of the moon; but then he was so weary and worn out that he was forced to rest for several days before he could go to his own home again.

Next morning the girl sat down beneath the castle window to play with the golden apple, and the first person she saw was the Princess with the long nose, who was to have the Prince. 'How much do you want for that gold apple of yours, girl?' said she, opening the window. 'It can't be bought either for gold or money,' answered the girl. 'If it cannot be bought either for gold or money, what will buy it? You may ask what you please,' said the Princess.

'Well, if I may go to the Prince who is here, and be with him to-night, you shall have it,' said the girl who had come with the North Wind. 'You may do that,' said the Princess, for she had made up her mind what she would do. So the Princess got the golden apple, but when the girl went up to the Prince's apartment that night he was asleep, for the Princess had so contrived it. The poor girl called to him and shook him, and between whiles she wept; but she could not wake him. In the morning, as soon as day dawned, in came the Princess with the long nose, and drove her out again. In the day-time she sat down once more beneath the windows of the castle, and began to card with her golden carding-comb; and then all happened as it had happened before. The Princess asked her what she wanted for it, and she replied that it was not for sale, either for gold or money, but that if she could get leave to go to the Prince, and be with him during the night, the Princess should have it. But when she went up to the Prince's room he was again asleep, and, let her call him, or shake him, or weep as she would, he still slept on, and she could not put any life in him. When daylight came, the Princess with the long nose came too, and once more drove her away.

So the girl seated herself under the castle windows, to spin with her golden spinning-wheel, and the Princess with the long nose wanted to have that also. She opened the window, and asked what the girl would take for it. The girl said what she had said on each of the former occasions – that it was not for sale either for gold or for money, but if she could get leave to go to the Prince who lived there, and be with him during the night, she should have it.

'Yes,' said the Princess, 'I will gladly consent to that.'

But in the castle there were some Christian folk who had been carried off, and they were in the chamber which was next to that of the Prince, and had heard how a woman wept and called on him two nights running, and they told the Prince of this. So that evening, when the Princess came once more with her sleeping-drink, he pretended to drink, but threw it away behind him, for he suspected that it was a sleeping-drink. So, when the girl went into the Prince's room this time he was awake, and she had to tell him how she had come there.

'You have come just in time,' said the Prince, 'for I should have been married to-morrow; but I will not have the long-nosed Princess, and you alone can save me. I will say that I want to see what my bride can do, and bid her wash the shirt which has the three drops of tallow on it. This she will consent to do, for she does not know that it is you who let them fall on it; but no one can wash them out but one born of Christian folk; it cannot be done by one of a pack of trolls; and then I will say that no one shall ever be my bride but the woman who can do this, and I know that you can.' So there was great joy and gladness between them all that night, and the next day, when the wedding was to take place, the Prince said, 'I must see what my bride can do.' 'That you may do,' said the step-mother.

'I have a fine shirt which I want to wear as my wedding shirt, but three drops of tallow have got upon it which must be washed off, and I have vowed to marry no one but the woman who is able to do it. If she can't, she's not worth having.'

Well, that was a very small matter, they thought, and agreed to do it. The Princess with the long nose began to wash as well as she could, but the more she washed and rubbed, the larger the spots grew. 'Ah! you can't wash at all,' said the old troll-hag, who was her mother. 'Give it to me.' But she too had not had the shirt very long in her hands before it looked worse still, and the more she washed it and rubbed it, the larger and blacker grew the spots.

So the other trolls had to come and wash, but, the more they did, the blacker and uglier grew the shirt, until at length it was as black as if it had been up the chimney. 'Oh!' cried the Prince, 'not one of you is good for anything at all! There is a beggar-girl sitting outside the window, and I'll be bound that she can wash better than any of you. Come in, you girl there!' he cried. So she came in. 'Can you wash this shirt clean?' he asked. 'Oh! I don't know,' she said, 'but I will try.' And no sooner had she taken the shirt and dipped it in the water than it was white as driven snow, and even whiter than that.

'I will marry *you*,' said the Prince.

Then the old troll-hag flew into such a rage that she burst, and the Princess with the long nose and all the little trolls must have burst too, for they have never been heard of since. The Prince and his bride set free all the Christian folk who were imprisoned there, and took away with them all the gold and silver that they could carry, and moved far away from the castle which lay east of the sun and west of the moon.

The Fairy Nurse

THERE WAS once a farmer and his wife living near Coolgarrow. They had three children, and my story happened while the youngest was a baby. The wife was a good wife enough, but her mind was all on her family and the farm, and she hardly ever went to her knees without falling asleep, and she thought the time spent in the chapel was twice as long as it need be. So, friends, she let her man and her two children go before her one day to Mass, while she called to consult a fairy man about a disorder one of her cows had. She was late at the chapel, and was sorry all the day after, for her husband was in grief about it, and she was very fond of him.

Late that night the man was wakened up by the cries of his children calling out 'Mother! mother!' When he sat up and rubbed his eyes, there was no wife by his side, and when he asked the little ones what was become of their mother, they said they saw the room full of little men and women, dressed in white and red and green, and their mother in the middle of them, going out by the door as if she were walking in her sleep. Out he ran, and searched everywhere round the house, but neither tale nor tidings did he get of her for many a day.

Well, the poor man was miserable enough, for he was as fond of his woman as she was of him. It used to bring the salt tears down his cheeks to see his poor children neglected and dirty, as they often were, and they'd have been bad enough only for a kind neighbour that used to look in whenever she could spare time. The infant was away with a nurse.

About six weeks after – just as he was going out to his work one morning – a neighbour, that used to mind women when they were ill, came up to him, and kept step by step with him to the field, and this is what she told him.

'Just as I was falling asleep last night, I heard a horse's tramp on the grass and a knock at the door, and there, when I came out, was a fine-looking dark man, mounted on a black horse, and he told me to get ready in all haste, for a lady was in great want of me. As soon as I put on my cloak and things, he took me by the hand, and I was sitting

73

behind him before I felt myself stirring. "Where are we going, sir?" says I. "You'll soon know," says he; and he drew his fingers across my eyes, and not a ray could I see. I kept a tight grip of him, and I little knew whether he was going backwards or forwards, or how long we were about it, till my hand was taken again, and I felt the ground under me. The fingers went the other way across my eyes, and there we were before a castle door, and in we went through a big hall and great rooms all painted in fine green colours, with red and gold bands and ornaments, and the finest carpets and chairs and tables and window curtains, and grand ladies and gentlemen walking about. At last we came to a bedroom, with a beautiful lady in bed, with a fine bouncing boy beside her. The lady clapped her hands, and in came the Dark Man and kissed her and the baby, and praised me, and gave me a bottle of green ointment to rub the child all over.

'Well, the child I rubbed, sure enough; but my right eye began to smart, and I put up my finger and gave it a rub, and then stared, for never in all my life was I so frightened. The beautiful room was a big, rough cave, with water oozing over the edges of the stones and through the clay; and the lady and the lord and the child were wizened, poverty-bitten creatures – nothing but skin and bone – and the rich dresses were old rags. I didn't let on that I found any difference, and after a bit says the Dark Man, "Go before me to the hall door, and I will be with you in a few moments, and see you safe home." Well, just as I turned into the outside cave, who should I see watching near the door but your poor Molly. She looked round all terrified, and says she to me in a whisper, "I'm brought here to nurse the child of the King and Queen of the fairies; but there is one chance of saving me. All the court will pass the cross near Templeshambo next Friday night, on a visit to the fairies of Old Ross. If John can catch me by the hand or cloak when I ride by, and has courage not to let go his grip, I'll be safe. Here's the King. Don't open your mouth to answer. I saw what happened with the ointment."

'The Dark Man didn't once cast his eye towards Molly, and he seemed to have no suspicion of me. When we came out I looked about me, and where do you think we were but in the dyke of the Rath of Cromogue. I was on the horse again, which was nothing but a big rag-weed, and I was in dread every minute I'd fall off; but nothing happened till I found myself in my own cabin. The King slipped five guineas into my hand as soon as I was on the ground, and thanked me, and bade me good night. I hope I'll never see his face again. I got into bed, and couldn't sleep for a long time; and when I examined my five guineas this morning, that I left in the table drawer the last thing, I found five withered leaves of oak – bad luck to the giver!'

Well, you may think of all the fright, and the joy, and the grief the poor man was in when the woman finished her story. They talked and they talked, but we needn't mind what they said till Friday night came, when both were standing where the mountain road crosses the one going to Ross.

There they stood, looking towards the bridge of Thuar, in the dead of the night, with a little moonlight shining from over Kilachdiarmid. At last she gave a start, and 'By this and by that,' says she, 'here they come, bridles jingling and feathers tossing!' He looked but could see nothing; and she stood trembling and her eyes wide open, looking down the way to the ford of Ballinacoola. 'I see your wife,' says she, 'riding on the outside just so as to rub against us. We'll walk on quietly, as if we suspected nothing, and when we are passing I'll give you a shove. If you don't do *your* duty then, woe be with you!'

Well, they walked on easy, and their poor hearts beating in their breasts; and though he could see nothing, he heard a faint jingle and trampling and rustling, and at last he got the push that she promised. He spread out his arms, and there was his wife's waist within them, and he could see her plain; but such a hullabulloo rose as if there was an earthquake, and he found himself surrounded by horrible-looking things, roaring at him and striving to pull his wife away. But he made the sign of the cross and bade them be gone in God's name, and held his wife as if it was iron his arms were made of. Bedad, in one moment everything was as silent as the grave, and the poor woman lying in a faint in the arms of her husband and her good neighbour. Well, all in good time she was minding her family and her business again; and I'll go bail, after the fright she got, she spent more time on her knees, and avoided fairy men all the days of the week, and particularly on Sunday.

It is hard to have anything to do with the good people without getting a mark from them. My brave nurse didn't escape no more than another. She was one Thursday at the market of Enniscorthy, when what did she see walking among the tubs of butter but the Dark Man, very hungry-looking, and taking a scoop out of one tub and out of another. 'Oh, sir,' says she, very foolish, 'I hope your lady is well, and the baby.' 'Pretty well, thank you,' says he, rather frightened like. 'How do I look in this new suit?' says he, getting to one side of her. 'I can't see you plain at all, sir,' says she. 'Well, now?' says he, getting round her back to the other side. 'Musha, indeed, sir, your coat looks no better than a withered dock-leaf.' 'Maybe, then,' says he, 'it will be different now,' and he struck the eye next him with a switch.

Friends, she never saw a glimmer after with that one eye till the day of her death.

The Finest Liar in the World

AT THE edge of a wood there lived an old man who had only one son. One day he called the boy to him and said he wanted some corn ground, but the youth must be sure never to enter any mill where the miller was beardless.

The boy took the corn and set out. Before he had gone very far he saw a large mill in front of him, with a beardless man standing in the doorway.

'Good greeting, beardless one!' cried he.

'Good greeting, sonny,' replied the man.

'Could I grind something here?'

'Yes, certainly! I will finish what I am doing and then you can grind as long as you like.'

But suddenly the boy remembered what his father had told him, and he bade farewell to the man. Going farther down the river, he came to another mill, not knowing that as soon as his back was turned the beardless man had picked up a bag of corn and run hastily to the same mill before him. When the boy reached the second mill, and saw a second beardless man sitting there, he did not stop but walked on till he came to a third mill. But this time also the beardless man had been too clever for him and had arrived first by another road.

When it happened a fourth time the boy grew cross, and said to himself, 'It is no good going on; there seems to be a beardless man in every mill.' He took the sack from his back and made up his mind to grind his corn where he was.

The beardless man finished grinding his own corn, and when he had done he said to the boy, who was beginning to grind his, 'Suppose, sonny, we make a cake of what you have there.'

Now the boy had been rather uneasy as he worked because of his father's warning, but he thought, 'What is done cannot be undone,' and answered, 'Very well, so let it be.'

Then the beardless one got up, threw the flour into the tub and made a hole in the middle, telling the boy to fetch some water from the river in his two hands, to mix the cake. When the cake was ready

77

for baking they put it on the fire and covered it
with hot ashes, till it was cooked through. Then
they leaned it up against the wall, for it was too
big to go into a cupboard, and the beardless
one said to the boy, 'Look here, if we share
this cake we shall neither of us have enough.
Let us see who can tell the biggest lie, and the
one who lies the better shall have the whole cake.'

The boy, not knowing what else to do, answered, 'All right; you
begin.'

So the beardless one began, and when he was tired of inventing
new stories, the boy said to him, 'My good fellow, if that is all you
can do it is not much! Listen to me, and I will tell you a true story.

'In my youth, when I was an old man we had a quantity of bee-
hives. Every morning when I got up I counted them over, and it was
quite easy to number the bees, but I never could reckon the hives
properly. One day, as I was counting the bees, I discovered that my
best bee was missing, and without losing a moment I saddled a cock
and went out to look for him. I traced him as far as the shore. I knew
then that he had crossed the sea and that I must follow. When I had
reached the other side I found a man had harnessed my bee to a
plough and, with his help, was sowing millet seed.

' "That is my bee!" I shouted. "Where did you get him?"

' "Brother," replied the man, "if he is yours, take him." And he not only gave me back my bee but a sack of millet seed into the bargain, because he had made use of my bee. Then I put the bag on my shoulders, took the saddle from the cock, and placed it on the back of the bee, which I mounted, leading the cock by a string so that he should have a rest.

'As we were flying home over the sea one of the strings that held the bag of millet broke in two, and the sack dropped straight into the ocean. It was quite lost, of course, and there was no use thinking about it, and by the time we were safe back again night had come. I then got down from my bee, and let him loose that he might get his supper, gave the cock some corn, and went to sleep myself.

'But when I awoke with the sun what a scene met my eyes! During the night wolves had come and eaten my bee. And honey lay ankle-deep in the valley and knee-deep on the hills. Then I began to consider how I could best collect some to take home with me.

'Now it happened that I had with me a small hatchet and this I took to the wood, hoping to meet some animal which I could kill, whose skin I might turn into a bag. As I entered the forest I saw two roe deer hopping on one foot, so I slew them with a single blow and made three bags from their skins, all of which I filled with honey and placed on the back of the cock. At length I reached home, where I was told that my father had just been born and that I must go at once to fetch some holy water to sprinkle him with.

'As I went I turned over in my mind if there was no way for me to get back my millet seed, which had dropped into the sea, and when I arrived at the place with the holy water, I saw the seed had fallen on fruitful soil and was growing before my eyes. And more than that, it was even cut by an invisible hand and made into a cake.

'So I took the cake as well as the holy water and was flying back with them over the sea, when there fell a great rain. The sea was swollen and swept away my millet cake. Ah, how vexed I was at its loss when I was safe on earth again.

'Suddenly I remembered that my hair was very long. If I stood it touched the ground, although if I was sitting it only reached my ears. I seized a knife and cut off a large lock, which I plaited together, and when night came tied it into a knot and prepared to use it for a pillow. But what was I to do for a fire? A tinder box I had, but no wood.

'Then it occurred to me that I had stuck a needle in my clothes, so I took the needle and split it in pieces and lit it, then laid myself down by the fire and went to sleep. But ill-luck still pursued me. While I was sleeping a spark from the fire lighted on the hair, which was burnt up in a moment.

'In despair I threw myself on the ground and instantly sank in it as far as my waist. I struggled to get out, but only fell in further; so I ran to the house, seized a spade, dug myself out, and took home the holy water. On the way I noticed that the ripe cornfields were full of reapers, and suddenly the air became so frightfully hot that the men dropped down in a faint.

'Then I called to them, "Why don't you bring out our mare, which is as tall as two days and as broad as half a day, and make a shade for yourselves?" My father heard what I said and jumped quickly on the mare, and the reapers worked with a will in the shadow, while I snatched up a wooden pail to bring them some water to drink.

'When I reached the well everything was frozen hard, and in order to draw some water I had to take off my head and break the ice with it. As I drew near them, carrying the water, the reapers all cried out, "Why, what has become of your head?" I put up my hand and discovered that I really had no head, and that I must have left it in the well.

'I ran back to look for it, but found that meanwhile a fox, which was passing by, had pulled my head out of the water and was tearing at it. I stole cautiously up to him and gave him such a kick that he uttered a loud scream and let fall a parchment on which was written, *The cake is mine, and the beardless one goes empty-handed.*'

With these words the boy rose, took the cake, and went home, while the beardless one remained behind to swallow his disappointment.

The Goose-Girl

AN OLD queen, whose husband had been dead for many years, had a beautiful daughter. When she grew up she was betrothed to a prince who lived a great way off, and when the time drew near for her to be married she made ready for the long journey. Her mother packed up many costly things: vessels of gold and silver, and jewels and trinkets, in fact, everything that became a royal bride, for she loved her daughter very dearly. She gave her a waiting-maid also, who was to ride with her and hand her over to the bridegroom, and she provided each of them with a horse for the journey. Now the Princess's horse was called Falada, and could speak.

When the hour for departure drew near the old Queen went to her bedroom, and taking a small knife she cut her finger till it bled. Then she let three drops of blood fall upon a handkerchief, and gave it to her daughter saying, 'Dear child, take great care of this; it may be of use to you on the journey.'

So they took a sad farewell of each other, and the Princess put the handkerchief in the front of her dress, mounted her horse, and set forth on the journey to her bridegroom's kingdom. After they had ridden for about an hour the Princess began to feel very thirsty, and said to her waiting-maid, 'Pray get down and fetch me some water in my golden cup out of yonder stream; I would like a drink.' 'If you're thirsty,' said the maid, 'dismount yourself, and lie down by the water and drink; I don't mean to be your servant any longer.' The Princess was so thirsty that she got down, bent over the stream, and drank, for she dared not use her golden goblet. As she drank she murmured, 'Oh! heaven, what am I to do?' and the three drops of blood replied:

> 'If your mother only knew,
> Her heart would surely break in two.'

But the Princess was meek, and said nothing about her maid's rude behaviour, and quietly mounted her horse again. They rode on their way for several miles, but the day was hot, and the sun's rays smote fiercely on them, so that the Princess was soon overcome by thirst again. And as they passed a brook she called once more to her waiting-maid, 'Pray get down and give me a drink from my golden cup,' for she had long ago forgotten her maid's rude words. But the waiting-maid replied, more haughtily even than before, 'If you want a drink, you can dismount and get it; I don't mean to be your servant.' Then the Princess was compelled by her thirst to get down, and bending over the flowing water she cried and said, 'Oh! heaven, what am I to do?' and the three drops of blood replied:

> 'If your mother only knew,
> Her heart would surely break in two.'

And as she drank thus, and leant right over the water, the handker-chief containing the three drops of blood fell from her bosom and floated down the stream, and she in her anxiety never even noticed her loss. But the waiting-maid had observed it with delight, as she knew it gave her power over the bride, for in losing the handker-chief the Princess had become weak and powerless. When she wished to get on her horse Falada again, the waiting-maid called out, 'I mean to ride Falada; you must mount my beast;' and this too she had to submit to. Then the waiting-maid commanded her harshly to take off her royal robes, and to put on her common ones, and finally she made her swear by heaven not to say a word about the matter when they reached the palace; and if she hadn't taken this oath she would have been killed on the spot. But Falada observed everything, and laid it all to heart.

The waiting-maid now mounted Falada, and the real bride the maid's horse, and so they continued their journey till at length they came to the palace yard. There was great rejoicing over their arrival, and the Prince sprang forward to meet them, and taking the waiting-maid for his bride, he lifted her down from her horse and led her upstairs to the royal chamber.

In the meantime the real Princess was left standing below in the courtyard. The old King, who was looking out of his window, beheld her in this plight, and it struck him how sweet and gentle, even beautiful, she looked. He went at once to the royal chamber, and asked the bride who it was she had brought with her and had left thus standing in the court below. 'Oh!' replied the bride, 'I brought her with me to keep me company on the journey; give the girl something to do, that she mayn't be idle.' But the old King had no work for her, and couldn't think of anything; so he said, 'I've a lad who looks after the geese, she'd better help him.' The youth's name was Curdken, and the real bride was made to assist him in herding geese.

Soon after this the false bride said to the Prince, 'Dearest husband, I pray you grant me a favour.' He answered, 'That I will.' 'Then let the slaughterer cut off the head of the horse I rode here, because it behaved very badly on the journey.' But the truth was she was afraid lest the horse should speak and tell how she had treated the Princess. She carried her point, and the faithful Falada was killed. When the news came to the ears of the real Princess she went to the slaughterer, and secretly promised him a piece of gold if he would do something for her. There was in the town a large dark gate, through which she had to pass night and morning with the geese; would he kindly hang up Falada's head there, that she might see it once again? The slaughterer said he would do as she desired, and that night he nailed the horse's head firmly over the gateway.

Early next morning, as she and Curdken were driving their flock through the gate, she said as she passed under:

'Oh! Falada, 'tis you hang there!'

and the head replied:

"'Tis you; pass under, Princess fair;
If your mother only knew,
Her heart would surely break in two.'

Then they drove the geese on out of the town. And when they had reached the common where the geese fed she sat down and unloosed her hair, which was the colour of spun gold. Curdken loved to see it glitter in the sun, and wanted much to pull out a hair. Then she said:

'Wind, wind, gently sway,
Blow Curdken's hat away;
Let him chase o'er field and wold
Till my locks of ruddy gold,
Now astray and hanging down,
Be combed and plaited in a crown.'

Then a gust of wind blew Curdken's hat away, and he had to chase it over hill and dale. When he returned from the pursuit she had finished her combing and curling, and his chance of getting any hair was gone. Curdken was very angry, and wouldn't speak to her. So they herded the geese till evening and then went home.

The next morning, as they passed under the gate, the girl said:

'Oh! Falada, 'tis you hang there!'

and the head replied:

''Tis you; pass under, Princess fair;
If your mother only knew,
Her heart would surely break in two.'

84

Then she went on her way till she came to the common, where she sat down and began to comb out her hair; then Curdken ran up to her and wanted to pull a hair from her head, but she called out hastily:

> 'Wind, wind, gently sway,
> Blow Curdken's hat away;
> Let him chase o'er field and wold
> Till my locks of ruddy gold,
> Now astray and hanging down,
> Be combed and plaited in a crown.'

Then a puff of wind came and blew Curdken's hat far away, so that he had to run after it; and when he returned she had long finished putting up her golden locks, and he couldn't get any hair; so they watched the geese till it was dark.

But that evening when they got home Curdken went to the old King, and said, 'I refuse to herd geese any longer with that girl.' 'For what reason?' asked the old King. 'Because she does nothing but annoy me all day long,' replied Curdken; and he proceeded to tell all that had happened. He said, 'Every morning as we drive the flock through the dark gate she says to a horse's head that hangs on the wall:

> ' "Oh! Falada, 'tis you hang there!"

and the head replies:

> ' " 'Tis you; pass under, Princess fair;
> If your mother only knew,
> Her heart would surely break in two." '

And Curdken went on to tell what passed on the common where the geese fed, and how he had always to chase his hat.

The old King bade him go and drive forth his flock as usual next day; and when morning came he himself took up his position behind the dark gate, and heard how the goose-girl greeted Falada. Then he followed her to the field, and hid himself behind a bush on the common. He soon saw with his own eyes how the goose-boy and the goose-girl looked after the geese, and how after a time the maiden sat down and loosed her hair, that glittered like gold, and repeated:

'Wind, wind, gently sway,
Blow Curdken's hat away;
Let him chase o'er field and wold
Till my locks of ruddy gold,
Now astray and hanging down,
Be combed and plaited in a crown.'

Then a gust of wind came and blew Curdken's hat away, so that he had to fly over hill and dale after it, and the girl in the meantime quietly combed and plaited her hair; all this the old King observed, and returned to the palace without anyone having noticed him. In the evening when the goose-girl came home he called her aside, and asked her why she behaved as she did. 'I mayn't tell you why, nor dare I confide my woes to anyone, for I swore not to by heaven, otherwise I should have lost my life.' The old King begged her to tell him all, and left her no peace, but he could get nothing out of her.

At last he said, 'Well, if you won't tell me, confide your trouble to the iron stove there;' and he went away. Then she crept to the stove, and began to sob and cry and to pour out her heart, and said, 'Here I sit, deserted by all the world, I who am a king's daughter. A false waiting-maid has forced me to put off my royal robes, and has taken my place with my bridegroom while I have to fulfil the lowly office of goose-girl.

'If my mother only knew,
Her heart would surely break in two.'

But the old King stood outside at the stove chimney, and listened to her words. Then he entered the room again, and bidding her leave the stove, he ordered royal apparel to be put on her, in which she looked amazingly lovely. Then he summoned his son, and revealed to him that he had got the false bride, who was nothing but a waiting-maid, while the real one, who had been in the guise of the goose-girl, was standing at his side.

The young King rejoiced from his heart when he saw her beauty and learnt how good she was, and a great banquet was prepared, to which everyone was bidden. The bridegroom sat at the head of the table, the Princess on one side of him and the waiting-maid on the other; but she was so dazzled that she did not recognise the Princess in her glittering garments. Now when they had eaten and drunk, and were merry, the old King asked the waiting-maid to solve a knotty problem for him. 'What,' said he, 'should be done to a certain person who has deceived everyone?' and he proceeded to relate the whole story, ending up with, 'Now what sentence should be passed?' Then the false bride answered, 'She deserves to be put stark naked into a barrel lined with sharp nails, which should be dragged by two white horses up and down the street till she is dead.'

'You are the person,' said the King, 'and you have passed sentence on yourself; and even so it shall be done to you.' And when the sentence had been carried out the young King was married to his real bride, and both reigned over the kingdom in peace and happiness.

The Groac'h of the Isle of Lok

IN OLD times, when all kinds of wonderful things happened in Brittany, there lived in the village of Lanillis a young man named Houarn and a girl called Bellah. They were cousins, and as their mothers were great friends, and constantly in and out of each other's houses, they had often been laid in the same cradle, and had played and fought over their games.

'When they are grown up they will marry,' said the mothers; but just as everyone was beginning to think of wedding bells, the two mothers died, and the cousins, who had no money, went as servants in the same house. This was better than being parted, of course, but not so good as having a little cottage of their own, where they could do as they liked, and soon they might have been heard bewailing to each other the hardness of their lots.

'If we could only manage to buy a cow and get a pig to fatten,' grumbled Houarn, 'I would rent a bit of ground from the master, and then we could be married.'

'Yes,' answered Bellah, with a deep sigh; 'but we live in such hard times, and at the last fair the price of pigs had risen again.'

'We shall have long to wait, that is quite clear,' replied Houarn, turning away to his work.

Whenever they met they repeated their grievances, and at length Houarn's patience was exhausted, and one morning he came to Bellah and told her that he was going away to seek his fortune.

The girl was very unhappy as she listened to this, and felt sorry that she had not tried to make the best of things. She implored Houarn not to leave her, but he would not listen.

'The birds,' he said, 'continue flying until they reach a field of corn, and the bees do not stop unless they find the honey-giving flowers, and why should a man have less sense than they? Like them, I shall seek till I get what I want – that is, money to buy a cow and a pig to fatten. And if you love me, Bellah, you won't attempt to hinder a plan which will hasten our marriage.'

The girl saw it was useless to say more, so she answered sadly, 'Well, go then, since you must. But first I will divide with you all that my parents left me,' and going to her room, she opened a small chest, and took from it a bell, a knife, and a little stick.

'This bell,' she said, 'can be heard at any distance, however far, but it only rings to warn us that our friends are in great danger. The knife frees all it touches from magic spells, while the stick will carry you wherever you want to go. I will give you the knife to guard you against the enchantment of wizards, and the bell to tell me of your perils. The stick I shall keep for myself, so that I can fly to you if ever you have need of me.'

Then they cried for a little on each other's necks, and Houarn started for the mountains.

But in those days beggars abounded, and through every village he passed they followed Houarn in crowds, mistaking him for a gentleman, because there were no holes in his clothes.

'There is no fortune to be made *here*,' he thought to himself; 'it is a place for spending, and not earning. I see I must go further,' and he walked on till he came to a little town.

He was sitting on a bench outside an inn, when he heard two men who were loading their mules talking about the Groac'h of the island of Lok.

'What is a Groac'h?' asked he. 'I have never come across one.' And the men answered that it was the name given to the fairy that dwelt in the lake, and that she was rich – oh! richer than all the kings in the world put together. Many had gone to the island to try and get possession of her treasures, but no one had ever come back.

As he listened Houarn made up his mind.

'I will go, and return too,' he said to the muleteers. They stared at him in astonishment, and besought him not to be so mad as to throw away his life in such a foolish manner; but he only laughed, and answered that if they could tell him of any other way in which to procure a cow and a pig to fatten, he would think no more about it. But the men did not know how this was to be done, and, shaking their heads over his obstinacy, left him to his fate.

So Houarn went down to the sea, and engaged a boatman to take him to the isle of Lok.

The island was large, and lying almost across it was a lake, with a narrow opening to the sea. Houarn paid the boatman and sent him away, and then proceeded to walk round the lake. At one end he perceived a small skiff, painted blue and shaped like a swan, lying under a clump of yellow broom. As far as he could see, the swan's head was tucked under its wing, and Houarn, who had never beheld a boat of the sort, went quickly towards it and stepped in, so as to examine it the better. But no sooner was he on board than the swan woke suddenly up; his head emerged from under his wing, his feet began to move in the water, and in another moment they were in the middle of the lake.

As soon as the young man had recovered from his surprise, he prepared to jump into the lake and swim to shore. But the bird had guessed his intentions, and plunged beneath the water, carrying Houarn with him to the palace of the Groac'h.

Now, unless you have been under the sea and beheld all the wonders that lie there, you can never have an idea what the Groac'h's palace was like. It was all made of shells, blue and green and pink and lilac and white, shading into each other till you could not tell where one colour ended and the other began. The staircases were of crystal, and every separate stair sang like a woodland bird as you put your foot on it. Round the palace were great gardens full of all the plants that grow in the sea, with diamonds for flowers.

In a large hall the Groac'h was lying on a couch of gold. Her colouring was the pink and white of shells, her long black hair was intertwined with strings of coral, and her dress of green silk seemed formed out of the sea. At the sight of her Houarn stopped, dazzled by her beauty.

'Come in,' said the Groac'h, rising to her feet. 'Strangers and handsome youths are always welcome here. Do not be shy, but tell me how you found your way, and what you want.'

'My name is Houarn,' he answered, 'Lanillis is my home, and I am trying to earn enough money to buy a little cow and a pig to fatten.'

'Well, you can easily get that,' replied she; 'it is nothing to worry about. Come in and enjoy yourself.' And she beckoned him to follow her into a second hall whose floors and walls were formed of pearls, and where there were tables laden with fruit and wines of all kinds; and as he ate and drank, the Groac'h talked to him and told him how the treasures he saw came from shipwrecked vessels, and were brought to her palace by a magic current of water.

'I do not wonder,' exclaimed Houarn, who now felt quite at home, 'I do not wonder that the people on the earth have so much to say about you.'

'The rich are always envied.'

'For myself,' he added, with a laugh, 'I only ask for the half of your wealth.'

'You can have it, if you will, Houarn,' answered the fairy.

'What do you mean?' cried he.

'My husband is dead,' she replied, 'and if you wish it, I will marry you.'

The young man gazed at her in surprise. Could anyone so rich and so beautiful really wish to be his wife? He looked at her again, and Bellah was forgotten as he answered, 'A man would be mad indeed to refuse such an offer. I can only accept it with joy.'

'Then the sooner it is done the better,' said the Groac'h, and gave orders to her servants. When the ceremony was over, she begged Houarn to accompany her to a fish-pond at the bottom of the garden.

'Come lawyer, come miller, come tailor, come singer!' cried she, holding out a net of steel; and at each call a fish appeared and jumped into the net. When it was full she went into a large kitchen and threw them all into a golden pot; but above the bubbling of the water Houarn seemed to hear the whispering of little voices.

'Who is it whispering in the golden pot, Groac'h?' he inquired at last.

'It is nothing but the noise of the wood hissing,' she answered; but it did not sound the least like that to Houarn.

'There it is again,' he said, after a short pause.

'The water is getting hot, and it makes the fish jump,' she replied; but soon the noise grew louder and sounded like cries.

'What *is* it?' asked Houarn, beginning to feel uncomfortable.

'Just the crickets on the hearth,' said she, and broke into a song which drowned the cries from the pot.

But though Houarn held his peace, he was not as happy as before. Something seemed to have gone wrong, and then he suddenly remembered Bellah.

'Is it possible I can have forgotten her so soon? What a wretch I am!' he thought to himself; and he remained apart and watched the Groac'h while she emptied the fish into a plate and bade him eat his dinner while she fetched wine from her cellar in a cave.

Houarn sat down and took out the knife which Bellah had given him, but as soon as the blade touched the fish the enchantment ceased, and four men stood before him.

'Houarn, save us, we entreat you, and save yourself too!' murmured they, not daring to raise their voices.

'Why, it must have been *you* who were crying out in the pot just now!' exclaimed Houarn.

'Yes, it was us,' they answered. 'Like you, we came to the isle of Lok to seek our fortunes, and like you we consented to marry the Groac'h, and no sooner was the ceremony over than she turned us into fishes, as she had done all our forerunners, who are in the fish-pond still, where you will shortly join them.'

On hearing this Houarn leaped into the air, as if he already felt himself frizzling in the golden pot. He rushed to the door, hoping to escape that way; but the Groac'h, who had heard everything, met him on the threshold. Instantly she threw the steel net over his head, and the eyes of a little green frog peeped through the meshes.

'You shall go and play with the rest,' she said, carrying him off to the fish-pond.

It was at this very moment that Bellah, who was skimming the milk in the farm dairy, heard the fairy bell tinkle violently.

At the sound she grew pale, for she knew it meant that Houarn was in danger; and, hastily changing from the rough dress she wore for her work, she left the farm with the magic stick in her hand.

Her knees were trembling under her, but she ran as fast as she could to the cross roads, where she drove her stick into the ground, murmuring as she did so a verse her mother had taught her:

> 'Little staff of apple-tree,
> Over the earth and over the sea,
> Up in the air be guide to me,
> Everywhere to wander free!'

and immediately the stick became a smart little horse, with a rosette at each ear and a feather on his forehead. He stood quite still while Bellah scrambled up, then he started off, his pace growing quicker and quicker, till at length the girl could hardly see the trees and houses as they flashed past. But, rapid as the pace was, it was not rapid enough for Bellah, who stooped and said:

'The swallow is less swift than the wind, the wind is less swift than the lightning. But you, my horse, if you love me, must be swifter than them all, for there is a part of my heart that suffers – the best part of my heart that is in danger.'

And the horse heard her, and galloped like a straw carried along by a tempest till they reached the foot of a rock called the Leap of the Deer. There he stopped, for no horse or mule that ever was born could climb that rock, and Bellah knew it, so she began to sing again:

> 'Horse of Léon, given to me,
> Over the earth and over the sea,
> Up in the air be guide to me,
> Everywhere to wander free!'

and when she had finished, the horse's fore-legs grew shorter and spread into wings, his hind legs became claws, feathers sprouted all over his body, and she sat on the back of a great bird, which bore her to the summit of the rock. Here she found a nest made of clay and lined with dried moss, and in the centre a tiny man, black and wrinkled, who gave a cry of surprise at the sight of Bellah.

'Ah! you are the pretty girl who was to come and save me!'

'To save you!' repeated Bellah. 'But who are you, my little friend?'

'I am the husband of the Groac'h of the isle of Lok, and it is because of her that I am here.'

'But what are you doing in this nest?'

'I am sitting on six eggs of stone, and I shall not be set free till they are hatched.'

On hearing this Bellah began to laugh.

'Poor little cock!' she said, 'and how am I to deliver you?'

'By delivering Houarn, who is in the power of the Groac'h.'

'Ah! tell me how I can manage that, and if I have to walk round the whole of Brittany on my bended knees I will do it!'

'Well, first you must dress yourself as a young man, and then go and seek the Groac'h. When you have found her you must contrive to get hold of the net of steel that hangs from her waist, and shut her up in it for ever!'

'But where am I to find a young man's clothes?' asked she.

'I will help you,' he replied, and as he spoke he pulled out four of his red hairs and blew them away, muttering something the while. In the twinkling of an eye the four hairs changed into four tailors, of whom the first carried a cabbage, the second a pair of scissors, the third a needle, and the fourth an iron. Without waiting for orders, they sat down in the nest and, crossing their legs comfortably, began to prepare the suit of clothes for Bellah.

With one of the leaves of the cabbage they made her a coat, and another served for a waistcoat; but it took two for the wide breeches which were then in fashion. The hat was cut from the heart of the cabbage, and a pair of shoes from the thick stem. And when Bellah had put them all on you would have taken her for a gentleman dressed in green velvet, lined with white satin.

She thanked the little men gratefully, and after a few more instructions, jumped on the back of her great bird and was borne away to the isle of Lok. Once there, she bade him transform himself back into a stick, and with it in her hand she stepped into the blue boat, which conducted her to the palace of shells.

The Groac'h seemed overjoyed to see her, and told her that never before had she beheld such a handsome young man. Very soon she led her visitor into the great hall, where wine and fruit were always waiting, and on the table lay the magic knife, left there by Houarn. Unseen by the Groac'h, Bellah hid it in a pocket of her green coat, and then followed her hostess into the garden, and to the pond which contained the fish, their sides shining with a thousand different colours.

'Oh, what beautiful, beautiful creatures!' said she. 'I'm sure I should never be tired of watching them.'

And she sat down on the bank, with her elbows on her knees and her chin in her hands, her eyes fixed on the fishes as they flashed past.

'Would you not like to stay here always?' asked the Groac'h; and Bellah answered that she desired nothing better.

'Then you have only to marry me,' said the Groac'h. 'Oh! don't say no, for I have fallen deeply in love with you!'

'Well, I won't say "No",' replied Bellah, with a laugh, 'but you must promise first to let me catch one of those lovely fish in your net.'

'It is not so easy as it looks,' rejoined the Groac'h, smiling, 'but take it, and try your luck.'

Bellah took the net which the Groac'h held out, and, turning rapidly, flung it over the witch's head.

'Become in body what you are in soul!' cried she, and in an instant the lovely fairy of the sea was a toad, horrible to look upon. She struggled hard to tear the net asunder, but it was no use. Bellah only drew it the tighter, and, flinging the sorceress into a pit, she rolled a great stone across the top, and left her.

As she drew near the pond she saw a great procession of fishes advancing to meet her, crying, 'This is our lord and master, who has saved us from the net of steel and the pot of gold!'

'And who will restore you to your proper shapes,' said Bellah, drawing the knife from her pocket.

But just as she was going to touch the foremost fish, her eyes fell on a green frog on his knees beside her, his little paws crossed over his little heart. Bellah felt as if fingers were tightening round her throat, but she managed to cry, 'Is this you, my Houarn? Is this you?'

'It is I,' croaked the little frog; and as the knife touched him he was a man again, and, springing up, he clasped her in his arms.

'But we must not forget the others,' she said at last, and began to transform the fishes to their proper shapes. There were so many of them that it took quite a long time. Just as she had finished there arrived the little dwarf from the Deer's Leap in a car drawn by six cockchafers, which once had been the six stone eggs.

'Here I am!' he exclaimed. 'You have broken the spell that held me, and now come and get your reward,' and, dismounting from his chariot, he led them down into the caves filled with gold and jewels, and bade Bellah and Houarn take as much as they wanted.

When their pockets were full, Bellah ordered her stick to become a winged carriage, large enough to bear them and the men they had rescued back to Lanillis.

There they were married the next day, but instead of setting up housekeeping with the little cow and pig to fatten that they had so long wished for, they were able to buy lands for miles round for themselves, and gave each man who had been delivered from the Groac'h a small farm, where he lived happily to the end of his days.

Hansel and Grettel

ONCE UPON a time there dwelt on the outskirts of a large forest a poor woodcutter with his wife and two children; the boy was called Hansel and the girl Grettel. He had always little enough to live on, and once, when there was a great famine in the land, the woodcutter couldn't even provide them with daily bread. One night, as he was tossing about in bed, full of cares and worry, he sighed and said to his wife, 'What's to become of us? How are we to support our poor children, now that we have nothing more for ourselves?'

'I'll tell you what, husband,' answered the woman; 'early to-morrow morning we'll take the children out into the thickest part of the wood; there we shall light a fire for them and give them each a piece of bread; then we'll go on to our work and leave them alone. They won't be able to find their way home, and we shall thus be rid of them.'

'No, wife,' said her husband, 'that I won't do; how could I find it in my heart to leave my children alone in the wood? The wild beasts would soon come and tear them to pieces.'

'Oh! you fool,' said she, 'then we must all four die of hunger, and you may just as well go and plane the boards for our coffins;' and she left him no peace till he consented. 'But I can't help feeling sorry for the poor children,' added the husband.

The children, too, had not been able to sleep for hunger, and had heard what their step-mother had said to their father. Grettel wept bitterly and spoke to Hansel, 'Now it's all up with us.' 'No, no, Grettel,' said Hansel, 'don't fret yourself; I'll be able to find a way of escape, never fear.' And when the old people had fallen asleep he got up, slipped on his little coat, opened the back door and stole out. The moon was shining clearly, and the white pebbles which lay in front of the house glittered like bits of silver. Hansel bent down and filled his pocket with as many of them as he could cram in. Then he went back and said to Grettel, 'Be comforted, my dear little sister, and go to sleep; God will not desert us;' and he lay down in bed again.

At daybreak, even before the sun was up, the woman came and woke the two children, saying, 'Get up, you lie-abeds, we're all going to the forest to fetch wood.' She gave them each a bit of bread and said, 'There's something for your dinner, but don't eat it up before then, for it's all you'll get.' Grettel took the bread under her apron, as Hansel had the stones in his pocket. Then they all set out together on the way to the forest. After they had walked for a little, Hansel stood still and looked back at the house, and this he did again and again. His father observed him and said, 'Hansel, what are you gazing at there, and why do you always remain behind? Take care, and don't lose your footing.' 'Oh! father,' said Hansel, 'I am looking back at my white kitten, which is sitting on the roof, waving me a farewell.' The woman exclaimed, 'What a donkey you are! that isn't your kitten, that's the morning sun shining on the chimney.' But Hansel had not looked back at his kitten, but had been dropping the white pebbles out of his pocket on to the path.

When they reached the middle of the forest the father said, 'Now, children, go and fetch a lot of wood, and I'll light a fire that you mayn't feel cold.' Hansel and Grettel heaped up brushwood till they had made a pile nearly the size of a small hill. The brushwood was set alight, and when the flames leaped high the woman said, 'Now lie down at the fire, children, and rest yourselves; we are going into the forest to cut down wood; when we've finished we'll come back and fetch you.'

Hansel and Grettel sat down beside the fire, and at midday ate their little bits of bread. They heard the strokes of the axe, so they thought their father was quite near. But it was no axe they heard, but a bough he had tied on to a dead tree, that was blown about by the wind. And when they had sat for a long time their eyes closed with fatigue, and they fell fast asleep. When they awoke at last it was pitch-dark. Grettel began to cry, and said, 'How are we ever to get out of the wood?' But Hansel comforted her. 'Wait a bit,' he said, 'till the moon is up, and then we'll find our way sure enough.'

And when the full moon had risen he took his sister by the hand and followed the pebbles, which shone like newly minted coins, and showed them the path. They walked all through the night, and at daybreak reached their father's house again. They knocked at the door, and when the woman opened it she exclaimed, 'You naughty children, what a time you've slept in the wood! we thought you were never going to come back.' But the father rejoiced, for his conscience had reproached him for leaving his children behind by themselves.

Not long afterwards there was again great dearth in the land, and the children heard their mother address their father thus in bed one night:

'Everything is eaten up once more; we have only half a loaf in the house, and when that's done it's all up with us. The children must be got rid of: we'll lead them deeper into the wood this time, so that they won't be able to find their way out again. There is no other way of saving ourselves.'

The man's heart smote him heavily, and he thought, 'Surely it would be better to share the last crust with one's children!' But his wife wouldn't listen to his arguments, and did nothing but scold and reproach him. If a man yields once he's done for, and so, because he had given in the first place, he was forced to do so again the second time.

But the children were awake, and had heard the conversation. When the old people were asleep, Hansel got up to go out and pick up pebbles again, as he had done the first time; but the woman had barred the door, and Hansel couldn't get out. But he consoled his little sister, and said, 'Don't cry, Grettel, and sleep peacefully, for God is sure to help us.'

At early dawn the woman came and made the children get up. They received their bit of bread, but it was even smaller than the time before. On the way to the wood Hansel crumbled it in his pocket, and every few minutes he stood still and dropped a crumb on the ground. 'Hansel, what are you stopping and looking about you for?' said the father. 'I'm looking back at my little pigeon, which is sitting on the roof waving me a farewell,' answered Hansel. 'Fool!' said the wife; 'that isn't your pigeon, it's the morning sun glittering on the chimney.' But Hansel gradually threw all his crumbs on to the path.

The woman led the children still deeper into the forest, farther than they had ever been in their lives before. Then a big fire was lit again, and the woman said, 'Just sit down there, children, and if you're tired you can sleep a little; we're going into the forest to cut down wood, and in the evening when we've finished we'll come back to fetch you.' At midday Grettel divided her bread with Hansel, for he had strewed his all along their path. Then they fell asleep, and evening passed away, but nobody came to the poor children. They didn't awake till it was pitch-dark, and Hansel comforted his sister, saying, 'Only wait, Grettel, till the moon rises, then we shall see the bread-crumbs I scattered along the path; they will show us the way back to the house.' When the moon appeared they got up, but they found no crumbs, for the thousands of birds that fly about the woods and fields had picked them all up. 'Never mind,' said Hansel to Grettel; 'you'll see we'll still find a way out;' but all the same they did not. They wandered about the whole night, and the next day, from morning till evening, but they could not find a path out of the wood. They were very hungry, too, for they had nothing to eat but a few berries they found growing on the ground. And at last they were so tired that their legs refused to carry them any longer, so they lay down under a tree and fell fast asleep.

On the third morning after they had left their father's house they
set about their wandering again, but only got deeper and deeper into
the wood, and now they felt that if help did not come to them soon
they must perish. At midday they saw a beautiful little snow-white
bird sitting on a branch, which sang so sweetly that they stopped still
and listened to it. And when its song was finished it flapped its wings
and flew on in front of them. They followed it and came to a little
house, on the roof of which it perched; and when they came quite
near they saw that the cottage was made of bread and roofed with
cakes, while the window was made of transparent sugar.

'Now we'll set to,' said Hansel, 'and have a good meal. I'll eat a
bit of the roof, and you, Grettel, can eat some of the window, which
will taste sweet.' Hansel stretched up his hand and broke off a little
bit of the roof to see what it was like, and Grettel went to the case-
ment and began to nibble at it. Thereupon a shrill voice called out
from the room inside:

> 'Nibble, nibble, little mouse,
> Who's nibbling my house?'

The children answered:

> ''Tis Heaven's own child,
> The tempest wild,'

and went on eating, without disturbing themselves. Hansel, who
thoroughly appreciated the roof, tore down a big bit of it, while
Grettel pushed out a whole round window-pane, and sat down the
better to enjoy it.

Suddenly the door opened, and an ancient dame leaning on a staff
hobbled out. Hansel and Grettel were so terrified that they let fall
what they had in their hands. But the old woman nodded to them
and said, 'Oh, ho! you dear children, what led you here? Just come
in and stay with me, no ill shall befall you.' She took them both by
the hand and led them into the house, and laid a most sumptuous
dinner before them – milk and sugared pancakes, with apples and
nuts. After they had finished, two beautiful little white beds were
prepared for them, and when Hansel and Grettel lay down in them
they felt as if they were in heaven.

The old woman appeared to be most friendly, but she was really an old witch who had waylaid the children, and had only built the little bread house in order to lure them in. When anyone came into her power she killed, cooked, and ate him, and held a regular feast-day for the occasion. Now witches have red eyes, and cannot see far, but, like beasts, they have a keen sense of smell, and know when human beings pass by. When Hansel and Grettel fell into her power she laughed maliciously to herself and said, 'I've got them now; they shan't escape me.'

Early in the morning, before the children were awake, she rose up, and when she saw them both with their round rosy cheeks sleeping so peacefully, she muttered to herself, 'That'll be a dainty bite.' Then she seized Hansel with her bony hand and carried him into a little stable, and barred the door on him; he might scream as much as he liked, it did him no good. Then she went to Grettel, shook her till she awoke, and cried, 'Get up, you lazy-bones, fetch water and cook something for your brother. When he's fat I'll eat him up.' Grettel began to cry bitterly, but it was of no use; she had to do what the wicked witch bade her.

So the best food was cooked for poor Hansel, but Grettel got nothing but crab-shells. Every morning the old woman hobbled out to the stable and cried, 'Hansel, put out your finger, that I may feel if you are getting fat.' But Hansel always stretched out a bone, and the old dame, whose sight was dim, thought it was Hansel's finger, and wondered why he fattened so slowly. When four weeks passed and Hansel still remained thin, she lost patience and determined to wait no longer. 'Hi! Grettel,' she called to the girl, 'be quick and get some water. Hansel may be fat or thin, I'm going to kill him to-morrow and cook him.' Oh! how the poor little sister sobbed as she carried the water, and how the tears rolled down her cheeks! 'Kind heaven help us now!' she cried; 'if only the wild beasts in the wood had eaten us, then at least we should have died together.' 'Just hold your peace,' said the old hag; 'crying won't help you.'

Early in the morning Grettel had to go out and hang up the kettle full of water, and light the fire. 'First we'll bake,' said the old dame; 'I've heated the oven already and kneaded the dough.' She pushed Grettel out to the oven, from under which fiery flames were already issuing. 'Creep in,' said the witch, 'and see if it's properly heated, so that we can shove in the bread.' For when she had got Grettel in she meant to close the oven and let the girl bake, that she might eat her up too. But Grettel perceived her intention, and said, 'I don't know how I'm to do it; how do I get in?' 'You silly goose!' said the witch, 'the opening is big enough see, I could get in myself;' and she crawled towards it, and poked her head into the oven. Then Grettel gave her a shove that sent her right in, shut the iron door, and drew the bolt. Gracious! how she yelled! It was quite horrible; but Grettel fled, and the wicked old woman was left to perish miserably.

Grettel fled straight to Hansel, opened the little stable-door, and cried, 'Hansel, we are free; the old witch is dead.' Then Hansel sprang like a bird out of a cage when the door is opened. How they rejoiced and embraced each other, and jumped for joy, and kissed one another! And as they had no longer any cause for fear, they went into the old hag's house, and there they found, in every corner of the room, boxes of pearls and precious stones. 'These are even better than pebbles,' said Hansel, and he crammed his pockets full of them; and Grettel said, 'I too will take something home;' and she filled her apron full. 'But now,' said Hansel, 'let's go and get well away from the witch's wood.' When they had wandered about for some hours they came to a big lake. 'We can't get over,' said Hansel; 'I see no bridge of any sort or kind.' 'No, and there's no ferry-boat either,' answered Grettel; 'but look, there swims a white duck; if I ask her she'll help us over;' and she called out:

> 'Here are two children, mournful very,
>   Seeing neither bridge nor ferry;
>   Take us upon your broad white back,
>   And row us over, quack, quack, quack!'

The duck swam towards them, and Hansel got on her back and bade his little sister sit beside him. 'No,' answered Grettel, 'we should be too heavy a load for the duck; she shall carry us across separately.' The good bird did this, and when they were landed safely on the other side, and had gone on for a while, the wood became more and more familiar to them, and at length they saw their father's house in the distance. Then they set off at a run, and bounding into the room fell on their father's neck. The man had not known one happy hour since he left them in the wood, but the woman had died. Grettel shook out her apron so that the pearls and precious stones rolled about the room, and Hansel threw down one handful after the other out of his pocket. Thus all their troubles were ended, and they all lived happily ever afterwards.

My story is done. See! there runs a little mouse; anyone who catches it may make himself a large fur cap out of it.

He wins who waits

ONCE UPON a time there reigned a king who had an only daughter. The child had been spoiled by everybody from her birth, and, besides being beautiful, was clever and wilful, and when she grew old enough to be married she refused to have anything to say to the prince whom her father favoured, but declared she would choose a husband for herself. By long experience the King knew that when once she had made up her mind, there was no use expecting her to change it, so he inquired meekly what she wished him to do.

'Summon all the young men in the kingdom to appear before me a month from to-day,' answered the Princess; 'and the one to whom I shall give this golden apple shall be my husband.'

'But, my dear – ' began the King, in tones of dismay.

'The one to whom I shall give this golden apple shall be my husband,' repeated the Princess, in a louder voice than before. And the King, with a sigh, proceeded to do her bidding.

The young men arrived – tall and short, dark and fair, rich and poor. They stood in rows in the great courtyard in front of the palace, and the Princess, clad in robes of green, with a golden veil flowing behind her, passed before all, holding the apple. Sometimes she stopped and hesitated, but in the end she always passed on, till she came to a youth near the end of the last row. There was nothing specially remarkable about him, the bystanders thought; nothing that was likely to take a girl's fancy. A hundred others were handsomer, and all wore finer clothes; but he met the Princess's eyes frankly and with a smile, and she smiled too, and held out the apple.

'There is some mistake,' cried the King, who had anxiously watched her progress, and hoped that none of the candidates would please her. 'It is impossible that she can wish to marry the son of a poor widow, who has not a farthing in the world! Tell her that I will not hear of it, and that she must go through the rows again and fix upon someone else.' The Princess went through the rows a second and a third time, and on each occasion she gave the apple to the widow's son. 'Well, marry him if you will,' exclaimed the angry

King; 'but at least you shall not stay here.' And the Princess answered nothing, but threw up her head, and taking the widow's son by the hand, they left the castle.

That evening they were married, and after the ceremony went back to the house of the bridegroom's mother, which, to the eyes of the Princess, did not look much bigger than a hen-coop.

The old woman was not at all pleased when her son entered bringing his bride with him.

'As if we were not poor enough before,' grumbled she. 'I dare say this is some fine lady who can do nothing to earn her living.' But the Princess caressed her arm, and said softly, 'Do not be vexed, dear mother; I am a famous spinner, and can sit at my wheel all day without breaking a thread.'

And she kept her word; but in spite of the efforts of all three, they became poorer and poorer; and at the end of six months it was agreed that the husband should go to the neighbouring town to get work. Here he met a merchant who was about to start on a long journey with a train of camels laden with goods of all sorts, and needed a man to help him. The widow's son begged to be taken as a servant, and to this the merchant assented, giving him his whole year's salary beforehand. The young man returned home with the news, and next day bade farewell to his mother and his wife, who were very sad at parting from him.

'Do not forget me while you are absent,' whispered the Princess as she flung her arms round his neck; 'and as you pass by the well which lies near the city gate, stop and greet the old man you will find sitting there. Kiss his hand, and then ask him what counsel he can give you for your journey.'

The youth set out, and when he reached the well where the old man was sitting he asked the question his wife had bidden him.

'My son,' replied the old man, 'you have done well to come to me, and in return remember three things: "She whom the heart loves, is ever the most beautiful." "Patience is the first step on the road to happiness." "He wins who waits." '

The young man thanked him and went on his way. Next morning early the caravan set out, and before sunset it had arrived at the first halting place, round some wells, where another company of merchants had already encamped. But no rain had fallen for a long while in that rocky country, and both men and beasts were parched with thirst. To be sure, there *was* another well, about half a mile away, where there was always water; but to get it a man had to be lowered deep down, and, besides, no one who had ever descended that well had been known to come back.

However, till they could store some water in their bags of goat-skin, the caravans dared not go further into the desert, and on the night of the arrival of the widow's son and his master, the merchants had decided to offer a large reward to anyone who was brave enough to go down into the enchanted well and bring some up. Thus it happened that at sunrise the young man was aroused from his sleep by a herald making his round of the camp, proclaiming that every merchant present would give a thousand piastres to the man who would risk his life to bring water for them and their camels.

The youth hesitated for a little while when he heard the proclamation. The story of the well had spread far and wide, and long ago had reached his ears. The danger was great, he knew; but then, if he came back alive, he would be the possessor of eighty thousand piastres. He turned to the herald who was passing the tent.

'*I* will go,' said he.

'What madness!' cried his master, who happened to be standing near. 'You are too young to throw away your life like that. Run after the herald and tell him you take back your offer.' But the young man shook his head, and the merchant saw that it was useless to try and persuade him.

'Well, it is your own affair,' he observed at last. 'If you must go, you must. Only, if you ever return, I will give you a camel's load of goods and my best mule besides.' And touching his turban in token of farewell, he entered the tent.

Hardly had he done so than a crowd of men were seen pouring out of the camp.

'How can we thank you!' they exclaimed, pressing round the youth. 'Our camels as well as ourselves are almost dead of thirst. See! here is the rope we have brought to let you down.'

'Come, then,' answered the youth. And they all set out.

On reaching the well, the rope was knotted securely under his arms, a big goat-skin bottle was given him, and he was gently lowered to the bottom of the pit. Here a clear stream was bubbling over the rocks, and, stooping down, he was about to drink, when a huge Arab appeared before him, saying in a loud voice, 'Come with me!'

The young man rose, never doubting that his last hour had come; but as he could do nothing, he followed the Arab into a brilliantly lighted hall, on the further side of the little river. There his guide sat down, and drawing towards him two boys, one black and the other white, he said to the stranger:

'I have a question to ask you. If you answer it right, your life shall be spared. If not, your head will be forfeit, as the head of many another has been before you. Tell me: which of my two children do I think the handsomer?'

The question did not seem a hard one, for while the white boy was as beautiful a child as ever was seen, his brother was equally ugly. But, just as the youth was going to speak, the old man's counsel flashed into the youth's mind, and he replied hastily, 'The one whom we love best is always the handsomest.'

'You have saved me!' cried the Arab, rising quickly from his seat, and pressing the young man in his arms. 'Ah! if you could only guess what I have suffered from the stupidity of all the people to whom I have put that question, and I was condemned by a wicked genius to remain here until it was answered! But what brought you to this place, and how can I reward you for what you have done for me?'

'By helping me to draw enough water for my caravan of eighty merchants and their camels, who are dying for want of it,' replied the youth.

'That is easily done,' said the Arab. 'Take these three apples, and when you have filled your skin, and are ready to be drawn up, lay one of them on the ground. Half-way to the earth, let fall another, and at the top drop the third. If you follow my directions no harm will happen to you. And take, besides, these three pomegranates, green, red and white. One day you will find a use for them!'

The young man did as he was told, and soon stepped out again on the rocky waste, where the merchants were anxiously awaiting him. Oh, how thirsty they all were! But even after the camels had drunk, the skin seemed as full as ever.

Full of gratitude for their deliverance, the merchants pressed the money into his hands, while his own master bade him choose what goods he liked, and a mule to carry them.

So the widow's son was rich at last and he hired a man by whom he sent the money and the mule back to his wife.

'I will send the pomegranates also,' thought he, 'for if I leave them in my turban they may some day fall out,' and he drew them out of his turban. But the fruit had vanished, and in their places were three precious stones, green, white and red.

For a long time he remained with the merchant, who gradually trusted him with all his business, and gave him a large share of the money he made. Then one day he realised with a start that twenty years had passed since he had gone away.

'I must return to my wife,' he said next morning, and, notwithstanding entreaties to remain, he mounted a camel and set out.

Now, it had happened that soon after he had taken service with the merchant a little boy had been born to him, and both the Princess and the old woman toiled hard all day to get the baby food and clothing. When the money and the pomegranates arrived there was no need for them to work any more, and the Princess saw at once that the pomegranates were not fruit at all, but precious stones of great value. The old woman, however, not being accustomed, like her daughter-in-law, to the sight of jewels, took them only for common fruit, and wished to give them to the child to eat. She was very angry when the Princess hastily took them from her and hid them in her dress, while she went to the market and bought the three finest pomegranates she could find, which she handed the old woman for the little boy.

Then she bought beautiful new clothes for all of them, and when they were dressed they looked as fine as could be. Next, she took out one of the precious stones which her husband had sent her, and placed it in a small silver box. This she wrapped up in a handkerchief embroidered in gold, and filled the old woman's pockets with gold and silver pieces.

'Go, dear mother,' she said, 'to the palace, and present the jewel to the King, and if he asks you what he can give you in return, tell him that you want a paper, with his seal attached, proclaiming that no one is to meddle with anything you may choose to do. Before you leave the palace distribute the money amongst the servants.'

The old woman took the box and started for the palace. No one there had ever seen a ruby of such beauty, and the most famous jeweller in the town was summoned to declare its value. But all he could say was:

'If a boy threw a stone into the air with all his might, and you could pile up gold as high as the flight of the stone, it would not be sufficient to pay for this ruby.'

At these words the King's face fell. Having once seen the ruby he could not bear to part with it, yet all the money in his treasury would not be enough to buy it. So for a little while he remained silent, wondering what offer he could make the old woman, and at last he said, 'If I cannot give you its worth in money, is there anything you will take in exchange?'

'A paper signed by your hand, and sealed with your seal, proclaiming that I may do what I will, without let or hindrance,' answered she promptly. And the King, delighted to have obtained what he coveted at so small a cost, gave her the paper without delay. Then the old woman took her leave and returned home.

The fame of this wonderful ruby soon spread far and wide, and envoys arrived at the little house to know if there were more stones to sell. Each king was so anxious to gain possession of the treasure that he bade his messenger outbid all the rest, and so the Princess sold the two remaining stones for a sum of money so large that if the gold pieces had been spread out they would have reached from here to the moon. The first thing she did was to build a palace by the side of the cottage, and it was raised on pillars of gold, in which were set great diamonds, which blazed night and day. Of course the news of this palace was the first thing that reached the King her father, on his return from the wars, and he hurried to see it. In the doorway stood a young man of twenty, who was his grandson, though neither of them knew it, and so pleased was the King with the appearance of the youth, that he carried him back to his own palace, and made him commander of the whole army.

Not long after this, the widow's son returned to his native land. There, sure enough, was the tiny cottage where he had lived with his mother, but the gorgeous building beside it was quite new to him. What had become of his wife and his mother, and who could be dwelling in that other wonderful place? These were the first thoughts that flashed through his mind; but not wishing to betray himself by asking questions of passing strangers, he climbed up into a tree that stood opposite the palace and watched.

By and by a lady came out, and began to gather some of the roses and jessamine that hung about the porch. The twenty years that had passed since he had last beheld her vanished in an instant, and he knew her to be his own wife, looking almost as young and beautiful as on the day of their parting. He was about to jump down from the tree and hasten to her side, when she was joined by a young man who placed his arm affectionately round her neck. At this sight the angry husband drew his bow, but before he could let fly the arrow, the counsel of the wise man came back to him, 'Patience is the first step on the road to happiness.' And he laid it down again.

At this moment the Princess turned, and drawing her companion's head down to hers, kissed him on each cheek. A second time blind rage filled the heart of the watcher, and he snatched up his bow from the branch where it hung, when words, heard long since, seemed to sound in his ears, 'He wins who waits.' And the bow dropped to his side. Then, through the silent air came the sound of the youth's voice:

'Mother, can you tell me nothing about my father? Does he still live, and will he never return to us?'

'Alas! my son, how can I answer you?' replied the lady. 'Twenty years have passed since he left us to make his fortune, and, in that time, only once have I heard aught of him. But what has brought him to your mind just now?'

'Because last night I dreamed that he was here,' said the youth, 'and then I remembered what I have so long forgotten, that I *had* a father, though even his very history was strange to me. And now, tell me, I pray you, all you can concerning him.'

And standing under the jessamine, the son learnt his father's history, and the man in the tree listened also.

'Oh,' exclaimed the youth, when it was ended, while he twisted his hands in pain, 'I am general-in-chief, you are the King's daughter, and we have the most splendid palace in the whole world, yet my father lives we know not where, and for all we can guess, may be poor and miserable. To-morrow I will ask the King to give me soldiers, and I will seek him over the whole earth till I find him.'

Then the man came down from the tree, and clasped his wife and son in his arms. All that night they talked, and when the sun rose it still found them talking. But as soon as it was proper, he went up to the palace to pay his homage to the King and to inform him of all that had happened and who they all really were. The King was overjoyed to think that his daughter, whom he had long since forgiven and sorely missed, was living at his gates, and was, besides, the

mother of the youth who was so dear to him. 'It was written beforehand,' cried the monarch. 'You are my son-in-law before the world,
and shall be king after me.'

And the man bowed his head.

He had waited; and he had won.

The History of Whittington

DICK WHITTINGTON was a very little boy when his father and mother died; so little indeed, that he never knew them, nor the place where he was born. He wandered about the country as ragged as a colt, till he met with a wagoner who was going to London, and who gave him leave to walk all the way by the side of his wagon without paying anything for his passage. This pleased little Whittington very much, as he wanted to see London sadly, for he had heard that the streets were paved with gold, and he was willing to get a bushel of it; but how great was his disappointment – poor boy! – when he saw the streets covered with dirt instead of gold, and found himself in a strange place, without a friend, without food, and without money.

Though the wagoner was so charitable as to let him walk up by the side of the wagon for nothing, he took care not to know him when he came to town, and the poor boy was, in a little time, so cold and so hungry that he wished himself in a good kitchen and by a warm fire in the country.

In this distress he asked charity of several people, and one of them bade him, 'Go to work for an idle rogue.' 'That I will,' says Whittington, 'with all my heart; I will work for you if you will let me.'

The man, who thought this savoured of wit and impertinence (though the poor lad had intended only to show his readiness to work), gave him a blow with a stick which broke his head so that the blood ran down. In this situation, and fainting for want of food, he laid himself down at the door of one Mr Fitzwarren, a merchant, where the cook saw him and, being an ill-natured hussy, ordered him to go about his business or she would scald him. At this time Mr Fitzwarren came from the Exchange, and began also to scold at the poor boy, bidding him to go to work.

Whittington answered that he should be glad to work if anybody would employ him, and that he should be able if he could get some victuals to eat, for he had had nothing for three days, and he was a poor country boy, and knew nobody, and nobody would employ him.

He then endeavoured to get up, but he was so very weak that he fell down again, which excited so much compassion in the merchant that he ordered the servants to take him in and give him some meat and drink, and let him help the cook to do any such dirty work as she could set him to.

Whittington would have lived happy in this worthy family had he not been bumped about by the cross cook, who must be always roasting or basting, and when the spit was idle employed her hands upon poor Whittington! At last Miss Alice, his master's daughter, was informed of it, and then she took compassion on the poor boy, and made the servants treat him kindly.

Besides the crossness of the cook, Whittington had another difficulty to get over before he could be happy. He had, by order of his master, a flock-bed placed for him in a garret, where there were a number of rats and mice that often ran over the poor boy's nose and disturbed him in his sleep. After some time, however, a gentleman who came to his master's house gave Whittington a penny for brushing his shoes. This he put into his pocket, being determined to lay it out to the best advantage; and the next day, seeing a woman in the street with a cat under her arm, he ran up to know the price of it. The woman (as the cat was a good mouser) asked a deal of money for it, but on Whittington's telling her he had but a penny in the world, and that he wanted a cat sadly, she let him have it.

This cat Whittington concealed in the garret, for fear she should be beat about by his mortal enemy the cook, and here she soon killed or frightened away the rats and mice, so that the poor boy could now sleep as sound as a top.

Soon after this the merchant, who had a ship ready to sail, called for his servants, as his custom was, in order that each of them might venture something to try their luck; and whatever they sent was to pay neither freight nor custom, for he thought justly that God Almighty would bless him the more for his readiness to let the poor partake of his fortune.

All the servants appeared but poor Whittington who, having neither money nor goods, could not think of sending anything to try his luck; but his good friend Miss Alice, thinking his poverty kept him away, ordered him to be called.

She then offered to lay down something for him, but the merchant told his daughter that would not do, it must be something of his own. Upon which poor Whittington said he had nothing but a cat which he bought for a penny that was given him. 'Fetch thy cat, boy,' said the merchant, 'and send her.' Whittington brought poor puss and delivered her to the captain, with tears in his eyes, for he said he should now be disturbed by the rats and mice as much as ever. All the company laughed at the adventure, except Miss Alice, who pitied the poor boy, and gave him something to buy another cat.

While puss was beating the billows at sea, poor Whittington was severely beaten at home by his tyrannical mistress the cook, who used him so cruelly, and made such game of him for sending his cat to sea, that at last the poor boy determined to run away from his place, and, having packed up the few belongings he had, he set out very early in the morning on All-hallows day. He travelled as far as Holloway, and there sat down on a stone to consider what course he should take; but while he was thus ruminating, Bow bells, of which there were only six, began to ring; and he thought their sounds addressed him in this manner:

'Turn again, Whittington,
Thrice Lord Mayor of London.'

'Lord Mayor of London!' said he to himself; 'what would not one endure to be Lord Mayor of London, and ride in such a fine coach? Well, I'll go back again, and bear all the pummelling and ill-usage of Cicely rather than miss the opportunity of being Lord Mayor!' So home he went, and happily got into the house and about his business before Mrs Cicely made her appearance.

We must now follow Miss Puss to the coast of Africa. How perilous are voyages at sea, how uncertain the winds and the waves, and how many accidents attend a naval life!

The ship which had the cat on board was long beaten at sea, and at last, by contrary winds, driven on a part of the coast of Barbary which was inhabited by Moors unknown to the English. These people received our countrymen with civility, and therefore the captain, in order to trade with them, showed them the patterns of the goods he had on board, and sent some of them to the King of the country, who was so well pleased that he sent for the captain and the factor to his palace, which was about a mile from the sea. Here they were placed, according to the custom of the country, on rich carpets, flowered with gold and silver; and the King and Queen being seated at the upper end of the room, dinner was brought in, which consisted of many dishes; but no sooner were the dishes put down than an amazing number of rats and mice came from all quarters, and devoured all the meat in an instant.

The factor, in surprise, turned round to the nobles and asked if these vermin were not offensive. 'Oh! yes,' said they, 'very offensive; and the King would give half his treasure to be freed of them, for they not only destroy his dinner, as you see, but they assault him in his chamber, and even in bed, so that he is obliged to be watched while he is sleeping, for fear of them.'

The factor jumped for joy; he remembered poor Whittington and his cat, and told the King he had a creature on board the ship that would despatch all these vermin immediately. The King's heart jumped so high at the joy which this news gave him that his turban dropped off his head. 'Bring this creature to me,' said he; 'vermin are dreadful in a court, and if she will perform what you say I will load your ship with gold and jewels in exchange for her.' The factor, who knew his business, took this opportunity to set forth the merits of Miss Puss. He told His Majesty that it would be inconvenient to part with her, as when she was gone, the rats and mice might destroy the goods in the ship – but to oblige his Majesty he would fetch her. 'Run, run,' said the Queen; 'I am impatient to see the dear creature.'

Away flew the factor, while another dinner was provided, and returned with the cat just as the rats and mice were devouring that also. He immediately put down Miss Puss, who killed a great number of them.

The King rejoiced greatly to see his old enemies destroyed by so small a creature, and the Queen was highly pleased, and desired the cat might be brought near that she might look at her. Upon which the factor called, 'Pussy, pussy, pussy!' and she came to him. He then presented her to the Queen, who started back, and was afraid to touch a creature who had made such a havoc among the rats and mice; however, when the factor stroked the cat and said, 'Pussy, pussy!' the Queen also touched her and cried, 'Putty, putty!' for she had not learned English.

He then put her down on the Queen's lap, where she, purring, played with Her Majesty's hand, and then sang herself to sleep.

The King having seen the exploits of Miss Puss, and being informed that her kittens would stock the whole country, bargained with the captain and the factor for the whole ship's cargo, and then gave them ten times as much for the cat as all the rest amounted to. On which, taking leave of Their Majesties and other great personages at court, they sailed with a fair wind for England, whither we must now attend them.

The morn had scarcely dawned when Mr Fitzwarren arose to count over the cash and settle the business for that day. He had just entered the counting-house, and seated himself at the desk, when somebody came tap, tap, at the door. 'Who's there?' said Mr Fitzwarren. 'A friend,' answered the other. 'What friend can come at this unseasonable time?' 'A real friend is never unseasonable,' answered the other. 'I come to bring you good news of your ship *Unicorn*.' The merchant bustled up in such a hurry that he forgot his gout; instantly opened the door, and who should be seen waiting but the captain and factor, with a cabinet of jewels, and a bill of lading, for which the merchant lifted up his eyes and thanked heaven for sending him such a prosperous voyage. Then they told him the adventures of the cat, and showed him the cabinet of jewels which they had brought for Mr Whittington. Upon which he cried out with great earnestness, but not in the most poetical manner:

> 'Go, send him in, and tell him of his fame,
> And call him Mr Whittington by name.'

Mr Fitzwarren was a good man, for when some who were present told him that this treasure was too much for such a poor boy as Whittington, he said, 'God forbid that I should deprive him of a penny; it is his own, and he shall have it to a farthing.' He then ordered Mr Whittington in, who was at this time cleaning the kitchen and would have excused himself from going into the counting-house, saying the room was swept and his shoes were dirty and full of hob-nails.

The merchant, however, made him come in, and ordered a chair to be set for him. Upon which, thinking they intended to make sport of him, as had been too often the case in the kitchen, he besought his master not to mock a poor simple fellow who intended them no harm, but let him go about his business. The merchant, taking him by the hand, said, 'Indeed Mr Whittington, I am in earnest with you, and sent for you to congratulate you on your great success. Your cat has procured you more money than I am worth in the world, and may you long enjoy it and be happy!'

At length, being shown the treasure, and convinced by them that all of it belonged to him, he fell upon his knees and thanked the Almighty for his providential care of such a poor and miserable creature. He then laid all the treasure at his master's feet, who refused to take any part of it, but told him he heartily rejoiced at his prosperity and hoped the wealth he had acquired would be a comfort to him, and would make him happy. He then applied to his mistress, and to his good friend Miss Alice, who refused to take any part of the money, but told him she heartily rejoiced at his good success, and wished him all imaginable felicity. He then gratified the captain, factor, and all the ship's crew for the care they had taken of his cargo. He likewise distributed presents to all the servants in the house, not forgetting his old enemy the cook, though she little deserved it.

After this Mr Fitzwarren advised Mr Whittington to send for the necessary people and dress himself like a gentleman, and made him the offer of his house to live in till he could provide himself with a better.

Now it came to pass when Mr Whittington's face was washed, his hair curled, and he was dressed in a rich suit of clothes, that he turned out a genteel young fellow; and as wealth contributes much to give a man confidence, he in a little time dropped that sheepish behaviour which was principally occasioned by a depression of spirits, and soon became a sprightly and good companion, insomuch that Miss Alice, who had formerly pitied him, now fell in love with him.

When her father perceived they had this good liking for each other, he proposed a match between them, to which both parties cheerfully consented, and the Lord Mayor, Court of Aldermen, Sheriffs, the Company of Stationers, the Royal Academy of Arts, and a number of eminent merchants attended the ceremony, and were elegantly treated at an entertainment made for that purpose.

History further relates that they lived very happy, had several children, and died at a good old age. Mr Whittington served Sheriff of London and was three times Lord Mayor. In the last year of his mayoralty he entertained King Henry V with his Queen, after his conquest of France, upon which occasion the King, in consideration of Whittington's merit, said, 'Never had prince such a subject;' which being told to Whittington at the table, he replied, 'Never had subject such a king.' His Majesty, out of respect to his good character, conferred the honour of knighthood on him soon after.

Sir Richard many years before his death constantly fed a great number of poor citizens, built a church and a college to it, with a yearly allowance for poor scholars, and near it erected a hospital.

He also built Newgate for criminals, and gave liberally to St Bartholomew's Hospital, and other public charities.

The House in the Wood

A POOR woodcutter lived with his wife and three daughters in a little hut on the borders of a great forest.

One morning as he was going to his work, he said to his wife, 'Let our eldest daughter bring me my lunch into the wood; and so that she shall not lose her way, I will take a bag of millet with me, and sprinkle the seed on the path.'

When the sun had risen high over the forest, the girl set out with a basin of soup. But the field and wood sparrows, the larks and finches, blackbirds and greenfinches had picked up the millet long ago, and the girl could not find her way.

She went on and on, till the sun set and night came on. The trees rustled in the darkness, the owls hooted, and she began to be very much frightened. Then she saw in the distance a light that twinkled between the trees. 'There must be people living yonder,' she thought, 'who will take me in for the night,' and she began walking towards it.

Not long afterwards she came to a house with lights in the windows.

She knocked at the door, and a gruff voice called, 'Come in!'

The girl stepped into the dark entrance, and tapped at the door of the room.

'Just walk in,' cried the voice, and when she opened the door there sat an old grey-haired man at the table. His face was resting on his hands, and his white beard flowed over the table almost down to the ground.

By the stove lay three beasts, a hen, a cock, and a brindled cow. The girl told the old man her story, and asked for a night's lodging.

The man said:

> 'Pretty cock,
> Pretty hen,
> And you, pretty brindled cow,
> What do you say now?'

'Duks,' answered the beasts; and that must have meant, 'We are quite willing,' for the old man went on, 'Here is abundance; go into the back kitchen and cook us a supper.'

The girl found plenty of everything in the kitchen, and cooked a good meal, but she did not think of the beasts.

She placed the full dishes on the table, sat down opposite the grey-haired man, and ate till her hunger was appeased.

When she was satisfied, she said, 'But now I am so tired, where is a bed in which I can sleep?'

The beasts answered:

> 'You have eaten with him,
> You have drunk with him,
> Of *us* you have not thought,
> Sleep then as you ought!'

Then the old man said, 'Go upstairs, and there you will find a bedroom; shake the bed, and put clean sheets on, and go to sleep.'

The maiden went upstairs, and when she had made the bed, she lay down.

After some time the grey-haired man came, looked at her by the light of his candle, and shook his head. And when he saw that she was sound asleep, he opened a trap-door and let her fall into the cellar.

The woodcutter came home late in the evening, and reproached his wife for leaving him all day without food.

'No, I did not,' she answered; 'the girl went off with your dinner. She must have lost her way, but will no doubt come back to-morrow.'

But at daybreak the woodcutter started off into the wood, and this time asked his second daughter to bring his food.

'I will take a bag of lentils,' said he; 'they are larger than millet, and the girl will see them better and be sure to find her way.'

At midday the second daughter took the food, but the lentils had all disappeared; as on the previous day, the wood birds had eaten them all.

The maiden wandered about the wood till nightfall, when she came in the same way to the old man's house, and asked for food and a night's lodging.

The man with the grey hair again asked the beasts:

> 'Pretty cock,
> Pretty hen,
> And you, pretty brindled cow,
> What do you say now?'

The beasts answered, 'Duks,' and everything happened as on the former day.

The girl cooked a good meal, ate and drank with the old man, and did not trouble herself about the animals.

And when she asked for a bed, they replied:

> 'You have eaten with him,
> You have drunk with him,
> Of *us* you have not thought,
> Now sleep as you ought!'

And when she was asleep, the old man shook his head over her, and let her fall into the cellar.

On the third morning the woodcutter said to his wife, 'Send our youngest child to-day with my dinner. She is always good and obedient, and will keep to the right path, and not wander away like her sisters, those idle drones!'

But the mother said, 'Must I lose my dearest child too?'

'Do not fear,' he answered; 'she is too clever and intelligent to lose her way. I will take plenty of peas with me and strew them along; they are even larger than lentils, and will show her the way.'

But when the maiden started off with the basket on her arm, the wood pigeons had eaten up the peas, and she did not know which way to go. She was much distressed, and thought constantly of her poor hungry father and her anxious mother. At last, when it grew dark, she saw the little light, and came to the house in the wood. She asked prettily if she might stay there for the night, and the man with the white beard asked his beasts again:

> 'Pretty cock,
> Pretty hen,
> And you, pretty brindled cow,
> What do you say now?'

'Duks,' they said. Then the maiden stepped up to the stove where the animals were lying, and stroked the cock and the hen, and scratched the brindled cow between its horns.

And when at the bidding of the old man she had prepared a good supper, and the dishes were standing on the table, she said, 'Shall I have plenty while the good beasts have nothing? There is food to spare outside; I will attend to them first.'

Then she went out and fetched barley and strewed it before the cock and hen, and brought the cow an armful of sweet-smelling hay. 'Eat that, dear beasts,' she said, 'and when you are thirsty you shall have a good drink.'

Then she fetched a bucket of water, and the cock and hen flew on to the edge, put their beaks in, and then held up their heads as birds do when they drink, and the brindled cow also drank her fill. When the beasts were satisfied, the maiden sat down beside the old man at the table and ate what was left for her. Soon the cock and hen began to tuck their heads under their wings, and the brindled cow blinked its eyes, so the maiden said, 'Shall we not go to rest now?'

The man said:

> 'Pretty cock,
> Pretty hen,
> And you, pretty brindled cow,
> What do you say now?'

The animals said, 'Duks:

> 'You have eaten with us,
> You have drunk with us,
> You have tended us right,
> So we wish you good night.'

The maiden therefore went upstairs, made the bed and put on clean sheets and fell asleep. She slept peacefully till midnight, when there was such a noise in the house that she awoke. Everything trembled and shook; the animals sprang up and dashed themselves in terror against the wall; the beams swayed as if they would be torn from their foundations, it seemed as if the stairs were tumbling down, and then the roof fell in with a crash. Then all became still, and as no harm came to the maiden she lay down again and fell asleep. But when she awoke again in broad daylight, what a sight met her eyes! She was lying in a splendid room furnished with royal splendour; the walls were covered with tapestry of golden flowers on a green ground; the bed was of ivory and the counterpane of velvet, and on a stool nearby lay a pair of slippers studded with pearls. The maiden thought she must be dreaming, but in came three servants richly dressed, who asked what were her commands. 'Go,' said the maiden, 'I will get up at once and cook the old man's breakfast for him, and then I will feed the pretty cock and hen and the brindled cow.'

But the door opened and in came a handsome young man, who said, 'I am a king's son, and was condemned by a wicked witch to live as an old man in this wood with no company but that of my three servants, who were transformed into a cock, a hen, and a brindled cow. The spell could only be broken by the arrival of a maiden who should show herself kind not only to men but to beasts. You are that maiden, and last night at midnight we were freed, and this poor house was again transformed into my royal palace.'

As they stood there the King's son told his three servants to go and fetch the maiden's parents to be present at the wedding feast.

'But where are my two sisters?' asked the maiden.

'I shut them up in the cellar, but in the morning they shall be led forth into the forest and shall serve a charcoal burner until they have learnt their lesson, and never again suffer poor animals to go hungry.'

How Ian Direach
got the Blue Falcon

LONG AGO a king and queen ruled over the islands of the west, and
they had one son, whom they loved dearly. The boy grew up to be
tall and strong and handsome, and he could run and shoot, and swim
and dive better than any lad of his own age in the country. Besides,
he knew how to sail a boat, and sing songs to the harp, and during
the winter evenings, when everyone was gathered round the huge
hall fire shaping bows or weaving cloth, Ian Direach would tell them
tales of the deeds of his fathers.

So the time slipped by till Ian was almost a man, as they reckoned
men in those days, and then his mother the queen died. There was
great mourning throughout all the isles, and the boy and his father
mourned her bitterly also; but before the new year came the King
had married another wife, and seemed to have forgotten his old one.
Only Ian remembered.

On a morning when the leaves were yellow in the trees of the glen,
Ian slung his bow over his shoulder, and filling his quiver with
arrows, went on the hill in search of game. But not a bird was to be
seen anywhere, till at length a blue falcon flew past him, and raising
his bow he took aim at her. His eye was straight and his hand steady,

but the falcon's flight was swift, and he only shot a feather from her wing. As the sun was now low over the sea he put the feather in his game bag, and set out homewards.

'Have you brought me much game to-day?' asked his step-mother as he entered the hall.

'Nought save this,' he answered, handing her the feather of the blue falcon, which she held by the tip and gazed at silently. Then she turned to Ian and said:

'I am setting it on you as crosses and as spells, and as the fall of the year! That you may always be cold, and wet and dirty, and that your shoes may ever have pools in them, till you bring me hither the blue falcon on which that feather grew.'

'If it is spells you are laying, I can lay them too,' answered Ian Direach; 'and you shall stand with one foot on the great house and another on the castle, till I come back again, and your face shall be to the wind, from wheresoever it shall blow.' Then he went away to seek the bird, as his step-mother bade him; and, looking homewards from the hill, he saw the Queen standing with one foot on the great house, and the other on the castle, and her face turned towards whatever tempest should blow.

On he journeyed, over hills, and through rivers till he reached a wide plain, and never a glimpse did he catch of the falcon. Darker and darker it grew, and the small birds were seeking their nests, and at length Ian Direach could see no more, and he lay down under some bushes and sleep came to him. And in his dream a soft nose touched him, and a warm body curled up beside him, and a low voice whispered to him:

'Fortune is against you, Ian Direach; I have but the cheek and the hoof of a sheep to give you, and with these you must be content.' With that Ian Direach awoke, and beheld Gille Mairtean the fox.

Between them they kindled a fire, and ate their supper. Then Gille Mairtean the fox bade Ian Direach lie down as before, and sleep till morning. And in the morning, when he awoke, Gille Mairtean said:

'The falcon that you seek is in the keeping of the Giant of the Five Heads, and the Five Necks, and the Five Humps. I will show you the way to his house, and I counsel you to do his bidding, nimbly and cheerfully, and, above all, to treat his birds kindly, for in this manner he may give you his falcon to feed and care for. And when this happens, wait till the giant is out of his house; then throw a cloth over the falcon and bear her away with you. Only see that not one of her feathers touches anything within the house, or evil will befall you.'

'I thank you for your counsel,' said Ian Direach, 'and I will be careful to follow it.' Then he took the path to the giant's house.

'Who is there?' cried the giant, as someone knocked loudly on the door of his house.

'One who seeks work as a servant,' answered Ian Direach.

'And what can you do?' asked the giant again.

'I can feed birds and tend pigs; I can feed and milk a cow, and also goats and sheep, if you have any of these,' replied Ian Direach.

'Then enter, for I have great need of such a one,' said the giant.

So Ian Direach entered, and tended so well and carefully all the birds and beasts, that the giant was better satisfied than ever he had been, and at length he thought that he might even be trusted to feed the falcon. And the heart of Ian was glad, and he tended the blue falcon till her feathers shone like the sky, and the giant was well pleased; and one day he said to him:

'For long my brothers on the other side of the mountain have besought me to visit them, but never could I go for fear of my falcon. Now I think I can leave her with you for one day, and before nightfall I shall be back again.'

Scarcely was the giant out of sight next morning when Ian Direach seized the falcon, and throwing a cloth over her head hastened with her to the door. But the rays of the sun pierced through the thickness of the cloth, and as they passed the doorpost she gave a spring, and the tip of one of her feathers touched the post, which gave a scream, and brought the giant back in three strides. Ian Direach trembled as he saw him; but the giant only said:

'If you wish for my falcon you must first bring me the White Sword of Light that is in the house of the Big Women of Dhiurradh.'

'And where do they live?' asked Ian. But the giant answered, 'Ah, that is for you to discover.'

And Ian dared say no more, and hastened down to the waste. There, as he hoped, he met his friend Gille Mairtean the fox, who bade him eat his supper and lie down to sleep. And when he had wakened next

morning the fox said to him, 'Let us go down to the shore of the sea.'
And to the shore of the sea they went. And after they had reached the
shore, and beheld the sea stretching before them, and the isle of
Dhiurradh in the midst of it, the soul of Ian sank, and he turned to
Gille Mairtean and asked why he had brought him thither, for the
giant, when he had sent him, had known full well that without a boat
he could never find the Big Women.

'Do not be cast down,' answered the fox, 'it is quite easy! I will
change myself into a boat, and you shall go on board me, and I will
carry you over the sea to the Seven Big Women of Dhiurradh. Tell
them that you are skilled in brightening silver and gold, and in the
end they will take you as servant, and if you are careful to please
them they will give you the White Sword of Light to make bright
and shining. But when you seek to steal it, take heed that its sheath
touches nothing inside the house, or ill will befall you.'

So Ian Direach did all things as the fox had told him, and the
Seven Big Women of Dhiurradh took him for their servant, and for
six weeks he worked so hard that his seven mistresses said to each
other, 'Never has a servant had the skill to make all bright and
shining like this one. Let us give him the White Sword of Light to
polish like the rest.'

Then they brought forth the White Sword of Light from the iron
closet where it hung, and bade him rub it till he could see his face in
the shining blade; and he did so. But one day, when the Seven Big
Women were out of the way, he bethought him that the moment had
come for him to carry off the sword, and, replacing it in its sheath,
he hoisted it on his shoulder. But just as he was passing through the
door the tip of the sheath touched it, and the door gave a loud shriek.
And the Big Women heard it, and came running back, and took the
sword from him, and said, 'If it is our sword you want, you must first
bring us the bay colt of the King of Erin.'

Humbled and abashed, Ian Direach left the house, and sat by the
side of the sea, and soon Gille Mairtean the fox came to him.

'Plainly I see that you have taken no heed to my words, Ian
Direach,' said the fox. 'But eat first, and yet once more will I help
you.'

At these words the heart returned again to Ian Direach, and he gathered sticks and made a fire and ate with Gille Mairtean the fox, and slept on the sand. At dawn next morning Gille Mairtean said to Ian Direach:

'I will change myself into a ship, and will bear you across the seas to Erin, to the land where dwells the King. And you shall offer yourself to serve in his stable, and to tend his horses, till at length so well content is he, that he gives you the bay colt to wash and brush. But when you run away with him see that nought except the soles of his hoofs touch anything within the palace gates, or it will go ill with you.'

After he had thus counselled Ian Direach, the fox changed himself into a ship, and set sail for Erin. And the King of that country gave into Ian Direach's hands the care of his horses, and never before did their skins shine so brightly or was their pace so swift. And the King was well pleased, and at the end of a month he sent for Ian and said to him, 'You have given me faithful service, and now I will entrust you with the most precious thing that my kingdom holds.' And when he had spoken, he led Ian Direach to the stable where stood the bay colt. And Ian rubbed him and fed him, and galloped with him all round the country, till he could leave one wind behind him and catch the other which was in front.

'I am going away to hunt,' said the King one morning while he was watching Ian tend the bay colt in his stable. 'The deer have come down from the hill, and it is time for me to give them chase.' Then he went away; and when he was no longer in sight, Ian Direach led the bay colt out of the stable, and sprang on his back. But as they rode through the gate, which stood between the palace and the outer world, the colt swished his tail against the post, which shrieked loudly. In a moment the King came running up, and he seized the colt's bridle.

'If you want my bay colt, you must first bring me the daughter of the King of the Franks.'

With slow steps went Ian Direach down to the shore where Gille Mairtean the fox awaited him.

'Plainly I see that you have not done as I bid you, nor will you ever do it,' spoke Gille Mairtean the fox; 'but I will help you yet again. For a third time I will change myself into a ship, and we will sail to France.'

And to France they sailed, and, as he was the ship, the *Gille Mairtean* sailed where he would, and ran himself into the cleft of a rock, high on to the land. Then he commanded Ian Direach to go up to the King's palace, saying that he had been wrecked, that his ship was made fast in a rock, and that none had been saved but himself only.

Ian Direach listened to the words of the fox, and he told a tale so pitiful, that the King and Queen, and the Princess their daughter, all came out to hear it. And when they had heard, nought would please them except to go down to the shore and visit the ship, which by now was floating, for the tide was up. Torn and battered was she, as if she had passed through many dangers, yet music of a wondrous sweetness poured forth from within.

'Bring hither a boat,' cried the Princess, 'that I may go and see for myself the harp that gives forth such music.' And a boat was brought, and Ian Direach stepped in to row it to the side of the ship.

To the further side he rowed, so that none could see, and when he helped the Princess on board he gave a push to the boat, so that she could not get back to it again. And the music sounded always sweeter, though they could never see whence it came, and sought it from one part of the vessel to another. When at last they reached the deck and looked around them, nought of land could they see, or anything save the rushing waters.

The Princess stood silent, and her face grew grim. At last she said, 'An ill trick have you played me! What is this that you have done, and whither are we going?'

'It is a queen you will be,' answered Ian Direach, 'for the King of Erin has sent me for you, and in return he will give me his bay colt, that I may take him to the Seven Big Women of Dhiurradh, in exchange for the White Sword of Light. This I must carry to the giant of the Five Heads and Five Necks and Five Humps, and in place of it he will bestow on me the blue falcon, which I have promised to my step-mother, so that she may free me from the spell which she has laid on me.'

'I would rather be wife to you,' answered the Princess.

By and by the ship sailed into a harbour on the coast of Erin, and cast anchor there. And Gille Mairtean the fox bade Ian Direach tell the Princess that she must bide yet a while in a cave amongst the rocks, for they had business on land, and after a while they would return to her. Then they took a boat and rowed up to some rocks, and as they touched the land Gille Mairtean changed himself into a fair woman, who laughed and said to Ian Direach, 'I will give the King a fine wife.'

Now the King of Erin had been hunting on the hill, and when he saw a strange ship sailing towards the harbour, he guessed that it might be Ian Direach, and left his hunting, and ran down the hill to the stable. Hastily he led the bay colt from his stall, and put the golden saddle on his back, and the silver bridle over his head, and with the colt's bridle in his hand, he hurried to meet the Princess.

'I have brought you the King of France's daughter,' said Ian Direach. And the King of Erin looked at the maiden, and was well pleased, not knowing that it was Gille Mairtean the fox. And he bowed low, and besought her to do him the honour to enter the palace; and Gille Mairtean, as he went in, turned to look back at Ian Direach, and laughed.

In the great hall the King paused and pointed to an iron chest which stood in a corner.

'In that chest is the crown that has waited for you for many years,' he said, 'and at last you have come for it.' And he stooped down to unlock the box.

In an instant Gille Mairtean the fox had sprung on his back, and gave him such a bite that he fell down unconscious. Quickly the fox took his own shape again, and galloped away to the sea shore, where Ian Direach and the Princess and the bay colt awaited him.

'I will become a ship,' cried Gille Mairtean, 'and you shall go on board me.' And so he did, and Ian Direach led the bay colt into the ship and the Princess went after them, and they set sail for Dhiurradh. The wind was behind them, and very soon they saw the rocks of Dhiurradh in front. Then spoke Gille Mairtean the fox.

'Let the bay colt and the King's daughter hide in these rocks, and I will change myself into the colt and go with you to the house of the Seven Big Women.'

Joy filled the hearts of the Big Women when they beheld the bay colt led up to their door by Ian Direach. And the youngest of them fetched the White Sword of Light, and gave it into the hands of Ian Direach, who took off the golden saddle and the silver bridle, and went down the hill with the sword to the place where the Princess and the real colt awaited him.

'Now we shall have the ride that we have longed for!' cried the Seven Big Women; and they saddled and bridled the colt, and the eldest one got upon the saddle. Then the second sister sat on the back of the first, and the third on the back of the second, and so on for the whole seven. And when they were all seated, the eldest struck his side with a whip and the colt bounded forward. Over the moors he flew, and round and round the mountains, and still the Big Women clung to him and snorted with pleasure. At last he leapt high in the air, and came down on top of Monadh the high hill, where the crag is. And he rested his fore-feet on the crag, and threw up his hind legs, and the Seven Big Women fell over the crag, and were dead when they reached the bottom. And the colt laughed, and became a fox again and galloped away to the sea shore, where Ian Direach and the Princess and the real colt and the White Sword of Light were awaiting him.

'I will make myself into a ship,' said Gille Mairtean the fox, 'and will carry you and the Princess, and the bay colt and the White Sword of Light, back to the land.' And when the shore was reached, Gille Mairtean the fox took back his own shape, and spoke to Ian Direach in this wise:

'Let the Princess and the White Sword of Light, and the bay colt, remain among the rocks, and I will change myself into the likeness of the White Sword of Light, and you shall bear me to the giant, and, instead, he will give you the blue falcon.'

And Ian Direach did as the fox bade him, and set out for the giant's castle. From afar the giant beheld the blaze of the White Sword of Light, and his heart rejoiced; and he took the blue falcon and put it in a basket, and gave it to Ian Direach, who bore it swiftly away to the place where the Princess, and the bay colt, and the real Sword of Light were awaiting him.

So well content was the giant to possess the sword he had coveted for many a year, that he began at once to whirl it through the air, and to cut and slash with it. For a little while Gille Mairtean let the giant play with him in this manner; then he turned in the giant's hand and cut through the Five Necks, so that the Five Heads rolled on the ground. Afterwards he went back to Ian Direach and said to him:

'Saddle the colt with the golden saddle, and bridle him with the silver bridle, and sling the basket with the falcon over your shoulders, and hold the White Sword of Light with its back against your nose. Then mount the colt, and let the Princess mount behind you, and ride thus to your father's palace. But see that the back of the sword is ever against your nose, else when your step-mother beholds you, she will change you into a dry faggot. If, however, you do as I bid you, she will become herself a bundle of sticks.'

Ian Direach hearkened to the words of Gille Mairtean, and his step-mother fell as a bundle of sticks before him; and he set fire to her, and was free from her spells for ever. After that he married the Princess, who was the best wife in all the islands of the West. Henceforth he was safe from harm, for had he not the bay colt who could leave one wind behind him and catch the other wind, and the blue falcon to bring him game to eat, and the White Sword of Light to pierce through his foes?

And Ian Direach knew that all this he owed to Gille Mairtean the fox, and he made a compact with him that he might choose any beast out of his herds, whenever hunger seized him, and that henceforth no arrow should be let fly at him or at any of his race. But Gille Mairtean the fox would take no reward for the help he had given to Ian Direach, only his friendship. Thus all things prospered with Ian Direach till he died.

How Six Men
travelled through the Wide World

THERE WAS once upon a time a man who understood all sorts of arts; he served in the war, and bore himself bravely and well; but when the war was over, he got his discharge, and set out on his travels with only three farthings in his pocket, which was all his pay.

'Wait,' he said; 'that does not please me; only let me find the right people, and the King shall yet give me all the treasures of his kingdom.' He strode angrily into the forest, and there he found a man standing who had uprooted six trees as if they were straws. He said to him, 'Will you be my servant and travel with me?'

'Yes,' he answered; 'but first of all I will take this little bundle of sticks home to my mother,' and he took one of the trees and wound it round the other five, raised the bundle on his shoulders and bore it off. Then he came back and went with his master, who said, 'We two ought to be able to travel through the wide world!' And when they had gone a little way they came upon a hunter, who was on his knees, his gun on his shoulder, aiming at something. The man said to him, 'Hunter, what are you aiming at?'

He answered, 'Two miles from this place sits a fly on a branch of an oak; I want to shoot out its left eye.'

'Oh, come with me,' said the man; 'if we three are together we shall easily travel through the wide world.'

The hunter agreed and went with him, and they came to seven windmills whose sails were going round quite fast, and yet there was not a breath of wind, nor was a leaf moving. The man said, 'I don't know what is turning those windmills; there is not the slightest breeze blowing.' So he walked on with his servants, and when they had gone two miles they saw a man sitting on a tree, holding one of his nostrils and blowing out of the other.

'Fellow, what are you puffing at up there?' asked the man.

He replied, 'Two miles from this place are standing seven windmills; see, I am blowing to drive them round.'

'Oh, come with me,' said the man; 'if we four are together we shall easily travel through the wide world.'

So the blower got down and went with him, and after a time they saw a man who was standing on one leg, and had unstrapped the other and laid it near him. Then said the master, 'You have made yourself very comfortable to rest!'

'I am a runner,' answered he; 'and so that I shall not go too quickly, I have unstrapped one leg; when I run with two legs, I go faster than a bird flies.'

'Oh, come with me; if we five are together we shall easily travel through the wide world.' So he went with him and, not long afterwards, they met a man who wore a little hat, but he had it slouched over one ear.

'Manners, manners!' said the master to him; 'straighten your hat; you look like a madman!'

'I dare not,' said the other, 'for if I were to put my hat on straight, there would come such a frost that the very birds in the sky would freeze and fall dead on the earth.'

'Oh, come with me,' said the master; 'if we six are together we shall easily travel through the wide world.'

Now the six went into the city where the King had proclaimed that whoever should run with his daughter in a race, and win, should become her husband; but if he lost, he must lose his head. This was reported to the master who declared he would compete. 'But,' he said, 'I shall let my servant run for me.'

The King replied, 'Then both your heads must be staked, and your head and his must be guaranteed for the winner.'

When this was agreed upon and settled, the master strapped on the runner's other leg, saying to him, 'Now be nimble, and see that we win!' It was arranged that whoever should first bring water from a far-off stream should be the winner. Then the runner took a pitcher, and the King's daughter another, and they began to run at the same time; but when the King's daughter was gone only just a little way, no spectator could see the runner, and it seemed as if the wind had whistled past. In a short time he reached the stream, filled his pitcher with water, and turned round again. But, half way back, a great drowsiness came over him; he put down his pitcher, lay down, and fell asleep. He had, however, put a horse's skull which was lying on the ground, for his pillow, so that he should not be too comfortable and might soon wake up.

In the meantime the King's daughter, who could also run well, and as fast as an ordinary man could, reached the stream, and hastened back with her pitcher full of water. When she saw the runner lying there asleep, she was delighted, and said, 'My enemy is given into my hands!' She emptied his pitcher and ran on.

Everything now would have been lost, if by good luck the hunter had not been standing on the castle tower and had seen everything with his sharp eyes.

'Ah,' said he, 'the King's daughter shall not overreach us;' and, loading his gun, he shot so cleverly that he shot away the horse's skull from under the runner's head, without its hurting him. Then the runner awoke, jumped up, and saw that his pitcher was empty and the King's daughter far ahead. But he did not lose courage, and ran back to the stream with his pitcher, filled it once more with water, and was home ten minutes before the King's daughter arrived.

'See,' said he, 'I have only just exercised my legs; that was nothing of a run.'

But the King was angry, and his daughter even more so, that she should be carried away by a common, discharged soldier. They consulted together how they could destroy both him and his companions.

Then the King said to her, 'I have found a way. Don't be frightened; they shall not get home again.' He went and said to them, 'You must now make merry together, and eat and drink,' and he led them into a room which had a floor of iron; the doors were also of iron, and the windows were barred with iron. In the room was a table spread with delicious food. The King said to them, 'Go in and enjoy yourselves,' and as soon as they were inside he had the doors shut and bolted. Then he made the cook come, and ordered him to keep up a large fire under the room until the iron was red-hot. The cook did so, and the six sitting round the table felt it grow very warm, and they thought this was because of their good fare; but when the heat became still greater and they wanted to go out, but found the doors and windows fastened, then they knew that the King meant them harm and was trying to suffocate them.

'But he shall not succeed,' cried he of the little hat, 'I will make a frost come which shall make the fire ashamed and die out!' So he put his hat on straight, and at once there came such a frost that all the heat disappeared and the food on the dishes began to freeze. When a couple of hours had passed, and the King thought they must be quite dead from the heat, he had the doors opened and went in himself to see.

But when the doors were opened, there stood all six, alive and well, saying they were glad they could come out to warm themselves, for the great cold in the room had frozen all the food hard in the dishes. Then the King went angrily to the cook, and scolded him, and asked him why he had not done what he was told.

But the cook answered, 'There is heat enough there; see for yourself.' Then the King saw a huge fire burning under the iron room, and understood that he could do no harm to the six in this way. The King now began again to think how he could free himself from his unwelcome guests. He commanded the master to come before him, and said, 'If you will take gold, and give up your right to my daughter, you shall have as much as you like.'

'Oh, yes, your Majesty,' answered he, 'give me as much as my servant can carry, and I will give up your daughter.'

The King was delighted, and the man said, 'I will come and fetch it in fourteen days.'

Then he called all the tailors in the kingdom together, and made them sit down for fourteen days sewing at a sack. When it was finished, he made the strong man who had uprooted the trees take the sack on his shoulder and go with him to the King. Then the King said, 'What a powerful fellow that is, carrying that bale of linen as large as a house on his shoulder!' and he was much frightened, and thought 'What a lot of gold he will make away with!' Then he had a ton of gold brought, which sixteen of the strongest men had to carry; but the strong man seized it with one hand, and put it in the sack, saying, 'Why don't you bring me more? That scarcely covers the bottom!' Then the King had to send again and again to fetch his treasures, which the strong man shoved into the sack, and the sack was only half full.

'Bring more,' he cried, 'these crumbs don't fill it.' So seven thousand wagons of the gold of the whole kingdom were driven up; these the strong man shoved into the sack, wagons and oxen and all. 'I will no longer be particular,' he said, 'and will take what comes, so that the sack shall be filled.'

When everything was put in and it was still not enough, he said, 'I will make an end of this; it is easier to fasten a sack when it is not full.' Then he threw it on his back and went off with his companions.

Now, when the King saw how a single man was carrying away the wealth of the whole country he was very angry, and made his cavalry mount and pursue the six, and bring back the strong man with the sack. Two regiments soon overtook them, and called to them, 'You are prisoners! lay down the sack of gold or you shall be cut down.'

'What do you say?' said the blower, 'we are prisoners? Before that, you shall dance in the air!' And he held one nostril and blew with the other at the two regiments; they were separated and blown away in the blue sky over the mountains, one this way, and the other that. A sergeant-major cried for mercy, saying he had nine wounds, and was a brave fellow, and did not deserve this disgrace. So the blower let him off, and he came down without hurt. Then he said to him, 'Now go home to the King, and say that if he sends any more cavalry I will blow them all into the air.'

When the King received the message, he said, 'Let the fellows go; they are bewitched.' Then the six brought the treasure home, shared it among themselves, and lived contentedly till the end of their days.

The Husband of the Rat's Daughter

ONCE UPON a time there lived in Japan a rat and his wife. They came of an old and noble race, and had one daughter, the loveliest girl in all the rat world. Her parents were very proud of her, and spared no pains to teach her all she ought to know. There was not another young lady in the whole town who was as clever as she was in gnawing through the hardest wood, or who could drop from such a height on to a bed, or run away so fast if anyone was heard coming. Great attention, too, was paid to her personal appearance, and her skin shone like satin, while her teeth were as white as pearls, and beautifully pointed.

Of course, with all these advantages, her parents expected her to make a brilliant marriage, and, as she grew up, they began to look round for a suitable husband.

But here a difficulty arose. The father was a rat from the tip of his nose to the end of his tail, outside as well as in, and desired that his daughter should wed among her own people. She had no lack of lovers, but her father's secret hopes rested on a fine young rat, with moustaches which almost swept the ground, whose family was still nobler and more ancient than his own. Unluckily, the mother had other views for her precious child. She was one of those people who always despise their own family and surroundings, and take pleasure in thinking that they themselves are made of finer material than the rest of the world. '*My* daughter shall never marry a mere rat,' she declared, holding her head high. 'With her beauty and talents she has a right to look for someone a little better than *that*.'

So she talked, as mothers will, to anyone that would listen to her. What the girl thought about the matter nobody knew or cared – it was not the fashion in the rat world.

Many were the quarrels which the old rat and his wife had upon the subject, and sometimes they bore on their faces certain marks which looked as if they had not kept to words only.

'Reach up to the stars is *my* motto,' cried the lady one day, when she was in a greater passion than usual. 'My daughter's beauty places her higher than anything upon earth,' she cried; 'and I am certainly not going to accept a son-in-law who is beneath her.'

'Better offer her in marriage to the sun,' answered her husband impatiently. 'As far as I know there is nothing greater than he.'

'Well, I *was* thinking of it,' replied the wife, 'and as you are of the same mind, we will pay him a visit to-morrow.'

So the next morning, the two rats, having spent hours in making themselves smart, set out to see the sun, leading their daughter between them.

The journey took some time, but at length they came to the golden palace where the sun lived.

'Noble king,' began the mother, 'behold our daughter! She is so beautiful that she is above everything in the whole world. Naturally, we wish for a son-in-law who, on his side, is greater than all. Therefore we have come to you.'

'I feel very much flattered,' replied the sun, who was so busy that he had not the least wish to marry anybody. 'You do me great honour by your proposal. Only, in one point you are mistaken, and it would be wrong of me to take advantage of your ignorance. There *is* something greater than I am, and that is the cloud. Look!' And as he spoke a cloud spread itself over the sun's face, blotting out his rays.

'Oh, well, we will speak to the cloud,' said the mother. And turning to the cloud she repeated her proposal.

'Indeed I am unworthy of anything so charming,' answered the cloud; 'but you make a mistake again in what you say. There is one thing that is even more powerful than I, and that is the wind. Ah, here he comes, you can see for yourself.'

And she *did* see, for catching up the cloud as he passed, the wind threw it on the other side of the sky. Then, tumbling father, mother and daughter down to earth again, he paused for a moment beside them, his foot on an old wall.

When she had recovered her breath, the mother began her little speech once more.

'The wall is the proper husband for your daughter,' answered the wind, whose home consisted of a cave, which he only visited when he was not rushing about elsewhere; 'you can see for yourself that he is greater than I, for he has power to stop me in my flight.' And the mother, who did not trouble to conceal her wishes, turned at once to the wall.

Then something happened which was quite unexpected by everyone.

'I won't marry that ugly old wall, which is as old as my grandfather,' sobbed the girl, who had not uttered one word all this time. 'I would have married the sun, or the cloud, or the wind, because it was my duty, although I love the handsome young rat, and him only. But that horrid old wall – I would sooner die!'

And the wall, rather hurt in his feelings, declared that he had no claim to be the husband of so beautiful a girl.

'It is quite true,' he said, 'that I can stop the wind who can part the clouds who can cover the sun; but there is someone who can do more than all these, and that is the rat who lives under me. He is stronger than I am, for he can reduce me to powder, simply by gnawing with his teeth. If, therefore, you want a son-in-law who is greater than the whole world, seek him among the rats.'

'Ah, what did I tell you?' cried the father. And his wife, though for the moment angry at being beaten, soon thought that a rat son-in-law was what she had always desired.

So all three returned happily home, and the wedding was celebrated three days after.

The Iron Stove

ONCE UPON a time when wishes came true there was a king's son who was enchanted by an old witch, so that he was obliged to sit in a large iron stove in a wood. There he lived for many years, and no one could free him. At last a king's daughter came into the wood; she had lost her way, and could not find her father's kingdom again. She had been wandering round and round for nine days, and she came at last to the iron stove.

A voice spoke from within and asked her, 'Where do you come from, and where do you want to go?' She answered, 'I have lost my way to my father's kingdom, and I shall never get home again.' Then the voice from the iron stove said, 'I will help you to find your home again, and that in a very short time, if you will promise to do what I ask you. I am a greater prince than you are a princess, and I will marry you.' Then she grew frightened, and thought, 'What can a young lassie do with an iron stove?' But as she wanted very much to go home to her father, she promised to do what he wished. He said, 'You must come again, and bring a knife with you to scrape a hole in the iron.'

Then he gave her someone for a guide, who walked near her and said nothing, but he brought her in two hours to her home. There was great joy in the castle when the Princess came back, and the old King fell on her neck and kissed her. But she was very much troubled, and said, 'Dear father, listen to what has befallen me! I should never have come home again out of the great wild wood if I had not come upon an iron stove, to whom I have had to promise that I will go back to free him and marry him!'

The old King was so frightened that he nearly fainted, for she was his only daughter. So they consulted together, and determined that the miller's daughter, who was very beautiful, should take her place. They took her there, gave her a knife, and said she must scrape at the iron stove. She scraped for twenty-four hours, but did not make the least impression. At daybreak, a voice called from the iron stove, 'It seems to me that it is day outside.' Then she answered, 'It seems so to me; I think I hear my father's mill rattling.'

'So you are a miller's daughter! Then go away at once, and tell the King's daughter to come.'

Then she went away, and told the old King that the thing inside the iron stove would not have her, but wanted the Princess. The old King was frightened, and his daughter wept. But the swineherd's daughter was even more beautiful than the miller's daughter, so they gave her a piece of gold to go to the iron stove instead of the Princess. Then she was taken to the wood, and had to scrape for four-and-twenty hours, but she could make no impression. As soon as the day broke the voice from the stove called out, 'It seems to be daylight outside.' Then she answered, 'It seems so to me too; I think I hear my father blowing his horn.' 'So you are a swineherd's daughter! Go away at once, and let the King's daughter come. And say to her that if she does not come everything in the kingdom shall fall into ruin, and not one stone shall be left upon another.'

When the Princess heard this she began to cry, but it was no good; she had to keep her word. She took leave of her father, put a knife in her belt, and went to the iron stove in the wood. As soon as she reached it she began to scrape, and the iron gave way and before two hours had passed she had made a little hole. Then she peeped in and saw such a beautiful youth all shining with gold and precious stones that she fell in love with him on the spot. So she scraped away harder than ever, and made the hole so large that he could get out. Then he said, 'You are mine, and I am thine; you are my bride and have set me free!'

He wanted to take her with him to his kingdom, but she begged him just to let her go once more to her father; and the Prince let her go, but told her not to say more than three words to her father, then to come back again. So she went home, but alas! she said more than three words; and immediately the iron stove vanished and went away over a mountain of glass and sharp swords. But the Prince was free, and was no longer shut up in it.

Then the Princess said good-bye to her father, and took a little money with her, and went again into the great wood to look for the iron stove; but she could not find it. She sought it for nine days, and then her hunger became so great that she did not know how she could live any longer. And when it was evening she climbed a little tree and wished that the night would not come, because she was afraid of the wild beasts. When midnight came she saw afar off a little light, and thought, 'Ah! if only I could reach that!' Then she got down from the tree and went towards the light.

She came to a little old house with a little heap of wood in front, and much rough grass growing round about it. She thought, 'Alas! what am I come to?' She peeped through the window; but she saw nothing inside except big and little toads, and a table laden with roast meats and wine, and beautifully set with dishes and drinking-cups of silver. Then she took heart and knocked. A fat toad called out:

> 'Little green toad with leg like crook,
> Open wide the door, and look
> Who it was the latch that shook.'

And a little toad came forward and let her in. When she entered they all bid her welcome, and made her sit down. They asked her how she came there and what she wanted. Then she told them everything that had happened to her, and how, because she had exceeded her permission only to speak three words, the stove had disappeared with the Prince; and how she had searched a very long time, and must wander over mountain and valley till she found him.

Then the old toad said:

> 'Little green toad whose leg doth twist,
> Go to the corner of which you wist,
> And bring to me the large old kist.'

And the little toad went and brought out a great chest. Then they gave her food and drink, and led her to a beautifully made bed of silk and samite, on which she lay down and slept soundly. When the day dawned she arose, and the old toad gave her three things out of the huge chest to take with her. She would have need of them, for she had to cross a high glass mountain, three cutting swords, and a great lake. When she had passed these she would find her lover again. So she was given three large needles, a plough-wheel, and three nuts, which she was to take great care of. The Princess set out with these gifts, and when she came to the glass mountain she stuck the three needles behind her feet and then in front, and so got over it, and when she was on the other side put them carefully away.

Then she reached the three cutting swords, and got on her plough-wheel and rolled over them. At last she came to a great lake, and, when she had crossed that, arrived at a beautiful castle. She went in and asked for a place as a servant; she said she was a poor maid who would gladly have employment. But she knew that the Prince, whom she had freed from the iron stove in the great wood, was in the castle. So she was taken on as a kitchen-maid for very small wages. Now the Prince was about to marry another, for he thought she was dead long ago.

In the evening when the Princess had washed up, she felt in her pocket and found the three nuts which the old toad had given her. She cracked one and was going to eat the kernel, when behold! there was a beautiful royal dress inside it! When the bride heard of this, she came and begged for the dress, and wanted to buy it, saying that it was not a dress for a serving-maid. Then the maid said she would not sell it unless she was granted one favour – namely, to sleep by the Prince's door. The bride granted her this, because the dress was so beautiful and she had none like it. When it was evening she said to her bridegroom, 'That stupid maid wants to sleep by your door.'

'If you are contented, I am,' he said. But she gave him a glass of wine in which she had poured a sleeping-draught, and he slept so soundly that the maid could not wake him. She wept all night long, and said, 'I freed you in the wild wood out of the iron stove; I have sought you, and have crossed a glassy mountain, three sharp swords, and a great lake before I found you, and will you not hear me now?' The servants outside heard how she cried the whole night, and they told their master in the morning.

When she had washed up the next evening she cracked the second nut, and there was a still more beautiful dress inside. When the bride saw it she wanted to buy it also. But the maid did not want money, and asked that she should sleep again by the Prince's door. The bride, however, gave him a sleeping-draught, and he slept so soundly that he heard nothing. But the kitchen-maid wept the whole night long, and said, 'I have freed you in a wood and from an iron stove; I sought you and have crossed a glassy mountain, three sharp swords, and a great lake to find you, and now you will not hear me!' The servants outside heard how she cried the whole night, and in the morning they told their master.

And when she had washed up on the third night she bit the third nut, and there was a still more beautiful dress inside that was made of pure gold. When the bride saw it she wanted to have it, but the maid would only give it her on condition that she should sleep for the third time by the Prince's door. But the Prince took care this time not to drink the sleeping-draught. When she began to weep and to say, 'Dearest sweetheart, I freed you in the horrible wild wood, and from an iron stove,' he jumped up and said, 'You are right. You are mine, and I am thine.' Though it was still night, he got into a carriage with her, and they took the false bride's clothes away, so that she could not follow them. When they came to the great lake they rowed across, and when they reached the three sharp swords they sat on the plough-wheel, and on the glassy mountain they stuck the three needles in. So they arrived at last at the little old house, but when they stepped inside it turned into a large castle. The toads were all freed from enchantment, and became again princes and princesses, and were full of joy.

Then the wedding was celebrated, and the Prince and Princess remained in the castle, which was much larger than her father's. But because the old man did not like being left alone, they went and fetched him. So they had two kingdoms and lived in great wealth and happiness.

> A mouse has run,
> My story's done.

Jesper who herded the Hares

THERE WAS once a king who ruled over a kingdom somewhere between sunrise and sunset. It was as small as kingdoms usually were in olden times, and when the King went up to the roof of his palace and took a look round he could see to the ends of it in every direction. But as it was all his own, he was very proud of it and often wondered how it would get along without him.

He had only one child, a daughter, so he foresaw that she must be provided with a husband who would be fit to be king after him. Where to find one rich enough and clever enough to be a suitable match for the Princess was what troubled the King and often kept him awake at night.

At last he devised a plan. He made a proclamation over all his kingdom (and asked his nearest neighbours to publish it in theirs as well) that whoever could bring him a dozen of the finest pearls the King had ever seen, and could perform certain tasks that would be set him, should have his daughter in marriage and in due time succeed to the throne. The pearls, he thought, could only be brought by a very wealthy man and the tasks would require unusual talents to accomplish them.

There were plenty who tried to fulfil the terms which the King proposed. Rich merchants and foreign princes presented themselves one after the other. On some days the number of them was quite annoying, but though they could all produce magnificent pearls, not one of them could perform even the simplest of the tasks set them.

Some turned up, too, who were mere adventurers and tried to deceive the old King with imitation pearls. But he was not to be taken in so easily and they were soon sent about their business. At the end of several weeks the stream of suitors began to fall off, and still there was no prospect of a suitable son-in-law.

Now it so happened that in a little corner of the King's dominions, beside the sea, there lived a poor fisher who had three sons, and their names were Peter, Paul and Jesper. Peter and Paul were grown men, while Jesper was just coming to manhood. The two elder brothers were much bigger and stronger than the youngest, but Jesper was by far the cleverest of the three, though neither Peter nor Paul would admit this. It was a fact, however, as we shall see in the course of our story.

One day the fisherman went out fishing, and among his catch for the day he brought home three dozen oysters. When these were opened, every shell was found to contain a large and beautiful pearl.

Hereupon the three brothers, at one and the same moment, fell upon the idea of offering themselves as suitors for the Princess. After some discussion, it was agreed that the pearls should be divided by lot, and that each should have his chance in the order of his age: of course, if the oldest was successful the other two would be saved the trouble of trying.

Next morning Peter put his pearls in a little basket and set off for the King's palace. He had not gone far on his way when he came upon the King of the Ants and the King of the Beetles who, with their armies behind them, were facing each other and preparing for battle.

'Come and help me,' said the King of the Ants; 'the beetles are too big for us. I may help you some day in return.'

'I have no time to waste on other people's affairs,' said Peter; 'just fight away as best you can.' And with that he walked off and left them.

A little farther on the way he met an old woman.

'Good morning, young man,' said she. 'You are early astir. What have you in your basket?'

'Cinders,' said Peter promptly. He walked on, adding to himself, 'Take that for being so inquisitive.'

'Very well, cinders be it,' the old woman called after him, but he pretended not to hear her.

Very soon he reached the palace, and was at once brought before the King. When he took the cover off the basket, the King and all his courtiers said with one voice that these were the finest pearls they had ever seen, and they could not take their eyes off them. But then a strange thing happened: the pearls began to lose their whiteness and grew quite dim in colour; then they grew blacker and blacker till at last they were just like so many cinders.

Peter was so amazed that he could say nothing for himself, but the

King said quite enough for both, and Peter was glad to get away home again as fast as his legs would carry him. To his father and brothers, however, he gave no account of his attempt, except that it had been a failure.

Next day Paul set out to try his luck. He soon came upon the King of the Ants and the King of the Beetles who, with their armies, had encamped on the field of battle all night and were ready to begin the fight again.

'Come and help me,' said the King of the Ants; 'we got the worst of it yesterday. I may help you some day in return.'

'I don't care, though you get the worst of it to-day too,' said Paul. 'I have more important business on hand than mixing myself up in your quarrels.'

So he walked on, and presently the same old woman met him. 'Good morning,' said she; 'what have you in your basket?'

'Cinders,' said Paul, who was quite as insolent as his brother and quite as anxious to teach other people good manners.

'Very well, cinders be it,' the old woman shouted after him, but Paul neither looked back nor answered her. He thought more of what she said, however, after his pearls also turned to cinders before the eyes of King and court. Then he lost no time in getting home again, and was very sulky when asked how he had succeeded.

The third day came and with it came Jesper's turn to try his fortune. He rose early and had his breakfast, while Peter and Paul lay in bed and made rude remarks, telling him that he would come back quicker than he went, for if they had failed it could not be supposed that he would succeed. Jesper made no reply, but put his pearls in the little basket and walked off.

The King of the Ants and the King of the Beetles were again marshalling their hosts, but the ants were greatly reduced in numbers and had little hope of holding out that day.

'Come and help us,' said their king to Jesper, 'or we shall be completely defeated. I may help you some day in return.'

Now Jesper had always heard the ants spoken of as clever and industrious little creatures, while he never heard anyone say a good word for the beetles, so he agreed to give the wished-for help. At the first charge he made, the ranks of the beetles broke and fled in dismay, and those escaped best that were nearest a hole and could get into it before Jesper's boots came down upon them. In a few minutes the ants had the field all to themselves; and their king made an eloquent speech to Jesper, thanking him for the service he had done them and promising to assist him in any difficulty.

'Just call on me when you want me,' he said, 'wherever you are. I'm never far away from anywhere, and if I can possibly help you, I shall not fail to do it.'

Jesper was inclined to laugh at this, but he kept a grave face, said he would remember the offer and walked on. At a turn of the road he suddenly came upon the old woman.

'Good morning,' said she; 'what have you in your basket?'

'Pearls,' said Jesper. 'I'm going to the palace to win the Princess with them.' And in case she might not believe him, he lifted the cover and let her see them.

'Beautiful,' said the old woman, 'very beautiful, indeed. But they will go a very little way towards winning the Princess, unless you can also perform the tasks that are set you. However,' she said, 'I see you have brought something with you to eat. Won't you give that to me? You are sure to get a good dinner at the palace.'

'Yes, of course,' said Jesper, 'I hadn't thought of that.' And he handed over the whole of his lunch to her.

He had already taken a few steps on the way again, when the old woman called him back.

'Here,' she said, 'take this whistle in return for your lunch. It isn't much to look at, but if you blow it, anything that you have lost or that has been taken from you will find its way back to you in a moment.'

Jesper thanked her for the whistle, though he did not see of what use it was to be to him just then, and held on his way to the palace.

When Jesper presented his pearls to the King there were exclamations of wonder and delight from everyone who saw them. It was not pleasant, however, for the King to discover that Jesper was a mere fisher-lad; that wasn't the kind of son-in-law he had expected, and he said so to the Queen.

'Never mind,' said she, 'you can easily set him such tasks as he will never be able to perform. We shall soon get rid of him.'

'Yes, of course,' said the King. 'Really I forget things nowadays, with all the bustle we have had of late.'

That day Jesper dined with the King and Queen and their nobles, and at night was put into a bedroom grander than any he had ever seen. It was all so new to him that he could not sleep a wink, especially as he was always wondering what kind of tasks would be set him to do, and whether he would be able to perform them. In spite of the softness of the bed, he was very glad when morning came at last.

After breakfast was over, the King said to Jesper, 'Just come with me and I'll show you what you must do first.' He led him out to the barn, and there in the middle of the floor was a large pile of grain.

'Here,' said the King, 'you have a mixed heap of wheat, barley, oats and rye, a sackful of each. By an hour before sunset you must have these sorted out into four heaps, and if a single grain is found to be in a wrong heap you have no further chance of marrying my daughter. I shall lock the door so no one can get in to assist you, and I shall return at the appointed time to see how you have succeeded.'

The King walked off, and Jesper looked in despair at the task before him. Then he sat down and tried what he could do at it, but it was soon very clear that single-handed he could never hope to accomplish it in the time.

Assistance was out of the question – unless, he suddenly thought – unless the King of the Ants could help. On him he began to call and before many minutes had passed that royal personage made his appearance. Jesper explained the trouble he was in.

'Is that all?' said the ant. 'We shall soon put that to rights.' He gave the royal signal, and in a minute or two a stream of ants came pouring into the barn, who under their king's orders set to work to separate the grain into the proper heaps.

Jesper watched them for a while, but through the continual movement of the little creatures, and his not having slept during the previous night, he soon fell sound asleep. When he woke again, the King had just come into the barn and was amazed to find that not only was the task accomplished but that Jesper had found time to take a nap as well.

'Wonderful!' said he. 'I wouldn't have believed it possible. However, the hardest is yet to come, as you will see to-morrow.'

Jesper thought so too when the next day's task was set before him. The King's gamekeepers had caught a hundred live hares, which were to be let loose in a large meadow, where Jesper must herd them all day and bring them safely home in the evening. If even one were missing, he must give up all thought of marrying the Princess. Before he had quite grasped the fact that this was an impossible task, the keepers had opened the sacks in which the hares were brought to the field and, with a whisk of the short tail and a flap of the long ears, each one of the hundred flew in a different direction.

'Now,' said the King, as he walked away, 'let's see what your cleverness can do here.'

Jesper stared round him in bewilderment, and having nothing better to do with his hands, thrust them into his pockets, as he was in the habit of doing. Here he found the whistle given to him by the old woman. He remembered what she had said about the virtues of the whistle, but was rather doubtful whether its powers would extend to a hundred hares, each of which had gone in a different direction and might be several miles distant by this time. However, he blew the whistle, and in a few minutes the hares came bounding through the hedge on all the four sides of the field and before long were all sitting round him in a circle. After that, Jesper allowed them to run about as they pleased, so long as they stayed in the field.

The King had told one of the keepers to hang about for a little and see what became of Jesper, not doubting, however, that as soon as he saw the coast clear he would use his legs to the best advantage and never show face at the palace again. It was therefore with great surprise and annoyance that he now learned of the mysterious return of the hares and the likelihood of Jesper carrying out his task with success.

'One of them must be got out of his hands by hook or by crook,' said he. 'I'll go and see the Queen about it; she's good at devising plans.'

A little later, a girl in a shabby dress came into the field and walked up to Jesper.

'Do give me one of those hares,' she said; 'we have visitors who are going to stay to dinner, and there's nothing we can give them to eat.'

'I can't,' said Jesper. 'For one thing, they're not mine; for another, a great deal depends on my having them all here in the evening.'

But the girl, and she was very pretty though so shabbily dressed, begged so hard for one of them that at last he said, 'Very well; give me a kiss and you shall have one of them.'

He could see that she didn't quite care for this, but she consented to the bargain, gave him the kiss, and went away with a hare in her apron. Scarcely was she outside the field, however, when Jesper blew his whistle, and immediately the hare wriggled out of its prison like an eel and went back to its master at the top of its speed.

Not long after this Jesper had another visitor. This time it was a stout old woman in the dress of a peasant, who also was after a hare to provide a dinner for unexpected visitors. Jesper again refused, but she was so pressing, and would take no refusal, that at last he said, 'Very well, you shall have a hare and pay nothing for it either, if you will only walk round me on tiptoe, look up to the sky, and cackle like a hen.'

'Fie,' said she, 'what a ridiculous thing to ask anyone to do. Just think what the neighbours would say if they saw me. They would think I had taken leave of my senses.'

'Just as you like,' said Jesper. 'You know best whether you want the hare or not.'

There was no help for it, and a pretty figure the old woman made in carrying out her task. The cackling wasn't very well done, but Jesper said it would do and gave her the hare. As soon as she had left the field, the whistle was sounded again and back came long-legs-and-ears at a marvellous speed.

The next to appear on the same errand was a fat old fellow in the dress of a groom. It was the royal livery he wore, and he plainly thought a good deal of himself.

'Young man,' said he, 'I want one of those hares; name your price, but I must have one of them.'

'All right,' said Jesper, 'you can have one at an easy rate. Just stand on your head, whack your heels together, and cry, "Hurrah," and the hare is yours.'

'Eh, what!' said the old fellow. 'Me stand on my head; what an idea!'

'Oh, very well,' said Jesper, 'you needn't unless you like, you know; but then you won't get the hare.'

It went very much against the grain, one could see, but after some efforts the old fellow had his head on the grass and his heels in the air. The whacking and the 'Hurrah' were rather feeble, but Jesper was not very exacting and the hare was handed over. Of course, it wasn't long in coming back again, like the others.

Evening came, and home went Jesper with the hundred hares behind him. Great was the wonder over all the palace. The King and Queen seemed very much put out, but it was noticed that the Princess actually smiled at Jesper.

'Well, well,' said the King, 'you have done that very well indeed. If you are as successful with a little task which I shall give you to-morrow we shall consider the matter settled, and you shall marry the Princess.'

Next day it was announced that the task would be performed in the great hall of the palace and everyone was invited to come and witness it. The King and Queen sat on their thrones, with the Princess beside them, and the lords and ladies were all round the hall. At a sign from the King, two servants carried in a large empty tub which they set down in the open space before the throne. Jesper was told to stand beside it.

'Now,' said the King, 'you must tell us as many undoubted truths as will fill that tub or you can't have the Princess.'

'But how are we to know when the tub is full?' said Jesper.

'Don't you trouble about that,' said the King; 'that's my part of the business.'

This seemed to everybody present rather unfair. But no one liked to be the first to say so, and Jesper had to put the best face he could on the matter and begin his story.

'Yesterday,' he said, 'when I was herding the hares, there came to me a girl, in a shabby dress, and begged me to give her one of them. She got the hare, but she had to give me a kiss for it; and that girl was the Princess! Isn't that true?' said he, looking at her.

The Princess blushed and looked very uncomfortable, but had to admit that it was true.

'That hasn't filled much of the tub,' said the King. 'Go on again.'

'After that,' said Jesper, 'a stout old woman, in a peasant's dress, came and begged for a hare. Before she got it, she had to walk round me on tiptoe, turn up her eyes and cackle like a hen; and that old woman was the Queen! Isn't that true, now?'

The Queen turned very red and hot, but couldn't deny it.

'H–m,' said the King, 'that is something, but the tub isn't full yet.' To the Queen he whispered, 'I didn't think you would be such a fool.'

'What did you do?' she whispered in return.

'Do you suppose I would do anything for him?' asked the King, and then hurriedly ordered Jesper to go on.

'In the next place,' said Jesper, 'there came a fat old fellow on the same errand. He was very proud and dignified, but in order to get the hare he actually stood on his head, whacked his heels together and cried, "Hurrah!" That old fellow was the –'

'Stop, stop!' shouted the King. 'You needn't say another word; the tub is full.'

Then all the court applauded, and the King and Queen accepted Jesper as their son-in-law. The Princess was very well pleased, for by this time she had quite fallen in love with him, because he was so handsome and so clever. When the old King had time to think it over, he was quite convinced that his kingdom would be safe in Jesper's hands if he looked after the people as well as he herded the hares.

Jorinde and Joringel

THERE WAS once upon a time a castle in the middle of a thick wood where lived an old woman quite alone, for she was an enchantress. In the day-time she changed herself into a cat or a night-owl, but in the evening she became like an ordinary woman again. She could entice animals and birds to come to her, and then she would kill and cook them. If any youth came within a hundred paces of the castle, he was obliged to stand still, and could not stir from the spot till she set him free; but if a pretty girl came within this boundary, the old enchantress changed her into a bird, and shut her up in a wicker cage, which she put in one of the rooms in the castle. She had quite seven thousand of such cages in the castle with very rare birds in them.

Now, there was once a maiden called Jorinde, who was more beautiful than other maidens. She and a youth named Joringel, who was just as good-looking as she was, were betrothed to one another. Their greatest delight was to be together, and so that they might get a good long talk, they went one evening for a walk in the wood. 'Take care,' said Joringel, 'not to come too close to the castle.' It was a beautiful evening; the sun shone brightly between the stems of the trees among the dark green leaves of the forest, and the turtle-dove sang clearly on the old may-bushes.

Jorinde wept from time to time, and she sat herself down in the sunshine and lamented, and Joringel lamented too. They felt as sad as if they had been condemned to die; they looked round and got quite confused, and did not remember which was their way home. Half the sun was still above the mountain and half was behind it when Joringel looked through the trees and saw the old wall of the castle quite near them. He was terrified and half dead with fright. Jorinde sang:

> 'My little bird with throat so red
> Sings sorrow, sorrow, sorrow;
> He sings to the little dove that's dead,
> Sings sorrow, sor – jug, jug, jug.'

Joringel looked up at Jorinde. She had been changed into a nightingale, who was singing 'jug, jug'. A night-owl with glowing eyes flew three times round her, and screeched three times 'tu-whit, tu-whit, tu-whoo'. Joringel could not stir; he stood there like a stone; he could not weep, or speak, or move hand or foot. Now the sun set; the owl flew into a bush, and immediately an old, bent woman came out of it; she was yellow-skinned and thin, and had large red eyes and a hooked nose, which met her chin. She muttered to herself, caught the nightingale, and carried her away in her hand. Joringel could say nothing; he could not move from the spot, and the nightingale was gone.

At last the woman came back again, and said in a gruff voice, 'Good evening, Zachiel; when the young moon shines in the basket, you are freed early, Zachiel.' Then Joringel was free. He fell on his knees before the old woman and implored her to give him back his Jorinde, but she said he would never have her again, and then went away. He called after her, he wept and lamented, but all in vain. 'What is to become of me!' he thought.

Then he went away, and came at last to a strange village, where he kept sheep for a long time. He often went round the castle while he was there, but never too close. At last he dreamt one night that he had found a blood-red flower, which had in its centre a beautiful large pearl. He plucked this flower and went with it to the castle; and there everything which he touched with the flower was freed from the enchantment, and he got his Jorinde back again through it.

When he awoke in the morning he began to seek mountain and valley to find such a flower. He sought it for eight days, and on the ninth early in the morning he found the blood-red flower. In its centre was a large dew-drop, as big as the most lovely pearl. He travelled day and night with this flower till he arrived at the castle. When he came within a hundred paces of it he did not cease to be able to move, but he went on till he reached the gate. He was delighted at his success, touched the great gate with the flower, and it sprang open. He entered, passed through the courtyard, and then stopped to listen for the singing of the birds; at last he heard it. He went in and found the hall in which was the enchantress, and with her seven thousand birds in their wicker cages.

When the enchantress saw Joringel she was furious, and breathed out poison and gall at him, but she could not move a step towards him. He took no notice of her, and went and looked over the cages of birds;

but there were many hundred nightingales, and how was he to find his Jorinde from among them? Whilst he was considering, he observed the old witch take up a cage secretly and go with it towards the door. Instantly he sprang after her, touched the cage with the flower, and the old woman as well. Now she could no longer work enchantments, and there stood Jorinde before him, with her arms round his neck, and more beautiful than ever. Then he turned all the other birds again into maidens, and he went home with his Jorinde, and they lived a long and happy life.

The King of the Waterfalls

WHEN THE young King of Easaidh Ruadh came into his kingdom, the first thing he thought of was how he could amuse himself best. The sports that all his life had pleased him best suddenly seemed to have grown dull, and he wanted to do something he had never done before. At last his face brightened.

'I know!' he said. 'I will go and play a game with the Gruagach.' Now the Gruagach was a kind of wicked fairy, with long curly brown hair, and his house was not very far from the King's house.

But though the King was young and eager, he was also prudent, and his father had told him on his death-bed to be very careful in his dealings with the 'good people', as the fairies were called. Therefore before going to the Gruagach the King sought out a wise man of the countryside.

'I am wanting to play a game with the curly-haired Gruagach,' said he.

'Are you, indeed?' replied the wizard. 'If you will take my counsel, you will play with someone else.'

'No; I will play with the Gruagach,' persisted the King.

'Well, if you must, you must, I suppose,' answered the wizard; 'but if you win that game, ask as a prize the ugly crop-headed girl that stands behind the door.'

'I will,' said the King.

So before the sun rose he got up and went to the house of the Gruagach, who was sitting outside.

'O King, what has brought you here to-day?' asked the Gruagach. 'But right welcome you are, and more welcome will you be still if you will play a game with me.'

'That is just what I want,' said the King, and they played; and sometimes it seemed as if one would win, and sometimes the other, but in the end it was the King who was the winner.

'And what is the prize that you will choose?' inquired the Gruagach.

'The ugly crop-headed girl that stands behind the door,' replied the King.

'Why, there are twenty others in the house, and each fairer than she!' exclaimed the Gruagach.

'Fairer they may be, but it is she whom I wish for my wife, and none other,' and the Gruagach saw that the King's mind was set upon her, so he entered his house, and bade all the maidens in it come out one by one, and pass before the King.

One by one they came; tall and short, dark and fair, plump and thin, and each said, 'I am she whom you want. You will be foolish indeed if you do not take me.'

But he took none of them, neither short nor tall, dark nor fair, plump nor thin, till at the last the crop-headed girl came out.

'This is mine,' said the King, though she was so ugly that most men would have turned from her. 'We will be married at once, and I will carry you home.' And married they were, and they set forth across a meadow to the King's house. As they went, the bride stooped and picked a sprig of shamrock, which grew amongst the grass, and when she stood upright again her ugliness had all gone, and the most beautiful woman that ever was seen stood by the King's side.

The next day, before the sun rose, the King sprang from his bed, and told his wife he must have another game with the Gruagach.

'If my father loses that game, and you win it,' said she, 'accept nothing for your prize but the shaggy young horse with the stick saddle.'

'I will do that,' answered the King, and he went.

'Does your bride please you?' asked the Gruagach, who was standing at his own door.

'Ah! does she not!' answered the King quickly. 'Otherwise I should be hard indeed to please. But will you play a game to-day?'

'I will,' replied the Gruagach, and they played, and sometimes it seemed as if one would win, and sometimes the other, but in the end the King was the winner.

'What is the prize that you will choose?' asked the Gruagach.

'The shaggy young horse with the stick saddle,' answered the King, but he noticed that the Gruagach held his peace, and his brow was dark as he led out the horse from the stable. Rough was its mane and dull was its skin, but the King cared nothing for that, and throwing his leg over the stick saddle rode away like the wind.

On the third morning the King got up as usual before dawn, and as soon as he had eaten food he prepared to go out, when his wife stopped him. 'I would rather,' she said, 'that you did not go to play with the Gruagach, for though twice *you* have won yet some day *he* will win, and then he will put trouble upon you.'

'Oh! I *must* have one more game,' cried the King; 'just this one.' And he went off to the house of the Gruagach.

Joy filled the heart of the Gruagach when he saw him coming, and without waiting to talk they played their game. Somehow or other, the King's strength and skill had departed from him, and soon the Gruagach was the victor.

'Choose your prize,' said the King, when the game was ended, 'but do not be too hard on me, or ask what I cannot give.'

'The prize I choose,' answered the Gruagach, 'is that the crop-headed creature should take thy head and thy neck, if thou dost not get for me the Sword of Light that hangs in the house of the King of the Oak Windows.'

'I will get it,' replied the young man bravely; but as soon as he was out of sight of the Gruagach he pretended no more, and his face grew dark and his steps lagging.

'You have brought nothing with you to-night,' said the Queen, who was standing on the steps awaiting him. She was so beautiful that the King was fain to smile when he looked at her, but then he remembered what had happened, and his heart grew heavy again.

'What is it? What is the matter? Tell me thy sorrow that I may bear it with thee, or, it may be, help thee!' Then the King told her everything that had befallen him, and she stroked his hair the while.

'That is nothing to grieve about,' she said, when the tale was finished. 'You have the best wife in Erin, and the best horse in Erin. Only do as I bid you, and all will go well.' And the King suffered himself to be comforted.

He was still sleeping when the Queen rose and dressed herself to make everything ready for her husband's journey; and the first place she went to was the stable, where she fed and watered the shaggy brown horse and put the saddle on it. Most people thought this saddle was of wood, and did not see the little sparkles of gold and silver that were hidden in it. She strapped it lightly on the horse's back, and then led it down before the house, where the King waited.

'Good luck to you, and victories in all your battles,' she said, as she kissed him before he mounted. 'I need not be telling you anything. Take the advice of the horse, and see you obey it.'

So he waved his hand and set out on his journey, and the wind was not swifter than the brown horse – no, not even the March wind which raced it and could not catch it. But the horse never stopped nor looked behind, till in the dark of the night he reached the castle of the King of the Oak Windows.

'We are at the end of the journey,' said the horse, 'and you will find the Sword of Light in the King's own chamber. If it comes to you without scrape or sound, the token is a good one. At this hour the King is eating his supper, and the room is empty, so none will see you. The sword has a knob at the end, and take heed that when you grasp it, you draw it softly out of its sheath. Now go! I will be under the window.'

Stealthily the young man crept along the passage, pausing now and then to make sure that no one was following him, and entered the chamber of the King of the Oak Windows. A strange white line of light told him where the sword was, and crossing the room on tiptoe, he seized the knob, and drew it slowly out of the sheath. He could hardly breathe with excitement lest it should make some noise, and bring all the people in the castle running to see what was the matter. But the sword slid swiftly and silently along the case till only the point was left touching it. Then a low sound was heard, as of the edge of a knife touching a silver plate, and the young man was so startled that he nearly dropped the knob.

'Quick! quick!' cried the horse, and the King scrambled hastily through the small window, and leapt into the saddle.

'He has heard and he will follow,' said the horse; 'but we have a good start.' And on they sped, on and on, leaving the winds behind them.

At length the horse slackened its pace. 'Look and see who is behind you,' it said; and the young man looked.

'I see a swarm of brown horses racing madly after us,' he answered.

'We are swifter than those,' said the horse, and flew on again.

'Look again, O King! Is anyone coming now?'

'A swarm of black horses, and one has a white face, and on that horse a man is seated. He is the King of the Oak Windows.'

'That is my brother, and swifter still than I,' said the horse, 'and he will fly past me with a rush. Then you must have your sword ready, and take off the head of the man who sits on him, as he turns and looks at you. And there is no sword in the world that will cut off his head, save only that one.'

'I will do it,' replied the King; and he listened with all his might, till he judged that the white-faced horse was close to him. Then he sat up very straight and made ready.

The next moment there was a rushing noise as of a mighty tempest, and the young man caught a glimpse of a face turned towards him. Almost blindly he struck, not knowing whether he had killed or only wounded the rider. But the head rolled off, and was caught in the brown horse's mouth.

'Jump on my brother, the black horse, and go home as fast as you can, and I will follow as quickly as I may,' cried the brown horse; and leaping forward the King alighted on the black horse, but so near the tail that he almost fell off again. But he stretched out his arm and clutched wildly at the mane and pulled himself into the saddle.

Before the sky was streaked with red he was at home again, and the Queen was sitting waiting till he arrived, for sleep was far from her eyes. Glad was she to see him enter, but she said little, only took her harp and sang softly the songs which he loved, till he went to bed, soothed and happy.

It was broad day when he woke, and he sprang up saying, 'Now I must go to the Gruagach, to find out if the spells he laid on me are loose.'

'Have a care,' answered the Queen, 'for it is not with a smile as on the other days that he will greet you. Furiously he will meet you, and will ask you in his wrath if you have got the sword, and you will reply that you have got it. Next he will want to know how you got it, and to this you must say that but for the knob you had not got it at all. Then he will raise his head to look at the knob, and you must stab him in the mole which is on the right side of his neck; but take heed, for if you miss the mole with the point of the sword, then my death and your death are certain. He is brother to the King of the Oak Windows, and sure will he be that the King must be dead, or the sword would not be in your hands.' After that she kissed him, and bade him good speed.

'Didst thou get the sword?' asked the Gruagach, when they met in the usual place.

'I got the sword.'

'And how didst thou get it?'

'If it had not had a knob on the top, then I had not got it,' answered the King.

'Give me the sword to look at,' said the Gruagach, peering forward; but like a flash the King had drawn it from under his nose and pierced the mole, so that the Gruagach rolled over on the ground.

'Now I shall be at peace,' thought the King. But he was wrong, for when he reached home he found his servants tied together back to back, with cloths bound round their mouths, so that they could not speak. He hastened to set them free, and he asked who had treated them in so evil a manner.

'No sooner had you gone than a great giant came, and dealt with us as you see, and carried off your wife and your two horses,' said the men.

'Then my eyes will not close nor will my head lay itself down till I fetch my wife and horses home again,' answered he, and he stooped and noted the tracks of the horses on the grass, and followed after them till he arrived at the wood, when the darkness fell.

'I will sleep here,' he said to himself, 'but first I will make a fire.' And he gathered together some twigs that were lying about, and then took two dry sticks and rubbed them together till the fire came, and he sat by it.

The twigs crackled and the flame blazed up, and a slim yellow dog pushed through the bushes and laid his head on the King's knee, and the King stroked his head.

'Wuf, wuf,' said the dog. 'Sore was the plight of thy wife and thy horses when the giant drove them last night through the forest.'

'That is why I have come,' answered the King; and suddenly his heart seemed to fail him and he felt that he could not go on.

'I cannot fight that giant,' he cried, looking at the dog with a white face. 'I am afraid, let me turn homewards.'

'No, don't do that,' replied the dog. 'Eat and sleep, and I will watch over you.' So the King ate and lay down, and slept till the sun waked him.

'It is time for you to start on your way,' said the dog, 'and if danger presses, call on me, and I will help you.'

'Farewell, then,' answered the King; 'I will not forget that promise,' and on he went, and on and on, till he reached a tall cliff with many sticks lying about.

'It is almost night,' he thought; 'I will make a fire and rest,' and thus he did, and when the flames blazed up, the hoary hawk of the grey rock flew on to a bough above him.

'Sore was the plight of thy wife and thy horses when they passed here with the giant,' said the hawk.

'Never shall I find them,' answered the King, 'and nothing shall I get for all my trouble.'

'Oh, take heart,' replied the hawk; 'things are never so bad but what they might be worse. Eat and sleep and I will watch thee,' and the King did as he was bidden by the hawk, and by the morning he felt brave again.

'Farewell,' said the bird, 'and if danger presses, call to me, and I will help you.'

On he walked, and on and on, till as the dusk was falling he came to a great river, and on the bank there were sticks lying about.

'I will make myself a fire,' he thought, and this he did, and by and by a smooth brown head peered at him from the water, and a long body followed it.

'Sore was the plight of thy wife and thy horses when they passed the river last night,' said the otter.

'I have sought them and not found them,' answered the King, 'and nought shall I get for my trouble.'

'Be not so downcast,' replied the otter; 'before noon to-morrow thou shalt behold thy wife. But eat and sleep and I will watch over thee.' So the King did as the otter bade him, and when the sun rose he woke and saw the otter lying on the bank.

'Farewell,' cried the otter as he jumped into the water, 'and if danger presses, call to me and I will help you.'

For many hours the King walked, and at length he reached a high rock, which was rent in two by a great earthquake. Throwing himself on the ground he looked over the side, and right at the very bottom he saw his wife and his horses. His heart gave a great bound, and all his fears left him, but he was forced to be patient, for the sides of the rock were smooth, and not even a goat could find foothold. So he got up again, and made his way round through the wood, pushing by trees, scrambling over rocks, wading through streams, till at last he was on flat ground again, close to the mouth of the cavern.

His wife gave a shriek of joy when he came in, and then burst into tears, for she was tired and very frightened. But her husband did not understand why she wept, and he was tired and bruised from his climb, and a little cross too.

'You give me but a sorry welcome,' grumbled he, 'when I have half-killed myself to get to you.'

'Do not heed him,' said the horses to the weeping woman; 'put him in front of us, where he will be safe, and give him food, for he is weary.' And she did as the horses told her, and he ate and rested, till by and by a long shadow fell over them, and their hearts beat with fear, for they knew that the giant was coming.

'I smell a stranger,' cried the giant, as he entered; but it was dark inside the chasm, and he did not see the King, who was crouching down between the feet of the horses.

'A stranger, my lord! no stranger ever comes here, not even the sun!' and the King's wife laughed gaily as she went up to the giant and stroked the huge hand which hung down by his side.

'Well, I perceive nothing, certainly,' answered he, 'but it is very odd. However, it is time that the horses were fed;' and he lifted down an armful of hay from a shelf of rock and held out a handful to each animal, who moved forward to meet him, leaving the King behind. As soon as the giant's hands were near their mouths they each made a snap, and began to bite them, so that his groans and shrieks might have been heard a mile off. Then they wheeled round and kicked him till they could kick no more. At length the giant crawled away, and lay quivering in a corner, and the Queen went up to him.

'Poor thing! poor thing!' she said, 'they seem to have gone mad; it was awful to behold.'

'If I had had my soul in my body they would certainly have killed me,' groaned the giant.

'It was lucky indeed,' answered the Queen; 'but tell me, where is thy soul, that I may take care of it?'

'Up there, in the Bonnach stone,' answered the giant, pointing to a stone which was balanced loosely on an edge of rock. 'But now leave me, that I may sleep, for I have far to go to-morrow.'

Soon snores were heard from the corner where the giant lay, and then the Queen lay down too, and the horses, and the King was hidden between them, so that none could see him.

Before the dawn the giant rose and went out, and immediately the Queen ran up to the Bonnach stone, and tugged and pushed at it till it was quite steady on its ledge, and could not fall over. And so it was in the evening when the giant came home; and when they saw his shadow, the King crept down in front of the horses.

'Why, what have you done to the Bonnach stone?' asked the giant.

'I feared lest it should fall over, and be broken, with your soul in it,' said the Queen, 'so I put it further back on the ledge.'

'It is not there that my soul is,' answered he, 'it is on the threshold. But it is time the horses were fed;' and he fetched the hay, and gave it to them, and they bit and kicked him as before, till he lay half dead on the ground.

Next morning he rose and went out, and the Queen ran to the threshold of the cave, and washed the stones, and pulled up some moss and little flowers that were hidden in the crannies, and by and by when dusk had fallen the giant came home.

'You have been cleaning the threshold,' said he.

'And was I not right to do it, seeing that your soul is in it?' asked the Queen.

'It is not there that my soul is,' answered the giant. 'Under the threshold is a stone, and under the stone is a sheep, and in the sheep's body is a duck, and in the duck is an egg, and in the egg is my soul. But it is late, and I must feed the horses;' and he brought them the hay, but they only bit and kicked him as before, and if his soul had been within him, they would have killed him outright.

It was still dark when the giant got up and went his way, and then the King and the Queen ran forward to take up the threshold, while the horses looked on. But sure enough! just as the giant had said, underneath the threshold was the flagstone, and they pulled and tugged till the stone gave way. Then something jumped out so suddenly that it nearly knocked them down, and as it fled past, they saw it was a sheep.

'If the slim yellow dog of the greenwood were only here, he would soon have that sheep,' cried the King; and as he spoke the slim yellow dog appeared from the forest, with the sheep in his mouth. With a blow from the King, the sheep fell dead, and they opened its body, only to be blinded by a rush of wings as the duck flew past.

'If the hoary hawk of the rock were only here, he would soon have that duck,' cried the King; and as he spoke the hoary hawk was seen hovering above them, with the duck in his mouth. They cut off the duck's head with a swing of the King's sword, and took the egg out of its body, but in his triumph the King held it carelessly, and it slipped from his hand, and rolled swiftly down the hill right into the river.

'If the brown otter of the stream were only here, he would soon have that egg,' cried the King; and the next minute there was the brown otter, dripping with water, holding the egg in his mouth. But beside the brown otter, a huge shadow came stealing along – the shadow of the giant.

The King stood staring at it, as if he were turned into stone, but the Queen snatched the egg from the otter and crushed it between her two hands. And after that the shadow suddenly shrank and was still, and they knew that the giant was dead, because they had found his soul.

Next day they mounted the two horses and rode home again, visiting their friends the brown otter and the hoary hawk and the slim yellow dog by the way.

Little One-eye,
Little Two-eyes, and Little Three-eyes

THERE WAS once a woman who had three daughters, of whom the eldest was called Little One-eye, because she had only one eye in the middle of her forehead; and the second, Little Two-eyes, because she had two eyes like other people; and the youngest, Little Three-eyes, because she had three eyes, and *her* third eye was also in the middle of her forehead. But because Little Two-eyes did not look any different from other children, her sisters and mother could not bear her. They would say to her, 'You with your two eyes are no better than common folk; you don't belong to us.' They pushed her here, and threw her wretched clothes there, and gave her to eat only what they left, and they were as unkind to her as ever they could be.

It happened one day that Little Two-eyes had to go out into the fields to take care of the goat, but she was still quite hungry because her sisters had given her so little to eat. So she sat down in the meadow and began to cry, and she cried so much that two little brooks ran out of her eyes. But when she looked up once in her grief there stood a woman beside her who asked, 'Little Two-eyes, what are you crying for?' Little Two-eyes answered, 'Have I not reason to cry? Because I have two eyes like other people, my sisters and my mother cannot bear me: they push me out of one corner into another, and give me nothing to eat except what they leave. To-day they have given me so little that I am still quite hungry.' Then the wise woman said, 'Little Two-eyes, dry your eyes, and I will tell you something so that you need never be hungry again. Only say to your goat:

> "Little goat, bleat,
> Little table, appear,"

and a beautifully spread table will stand before you, with the most delicious food on it, so that you can eat as much as you want. And when you have had enough and don't want the little table any more, you have only to say:

> "Little goat, bleat,
> Little table, away,"

and then it will vanish.' Then the wise woman went away.

But Little Two-eyes thought, 'I must try at once if what she has told me is true, for I am more hungry than ever;' and she said:

> 'Little goat, bleat,
> Little table, appear,'

and scarcely had she uttered the words, when there stood a little table before her covered with a white cloth, on which were arranged a plate, with a knife and fork and a silver spoon, and the most beautiful dishes, which were smoking hot, as if they had just come out of the kitchen. Then Little Two-eyes said the shortest grace she knew, and set to work and made a good dinner. And when she had had enough, she said, as the wise woman had told her:

> 'Little goat bleat,
>   Little table, away,'

and immediately the table and all that was on it disappeared again.

'That is a splendid way of housekeeping,' thought Little Two-eyes, and she was quite happy and contented.

In the evening, when she went home with her goat, she found a little earthenware dish with the food that her sisters had thrown to her, but she did not touch it. The next day she went out again with her goat, and left the few scraps which were given her. The first and second times her sisters did not notice this, but when it happened continually, they remarked it and said, 'Something is the matter with Little Two-eyes, for she always leaves her food now, and she used to gobble up all that was given her. She must have found other means of getting food.' So in order to get at the truth, Little One-eye was told to go out with Little Two-eyes when she drove the goat to pasture, and to notice particularly what she did there, and whether anyone brought her food and drink.

Now when Little Two-eyes was setting out, Little One-eye came up to her and said, 'I will go into the field with you and see if you take good care of the goat, and if you drive him properly to get grass.' But Little Two-eyes saw what Little One-eye had in her mind, and she drove the goat into the long grass and said, 'Come, Little One-eye, we will sit down here, and I will sing you something.'

Little One-eye sat down, and as she was very much tired by the long walk to which she was not used, and by the hot day, and as Little Two-eyes went on singing:

> 'Little One-eye, are you awake?
>   Little One-eye, are you asleep?'

she shut her one eye and fell asleep. When Little Two-eyes saw that Little One-eye was asleep and could find out nothing, she said:

> 'Little goat, bleat,
>   Little table, appear,'

and sat down at her table and ate and drank as much as she wanted. Then she said again:

> 'Little goat, bleat,
> Little table, away,'

and in the twinkling of an eye all had vanished.

Little Two-eyes then woke Little One-eye and said, 'Little One-eye, you meant to watch, and, instead, you went to sleep; in the meantime the goat might have run far and wide. Come, we will go home.' So they went home, and Little Two-eyes again left her little dish untouched, and Little One-eye could not tell her mother why she would not eat, and said as an excuse, 'I was so sleepy out-of-doors.'

The next day the mother said to Little Three-eyes, 'This time you shall go with Little Two-eyes and watch whether she eats anything out in the fields, and whether anyone brings her food and drink, for eat and drink she must secretly.' So Little Three-eyes went to Little Two-eyes and said, 'I will go with you and see if you take good care of the goat, and if you drive him properly to get grass.' But Little Two-eyes knew what Little Three-eyes had in her mind, and she drove the goat out into the tall grass and said, 'We will sit down here, Little Three-eyes, and I will sing you something.' Little Three-eyes sat down; she was tired by the walk and the hot day, and Little Two-eyes sang the same little song again:

> 'Little Three-eyes, are you awake?'

but instead of singing as she ought to have done:

> 'Little Three-eyes, are you asleep?'

she sang, without thinking:

> 'Little *Two-eyes*, are you asleep?'

She went on singing:

> 'Little Three-eyes, are you awake?
> Little *Two-eyes*, are you asleep?'

so that the two eyes of Little Three-eyes fell asleep, but the third, which was not spoken to in the little rhyme, did not fall asleep. Of course Little Three-eyes shut that eye also out of cunning, to look as if she were asleep, but it was blinking and could see everything quite well.

And when Little Two-eyes thought that Little Three-eyes was sound asleep, she said her rhyme:

> 'Little goat, bleat,
> Little table, appear,'

and ate and drank to her heart's content, and then made the table go away again, by saying:

> 'Little goat, bleat,
> Little table, away.'

But Little Three-eyes had seen everything. Then Little Two-eyes came to her, and woke her and said, 'Well, Little Three-eyes, have you been asleep? You watch well! Come, we will go home.' When they reached home, Little Two-eyes did not eat again, and Little Three-eyes said to the mother, 'I know now why that proud thing eats nothing. When she says to the goat in the field:

> "Little goat, bleat,
> Little table, appear,"

a table stands before her, spread with the best food, much better than we have; and when she has had enough, she says:

> "Little goat, bleat,
> Little table, away,"

and everything disappears again. I saw it all exactly. She made two of my eyes go to sleep with a little rhyme, but the one in my forehead remained awake, luckily!'

Then the envious mother cried out, 'Will you fare better than we do? You shall not have the chance to do so again!' and she fetched a knife, and killed the goat.

When Little Two-eyes saw this, she went out full of grief, and sat down in the meadow and wept bitter tears. Then again the wise woman stood before her, and said, 'Little Two-eyes, what are you crying for?' 'Have I not reason to cry?' she answered. 'The goat, which when I said the little rhyme, spread the table so beautifully, my mother has killed, and now I must suffer hunger and want again.'

The wise woman said, 'Little Two-eyes, I will give you a good piece of advice. Ask your sisters to give you the heart of the dead goat, and bury it in the earth before the house-door; that will bring you good luck.' Then she disappeared, and Little Two-eyes went home, and said to her sisters, 'Dear sisters, do give me something of my goat; I ask nothing better than its heart.' Then they laughed and said, 'You can have that if you want nothing more.' And Little Two-eyes took the heart and buried it in the evening when all was quiet, as the wise woman had told her, before the house-door.

The next morning when they all awoke and came to the house-door, there stood a most wonderful tree, which had leaves of silver and fruit of gold growing on it – you never saw anything more lovely and gorgeous in your life! But they did not know how the tree had grown up in the night; only Little Two-eyes knew that it had sprung from the heart of the goat, for it was standing just where she had buried it in the ground.

Then the mother said to Little One-eye, 'Climb up, my child, and break us off the fruit from the tree.' Little One-eye climbed up, but just when she was going to take hold of one of the golden apples the bough sprang out of her hands; and this happened every time, so that she could not break off a single apple, however hard she tried.

Then the mother said, 'Little Three-eyes, do you climb up; you with your three eyes can see round better than Little One-eye.' So Little One-eye slid down, and Little Three-eyes climbed up; but she was not any more successful; look round as she might, the golden apples bent themselves back.

At last the mother got impatient and climbed up herself, but she was even less successful than Little One-eye and Little Three-eyes in catching hold of the fruit, and only grasped at the empty air.

Then Little Two-eyes said, 'I will try just once, perhaps I shall succeed better.' The sisters called out, 'You with your two eyes will no doubt succeed!' But Little Two-eyes climbed up, and the golden apples did not jump away from her, but behaved quite properly, so that she could pluck them off, one after the other, and brought a whole apron-full down with her. The mother took them from her, and, instead of treating poor Little Two-eyes more kindly, as they ought to have done, they were jealous that she only could reach the fruit and behaved still more harshly to her.

It happened one day that when they were all standing together by the tree that a young knight came riding along. 'Be quick, Little Two-eyes,' cried the two sisters, 'creep under this, so that you shall not disgrace us,' and they put poor Little Two-eyes as quickly as possible under an empty cask, which was standing close to the tree, and they pushed the golden apples which she had broken off in with her.

When the knight, who was a very handsome young man, rode up, he wondered to see the marvellous tree of gold and silver, and said to the two sisters, 'Whose is this beautiful tree? Whoever will give me a twig of it shall have whatever she wants.'

Then Little One-eye and Little Three-eyes answered that the tree belonged to them, and they would certainly break him off a twig. They gave themselves a great deal of trouble but in vain; the twigs and fruit bent back every time from their hands. Then the knight said, 'It is very strange that the tree should belong to you, and yet that you have not the power to break anything from it!' But they would have it that the tree was theirs; and while they were saying this, Little Two-eyes rolled a couple of golden apples from under the cask, so that they lay at the knight's feet, for she was angry with Little One-eye and Little Three-eyes for not speaking the truth.

When the knight saw the apples he was astonished, and asked where they came from. Little One-eye and Little Three-eyes answered that they had another sister, but she could not be seen because she only had two eyes, like ordinary people. But the knight demanded to see her, and called out, 'Little Two-eyes, come forth.'

Then Little Two-eyes came out from under the cask quite happily, and the knight was astonished at her great beauty, and said, 'Little Two-eyes, I am sure you can break me off a twig from the tree.' 'Yes,' answered Little Two-eyes, 'I can, for the tree is mine.' So she climbed up and broke off a small branch with its silver leaves and golden fruit without any trouble, and gave it to the knight.

Then he said, 'Little Two-eyes, what shall I give you for this?' 'Ah,' answered Little Two-eyes, 'I suffer hunger and thirst, want and sorrow, from early morning till late in the evening; if you would take me with you, and free me from this, I should be happy!' Then the knight lifted Little Two-eyes on his horse, and took her home to his father's castle. There he gave her beautiful clothes, and food and drink, and because he loved her so much he married her, and the wedding was celebrated with great joy.

When the handsome knight carried Little Two-eyes away with him, the two sisters envied her good luck at first. 'But the wonderful tree is still with us, after all,' they thought, 'and although we cannot break any fruit from it, everyone will stop and look at it, and will come to us and praise it; who knows whether *we* may not reap a harvest from it?' But the next morning the tree had flown, and their hopes with it; and when Little Two-eyes looked out of her window there it stood beneath, to her great delight.

Little Two-eyes lived happily for a long time. Once two poor women came to the castle to beg alms. Then Little Two-eyes looked at them and recognised both her sisters, Little One-eye and Little Three-eyes, who had become so poor that they came to beg bread at her door. But Little Two-eyes bade them welcome, and was so good to them that they both repented from their hearts of having been so unkind to their sister.

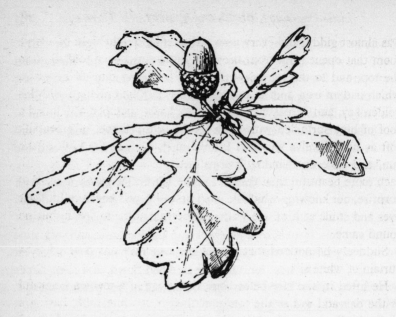

Long, Broad, and Quickeye

ONCE UPON a time there lived a king who had an only son whom he loved dearly. Now one day the King sent for his son and said to him, 'My dearest child, my hair is grey and I am old, and soon I shall feel no more the warmth of the sun, or look upon the trees and flowers. But before I die I should like to see you with a good wife; therefore marry, my son, as speedily as possible.'

'My father,' replied the Prince, 'now and always, I ask nothing better than to do your bidding, but I know of no daughter-in-law that I could give you.'

On hearing these words the old King drew from his pocket a key of gold, and gave it to his son, saying, 'Go up the staircase, right up to the top of the tower. Look carefully round you, and then come and tell me what you like best of all that you see.'

So the young man went up. He had never before been in the tower, and had no idea what it might contain.

The staircase wound round and round and round, till the Prince was almost giddy, and every now and then he caught sight of a large room that opened out from the side. But he had been told to go to the top, and to the top he went. Then he found himself in a hall, which had an iron door at one end. This door he unlocked with his golden key, and he passed through into a vast chamber which had a roof of blue sprinkled with golden stars, and a carpet of green silk soft as turf. Twelve windows framed in gold let in the light of the sun, and on every window was painted the figure of a young girl, each more beautiful than the last. While the Prince gazed at them in surprise, not knowing which he liked best, the girls began to lift their eyes and smile at him. He waited, expecting them to speak, but no sound came.

Suddenly he noticed that one of the windows was covered by a curtain of white silk.

He lifted it, and saw before him the image of a maiden beautiful as the day and sad as the tomb, clothed in a white robe, having a girdle of silver and a crown of pearls. The Prince stood and gazed at her, as if he had been turned into stone, but as he looked the sadness which was on her face seemed to pass into his heart, and he cried out, 'This one shall be my wife. This one and no other.'

As he said the words the young girl blushed and hung her head, and all the other figures vanished.

The young Prince went quickly back to his father, and told him all he had seen and which wife he had chosen. The old man listened to him full of sorrow, and then he spoke:

'You have done ill, my son, to search out that which was hidden, and you are running to meet a great danger. This young girl has fallen into the power of a wicked sorcerer, who lives in an iron castle. Many young men have tried to deliver her, and none have ever come back. But what is done is done! You have given your word, and it cannot be broken. Go, dare your fate, and return to me safe and sound.'

So the Prince embraced his father, mounted his horse, and set forth to seek his bride. He rode on gaily for several hours, till he found himself in a wood where he had never been before, and soon lost his way among its winding paths and deep valleys. He tried in vain to see where he was; the thick trees shut out the sun, and he could not tell which was north and which was south, so that he might know what direction to make for. He felt in despair, and had quite given up all hope of getting out of this horrible place, when he heard a voice calling to him.

'Hey! hey! stop a minute!'

The Prince turned round and saw behind him a very tall man, running as fast as his legs would carry him.

'Wait for me,' he panted, 'and take me into your service. If you do, you will never be sorry.'

'Who are you?' asked the Prince, 'and what can you do?'

'Long is my name, and I can lengthen my body at will. Do you see that nest up there on the top of that pine-tree? Well, I can get it for you without taking the trouble of climbing the tree,' and Long stretched himself up and up and up, till he was very soon as tall as the pine itself. He put the nest in his pocket, and before you could wink your eyelid he had made himself small again, and stood before the Prince.

'Yes; you know your business,' said he, 'but birds' nests are no use to me. I am too old for them. Now if you were only able to get me out of this wood, you would indeed be good for something.'

'Oh, there's no difficulty about that,' replied Long, and he stretched himself up and up and up till he was three times as tall as the tallest tree in the forest. Then he looked all round and said, 'We must go in this direction in order to get out of the wood,' and shortening himself again, he took the Prince's horse by the bridle, and led him along. Very soon they got clear of the forest, and saw before them a wide plain covered here and there with trees, ending in a pile of high rocks, as solid as the fortifications of a town.

As they left the wood behind, Long turned to the Prince and said, 'My lord, here comes my comrade. You should take him into your service too, as you will find him a great help.'

'Well, call him then, so that I can see what sort of a man he is.'

'He is a little too far off for that,' replied Long. 'He would hardly hear my voice, and he couldn't be here for some time yet, as he has so much to carry. I think I had better go and bring him myself,' and this time he stretched himself to such a height that his head was lost in the clouds. He made two or three strides, took his friend on his back, and set him down before the Prince. The new-comer was a very fat man, and as round as a barrel.

'Who are you?' asked the Prince, 'and what can you do?'

'Your worship, Broad is my name, and I can make myself as wide as I please.'

'Let me see how you manage it.'

'Run, my lord, as fast as you can, and hide yourself in the wood,' cried Broad, and he began to swell himself out.

The Prince did not understand why he should run to the wood, but when he saw Long flying towards it, he thought he had better follow his example. He was only just in time, for Broad had so suddenly inflated himself that he very nearly knocked over the Prince and his horse too. He covered all the space for acres round. You would have thought he was a mountain!

At length Broad ceased to expand, drew a deep breath that made the whole forest tremble, and shrank into his usual size.

'You have made me run away,' said the Prince. 'But it is not every day one meets with a man of your sort. I will take you into my service.'

So the three companions continued their journey, and when they were drawing near the rocks they met a man whose eyes were covered by a bandage.

'Your excellency,' said Long, 'this is our third comrade. You will do well to take him into your service, and, I assure you, you will find him worth his salt.'

'Who are you?' asked the Prince. 'And why are your eyes bandaged? You can never see your way!'

'It is just the contrary, my lord! It is because I see only too well that I am forced to bandage my eyes. Even so I see as well as people who have no bandage. When I take it off my eyes pierce through everything. Everything I look at catches fire, or, if it cannot catch fire, it falls into a thousand pieces. They call me Quickeye.'

And so saying he took off his bandage and turned towards the rock. As he fixed his eyes upon it a crack was heard, and in a few moments it was nothing but a heap of sand. In the sand something might be detected glittering brightly. Quickeye picked it up and brought it to the Prince. It turned out to be a lump of pure gold.

'You are a wonderful creature,' said the Prince, 'and I should be a fool not to take you into my service. But since your eyes are so good, tell me if I am very far from the Iron Castle, and what is happening there just now.'

'If you were travelling alone,' replied Quickeye, 'it would take you at least a year to get to it; but as we are with you, we shall arrive there to-night. Just now they are preparing supper.'

'There is a princess in the castle. Do you see her?'

'A wizard keeps her in a high tower, guarded by iron bars.'

'Ah, help me to deliver her!' cried the Prince.

And they promised they would.

Then they all set out through the grey rocks, by the breach made by the eyes of Quickeye, and passed over great mountains and through deep woods. And every time they met with any obstacle the three friends contrived somehow to put it aside. As the sun was setting, the Prince beheld the towers of the Iron Castle, and before it sank beneath the horizon he was crossing the iron bridge which led to the gates. He was only just in time, for no sooner had the sun disappeared altogether, than the bridge drew itself up and the gates shut themselves.

There was no turning back now!

The Prince put up his horse in the stable, where everything looked as if a guest was expected, and then the whole party marched straight up to the castle. In the courtyard, in the stables, and in the great halls, they saw men richly dressed, but every one turned into stone. They crossed many sets of rooms, all opening into each other, till they reached the dining-hall. It was brilliantly lighted; the table was covered with wine and fruit, and was laid for four. They waited a few minutes expecting someone to come, but as nobody did, they sat down and began to eat and drink, for they were very hungry.

When they had done their supper they looked about for some place to sleep. But suddenly the door burst open, and the wizard entered the hall. He was old and hump-backed, with a bald head and a grey beard that fell to his knees. He wore a black robe, and instead of a belt three iron circlets clasped his waist. He led by the hand a lady of wonderful beauty, dressed in white, with a girdle of silver and a crown of pearls, but her face was pale and sad as death itself.

The Prince knew her in an instant, and moved eagerly forward; but the wizard gave him no time to speak, and said, 'I know why you are here. Very good; you may have her if for three nights following you can prevent her making her escape. If you fail in this, you and your servants will all be turned into stone, like those who have come before you.' And offering the Princess a chair, he left the hall.

The Prince could not take his eyes from the Princess, she was so lovely! He began to talk to her, but she neither answered nor smiled, and sat as if she were made of marble. He seated himself by her, and determined not to close his eyes that night, for fear she should escape him. And in order that she should be doubly guarded, Long stretched himself like a strap all round the room, Broad took his stand by the door and puffed himself out, so that not even a mouse could slip by, and Quickeye leant against a pillar which stood in the middle of the floor and supported the roof. But in half a second they were all sound asleep, and they slept sound the whole night long.

In the morning, at the first peep of dawn, the Prince awoke with a start. But the Princess was gone. He aroused his servants and implored them to tell him what he must do.

'Calm yourself, my lord,' said Quickeye. 'I have found her already. A hundred miles from here there is a forest. In the middle of the forest, an old oak, and on the top of the oak, an acorn. This acorn is the Princess. If Long will take me on his shoulders, we shall soon bring her back.' And sure enough, in less time than it takes to walk round a cottage, they had returned from the forest, and Long presented the acorn to the Prince.

'Now your excellency, throw it on the ground.'

The Prince obeyed, and was enchanted to see the Princess appear at his side. But when the sun peeped for the first time over the mountains, the door burst open as before, and the wizard entered with a loud laugh. Suddenly he caught sight of the Princess; his face darkened, he uttered a low growl, and one of the iron circlets gave way with a crash. He seized the young girl by the hand and bore her away with him.

All that day the Prince wandered about the castle, studying the curious treasures it contained, but everything looked as if life had suddenly come to a standstill. In one place he saw a prince who had been turned into stone in the act of brandishing a sword round which his two hands were clasped. In another, the same doom had fallen upon a knight in the act of running away. In a third, a serving man was standing eternally trying to convey a piece of beef to his mouth, and all around them were others, still preserving for evermore the attitudes they were in when the wizard had commanded 'From henceforth be turned into marble.' In the castle, and round the castle, all was dismal and desolate. Trees there were, but without leaves; fields there were, but no grass grew on them. There was one river, but it never flowed, and no fish lived in it. No flowers blossomed, and no birds sang.

Three times during the day food appeared, as if by magic, for the Prince and his servants. And it was not until supper was ended that the wizard appeared, as on the previous evening, and delivered the Princess into the care of the Prince.

All four determined that this time they would keep awake at any cost. But it was no use. Off to sleep they went as they had done before, and when the Prince awoke the next morning the Princess was gone.

With a pang of shame, he rushed to find Quickeye. 'Awake! Awake! Quickeye! Do you know what has become of the Princess?'

Quickeye rubbed his eyes and answered, 'Yes, I see her. Two hundred miles from here there is a mountain. In this mountain is a rock. In the rock, a precious stone. This stone is the Princess. Long shall take me there, and we will be back before you can turn round.'

So Long took him on his shoulders and they set out. At every stride they covered twenty miles, and as they drew near Quickeye fixed his burning eyes on the mountain; in an instant it split into a thousand pieces, and in one of these sparkled the precious stone. They picked it up and brought it to the Prince, who flung it hastily down, and as the stone touched the floor the Princess stood before him. When the wizard came, his eyes shot forth flames of fury. There was a sharp noise, cric-crac! and another of his iron bands broke and fell. He seized the Princess by the hand and led her off, growling louder than ever.

All that day things went on exactly as they had done the day before. After supper the wizard brought back the Princess, and looking the

Prince straight in the eyes he said, 'We shall see which of us two will gain the prize after all!'

That night they struggled their very hardest to keep awake, and even walked about instead of sitting down. But it was quite useless. One after another they had to give in, and for the third time the Princess slipped through their fingers.

When morning came, it was as usual the Prince who awoke the first, and as usual, the Princess being gone, he rushed to Quickeye. 'Get up, get up, Quickeye, and tell me where is the Princess?'

Quickeye looked about for some time without answering. 'Oh, my lord, she is far, very far. Three hundred miles away there lies a black sea. In the middle of this sea is a little shell, and in the middle of the shell is fixed a gold ring. That gold ring is the Princess. But do not vex your soul; we will get her. Only to-day, Long must take Broad with him. He will be wanted badly.'

So Long took Quickeye on one shoulder, and Broad on the other, and they set out. At each stride they left thirty miles behind them. When they reached the black sea, Quickeye showed them the spot where they must seek the shell. But though Long stretched down his hand as far as it would go, he could not find the shell, for it lay at the bottom of the sea.

'Wait a moment, comrades, it will be all right. I will help you,' said Broad.

Then he swelled himself out so that you would have thought the world could hardly have held him, and stooping down he drank. He drank so much at every mouthful, that only a minute or so passed before the water had sunk enough for Long to put his hand to the bottom. He soon found the shell and pulled the ring out. But time had been lost, and Long had a double burden to carry. The dawn was breaking fast before they got back to the castle, where the Prince was waiting for them in an agony of fear.

Soon the first rays of the sun were seen peeping over the tops of the mountains. The door burst open, and finding the Prince standing alone the wizard broke into peals of wicked laughter. But as he laughed a loud crash was heard, the window fell into a thousand pieces, a gold ring glittered in the air, and the Princess stood before the enchanter. For Quickeye, who was watching from afar, had told

Long of the terrible danger now threatening the Prince, and Long, summoning all his strength for one gigantic effort, had thrown the ring right through the window.

The wizard shrieked and howled with rage, till the whole castle trembled to its foundations. Then a crash was heard, the third band split in two, and a crow flew out of the window.

Then the Princess at length broke the enchanted silence, and blushing like a rose, gave the Prince her thanks for her unlooked-for deliverance.

But it was not only the Princess who was restored to life by the flight of the wicked black crow. The marble figures became men once more, and took up their occupations just as they had left them off. The horses neighed in the stables, the flowers blossomed in the garden, the birds flew in the air, the fish darted in the water. Everywhere you looked, all was life, all was joy!

And the knights who had been turned into stone came in a body to offer their homage to the Prince who had set them free.

'Do not thank me,' he said, 'for I have done nothing. Without my faithful servants, Long, Broad, and Quickeye, I should even have been as one of you.'

With these words he bade them farewell, and departed with the Princess and his faithful companions for the kingdom of his father.

The old King, who had long since given up all hope, wept for joy at the sight of his son, and insisted that the wedding should take place as soon as possible.

All the knights who had been enchanted in the Iron Castle were invited to the ceremony, and after it had taken place, Long, Broad, and Quickeye took leave of the young couple, saying that they were going to look for more work.

The Prince offered them all their hearts could desire if they would only remain with him, but they replied that an idle life would not please them, and that they could never be happy unless they were busy, so they went away to seek their fortunes, and for all I know are seeking still.

The Many-Furred Creature

THERE WAS once upon a time a king who had a wife with golden hair, and she was so beautiful that you couldn't find anyone like her in the world. It happened that she fell ill, and when she felt that she must soon die, she sent for the King, and said, 'If you want to marry after my death, make no one queen unless she is just as beautiful as I am, and has just such golden hair as I have. Promise me this.' After the King had promised her this, she closed her eyes and died.

For a long time the King was not to be comforted, and he did not even think of taking a second wife. At last his councillors said, 'The

King *must* marry again, so that we may have a queen.' So messengers were sent far and wide to seek for a bride equal to the late Queen in beauty. But there was no one in the wide world, and if there had been she could not have had such golden hair. Then the messengers came home again, not having been able to find a queen.

Now, the King had a daughter, who was just as beautiful as her dead mother, and had just such golden hair. One day when she had grown up, her father looked at her, and saw that she was exactly like her mother, so he said to his councillors, 'I will marry my daughter to one of you, and she shall be queen, for she is exactly like her dead mother, and when I die her husband shall be king.'

But when the Princess heard of her father's decision, she was not at all pleased, and said to him, 'Before I do your bidding, I must have three dresses; one as golden as the sun, one as silver as the moon, and one as shining as the stars. Besides these, I want a cloak made of a thousand different kinds of skin; every animal in your kingdom must give a bit of his skin to it.' But she thought to herself, 'This will be quite impossible, and I shall not have to marry someone I do not care for.'

The King, however, was not to be turned from his purpose, and he commanded the most skilled maidens in his kingdom to weave the three dresses, one as golden as the sun, and one as silver as the moon, and one as shining as the stars; and he gave orders to all his huntsmen to catch one of every kind of beast in the kingdom, and to get a bit of its skin to make the cloak of a thousand pieces of fur. At last, when all was ready, the King commanded the cloak to be brought to him, and he spread it out before the Princess, and said, 'To-morrow shall be your wedding day.'

When the Princess saw that there was no more hope of changing her father's resolution, she determined to flee away. In the night, when everyone else was sleeping, she got up and took three things from her treasures, a gold ring, a little gold spinning-wheel, and a gold reel; she put the sun, moon, and star dresses in a nut-shell, drew on the cloak of many skins, and made her face and hands black with soot. Then she commended herself to God, and went out and travelled the whole night till she came to a large forest. And as she was very much tired she sat down inside a hollow tree and fell asleep.

The sun rose and she still slept on and on, although it was nearly noon. Now, it happened that the King to whom this wood belonged was hunting in it. When his dogs came to the tree, they sniffed, and ran round and round it, barking. The King said to the huntsmen, 'See what sort of a wild beast is in there.' The huntsmen went in, and then came back and said, 'In the hollow tree there lies a wonderful animal that we don't know, and we have never seen one like it; its skin is made of a thousand pieces of fur; but it is lying down asleep.'

The King said, 'See if you can catch it alive, and then fasten it to the cart, and we will take it with us.' When the huntsmen seized the maiden, she awoke and was frightened, and cried out to them, 'I am a poor child, forsaken by father and mother; take pity on me, and let me go with you.' Then they said to her, 'Many-furred Creature, you can work in the kitchen; come with us and sweep the ashes together.'

So they put her in the cart and they went back to the palace. There they showed her a tiny room under the stairs, where no daylight came, and said to her, 'Many-furred Creature, you can live and sleep here.' Then she was sent into the kitchen, where she carried wood and water, raked the fire, washed vegetables, plucked fowls, swept up the ashes, and did all the dirty work.

So the Many-furred Creature lived for a long time in great poverty. Ah, beautiful King's daughter, what is going to befall you now?

It happened once when a great feast was being held in the palace, that she said to the cook, 'Can I go upstairs for a little bit and look on? I will stand outside the doors.' The cook replied, 'Yes, you can go up, but in half-an-hour you must be back here to sweep up the ashes.' Then she took her little oil-lamp, and went into her little room, drew off her fur cloak, and washed off the soot from her face and hands, so that her beauty shone forth, and it was as if one sunbeam after another were coming out of a black cloud. Then she opened the nut, and took out the dress as golden as the sun. And when she had done this, she went up to the feast, and everyone stepped out of her way, for nobody knew her, and they thought she must be a king's daughter. But the King came towards her and gave her his hand, and danced with her, thinking to himself, 'My eyes have never beheld anyone so fair!' When the dance was ended, she curtsied to him, and when the King looked round she had disappeared, no one knew whither. The guards who were standing before the palace were called and questioned, but no one had seen her.

She had run to her little room and had quickly taken off her dress, made her face and hands black, put on the fur cloak, and was once more the Many-furred Creature. When she came into the kitchen and was setting about her work of sweeping the ashes together, the cook said to her, 'Let that wait till to-morrow, and just cook the King's soup for me: I want to have a little peep at the company upstairs; but be sure that you do not let a hair fall into it, otherwise you will get nothing to eat in future!' So the cook went away, and the Many-furred Creature cooked the soup for the King. She made a bread-soup as well as she possibly could, and when it was done, she fetched her gold ring from her little room, and laid it in the tureen in which the soup was to be served up.

When the dance was ended, the King had his soup brought to him and ate it, and it was so good that he thought he had never tasted such soup in his life. But when he came to the bottom of the dish he saw a gold ring lying there, and he could not imagine how it got in. Then he commanded the cook to be brought before him. The cook was terrified when he heard the command, and said to the Many-furred Creature, 'You must have let a hair fall into the soup, and if you have you deserve a good beating!' When he came before the King, the King asked who had cooked the soup. The cook answered, 'I cooked it.' But the King said, 'That's not true, for it was quite different and much better soup than you have ever cooked.' Then the cook said, 'I must confess; I did not cook the soup; the Many-furred Creature did.' 'Let her be brought before me,' said the King. When the Many-furred Creature came, the King asked her who she was. 'I am a poor child without father or mother.' Then he asked her, 'What do you do in my palace?' 'I am of no use except to have boots thrown at my head.' 'How did you get the ring which was in the soup?' he asked. 'I know nothing at all about the ring,' she answered. So the King could find out nothing, and was obliged to send her away.

After a time there was another feast, and the Many-furred Creature begged the cook as before to let her go and look on. He answered, 'Yes, but come back again in half-an-hour and cook the King the bread-soup that he likes so much.' So she ran away to her little room, washed herself quickly, took out of the nut the dress as silver as the moon and put it on. Then she went upstairs looking just like a king's daughter, and the King came towards her, delighted to see her again, and as the dance had just begun, they danced together. But when the dance was ended, she disappeared again so quickly that the King could not see which way she went. She ran to her little room and changed herself once more into the Many-furred Creature, and went into the kitchen to cook the bread-soup. When the cook was upstairs, she fetched the golden spinning-wheel and put it in the dish so that the soup was poured over it. It was brought to the King, who ate it, and liked it as much as the last time. He had the cook sent to him, and again he had to confess that the Many-furred Creature had cooked the soup. Then the Many-furred Creature came before the King, but she said again that she was of no use except to have boots thrown at her head, and that she knew nothing at all of the golden spinning-wheel.

When the King had a feast for the third time, things did not turn out quite the same as at the other two. The cook said, 'You must be a witch, Many-furred Creature, for you always put something in the soup, so that it is much better and tastes nicer to the King than any that I cook.' But because she begged hard, he let her go up for the usual time. Now she put on the dress as shining as the stars, and stepped into the hall in it.

The King danced again with the beautiful maiden, and thought she had never looked so beautiful. And while he was dancing, he put a gold ring on her finger without her seeing it, and he commanded that the dance should last longer than usual. When it was finished he wanted to keep her hands in his, but she broke from him, and sprang so quickly away among the people that she vanished from his sight. She ran as fast as she could to her little room under the stairs, but because she had stayed too long beyond the half-hour, she could not stop to take off the beautiful dress, but only threw the fur cloak over it, and in her haste she did not make herself quite black with the soot, one finger remaining white. The Many-furred Creature now ran into the kitchen, cooked the King's bread-soup, and when the cook had gone, she laid the gold reel in the dish.

When the King found the reel at the bottom, he had the Many-furred Creature brought to him, and then he saw the white finger and the ring which he had put on her hand in the dance. Then he took her hand and held her tightly, and as she was trying to get away, the fur cloak came apart and the star-dress shone out. The King seized the cloak and tore it off her. Her golden hair came down, and she stood there in her full splendour, and could not hide herself away any more. And when the soot and ashes had been washed from her face, she looked more beautiful than anyone in the world. But the King said, 'You are my dear bride, and we will never be separated from one another.' So the wedding was celebrated and they lived happily ever after.

Mother Holle

ONCE UPON a time there was a widow who had two daughters; one of them was pretty and clever, and the other ugly and lazy. But as the ugly one was her own daughter, she liked her far the best, and the pretty one had to do all the work of the house, and was in fact the regular maid of all work. Every day she had to sit by a well on the high road, and spin till her fingers were so sore that they often bled.

One day some drops of blood fell on her spindle, so she dipped it into the well meaning to wash it, but, as luck would have it, it dropped from her hand and fell right in. She ran weeping to her step-mother, and told her what had happened, but she scolded her harshly, merciless in her anger, and she said, 'Well, since you've dropped the spindle down, you must just go after it yourself, and don't let me see your face again until you bring it back with you.'

Then the poor girl returned to the well, and not knowing what she was about, in the despair and misery of her heart she sprang into the well and sank to the bottom. For a time she lost all consciousness, and when she came to herself again she was lying in a lovely meadow, with the sun shining brightly overhead, and a thousand flowers blooming at her feet. She rose up and wandered through this enchanted place, till she came to a baker's oven full of bread, and the bread called out to her as she passed:

'Oh! take me out, take me out, or I shall be burnt to a cinder. I am quite done enough.'

So she stepped up quickly to the oven and took out all the loaves one after the other. Then she went on a little farther and came to a tree laden with beautiful rosy-cheeked apples, and as she passed by it called out:

'Oh! shake me, shake me, my apples are all quite ripe.'

She did as she was asked, and shook the tree till the apples fell like rain and none were left hanging. When she had gathered them all up into a heap she went on her way again, and came at length to a little house, at the door of which sat an old woman. The old dame had such large teeth that the girl felt frightened and wanted to run away, but the old woman called after her:

'What are you afraid of, dear child? Stay with me and be my little maid, and if you do your work well I will reward you handsomely; but you must be very careful how you make my bed – you must shake it well till the feathers fly; then people in the world below say it snows, for I am Mother Holle.'

She spoke so kindly that the girl took heart and agreed readily to enter her service. She did her best to please the old woman, and shook her bed with such a will that the feathers flew about like snow-flakes; so she led a very easy life, was never scolded, and lived on the fat of the land. But after she had been some time with Mother Holle she grew sad and depressed, and at first she hardly knew herself what was the matter. At last she discovered that she was homesick, so she went to Mother Holle and said:

'I know I am a thousand times better off here than I ever was in my life before, but notwithstanding, I have a great longing to go home. In spite of all your kindness to me, I can remain with you no longer, but must return to my own people.'

'Your desire to go home pleases me,' said Mother Holle, 'and because you have served me so faithfully, I will show you the way back into the world myself.'

So she took her by the hand and led her to an open door, and as the girl passed through it there fell a heavy shower of gold all over her, till she was covered with it from top to toe.

'That's a reward for being such a good little maid,' said Mother Holle, and she gave her the spindle too that had fallen into the well. Then she shut the door, and the girl found herself back in the world again, not far from her own house; and when she came to the court-yard the old hen, who sat on the top of the wall, called out:

'Click, clock, clack,
Our golden maid's come back.'

Then she went in to her step-mother, and as she had returned covered with gold she was welcomed home.

She proceeded to tell all that had happened to her, and when the mother heard how she had come by her riches, she was most anxious to secure the same luck for her own idle, ugly daughter; so she told her to sit at the well and spin. In order to make her spindle bloody, she stuck her hand into a hedge of thorns and pricked her finger. Then she threw the spindle into the well, and jumped in herself after it. Like her sister she came to the beautiful meadow, and followed the same path. When she reached the baker's oven the bread called out as before:

'Oh! take me out, take me out, or I shall be burnt to a cinder. I am quite done enough.'

But the good-for-nothing girl answered:

'A pretty joke, indeed; just as if I should dirty my hands for you!'

And on she went. Soon she came to the apple tree, which cried:

'Oh! shake me, shake me, my apples are all quite ripe.'

'I'll see myself farther,' she replied, 'one of them might fall on my head.'

And so she pursued her way. When she came to Mother Holle's house she wasn't the least afraid, for she had been warned about her big teeth, and she readily agreed to become her maid. The first day she worked very hard, and did all her mistress told her, for she thought of the gold she would give her; but on the second day she began to be lazy, and on the third she wouldn't even get up in the morning. She didn't make Mother Holle's bed as she ought to have done, and never shook it enough to make the feathers fly. So her mistress soon grew weary of her, and dismissed her, much to the lazy creature's delight.

'For now,' she thought, 'the shower of golden rain will come.'

Mother Holle led her to the same door as she had done her sister, but when she passed through it, instead of the gold rain a kettle full of pitch came showering over her.

'That's a reward for your service,' said Mother Holle, and she closed the door behind her.

So the lazy girl came home all covered with pitch, and when the old hen on the top of the wall saw her, it called out:

> 'Click, clock, clack,
>   Our dirty slut's come back.'

But the pitch remained sticking to her, and never as long as she lived could it be got off.

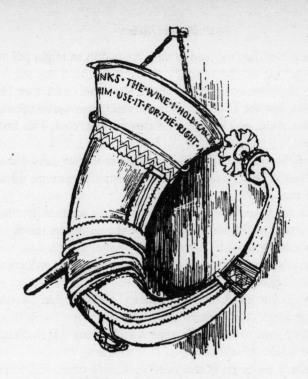

Niels and the Giants

ON ONE of the great moors over in Jutland, where trees won't grow because the soil is so sandy and the wind so strong, there once lived a man and his wife. They had a little house and some sheep, and two sons who helped to herd them. The elder of the two was called Rasmus, and the younger Niels. Rasmus was quite content to look after sheep, as his father had done before him, but Niels had a fancy to be a hunter, and was not happy till he got hold of a gun and learned to shoot. It was only an old muzzle-loading flint-lock after all, but Niels thought it a great prize, and went about shooting at everything he could see. So much did he practise that in the long run he became a wonderful shot, and his fame was known even where he had never been seen. Some people said there was very little in him beyond this, but that was a judgement they found reason to change in the course of time.

The parents of Rasmus and Niels were good Catholics, and when they were getting old the mother took it into her head that she would like to go to Rome and see the Pope. The others didn't see much point in this, but she had her way in the end: they sold all the sheep, shut up the house, and set out for Rome on foot. Niels took his gun with him.

'What do you want with that?' said Rasmus; 'we have plenty to carry without it.' But Niels could not be happy without his gun, and took it all the same.

It was in the hottest part of summer that they began their journey, so hot that they could not travel at all in the middle of the day, and they were afraid to do it by night lest they might lose their way or fall into the hands of robbers. One day, a little before sunset, they came to an inn which lay at the edge of a forest.

'We had better stay here for the night,' said Rasmus.

'What an idea!' said Niels, who was growing impatient at the slow progress they were making. 'We can't travel by day for the heat, and we remain where we are all night. It will be long enough before we get to Rome if we go on at this rate.'

Rasmus was unwilling to go on, but the two old people sided with Niels, who said, 'The nights aren't dark, and the moon will soon be up. We can ask at the inn here, and find out which way we ought to take.'

So they journeyed on for some time, but at last they came to a small opening in the forest, and here they found that the road split in two. There was no sign-post to direct them, and the people in the inn had not told them which of the two roads to take.

'What's to be done now?' said Rasmus. 'I think we had better have stayed at the inn.'

'There's no harm done,' said Niels. 'The night is warm, and we can wait here till morning. One of us will keep watch till midnight and then waken the other.'

Rasmus chose to take the first watch, and the others lay down to sleep. It was very quiet in the forest, and Rasmus could hear the deer and foxes and other animals moving about among the rustling leaves. After the moon rose he could see them occasionally, and when a big stag came quite close to him he got hold of Niels' gun and shot it.

Niels was wakened by the report. 'What's that?' he said.

'I've just shot a stag,' said Rasmus, highly pleased with himself.

'That's nothing,' said Niels. 'I've often shot a sparrow, which is a much more difficult thing to do.'

It was now close on midnight, so Niels took his turn to watch, and Rasmus went to sleep. It began to get colder, and Niels walked about a little to keep himself warm. He soon found that they were not far from the edge of the forest, and when he climbed up one of the trees he could see out over the open country beyond. At a little distance he saw a fire, and beside there sat three giants, busy with broth and beef. They were so huge that the spoons they used were as large as spades, and their forks as big as hay-forks: with these they lifted whole bucketfuls of broth and great joints of meat out of an enormous pot which was set on the ground between them. Niels was startled and rather scared at first, but he comforted himself with the thought that the giants were a good way off, and that if they came nearer he could easily hide among the bushes. After watching them for a little, however, he began to get over his alarm, and finally slid down the tree again, resolved to get his gun and play some tricks on them.

When he had climbed back to his former position, he took good aim, and waited till one of the giants was just in the act of putting a large piece of meat into his mouth. *Bang!* went Niels' gun, and the bullet struck the handle of the fork so hard that the point went into the giant's chin, instead of his mouth.

'None of your tricks,' growled the giant to the one who sat next him. 'What do you mean by hitting my fork like that, and making me prick myself?'

'I never touched your fork,' said the other. 'Don't try to pick a quarrel with me.'

'Look at it, then,' said the first. 'Do you suppose I stuck it into my own chin for fun?'

The two got so angry over the matter that each offered to fight the other there and then, but the third giant acted as peace-maker, and they again fell to their eating. While the quarrel was going on, Niels had loaded the gun again, and just as the second giant was about to

put a nice tit-bit into his mouth, *bang!* went the gun again, and the
fork flew into a dozen pieces.

This giant was even more furious than the first had been, and
words were just turning to blows, when the third giant again inter-
posed.

'Don't be fools,' he said to them; 'what's the good of beginning
to fight among ourselves, when it is so necessary for the three of us
to work together and get the upper hand over the king of this country.
It will be a hard enough task as it is, but it will be altogether hopeless
if we don't stick together. Sit down again, and let us finish our meal;
I shall sit between you, and then neither of you can blame the other.'

Niels was too far away to hear their talk, but from their gestures
he could guess what was happening, and thought it good fun.

'Thrice is lucky,' said he to himself. 'I'll have another shot yet.'

This time it was the third giant's fork that caught the bullet, and
snapped in two.

'Well,' said he, 'if I were as foolish as you two, I would also fly
into a rage, but I begin to see what time of day it is, and I'm going
off this minute to see who is playing these tricks with us.'

So well had the giant made his observations, that though Niels
climbed down the tree as fast as he could, so as to hide among the
bushes, he had just got to the ground when the enemy was upon him.

'Stay where you are,' said the giant, 'or I'll put my foot on you,
and there won't be much left of you after that.'

Niels gave in, and the giant carried him back to his comrades.

'You don't deserve any mercy at our hands,' said his captor, 'but
as you are such a good shot you may be of great use to us, so we shall
spare your life, if you will do us a service. Not far from here there
stands a castle, in which the King's daughter lives; we are at war with
the King, and want to get the upper hand of him by carrying off the
Princess, but the castle is so well guarded that there is no getting into
it. By our skill in magic we have cast sleep on every living thing in
the castle, except a black dog, and, as long as he is awake, we are no
better off than before; for, as soon as we begin to climb over the wall,
the dog will hear us, and its barking will waken all the others again.
Having got you, we can place you where you will be able to shoot the
dog before it begins to bark, and then no one can hinder us from

getting the Princess into our hands. If you do that, we shall not only let you off, but reward you handsomely.'

Niels had to consent, and they set out for the castle at once. It was surrounded by a very high rampart, so high that even the giants could not touch the top of it. 'How am I to get over that?' said Niels.

'Quite easily,' said the third giant. 'I'll throw you up on it.'

'No, thanks,' said Niels. 'I might fall down on the other side, or break my leg, or neck, and then the dog wouldn't get shot after all.'

'No fear of that,' said the giant; 'the rampart is quite wide on the top, and covered with long grass, so that you will come down as softly as though you fell on a feather-bed.'

Niels had to believe him, and allowed the giant to throw him up. He came down on his feet quite unhurt, but the black dog heard the thump, and rushed out of its kennel at once. It was just opening its mouth to bark, when Niels fired, and it fell dead on the spot.

'Go down on the inside now,' said the giant, 'and see if you can open the gate to us.'

Niels made his way down into the courtyard, but on his way to the outer gate he found himself at the entrance to the large hall of the castle. The door was open, and the hall was brilliantly lighted, though there was no one to be seen. Niels went in here and looked round him; on the wall there hung a huge sword without a sheath, and beneath it was a large drinking-horn, mounted with silver. Niels went closer to look at these, and saw that the horn had letters engraved on the silver rim; when he took it down and turned it round, he found that the inscription was:

> Whoever drinks the wine I hold
> Can wield the sword that hangs above;
> Then let him use it for the right,
> And win a royal maiden's love.

Niels took out the silver stopper of the horn, and drank some of the wine, but when he tried to take down the sword he found himself unable to move it. So he hung up the horn again, and went further into the castle. 'The giants can wait a little,' he said.

Before long he came to an apartment in which a beautiful princess lay asleep in a bed, and on a table by her side there lay a gold-hemmed handkerchief. Niels tore this in two, and put one half in his pocket, leaving the other half on the table. On the floor he saw a pair of gold-embroidered slippers, and one of these he also put in his pocket. After that he went back to the hall, and took down the horn again. 'Perhaps I have to drink all that is in it before I can move the sword,' he thought; so he put it to his lips again and drank till it was quite empty. When he had done this, he could wield the sword with the greatest of ease, and felt himself strong enough to do anything, even to fight the giants he had left outside, who were no doubt wondering why he had not yet opened the gate to them. To kill the giants, he thought, would be using the sword for the right; but as to winning the love of the Princess, that was a thing which the son of a poor sheep-farmer need not hope for.

When Niels came to the gate of the castle, he found that there was a large door and a small one. He opened the latter.

'Can't you open the big door?' said the giants. 'We shall hardly be able to get in at this one.'

'The bars are too heavy for me to draw,' said Niels; 'if you stoop a little you can quite well come in here.' The first giant accordingly bent down and entered in a stooping posture, but before he had time to straighten his back again Niels made a sweep with the sword, and off went the giant's head. To push the body aside as it fell was quite easy for Niels, so strong had the wine made him, and the second giant as he entered met the same reception. The third was slower in coming, so Niels called out to him.

'Be quick,' he said, 'you are surely the oldest of the three, since you are so slow in your movements, but I can't wait here long: I must get back to my own people as soon as possible.' So the third also came in, and was served in the same way.

By now day was beginning to break, and Niels thought that his folks might already be searching for him, so instead of waiting to see what took place at the castle, he ran off to the forest as fast as he could, taking the sword with him. He found the others still asleep, so he woke them up, and they again set out on their journey. Of the night's adventures he said not a word, and when they asked where he got the sword, he only pointed in the direction of the castle, and said,

'Over that way.' They thought he had found it, and asked no more questions.

When Niels left the castle, he pulled the door behind him, and it closed with such a bang that the porter woke up. He could scarcely believe his eyes when he saw the three headless giants lying in a heap in the courtyard, and could not imagine what had taken place. The whole castle was soon aroused, and then everybody wondered at the affair: it was soon seen that the bodies were those of the King's great enemies, but how they came to be there and in that condition was a perfect mystery. Then it was noticed that the drinking-horn was empty and the sword gone, while the Princess reported that half of her handkerchief and one of her slippers had been taken away. *How* the giants had been killed seemed a little clearer now, but *who* had done it was as great a puzzle as before. The old knight who had charge of the castle said that in his opinion it must have been some young knight, who had immediately set off to the King to claim the hand of the Princess. This sounded likely, but the messenger who was sent to the Court returned with the news that no one there knew anything about the matter.

'We must find him, however,' said the Princess: 'for if he is willing to marry me I cannot in honour refuse him, after what my father put on the horn.' She took counsel with her father's wisest men as to what ought to be done, and among other things they advised her to build a house beside the highway, and put over the door this inscription:

'Whoever will tell the story of his life, may stay here three nights for nothing.'

This was done, and many strange tales were told to the Princess, but none of the travellers said a word about the three giants.

In the meantime Niels and the others tramped on towards Rome. Autumn passed, and winter was just beginning when they came to the foot of a great range of mountains towering up to the sky. 'Must we go over these?' said they. 'We shall be frozen to death or buried in the snow.'

'Here comes a man,' said Niels. 'Let us ask him the way to Rome.' They did so, and were told that there was no other way.

'And is it far yet?' said the old people, who were beginning to be worn out by the long journey. The man held up his foot so that they could see the sole of his shoe; it was worn as thin as paper, and there was a hole in the middle of it.

'These shoes were quite new when I left Rome,' he said, 'and look at them now; that will tell you whether you are far from it or not.'

This discouraged the old people so much that they gave up all thought of finishing the journey, and only wished to get back to Denmark as quickly as they could. What with the winter and bad roads they took longer to return than they had taken to go. At length they found themselves in sight of the forest where they had slept before.

'What's this?' said Rasmus. 'Here's a big house built since we passed this way before.'

'So it is,' said Niels. 'Let's stay all night in it.'

'No, we can't afford that,' said the old people. 'It will be too dear for the like of us.'

However, when they saw what was written above the door, they were all well pleased to get a night's lodging for nothing. They were well received, and had so much attention given to them, that the old people were quite put out by it. After they had got time to rest themselves, the Princess's steward came to hear their story.

'You saw what was written above the door,' he said to the father. 'Tell me who you are and what your history has been.'

'Dear me, I have nothing of any importance to tell you,' said the old man, 'and I am sure we should never have made so bold as to trouble you at all if it hadn't been for the youngest of our two sons here.'

'Never mind that,' said the steward. 'You are very welcome if you will only tell me the story of your life.'

'Well, well, I will,' said he, 'but there is nothing to tell about it. I and my wife have lived all our days on a moor in North Jutland, until this last year, when she took a fancy to go to Rome. We set out with our two sons, but turned back long before we got there, and are now on our way home again. That's all my own story, and our two sons have lived with us all their days, so there is nothing more to be told about them either.'

'Yes there is,' said Rasmus. 'When we were on our way south, we slept in the wood near here one night, and I shot a stag.'

The steward was so much accustomed to hearing stories of no importance that he thought there was no use going further with this, and reported to the Princess that the newcomers had nothing to tell.

'Did you question them all?' she said.

'Well, no; not directly,' said he, 'but the father said that none of them could tell me any more than he had done.'

'You are getting careless,' said the Princess. 'I shall go and talk to them myself.'

Niels knew the Princess again as soon as she entered the room, and was greatly alarmed, for he immediately supposed that all this was a device to discover the person who had run away with the sword, the slipper and the half of the handkerchief, and that it would fare badly with him if he were discovered. So he told his story much the same as the others did, and thought he had escaped all further trouble, when Rasmus put in his word.

'You've forgotten something, Niels,' he said. 'You remember you found a sword near here that night I shot the stag.'

'Where is the sword?' said the Princess.

'I know,' said the steward. 'I saw where he laid it down when they came in;' and off he went to fetch it, while Niels wondered whether he could make his escape in the meantime. Before he had made up his mind, however, the steward was back with the sword, which the Princess recognised at once.

'Where did you get this?' she said to Niels.

Niels was silent, and wondered what the usual penalty was for a poor sheep-farmer's son who was so unfortunate as to deliver a princess and carry off things from her bedroom.

'See what else he has about him,' said the Princess to the steward, and Niels had to submit to be searched; out of one pocket came a gold-embroidered slipper, and out of another the half of a gold-hemmed handkerchief.

'That is enough,' said the Princess. '*Now* we needn't ask any more questions. Send for my father the King at once.'

'Please let me go,' said Niels. 'I did you as much good as harm, at any rate.'

'Why, who said anything about doing harm?' said the Princess. 'You must stay here till my father comes.'

The way in which the Princess smiled when she said this gave Niels some hope that things might not be bad for him after all, and he was yet more encouraged when he thought of the words engraven on the horn, though the last line still seemed too good to be true. However, the arrival of the King soon settled the matter; the Princess was willing and so was Niels, and in a few days the wedding bells were ringing. Niels was made an earl by that time, and looked as handsome as any of them when dressed in all his robes. Before long the old King died, and Niels reigned after him; but whether his father and mother stayed with him, or went back to the moor in Jutland, or were sent to Rome in a carriage and four, is something that all the historians of his reign have forgotten to mention.

The Ogre

THERE LIVED, once upon a time, in the land of Marigliano, a poor woman called Masella, who had six pretty daughters, all as upright as young fir-trees, and an only son called Antonio, who was so simple as to be almost an idiot. Hardly a day passed without his mother saying to him, 'What are you doing, you useless creature? If you weren't too stupid to look after yourself, I would order you to leave the house and never to let me see your face again.'

Every day the youth committed some fresh piece of folly, till at last Masella, losing all patience, gave him a good beating, which so startled Antonio that he took to his heels and never stopped running till it was dark and the stars were shining in the heavens. He wandered on for some time, not knowing where to go, and at last he came to a cave, at the mouth of which sat an ogre, uglier than anything you can conceive.

He had a huge head and wrinkled brow – eyebrows that met, squinting eyes, a flat broad nose, and a great gash of a mouth from which two huge tusks stuck out. His skin was hairy, his arms enormous, his legs like sword blades, and his feet as flat as ducks'.

In short, he was the most hideous and laughable object in the world.

But Antonio, who, with all his faults, was no coward and was moreover a very civil-spoken lad, took off his hat, and said, 'Good-day, sir; I hope you are pretty well. Could you kindly tell me how far it is from here to the place where I wish to go?'

When the ogre heard this extraordinary question he burst out laughing, and as he liked the youth's polite manners he said to him, 'Will you enter my service?'

'What wages do you give?' replied Antonio.

'If you serve me faithfully,' returned the ogre, 'I'll be bound you'll get enough wages to satisfy you.'

So the bargain was struck, and Antonio agreed to become the ogre's servant. He was very well treated, in every way, and he had little or no work to do, with the result that in a few days he became as fat as a quail, as round as a barrel, as red as a lobster, and as impudent as a bantam-cock.

But, after two years, the lad got weary of this idle life, and longed desperately to visit his home again. The ogre, who could see into his heart and knew how unhappy he was, said to him one day, 'My dear Antonio, I know how much you long to see your mother and sisters again, and because I love you as the apple of my eye, I am willing to allow you to go home for a visit. Therefore, take this donkey, so that you may not have to go on foot, but see that you never say "Brickle-brit" to him before you reach home, for if you do you'll be sure to regret it.'

Antonio took the beast without as much as saying 'thank you', and jumping on its back he rode away in great haste; but he hadn't gone two hundred yards when he dismounted and called out 'Bricklebrit'.

No sooner had he pronounced the word than the donkey opened its mouth and poured forth rubies, emeralds, diamonds and pearls, as big as walnuts.

Antonio gazed in amazement at the sight of such wealth, and joyfully filling a huge sack with the precious stones, he mounted the donkey again and rode on till he came to an inn. Here he got down, and going straight to the landlord, he said to him, 'My good man, I must ask you to stable this donkey for me. Be sure you give the poor

beast plenty of oats and hay, but beware of saying the word "Bricklebrit" to him, for if you do I can promise you will regret it. Take this
heavy sack, too, and put it carefully away for me.'

The landlord, who was no fool, on receiving this strange warning,
and seeing the precious stones sparkling through the canvas of the
sack, was most anxious to see what would happen if he used the
forbidden word. So he gave Antonio an excellent dinner, with a bottle
of fine old wine, and prepared a comfortable bed for him. As soon as
he saw the poor simpleton close his eyes and heard his lusty snores,
he hurried to the stables and said to the donkey, 'Bricklebrit', and
the animal as usual poured out any number of precious stones.

When the landlord saw all these treasures he longed to get possession of so valuable an animal, and determined to steal the donkey
from his foolish guest. As soon as it was light next morning Antonio
awoke, and having rubbed his eyes and stretched himself about a
hundred times he called the landlord and said to him, 'Come here,
my friend, and produce your bill, for short reckonings make long
friends.'

When Antonio had paid his account he went to the stables and
took out his donkey, as he thought, and fastening a sack of gravel,
which the landlord had substituted for his precious stones, on the
creature's back, he set out for his home.

No sooner had he arrived there than he called out, 'Mother, come
quickly, and bring table-cloths and sheets with you, and spread
them out on the ground, and you will soon see what wonderful
riches I have brought you.'

His mother hurried into the house, and opening the linen-chest
where she kept her daughters' wedding outfits, she took out table-
cloths and sheets made of the finest linen, and spread them flat and
smooth on the ground. Antonio placed the donkey on them, and
called out 'Bricklebrit'. But this time the donkey took no more
notice of the magic word than he would have done if a lyre had been
twanged in his ear. Two, three, and four times did Antonio pronounce
'Bricklebrit', but all in vain. He might as well have spoken to the
wind.

Disgusted and furious with the poor creature, he seized a thick
stick and began to beat it. The miserable donkey was so distracted

at such treatment that, far from pouring out precious stones, it only tore and dirtied all the fine linen.

When poor Masella saw her table-cloths and sheets being destroyed, and that instead of becoming rich she had only been made a fool of, she seized another stick and belaboured Antonio so unmercifully with it, that he fled before her, and never stopped till he reached the ogre's cave.

When his master saw the lad returning in such a sorry plight, he understood at once what had happened to him, and making no bones about the matter, he told Antonio what a fool he had been to allow himself to be so imposed upon by the landlord, and to let a worthless animal be palmed off on him instead of his magic donkey.

Antonio listened humbly to the ogre's words, and vowed solemnly that he would never act so foolishly again. And so a year passed, and once more Antonio was overcome by a fit of home-sickness, and felt a great longing to see his own people again.

Now the ogre, although he was so hideous to look upon, had a very kind heart, and when he saw how restless and unhappy Antonio was, he at once gave him leave to go home on a visit. At parting he gave him a beautiful table-cloth, and said, 'Give this to your mother; but see that you don't lose it as you lost the donkey, and till you are safely in your own house beware of saying "Table-cloth, open", and "Table-cloth, shut". If you do, the misfortune be on your own head, for I have given you fair warning.'

Antonio set out on his journey, but hardly had he got out of sight of the cave than he laid the table-cloth on the ground and said, 'Table-cloth, open'. In an instant the table-cloth unfolded itself and disclosed a whole mass of precious stones and other treasures.

When Antonio perceived this he said, 'Table-cloth, shut', and continued his journey. He came to the same inn again, and calling the landlord to him, he told him to put the table-cloth carefully away, and whatever he did not to say, 'Table-cloth, open', or 'Table-cloth, shut', to it.

The landlord, who was a regular rogue, answered, 'Just leave it to me, I will look after it as if it were my own.'

After he had given Antonio plenty to eat and drink, and had

provided him with a comfortable bed, he went straight to the table-cloth and said, 'Table-cloth, open'. It opened at once, and displayed such costly treasures that the landlord made up his mind on the spot to steal it.

When Antonio awoke next morning, the host handed him over a table-cloth exactly like his own, and carrying it carefully over his arm, the foolish youth went straight to his mother's house, and said, 'Now we shall be rich beyond the dreams of avarice, and need never go about in rags again, or lack the best of food.'

With these words he spread the table-cloth on the ground and said, 'Table-cloth, open'.

But he might repeat the injunction as often as he pleased, it was only waste of breath, for nothing happened. When Antonio saw this he turned to his mother and said, 'That old scoundrel of a landlord has done me once more; but he will live to repent it, for if I ever enter his inn again, I will make him suffer for the loss of my donkey and the other treasures he has robbed me of.'

Masella was in such a rage over her fresh disappointment that she could not restrain her impatience, and, turning on Antonio, she abused him soundly, and told him to get out of her sight at once, for she would never acknowledge him as a son of hers again. The poor boy was very depressed by her words, and slunk back to his master like a dog with his tail between his legs. When the ogre saw him, he guessed at once what had happened. He gave Antonio a good scolding, and said, 'I don't know what prevents me breaking your head, you useless ne'er-do-well! You blurt everything out, and your long tongue never ceases wagging for a moment. If you had remained silent in the inn this misfortune would never have overtaken you, so you have only yourself to blame for your present suffering.'

Antonio listened to his master's words in silence, looking for all the world like a whipped dog. When he had been three more years in the ogre's service he had another bad fit of home-sickness, and longed very much to see his mother and sisters again.

So he asked for permission to go home on a visit, and it was at once granted to him. Before he set out on his journey the ogre presented him with a beautifully carved stick and said, 'Take this stick as a remembrance of me; but beware of saying, "Rise up,

Stick", and "Lie down, Stick", for if you do, I can only say I wouldn't be in your shoes for anything.'

Antonio took the stick and said, 'Don't be in the least alarmed, I'm not such a fool as you think, and know better than most people what two and two make.'

'I'm glad to hear it,' replied the ogre, 'but words are women, deeds are men. You have heard what I said, and forewarned is forearmed.'

This time Antonio thanked his master warmly for all his kindness, and started on his homeward journey in great spirits; but he had not gone half a mile when he said 'Rise up, Stick'.

The words were hardly out of his mouth when the stick rose and began to rain down blows on his back with such lightning-like rapidity that he had hardly strength to call out, 'Lie down, Stick'; but as soon as he uttered the words the stick lay down, and ceased beating his back black and blue.

Although he had learnt a lesson at some cost to himself, Antonio was full of joy, for he saw a way now of revenging himself on the wicked landlord. Once more he arrived at the inn, and was received in the most friendly and hospitable manner by his host. Antonio greeted him cordially, and said: 'My friend, will you kindly take care of this stick for me? But, whatever you do, don't say "Rise up, Stick". If you do, you will be sorry for it, and you needn't expect any sympathy from me.'

The landlord, thinking he was coming in for a third piece of good fortune, gave Antonio an excellent supper; and after he had seen him comfortably to bed, he ran to the stick, and calling to his wife to come and see the fun, he lost no time in pronouncing the words, 'Rise up, Stick'.

The moment he spoke the stick jumped up and beat the landlord so unmercifully that he and his wife ran screaming to Antonio, and, waking him up, pleaded for mercy.

When Antonio saw how successful his trick had been he said, 'I refuse to help you, unless you give me all that you have stolen from me, otherwise you will be beaten to death.'

The landlord, who felt himself at death's door already, cried out, 'Take back your property, only release me from this terrible stick;'

and with these words he ordered the donkey, the table-cloth, and other treasures to be restored to their rightful owner.

As soon as Antonio had recovered his belongings he said 'Stick, lie down', and it stopped beating the landlord at once.

Then Antonio took his donkey and table-cloth and arrived safely at his home with them. This time the magic words had the desired effect, and the donkey and table-cloth provided the family with treasures untold. Antonio very soon married off his sisters, made his mother rich for life, and they all lived happily for ever after.

The Princess on the Glass Hill

ONCE UPON a time there was a man who had a meadow which lay
on the side of a mountain, and in the meadow there was a barn in
which he stored hay. But there had not been much hay in the barn
for the last two years, for every St John's eve, when the grass was in
the height of its vigour, it was all eaten clean up, just as if a whole
flock of sheep had gnawed it down to the ground during the night.
This happened once, and it happened twice, but then the man got
tired of losing his crop, and said to his sons – he had three of them,
and the third was called Cinderlad – that one of them must go and
sleep in the barn on St John's night, for it was absurd to let the grass
be eaten up again, blade and stalk, as it had been the last two years,
and the one who went to watch must keep a sharp look-out, the man
said.

The oldest was quite willing to go to the meadow; he would watch
the grass, he said, and he would do it so well that neither man, nor
beast, nor even the devil himself should have any of it. So when
evening came he went to the barn, and lay down to sleep, but when
night was drawing near there was such a rumbling and such an
earthquake that the walls and roof shook again, and the lad jumped

up and took to his heels as fast as he could, and never even looked back, and the barn remained empty that year just as it had been for the last two.

Next St John's eve the man again said that he could not go on in this way, losing all the grass in the outlying field year after year, and that one of his sons must go there and watch it, and watch well too. So the next oldest son was willing to show what he could do. He went to the barn and lay down to sleep, as his brother had done; but when night was drawing near there was a great rumbling, and then an earthquake, which was even worse than that on the former St John's night, and when the youth heard it he was terrified, and went off, running as if for a wager.

The year after, it was Cinderlad's turn, but when he made ready to go the others laughed at him, and mocked him. 'Well, you are just the right one to watch the hay, you who have never learnt anything but how to sit among the ashes and bake yourself!' said they. Cinderlad, however, did not trouble himself about what they said, but when evening drew near rambled away to the outlying field. When he got there he went into the barn and lay down, but in about an hour's time the rumbling and creaking began, and it was frightful to hear it.

'Well, if it gets no worse than that, I can manage to stand it,' thought Cinderlad. Soon the creaking began again, and the earth quaked, and the litter in the barn flew about the boy's head. 'Oh! if it gets no worse than that I can manage to stand it,' thought Cinderlad. But then came a third rumbling, and a third earthquake, so violent that the boy thought the walls and roof had fallen down, but when it was over everything suddenly grew as still as death around him. 'I am pretty sure that it will come again,' thought Cinderlad; but no, it did not. Everything was quiet, and everything stayed quiet, and when he had lain still a short time he heard something that sounded as if a horse were standing chewing just outside the barn door. He stole away to the door, which was ajar, to see what was there, and a horse was standing eating. So big, and fat, and fine a horse Cinderlad had never seen before, and a saddle and bridle lay beside it, and a complete suit of armour for a knight, and everything was of copper, and so bright that it shone again.

'Ha, ha! it is you then who eats up our hay,' said the boy to himself; 'but I will stop that.' So he made haste, and took out his steel for striking fire, and threw it over the horse, and then it had no power to stir from the spot, and became so tame that the boy could do what he liked with it. So he mounted it and rode away to a place which no one knew of but himself, and there he tied it up. When he went home again his brothers laughed and asked how he had got on.

'You didn't lie long in the barn, even if you have been so far as the field!' said they.

'I lay in the barn till the sun rose, but I saw nothing and heard nothing, not I,' said the boy. 'Heaven knows what there was to make you two so frightened.'

'Well, we shall soon see whether you have watched the meadow or not,' answered the brothers, but when they got there the grass was all standing just as long and as thick as it had been the night before.

The next St John's eve it was the same thing once again: neither of the two brothers dared to go to the outlying field to watch the crop, but Cinderlad went, and everything happened exactly the same as on the previous St John's eve. First there was a rumbling and an earthquake, and then there was another, and then a third; but all three earthquakes were much, very much more violent than they had been the year before. Then everything became still as death again, and the boy heard something chewing outside the barn door, so he stole as softly as he could to the door, which was slightly ajar, and again there was a horse standing close by the wall of the house, eating and chewing, and it was finer and bigger than the first horse, and it had a saddle on its back, and a bridle was on it too, and beside it lay a full suit of armour for a knight, all of bright silver, and as beautiful as anyone could wish to see.

'Ho, ho!' said the boy, 'is it you who eats up our hay in the night? But I will put a stop to that.' So he took out his steel for striking fire, and threw it over the horse's mane, and the beast stood there as quiet as a lamb. Then the boy rode this horse, too, away to the place where he kept the other, and then went home again.

'I suppose you will tell us that you have watched well again this time,' said the brothers.

'Well, so I have,' said Cinderlad. So they went, and there the grass was, standing as high and as thick as it had been before, but that did not make them any kinder to Cinderlad.

When the third St John's night came neither of the two elder brothers dared to lie out in the barn to watch the grass, for they had been so heartily frightened the night that they had slept there that they could not get over it, but Cinderlad dared to go, and everything happened just the same as on the two former nights. There were three earthquakes, each worse than the other, and the last flung the boy from one wall of the barn to the other, but then everything suddenly became still as death. When he had lain quietly a short time, he heard something chewing outside the barn door; then he once more stole to the door, which was slightly ajar, and behold, a horse was standing just outside it, which was much bigger and far more splendid than the two others he had caught, and the suit of armour, which lay beside it, was all of burnished gold. 'Ho, ho! it is you, then, who is eating up our hay this time,' said the boy; 'but I will put a stop to that.' So he pulled out his steel for striking fire, and threw it over the horse, and it stood as still as if it had been nailed to the field, and the boy could do just what he liked with it. Then he mounted it and rode away to the place where he had the two others, and then he went home again. Then the two brothers mocked him just as they had done before, and told him that they could see that he must have watched the grass very carefully that night, for he looked just as if he were walking in his sleep; but Cinderlad did not trouble about that, he just bade them go to the field and see. They did go, and this time too the grass was standing, looking as fine and as thick as ever.

Now the King of the country in which Cinderlad's father dwelt had a daughter whom he would only give in marriage to the man who could ride up to the top of the glass hill, for there was a high, high hill of glass, slippery as ice, close to the King's palace. Upon the very top of this hill the King's daughter was to sit with three gold apples in her lap, and the man who could ride up and take the three golden apples should marry her, and have half the kingdom. The King had this proclaimed in every church in his kingdom, and in many other kingdoms too. The Princess was very beautiful, and all who saw her fell violently in love with her, even in spite of themselves. So it is needless to say that all the princes and knights were eager to win her, and half the kingdom besides. They came riding from the very end of the world, dressed so splendidly that their raiments gleamed in the sunshine, and riding on horses which seemed to dance as they went, and there was not one of these princes who did not think that he was sure to win the Princess.

When the day appointed by the King had come, there was a great host of knights and princes collected under the glass hill, and everyone who could walk or even creep was there too, to see who won the King's daughter. Cinderlad's two brothers went too, but they would not hear of letting him go with them, for he was so dirty and black with sleeping and grubbing among the ashes that they said everyone would laugh at them if they were seen in the company of such an oaf.

'Well, then, I will go all alone by myself,' said Cinderlad.

When the two brothers came to the glass hill, the trial had begun. The princes and knights tried to ride up it, till their horses were in a foam; but it was all in vain, for no sooner did the horses set foot upon the hill than down they slipped, and there was not one which could get even so much as a couple of yards up. Nor was that strange, for the hill was as smooth as glass window-pane, and as steep as the side of a house. But they were all eager to win the King's daughter and half the kingdom, so they rode and they slipped, and thus it went on. At length all the horses were so tired that they could do no more, and so hot that the sweat ran off them and their riders were forced to give up the attempt.

The King was just thinking that he would cause it to be proclaimed that the riding should begin afresh on the following day, when perhaps it might go better, when suddenly a knight came riding up on so fine a horse that no one had ever seen the like of it before, and the knight had armour of copper, and his bridle was of copper too, and all his accoutrements were so bright that they shone again. The other knights all called out to him that he might just as well spare himself the trouble of trying to ride up the glass hill, for it was of no use to try; but he did not heed them, and rode straight at it, and went up as if it were nothing at all. Thus he rode for some way – it may have been a third part of the way up – but when he got so far he

turned his horse round and rode down again. But the Princess thought that she had never seen so handsome a knight, and while he was riding up she sat and thought, 'Oh! how I hope he may be able to come up to the top!' And when she saw that he was turning his horse back she threw one of the golden apples down after him, and it rolled into his shoe. But when he had come down from off the hill he rode away, and that so fast that no one knew what had become of him.

All the princes and knights were bidden to present themselves before the King that night, so that he who had ridden so far up the glass hill might show the golden apple which the King's daughter had thrown down. But no one had anything to show. One knight after another presented himself, and none could show the apple.

At night, too, Cinderlad's brothers came home and had a long story to tell about the riding up the glass hill. 'At first,' they said, 'there was not one who was able to get even so much as one step up, but then came a knight who had armour of copper, and a bridle of copper, and his armour and trappings were so bright that they shone from a great distance, and it was something like a sight to see him riding. He rode one-third of the way up the glass hill, and he could easily have ridden the whole of it if he had liked; but he turned back, as though he had made up his mind that that was enough for once.'

'Oh! I should have liked to see him, that I should,' said Cinderlad, who was as usual sitting by the chimney among the cinders.

'You indeed!' said the brothers, 'you look as if you were fit to be among such great lords, dirty lout that you are to sit there!'

Next day the brothers were for setting out again, and this time too Cinderlad begged them to let him go with them; but no, they said he was not fit to do that, for he was much too ugly and dirty. 'Well, well, then I will go all alone by myself,' said Cinderlad. So the brothers went to the glass hill, and all the princes and knights began to ride again, and this time they had taken care to roughen the shoes of their horses; but that did not help them; they rode and they slipped as they had done the day before, and not one of them could even get so far as a yard up the hill. When they had tired out their horses, so that they could do no more, they again had to stop altogether. But just as the King had decided that it would be well to proclaim that the riding should take place next day for the last time, so that they might have one more chance, he suddenly thought that it would be well to wait a little longer to see if the knight in copper armour would come on this day too. But nothing was to be seen of him. While they were still looking for him, however, there came a knight riding on a steed that was much, much finer than that which the knight in copper armour had ridden, and this knight had silver armour and a silver saddle and bridle, all so bright that they shone and glistened when he was a long way off. Again the other knights called to him, and said that he might just as well give up the attempt to ride up the glass hill, for it was useless to try; but the knight paid no heed to that, but rode straight away to the glass hill, and went still farther up than the knight in copper armour had gone; but when he had ridden two-thirds of the way up he turned his horse round, and rode down again. The Princess liked this knight still better than she had liked the other, and sat longing that he might be able to get up above, and when she saw him turning back she threw the second apple after him, and it rolled into his shoe, and as soon as he had got down the glass hill he rode away so fast that no one could see what had become of him.

In the evening, when everyone was to appear before the King and Princess, in order that he who had the golden apple might show it, one knight after another went in, but none of them had a golden apple to show.

At night the two brothers went home as they had done the night before, and told how things had gone, and how everyone had ridden, but no one had been able to get up the hill. 'But last of all,' they said, 'came one in silver armour, and he had a silver bridle on his horse, and a silver saddle, and oh, but he could ride! He took his horse two-thirds of the way up the hill, but then he turned back. He was a fine fellow,' said the brothers, 'and the Princess threw the second golden apple to him!'

'Oh, how I should have liked to see him too!' said Cinderlad.

'Oh, indeed! He was a little brighter than the ashes that you sit grubbing among, you dirty black creature!' said the brothers.

On the third day everything went just as on the former days. Cinderlad wanted to go with them to see the riding, but the two brothers would not have him in their company, and when they got

to the glass hill there was no one who could ride even so far as a yard
up it, and everyone waited for the knight in silver armour, but he was
neither to be seen nor heard of. At last, after a long time, came a knight
riding upon a horse that was such a fine one, its equal had never yet
been seen. The knight had golden armour, and the horse a golden
saddle and bridle, and these were all so bright that they shone and
dazzled everyone, even while the knight was still at a great distance.
The other princes and knights were not able even to call to tell him
how useless it was to try to ascend the hill, so amazed were they at the
sight of his magnificence. He rode straight away to the glass hill, and
galloped up it as if it were no hill at all, so that the Princess had not
even time to wish that he might get up the whole way. As soon as he
had ridden to the top, he took the third golden apple from the lap of
the Princess, and then turned his horse about and rode down again,
and vanished from their sight before anyone was able to say a word to
him.

When the two brothers came home again at night, they had much
to tell of how the riding had gone off that day, and in particular about
the knight in the golden armour. 'He was a fine fellow, he was! Such
another splendid knight is not to be found on earth!' said the
brothers.

'Oh, how I should have liked to see him too!' said Cinderlad.

'Well, he shone nearly as brightly as the coal-heaps that you lie
about in, dirty black creature that you are!' said the brothers.

Next day all the knights and princes were to appear before the
King and the Princess – it had been too late for them to do it the
night before – in order that he who had the golden apple might
produce it. They all went in turn, first princes, and then knights, but
none of them had a golden apple.

'But somebody must have it,' said the King, 'for with our own eye
we all saw a man ride up and take it.' So he commanded that everyone in the kingdom should come to the palace, and see if he could
show the apple. And one after the other they all came, but no one
had the golden apple, and after a long time Cinderlad's two brothers
came likewise. They were the last of all, so the King inquired of them
if there was no one else in the kingdom left to come.

'Oh! yes, we have a brother,' said the two, 'but he could not have the golden apple! He never left the cinder-heap on any of the three days.'

'Never mind that,' said the King. 'As everyone else has come to the palace, let him come too.'

So Cinderlad was forced to go to the King's palace.

'Have you the golden apple?' asked the King.

'Yes, here is the first, here is the second, and here is the third, too,' said Cinderlad, and he took all the three apples out of his pocket, and with that threw off his sooty rags, and appeared there before them in his bright golden armour, which gleamed as he stood.

'You shall have my daughter, and the half of my kingdom, and you have well earned both!' said the King. So there was a wedding, and Cinderlad got the King's daughter, and everyone made merry at the wedding, for all of them could make merry, though they could not ride up the glass hill, and if they have not left off their merry-making they must be at it still.

Rapunzel

ONCE UPON a time there lived a man and his wife who were very unhappy because they had no children. These good people had a little window at the back of their house, which looked into the most lovely garden, full of all manner of beautiful flowers and vegetables; but the garden was surrounded by a high wall, and no one dared to enter it, for it belonged to a witch of great power, who was feared by the whole world. One day the woman stood at the window overlooking the garden, and saw there a bed full of finest rampion: the leaves looked so fresh and green that she longed to eat them. The desire grew day by day, and just because she knew she couldn't possibly get any, she pined away and became quite pale and wretched. Then her husband grew alarmed and said, 'What ails you, dear wife?'

'Oh,' she answered, 'if I don't get some rampion to eat out of the garden behind the house, I know I shall die.'

The man, who loved her dearly, thought to himself, 'Come! rather than let your wife die you shall fetch her some rampion, no matter the cost.' So at dusk he climbed over the wall into the witch's garden, and, hastily gathering a handful of rampion leaves, he returned with them to his wife. She made them into a salad, which tasted so good that her longing for the forbidden food was greater than ever. If she were to know any peace of mind, there was nothing for it but that her husband should climb over the garden wall again, and fetch her some more. So at dusk over he got, but when he reached the other side, he drew back in terror, for there, standing before him, was the old witch.

'How dare you,' she said, with a wrathful glare, 'climb into my garden and steal my rampion like a common thief? You shall suffer for your foolhardiness.'

'Oh!' he implored, 'pardon my presumption; necessity alone drove me to the deed. My wife saw your rampion from her window, and conceived such a desire for it that she would certainly have died if her wish had not been gratified.' Then the witch's anger was a little appeased, and she said:

'If it's as you say, you may take as much rampion away with you as you like, but on one condition only – that you give me the child your wife will shortly bring into the world. All shall go well with it, and I will look after it like a mother.'

The man in his terror agreed to everything she asked, and as soon as the child was born the witch appeared, and having given it the name of Rapunzel, which is the same as rampion, she carried it off with her.

Rapunzel was the most beautiful child under the sun. When she was twelve years old the witch shut her up in a tower, in the middle of a great wood, and the tower had neither stairs nor doors, only high up at the very top a small window. When the old witch wanted to get in she stood underneath and called out:

> 'Rapunzel, Rapunzel,
> Let down your golden hair!'

for Rapunzel had wonderful long hair, and it was as fine as spun gold. Whenever she heard the witch's voice she unbound her plaits, and let her hair fall down out of the window about twenty yards below, and the old witch climbed up by it.

After they had lived like this for a few years, it happened one day that a prince was riding through the wood and passed by the tower. As he drew near it he heard someone singing so sweetly that he stood still spell-bound, and listened. It was Rapunzel in her loneliness singing to while away the time. The Prince longed to see the owner of the voice, but he sought in vain for a door in the tower. He rode home, but he was so haunted by the song he had heard that he returned every day to the wood and listened. One day, when he was standing thus behind a tree, he saw the old witch approach and heard her call out:

> 'Rapunzel, Rapunzel,
> Let down your golden hair!'

Then Rapunzel let down her plaits, and the witch climbed up by them.

'So that's the staircase, is it?' said the Prince. 'Then I too will climb it and try my luck.'

So on the following day, at dusk, he went to the foot of the tower and cried:

> 'Rapunzel, Rapunzel,
> Let down your golden hair!'

and as soon as she had let it down the Prince climbed up.

At first Rapunzel was terribly frightened when a man came in, for she had never seen one before; but the Prince spoke to her so kindly, and told her at once that his heart had been so touched by her singing, that he felt he should know no peace of mind till he had seen her. Very soon Rapunzel forgot her fear, and when he asked her to marry him she consented at once. 'For,' she thought, 'he is young and handsome, and I'll certainly be happier with him than with the old witch.' So she put her hand in his and said:

'Yes, I will gladly go with you, only how am I to get down out of the tower? Every time you come to see me you must bring a skein of silk with you, and I will make a ladder of them, and when it is finished I will climb down by it, and you will take me away on your horse.'

They arranged that, till the ladder was ready, he was to come to her every evening, because the old woman was with her during the day. The old witch, of course, knew nothing of what was going on, till one day Rapunzel, not thinking of what she was about, turned to the witch and said:

'How is it, good mother, that you are so much harder to pull up than the young Prince? He is always with me in a moment.'

'Oh! you wicked child,' cried the witch. 'What is this I hear? I thought I had hidden you safely from the whole world, and in spite of it you have managed to deceive me.'

In her wrath she seized Rapunzel's beautiful hair, wound it round and round her left hand, and then grasping a pair of scissors in her right, snip snap, off it came, and the beautiful plaits lay on the ground. And, worse than this, she was so hard-hearted that she took Rapunzel to a lonely desert place, and there left her to live in loneliness and misery.

But on the evening of the day in which she had driven poor Rapunzel away, the witch fastened the plaits on to a hook in the window, and when the Prince came and called out:

> 'Rapunzel, Rapunzel,
>   Let down your golden hair!'

she let them down, and the Prince climbed up as usual, but instead
of his beloved Rapunzel he found the old witch, who fixed her evil,
glittering eyes on him, and cried mockingly:

'Ah, ah! you thought to find your lady love, but the pretty bird has
flown and sings no longer; the cat caught it, and will scratch out your
eyes too. Rapunzel is lost to you for ever – you will never see her
more.'

The Prince was beside himself with grief, and in his despair he
jumped right down from the tower, and, though he escaped with his
life, the thorns among which he fell pierced his eyes out. Then he
wandered, blind and miserable, through the wood, eating nothing
but roots and berries, and weeping and lamenting the loss of his
lovely bride.

So he wandered about for some years, as wretched and unhappy as
he could well be, and at last he came to the desert place where
Rapunzel was living. Of a sudden he heard a voice which seemed
strangely familiar to him. He walked eagerly in the direction of the
sound, and when he was quite close, Rapunzel recognised him and
fell on his neck and wept. But two of her tears touched his eyes, and
in a moment they became quite clear again, and he saw as well as he
had ever done. Then he led her to his kingdom, where they were
received and welcomed with great joy, and they lived happily ever
after.

The Ratcatcher

A VERY long time ago the town of Hamel in Germany was invaded by rats, the like of which had never been seen before nor will ever be again.

They were great black creatures that ran boldly in broad daylight through the streets, and swarmed so, all over the houses, that people at last could not put their hand or foot down anywhere without touching one. When dressing in the morning they found them in their breeches and petticoats, in their pockets and in their boots; and when they wanted a morsel to eat, the voracious horde had swept away everything from cellar to garret. The night was even worse. As soon as the lights were out, these untiring nibblers set to work. And every-where, in the ceilings, in the floors, in the cupboards, at the doors, there was a chase and a rummage, and so furious a noise of gimlets, pincers, and saws, that even a deaf man could not have rested for one hour together.

Neither cats nor dogs, nor poison nor traps, nor prayers nor candles burnt to all the saints – nothing would do anything. The more the rats were killed the more they came. And the inhabitants of Hamel began to go to the dogs (not that *they* were of much use), when one Friday there arrived in the town a man with a queer face, who played the bagpipes and sang this refrain:

> '*Qui vivra verra:*
> *Le voilà,*
> *Le preneur des rats.*'

He was a great gawky fellow, dry and bronzed, with a crooked nose, a long rat-tail moustache, two great yellow piercing and mocking eyes, under a large felt hat set off by a scarlet cock's feather. He was dressed in a green jacket with a leather belt and red breeches, and on his feet were sandals fastened by thongs passed round his legs in gipsy fashion.

That is how he may be seen to this day, painted on a window of the cathedral of Hamel.

He stopped in the great market-place before the town hall, turned his back on the church and went on with his music, singing:

> 'Who lives shall see:
> This is he,
> The ratcatcher.'

The town council had just assembled to consider once more this 'plague of Egypt', from which no one could save the town.

The stranger sent word to the councillors that, if they would make it worth his while, he would rid them of all their rats before night, down to the very last one.

'Then he is a sorcerer!' cried the citizens with one voice. 'We must beware of him.'

The Mayor of the town, who was considered clever, reassured them.

He said: 'Sorcerer or no, if this piper speaks the truth, it was he who sent us this horrible vermin that he wants to rid us of to-day for money. Well, we must learn to catch the devil in his own snares. You leave it to me.'

'Leave it to the Mayor,' said the citizens one to another.

And the stranger was brought before them.

'Before night,' said he, 'I shall have despatched all the rats in Hamel if you will but pay me a *groschen* a head.'

'A *groschen* a head!' cried the citizens, 'but that will come to millions of florins!'

The Mayor simply shrugged his shoulders and said to the stranger:

'A bargain! To work; the rats will be paid for, one *groschen* a head as you ask.'

The piper announced that he would set to work that very evening when the moon rose. He added that the inhabitants should at that hour leave the streets free, and content themselves with looking out of their windows at what was passing, and that it would be a pleasant spectacle. When the people of Hamel heard of the bargain, they too exclaimed, 'A *groschen* a head! But this will cost us a deal of money!'

'Leave it to the Mayor,' said the town councillors with a malicious air. And the good people of Hamel repeated with their councillors, 'Leave it to the Mayor.'

Towards nine at night the piper re-appeared on the market-place. As at first, he turned his back to the church, and the moment the moon rose on the horizon, 'Trarira, trari!' the bagpipes resounded.

It was first a slow, caressing sound. Then it became more and more lively and urgent, and so sonorous and piercing that it penetrated as far as the farthest alleys and retreats of the town.

Soon from the bottom of the cellars, the top of the garrets, from under all the furniture, from all the nooks and corners of the houses, out came the rats, searching for the door, flinging themselves into the street, and trip, trip, trip, they began to run in file towards the front of the town hall, so squeezed together that they covered the pavement like the waves of flooded torrent.

When the square was quite full the piper faced about, and, still playing briskly, turned towards the river that runs at the foot of the walls of Hamel.

There he turned round; the rats were following.

'Hop! hop!' he cried, pointing with his finger to the middle of the stream, where the water whirled and was drawn down as if through a funnel. And hop! hop! without hesitating, the rats took the leap, swam straight to the whirlpool, plunged in head foremost and disappeared.

The plunging continued thus without ceasing till midnight.

At last, dragging himself with difficulty, came a big rat, white with age, and stopped on the bank.

It was the king of the band.

'Are they all there, friend Blanchet?' asked the piper.

'They are all there,' replied friend Blanchet.

'And how many were they?'

'Nine hundred and ninety thousand, nine hundred and ninety-nine.'

'Well reckoned?'

'Well reckoned.'

'Then go and join them, old sire, and *au revoir*.'

Then the old white rat sprang in his turn into the river, swam to the whirlpool and disappeared.

When the piper had thus concluded his business he went to bed at his inn. And for the first time during three months the people of Hamel slept quietly through the night.

The next morning, at nine o'clock, the piper repaired to the town hall, where the town councillors awaited him.

'All your rats took a jump into the river yesterday,' said he to the councillors, 'and I guarantee that not one of them comes back. They were nine hundred and ninety thousand, nine hundred and ninety-nine, at one *groschen* a head. Reckon!'

'Let us reckon the heads first. One *groschen* a head is one head the *groschen*. Where are the heads?'

The ratcatcher did not expect this treachery. He paled with anger and his eyes flashed fire.

'The heads!' cried he. 'If you care about them, go and find them in the river.'

'So,' replied the Mayor, 'you refuse to hold to the terms of your agreement? We ourselves could refuse you all payment. But you have

been of use to us, and we will not let you go without a recompense.'
And he offered him fifty crowns.

'Keep your recompense for yourself,' replied the ratcatcher
proudly. 'If you do not pay me I will be paid by your heirs.'

Thereupon he pulled his hat down over his eyes, went hastily out
of the hall, and left the town without speaking to a soul.

When the Hamel people heard how the affair had ended they
rubbed their hands, and with no more scruple than their Mayor, they
laughed over the ratcatcher, who, they said, was caught in his own
trap.

Next day, which was a Sunday, they all went gaily to church,
thinking that after Mass they would at last be able to eat some good
things that the rats had not tasted before them.

They never suspected the terrible surprise that awaited them on
their return home. No children anywhere, they had all disappeared!

'Our children! where are our poor children?' was the cry that
was soon heard in all the streets.

Then through the east gate of the town came three little boys, who
cried and wept, and this is the story they told.

While the parents were at church a wonderful music had been
heard. Soon all the little boys and all the little girls left at home had
gone out, attracted by the magic sounds, and had rushed to the great
market-place. There they found the ratcatcher playing his bagpipes
at the same spot as the evening before. Then he had begun to walk
away quickly, and they had followed, running, singing and dancing
to the sound of the music, as far as the foot of the mountain which
one sees on entering Hamel. At their approach the mountain had
opened a little, and the piper had gone in with them, after which it
had closed again. Only the three little ones who told the adventure
had remained outside, as if by a miracle. One was bandy-legged and
could not run fast enough; the second, who had left the house in
haste, one foot shod, the other bare, had hurt himself against a big
stone and could not walk without difficulty; the third had arrived in
time, but in hurrying to go in with the others had struck so violently
against the wall of the mountain that he fell backwards at the moment
it closed upon his comrades.

At this story the parents redoubled their lamentations. They ran

with pikes and mattocks to the mountain, and searched till evening
to find the opening by which their children had disappeared, without
being able to find it. At last, the night falling, they returned desolate
to Hamel.

But the most unhappy of all was the Mayor, for he had lost three
little boys and two pretty little girls, and to crown all, the people of
Hamel overwhelmed him with reproaches, forgetting that the evening
before they had all agreed with him.

What had become of all these unfortunate children?

The parents always hoped they were not dead and that the ratcatcher, who certainly must have come out of the mountain, would
have taken them with him to his own country. That is why for several
years they sent in search of them to different countries, but no one
ever came on any trace of the poor little ones.

It was not till much later that anything was to be heard of them.

About one hundred and fifty years after the event, when there was
no longer anyone left of the fathers, mothers, brothers or sisters of
that day, there arrived one evening in Hamel some merchants of
Bremen returning from the East, who asked to speak with the
citizens. Then they told that, in crossing Hungary, they had sojourned
in a mountainous country called Transylvania, where the inhabitants
only spoke German, while all around them nothing was spoken but
Hungarian. These people also declared that they came from Germany,
but they did not know how they chanced to be in this strange
country. 'Now,' said the merchants of Bremen, 'these Germans
cannot be other than the descendants of the lost children of Hamel.'

The people of Hamel did not doubt it; and since that day they
regard it as certain that the Transylvanians of Hungary are their own
country folk, whose ancestors, as children, were brought there by the
ratcatcher. There are things more difficult to believe than this.

The Riddle

A KING'S son once had a great desire to travel through the world, so he started off, taking no one with him but one trusty servant. One day he came to a great forest, and as evening drew on he could find no shelter, and could not think where to spend the night. All of a sudden he saw a girl going towards a little house, and as he drew nearer he remarked that she was both young and pretty. He spoke to her, and said, 'Dear child, could I and my servant spend the night in this house?'

'Oh, yes,' said the girl in a sad tone, 'you can if you like, but I should not advise you to do so. Better not go in.'

'Why not?' asked the King's son.

The girl sighed and answered, 'My step-mother deals in the black arts, and she is not very friendly to strangers.'

The Prince guessed easily that he had fallen on a witch's house, but as by this time it was quite dark and he could go no further, and as moreover he was not at all afraid, he stepped in.

An old woman sat in an armchair near the fire, and as the strangers entered she turned her red eyes on them. 'Good evening,' she muttered, pretending to be quite friendly. 'Won't you sit down?'

She blew up the fire on which she was cooking something in a little pot, and her daughter secretly warned the travellers to be very careful not to eat or drink anything, as the old woman's brews were apt to be dangerous.

They went to bed, and slept soundly till morning. When they were ready to start and the King's son had already mounted his horse the old woman said: 'Wait a minute, I must give you a stirrup cup.' Whilst she went to fetch it the King's son rode off, and the servant who had waited to tighten his saddle-girths was alone when the witch returned.

'Take that to your master,' she said; but as she spoke the glass cracked and the poison spurted over the horse, and it was so powerful that the poor creature sank down dead. The servant ran after his master and told him what had happened, and then, not wishing to lose the saddle as well as the horse, he went back to fetch it. When he got to the spot he saw that a raven had perched on the carcase and was pecking at it. 'Who knows whether we shall get anything better to eat to-day!' said the servant, and he shot the raven and carried it off.

The Prince and his servant rode on all day through the forest without coming to the end. At night-fall they reached an inn, which they entered, and the servant gave the landlord the raven to dress for their supper. Now, as it happened, this inn was the regular resort of a band of murderers, and the old witch too was in the habit of frequenting it.

As soon as it was dark twelve murderers arrived, with the full intention of killing and robbing the strangers. Before they set to work, however, they sat down to table, and the landlord and the old witch joined them, and they all ate some broth in which the flesh of the raven had been stewed down. They had hardly taken a couple of spoonfuls when they all fell down dead, for the poison had passed from the horse to the raven and so into the broth. So there was no one left belonging to the house but the landlord's daughter, who was a good, well-meaning girl, and had taken no part in all the evil doings.

She opened all the doors, and showed the strangers the treasure the robbers had gathered together; but the Prince bade her keep them all for herself, as he wanted none of them, and so he rode further with his servant.

After travelling about for some length of time they reached a town where lived a lovely but most arrogant princess. She had given out that anyone who asked her a riddle which she found herself unable to guess should be her husband, but should she guess it he must forfeit his head. She claimed three days in which to think over the riddles, but she was so very clever that she invariably guessed them in a much shorter time. Nine suitors had already lost their lives when the King's son arrived, and, dazzled by her beauty, determined to risk his life in hopes of winning her.

So he came before her and propounded his riddle. 'What is this?' he asked. 'One slew none and yet killed twelve.'

She could not think what it was! She thought, and thought, and looked through all her books of riddles and puzzles, but she found nothing to help her, and could not guess; in fact, she was at her wits' end. As she could think of no way to guess the riddle, she ordered her maid to steal at night into the Prince's bedroom and to listen, for she thought that he might perhaps talk aloud in his dreams and so betray the secret. But the clever servant had taken his master's place, and when the maid came he tore off the cloak she had wrapped herself in and chased her off with a whip.

On the second night the Princess sent her lady-in-waiting, hoping that she might succeed better, but the servant took away her mantle and chased her away also.

On the third night the King's son thought he really might be safe, so he went to bed. But in the middle of the night the Princess came herself, all huddled up in a misty grey mantle, and sat down near him. When she thought he was fast asleep, she spoke to him, hoping he would answer in the midst of his dreams, as many people do; but he was wide awake all the time, and heard and understood everything very well.

Then she asked, 'One slew none – what is that?' and he answered: 'A raven which fed on the carcase of a poisoned horse.'

She went on, 'And yet killed twelve – what is that?' 'Those twelve murderers who ate the raven and died of it.'

As soon as she knew the riddle she tried to slip away, but he held her mantle so tightly that she was obliged to leave it behind.

Next morning the Princess announced that she had guessed the riddle, and sent for the twelve judges, before whom she declared it. But the young man begged to be heard, too, and said, 'She came by night to question me, otherwise she never could have guessed it.'

The judges said: 'Bring us some proof.' So the servant brought out the three cloaks, and when the judges saw the grey one, which the Princess was in the habit of wearing, they said, 'Let it be embroidered with gold and silver; it shall be your wedding mantle.'

The Seven Foals

ONCE UPON a time there was a poor couple who lived in a wretched hut, far away from everyone else, in a wood. They only just managed to live from hand to mouth, and had great difficulty in doing even so much as that. They had three sons, and the youngest of them was called Cinderlad, for he did little else but lie and poke about among the ashes.

One day the eldest lad said that he would go out into the world to earn his living; he soon got leave to do that, and set out on his way. He walked on and on for the whole day, and when night was beginning to fall he came to a royal palace. The King was standing outside on the steps, and asked where he was going.

'Oh, I am going about seeking a place, my father,' said the youth.

'Will you serve me, and watch my seven foals?' asked the King. 'If you can watch them for a whole day and tell me at night what they eat and drink, you shall have the Princess to wife and half my kingdom, but if you can't, I'll cut three red stripes on your back.'

The youth thought that it was easy work to watch the foals, and that he could do it well enough.

Next morning, when day was beginning to dawn, the King's Master of the Horse let out the seven foals; off they went over hill and dale, through wood and bog, with the youth after them. When the lad had run thus for a long time he began to feel tired, and when he had held on a little longer he had had more than enough of his watching. At that same moment he came to a cleft in a rock where an old woman sat spinning her distaff in her hand.

As soon as she caught sight of the youth, who had run after the foals till the sweat streamed down his face, she cried, 'Come hither, come hither, my handsome son, and let me comb your hair for you.'

The lad was willing enough, so he sat down in the cleft of the rock beside the old hag, and laid his head on her lap, and she combed his hair all day while he lay there and gave himself up to idleness.

When evening was drawing near, the youth wanted to go.

'I may just as well go straight home again,' said he, 'for it is no use to go to the King's palace.'

'Wait till it is dusk,' said the old hag, 'and then the King's foals will pass by this place again, and you can run home with them; no one will ever know that you have been lying here all day instead of watching them.'

So when they came she gave the lad a bottle of water and a tuft of moss, and told him to show these to the King and say that this was what his seven foals ate and drank.

'Have you watched faithfully and well the whole day long?' said the King, when the lad came into his presence in the evening.

'Yes, that I have!' said the youth.

'Then you are able to tell me what it is that my seven foals eat and drink,' said the King.

So the youth produced the bottle of water and the tuft of moss which he had got from the old woman, saying, 'Here you see their meat, and here you see their drink.'

Then the King knew how his watching had been done, and fell into such a rage that he ordered his men to chase the youth back to his own home at once; but first they were to cut three red stripes in his back, and rub salt into them.

When the youth reached home again, you can imagine what a state of mind he was in. He had gone out once to seek a place, he said, but never would he do such a thing again.

Next day the second son said that he would now go out into the world to seek his fortune. His father and mother said 'No', and bade him look at his brother's back, but the youth would not give up his design, and stuck to it, and at last he got leave to go, and set forth on his way. When he had walked all day he too came to the King's palace, and the King was standing outside on the steps, and asked where he was going; and when the youth replied that he was in search of a place, the King said that he might enter into his service and watch his seven foals. Then the King promised him the same punishment and the same reward that he had promised his brother.

The youth at once consented to this and entered into the King's service, for he thought he could easily watch the foals and tell the King what they ate and drank.

In the grey light of dawn the Master of the Horse let out the seven foals, and off they went again over hill and dale, and off went the lad after them. But all went with him as it had gone with his brother. When he had run after the foals for a long, long time and was hot and tired, he passed by a cleft in the rock where an old woman sat spinning with a distaff, and she called to him, 'Come hither, come hither, my handsome son, and let me comb your hair.'

The youth liked the thought of this, let the foals run where they chose, and seated himself in the cleft of the rock by the side of the old hag. So there he sat, with his head on her lap, taking his ease the livelong day.

The foals came back in the evening, and then he too got a tuft of moss and a bottle of water from the old hag to show to the King. But when the King asked him, 'Can you tell me what my seven foals eat and drink?' and the youth showed him the moss and the water, saying, 'Yes, here may you behold their meat, and here their drink,' the King once more became wroth, and commanded that three red stripes should be cut on the lad's back, that salt should be strewn upon them, and that he should then be instantly chased back to his own home. So when the youth got home again he also told all that had happened to him, and said that he had gone out in search of a place once, but never would do that again.

On the third day Cinderlad wanted to set out. He had a fancy to try to watch the seven foals himself, he said.

The two others laughed at him, and mocked him. 'What! when all went so ill with us, do you suppose that you are going to succeed? You look like succeeding – you who have never done anything else but lie and poke about among the ashes!'

'Yes, I will go too,' said Cinderlad, 'for I have made up my mind.'

The two brothers laughed at him, and his father and mother begged him not to go, but all to no purpose, and Cinderlad set out on his way. So when he had walked the whole day, he too came to the King's palace as darkness began to fall.

There stood the King outside on the steps, and asked whither he was bound.

'I am in search of a place,' said Cinderlad.

'From whence do you come, then?' asked the King, for by this time he wanted to know a little more about the men he took into his service.

So Cinderlad told him whence he came, and that he was brother to the two who had watched the seven foals for the King, and then he asked if he might be allowed to try to watch them the next day.

'Oh, shame on those two!' said the King, for it enraged him even to think of them. 'If you are their brother you are not good for much. I have had enough of such fellows.'

'Well, but since I am here, you might just give me leave to try,' said Cinderlad.

'Oh, very well,' said the King. 'If you are determined to have your back flayed, have your own way.'

'I would much rather have the Princess,' said Cinderlad.

Next morning, in the grey light of dawn, the Master of the Horse let out the seven foals again, and off they went over hill and dale, through wood and bog, and off went Cinderlad after them. When he had run thus for a long time, he too came to the cleft in the rock, where the old hag sat spinning at her distaff, and she cried to Cinderlad, 'Come hither, come hither, my handsome son, and let me comb your hair for you.'

'Come and catch me, then; come and catch me!' said Cinderlad, as he passed by, jumping and running, and keeping tight hold of one of the foals by its tail.

When he had got safely past the cleft in the rock, the youngest foal said, 'Get on my back, for we have still a long way to go.' So the lad did this. And thus they journeyed onwards a long, long way.

'Do you see anything now?' said the foal.

'No,' said Cinderlad.

So they journeyed onwards a good bit farther.

'Do you see anything now?' asked the foal.

'Oh, no,' said the lad.

When they had gone thus for a long, long way, the foal again asked, 'Do you see anything now?'

'Yes, now I see something that is white,' said Cinderlad. 'It looks like the trunk of a great thick birch tree.'

'Yes, that is where we are to go in,' said the foal.

When they got to the tree, the eldest foal pushed it down on one side, and then they saw a door where the tree-trunk had stood, and inside this there was a small room, and in the room there was nothing but a small fire-place and a couple of benches, but behind the door hung a great rusty sword and a small pitcher.

'Can you wield that sword?' asked the foals.

Cinderlad tried, but could not do it; so they made him take a draught from the pitcher, and then one more, and after that still another, and then he was able to wield the sword with perfect ease.

'Good,' said the foals; 'and now you must take the sword away with you, and with it you must cut off the heads of all seven of us on your wedding-day, and then we shall become princes again as we were before. For we are brothers of the Princess you are to have when you tell the King what we eat and drink, but a mighty troll has cast a spell over us. When you have cut off our heads, you must take the greatest care to lay each head at the tail of the body to which it belonged before, and then the spell which the troll has cast upon us will lose all its power.'

Cinderlad promised to do this, and then they went on farther.

When they had travelled a long, long way, the youngest foal said, 'Do you see anything?'

'No,' said Cinderlad.

So they went on a great distance farther.

'And now?' inquired the foal. 'Do you see anything?'

'Alas! no,' said Cinderlad.

So they travelled onwards again, for many and many a mile, over hill and dale.

'Now, then,' said the foal. 'Do you not see anything now?'

'Yes,' said Cinderlad; 'now I see something like a bluish streak, far, far away.'

'That is a river,' said the foal, 'and we have to cross it.'

There was a long, splendid bridge over the river, and when they had got to the other side of it they again travelled on a long, long way, and then once more the foal inquired if Cinderlad saw anything. Yes, this time he saw something that looked black, far, far away, and was rather like a church tower.

'Yes,' said the foal, 'we shall go there.'

When the foals got into the churchyard they turned into men, and looked like the sons of a king, and their clothes were so magnificent that they shone with splendour. They went into the church and received bread and wine from the priest, who was standing before the altar. And Cinderlad went in too, and when the priest had laid his hands on the princes and blessed them, they went out of the church again, and Cinderlad went out too, but he took with him a flask of wine and some consecrated bread. No sooner had the seven princes come out into the churchyard than they became foals again, and Cinderlad got upon the back of the youngest, and they returned by the way they had come, only they went much, much faster.

First they went over the bridge, and then past the trunk of the birch tree, and then past the old hag who sat in the cleft of the rock spinning, and they went by so fast that Cinderlad could not hear what the old hag screeched after him, but he heard enough to understand that she was terribly enraged.

It was all but dark when they got back to the palace, and the King himself was standing in the courtyard waiting for them.

'Have you watched well and faithfully the whole day?' said the King to Cinderlad.

'I have done my best,' replied Cinderlad.

'Then can you tell me what my seven foals eat and drink?' asked the King.

So Cinderlad pulled out the consecrated bread and the flask of wine, and showed them to the King. 'Here may you behold their meat, and here their drink,' said he.

'Yes, diligently and faithfully have you watched,' said the King, 'and you shall have the Princess and half the kingdom.'

So all was made ready for the wedding, and the King said that it was to be so stately and magnificent that it should be talked of far and wide.

But when they sat down to the marriage-feast, the bridegroom arose and went down to the stable, for he said that he had forgotten something which he must go and look to. When he got there, he did what the foals had bidden him, and cut off the heads of all the seven. First the eldest, and then the second, and so on according to their age, and he was extremely careful to lay each head at the tail of the foal to which it had belonged, and when that was done, all the foals became princes again. When Cinderlad returned to the marriage-feast with the seven princes, the King was so joyful that he both kissed Cinderlad and clapped him on the back, and his bride was still more delighted with him than she had been before.

'Half my kingdom is yours already,' said the King, 'and the other half you shall have at my death, for my sons can get countries and kingdoms for themselves now that they have become princes again.'

Therefore, as all may well believe, there was great joy and merriment at that wedding.

Shepherd Paul

ONCE UPON a time a shepherd was taking his flock out to pasture, when he found a little baby lying in a meadow, left there by some wicked person, who thought it was too much trouble to look after it. The shepherd was fond of children, so he took the baby home with him and gave it plenty of milk. By the time the boy was fourteen he was tall and very strong; he could tear up oaks as if they were weeds. Then Paul, as the shepherd had called him, grew tired of living at home, and went out into the world to try his luck.

He walked for many miles, seeing nothing that surprised him, but in a clearing in a wood he was astonished to find a man combing trees as another man would comb flax.

'Good morning, friend,' said Paul, 'upon my word, you must be a strong man!'

The man stopped his work and laughed. 'I am Tree Comber,' he answered proudly; 'and the greatest wish of my life is to wrestle with Shepherd Paul.'

'May all your wishes be fulfilled as easily, for I am Shepherd Paul, and can wrestle with you at once,' replied the lad; and he seized Tree Comber and flung him with such force to the ground that he sank up to his knees in the earth. However, in a moment he was up again, and catching hold of Paul, threw him so that he sank up to his waist; but then it was Paul's turn again, and this time the man was buried up to his neck. 'That is enough,' cried he; 'I see you are a smart fellow, let us become friends.'

'Very good,' answered Paul, and they continued their journey together.

By and by they reached a man who was grinding stones to powder in his hands, as if they had been nuts.

'Good morning,' said Paul politely, 'upon my word, you must be a strong fellow!'

'I am Stone Crusher,' answered the man, 'and the greatest wish of my life is to wrestle with Shepherd Paul.'

'May all your wishes be as easily fulfilled, for I am Shepherd Paul, and will wrestle with you at once,' replied the lad; and the sport began. After a short time the man declared himself beaten, and begged leave to go with them; so they all three travelled together.

A little further on they came upon a man who was kneading iron as if it had been dough. 'Good morning,' said Paul, 'you must be a strong fellow.'

'I am Iron Kneader, and above all else I should like to wrestle with Shepherd Paul,' answered he.

'Let us begin at once then,' replied Paul; and on this occasion also, Paul got the better of his foe, and they all four continued their journey.

At midday they entered a forest, and Paul stopped suddenly. 'We three will go and look for game,' he said, 'and you, Tree Comber, will stay behind to prepare a good supper for us.' So Tree Comber set to work to boil and roast, and when dinner was nearly ready, a little dwarf with a pointed beard strolled up to the place. 'What are you cooking?' asked he. 'Give me some of it.'

'I'll give you some on your back, if you like,' answered Tree

Comber rudely. The dwarf took no notice, but waited patiently till the dinner was cooked, then suddenly throwing Tree Comber on the ground, he ate up the contents of the pot and vanished. Tree Comber felt rather ashamed of himself, and set about boiling some more vegetables, but they were still very hard when the hunters returned, and though they complained of his bad cooking, he did not tell them about the dwarf.

Next day Stone Crusher was left behind, and after him Iron Kneader, and each time the dwarf appeared, and they fared no better than Tree Comber had done. The fourth day Paul said to them, 'My friends, there must be some reason why your cooking has always been so bad, now you shall go and hunt and I will stay behind.' So they went off, laughing as they thought of what was in store for Paul.

He set to work at once, and had just got all his vegetables simmering in the pot when the dwarf appeared as before, and asked to have some of the stew. 'Be off,' cried Paul, snatching up the saucepan as he spoke. The dwarf tried to get hold of his collar, but Paul seized him by the beard, and tied him to a big tree so that he could not stir, and went on quietly with his cooking. The hunters came back early, longing to see how Paul had got on, and, to their surprise, dinner was quite ready for them.

'You are great useless creatures,' said he, 'who couldn't even outwit that little dwarf. When we have finished supper I will show you what I have done with him!' But when they reached the place where Paul had left the dwarf, neither he nor the tree was to be seen, for the little fellow had pulled it up by the roots and run away, dragging it after him. The four friends followed the track of the tree and found that it ended in a deep, deep hole. 'He must have gone down here,' said Paul, 'and I will go after him. See! there is a basket that will do for me to sit in, and a cord to lower me with. But when I pull the cord again, lose no time in drawing the basket up.'

And he stepped into the basket, which was lowered by his friends.

At last it touched the ground and he jumped out and looked about him. He was in a beautiful valley of fair meadows in which stood a splendid castle. As the door was open he walked in, but a lovely maiden met him and implored him to go back, for the owner of the castle was a dragon with six heads, who had stolen her from her home and brought her to this underground spot. But Paul refused to listen to her entreaties, and declared that he was not afraid of the dragon, and did not care how many heads he had; and he sat down calmly to wait for him.

In a little while the dragon came in, and all the long teeth in his six heads chattered with anger at the sight of the stranger.

'I am Shepherd Paul,' said the young man, 'and I have come to fight you, and as I am in a hurry we had better begin at once.'

'Very good,' answered the dragon. 'I am sure of my supper, but let us have a mouthful of something first, just to give us an appetite.'

Whereupon he began to eat some huge boulders as if they had been cakes, and when he had quite finished, he offered Paul one. Paul was not fond of boulders, but he took a wooden knife and cut one in two, then he snatched up both halves in his hands and threw them with all his strength at the dragon, so that two out of the six heads were smashed in. At this the dragon, with a mighty roar, rushed upon Paul, but Paul sprang on one side, and with a swinging blow cut off two more heads. Then, seizing the monster by the neck, he dashed the remaining heads against the rock.

When the maiden heard that the dragon was dead, she thanked her deliverer with tears in her eyes, but told him that her two younger sisters were in the power of dragons still fiercer and more horrible than this one. He vowed that his sword should never rest in its sheath till they were set free, and bade the girl come with him and show him the way.

The maiden gladly consented to go with him, but first she gave him a golden rod, and bade him strike the castle with it. He did so, and it instantly changed into a golden apple, which he put in his pocket. After that, they started on their search.

They had not gone far before they reached the castle where the second girl was confined by the power of the dragon with twelve heads. She was overjoyed at the sight of her sister and of Paul, and brought him a shirt belonging to the dragon, which made its wearer twice as strong as he was before. Scarcely had he put it on when the dragon came back, and the fight began. Long and hard was the struggle, but Paul's sword and his shirt helped him, and soon the twelve heads lay upon the ground.

Then Paul changed the castle into an apple, which he put into his pocket, and set out with the two girls in search of the third castle.

It was not long before they found it, and within the walls was

the third sister, who was younger and prettier than either of the other two. The dragon of this castle had eighteen heads, but when he quitted the lower regions for the surface of the earth, he left them all at home except one, and changed himself into a little dwarf, with a pointed beard.

The moment Paul knew that this terrible dragon was no other than the dwarf whom he had tied to the tree, he longed more than ever to fly at his throat. But the thought of the eighteen heads warned him to be careful, and the third sister brought him a silk shirt which would make him ten times stronger than he was before.

He had scarcely put it on, when the whole castle began to shake violently, and the dragon flew up the steps into the hall.

'Well, my friend, so we meet once more! Have you forgotten me?

I am Shepherd Paul, and I have come to wrestle with you, and to free this maiden from your clutches.'

'Ah, I am glad to see you again,' said the dragon. 'Those were my two brothers whom you killed, and now your blood shall pay for them.' And he went into his room to look for his shirt and to drink some magic wine, but the shirt was on Paul's back, and as for the wine, the girl had given a cupful to Paul and then had allowed the rest to run out of the cask.

At this the dragon grew rather frightened, but in a moment had recollected his eighteen heads, and was bold again.

'Come on,' he cried, rearing himself up and preparing to dart all his heads at once at Paul. But Paul jumped underneath, and gave an upward cut so that six of the heads went rolling down. They were the best heads too, and very soon the other twelve lay beside them. Then Paul changed the castle into an apple, and put it in his pocket. Afterwards he and the three girls set off for the opening which led upwards to the earth.

The basket was still there, dangling from the rope, but it was only big enough to hold the three girls, so Paul sent them up, and told them to be sure and let down the basket for him. Unluckily, at the sight of the maidens' beauty, so far beyond anything they had ever seen, the friends forgot all about Paul, and carried the girls straight away into a far country, so that they were not much better off than before. Meanwhile Paul, mad with rage at the ingratitude of the three sisters, vowed he would be revenged upon them, and set about finding some way of getting back to earth. But it was not very easy, and for months, and months, and months, he wandered about underground, and, at the end, seemed no nearer to fulfilling his purpose than he was at the beginning.

At length, one day, he happened to pass the nest of a huge griffin, who had left her young ones all alone. Just as Paul came along a cloud containing fire instead of rain burst overhead, and all the little griffins would certainly have been killed had not Paul spread his cloak over the nest and saved them. When their father returned the young ones told him what Paul had done, and he lost no time in flying after Paul, and asking how he could reward him for his goodness.

'By carrying me up to the earth,' answered Paul; and the griffin agreed, but first went to fetch some food to eat on the way, as it was a long journey.

'Now get on my back,' he said to Paul, 'and when I turn my head to the right, cut a slice off the bullock that hangs on that side, and put it in my mouth, and when I turn my head to the left, draw a cupful of wine from the cask that hangs on that side, and pour it down my throat.'

For three days and three nights Paul and the griffin flew upwards, and on the fourth morning it touched the ground just outside the city where Paul's friends had gone to live. Then Paul thanked him and bade him farewell, and he returned home again.

At first Paul was too tired to do anything but sleep, but as soon as he was rested he started off in search of the three faithless ones, who almost died from fright at the sight of him, for they had thought he would never come back to reproach them for their wickedness.

'You know what to expect,' Paul said to them quietly. 'You shall never see me again. Off with you!' Then he took the three apples out of his pocket and placed them in the prettiest places he could find; after which he tapped them with his golden rod, and they became castles again. He gave two of the castles to the eldest sisters, and kept the other for himself and the youngest, whom he married, and there they are living still.

Snowdrop

ONCE UPON a time, in the middle of winter when the snow-flakes were falling like feathers on the earth, a queen sat at a window framed in black ebony and sewed. And as she sewed and gazed out to the white landscape, she pricked her finger with the needle, and three drops of blood fell on the snow outside, and because the red showed up so well against the white she thought to herself, 'Oh! what wouldn't I give to have a child as white as snow, as red as blood, and as black as ebony!'

And her wish was granted, for not long after a little daughter was born to her, with a skin as white as snow, lips and cheeks as red as blood, and hair as black as ebony. They called her Snowdrop, and not long after her birth the Queen died.

After a year the King married again. His new wife was a beautiful woman, but so proud and overbearing that she couldn't stand any rival to her beauty. She possessed a magic mirror, and when she stood before it gazing at her own reflection and asked:

> 'Mirror, mirror, hanging there,
> Who in all the land's most fair?'

it always replied:

> 'You are most fair, my Lady Queen,
> None fairer in the land, I ween.'

Then she was quite happy, for she knew the mirror always spoke the truth.

But Snowdrop was growing prettier and prettier every day, and when she was seven years old she was as beautiful as she could be, and fairer even than the Queen herself. One day when the Queen asked her mirror the usual question, it replied:

> 'My Lady Queen, you are fair, 'tis true,
> But Snowdrop is fairer far than you.'

Then the Queen flew into the most awful passion and turned every shade of green in her jealousy. From that hour she hated poor Snow-drop, and every day her envy, hatred and malice grew, for envy and jealousy are like evil weeds which spring up and choke the heart. At last she could endure Snowdrop's presence no longer, and, calling a huntsman to her, she said, 'Take the child out into the wood, and never let me see her face again. You must kill her, and bring me back her heart, that I may know for certain she is dead.'

The huntsman did as he was told and led Snowdrop out into the wood, but as he was in the act of drawing out his knife to slay her, she began to cry, and said, 'Oh, dear huntsman, spare my life, and I will promise to go forth into the wide wood and never to return home again.'

And because she was so young and pretty the huntsman had pity on her, and said, 'Well, run along, poor child.' For he thought to himself, 'The wild beasts will soon eat her up.'

And his heart felt lighter because he hadn't had to do the deed himself. And as he turned away a young boar came running past, so he shot it, and brought its heart home to the Queen as a proof that Snowdrop was really dead. And the wicked woman stewed it with salt, and ate it, thinking she had made an end of Snowdrop for ever.

Now when the poor child found herself alone in the big wood the very trees around her seemed to assume strange shapes, and she felt so frightened she didn't know what to do. Then she began to run over the sharp stones, and through the bramble bushes, and the wild beasts ran past her, but they did her no harm. She ran as fast as her legs would carry her, and as evening approached, she saw a little house, and she stepped inside to rest. Everything was very small in the little house, but cleaner and neater than anything you can imagine. In the middle of the room there stood a little table, covered with a white tablecloth, and seven little plates and forks and spoons and knives and tumblers. Side by side against the wall were seven little beds, covered with snow-white counterpanes. Snowdrop felt so hungry and so thirsty that she ate a bit of bread and a little porridge from each plate, and drank a drop of wine out of each tumbler. Then feeling tired and sleepy she lay down on one of the beds, but it wasn't comfortable; then she tried all the others in turn, but one was too long, and another too short, and it was only when she got to the seventh that she found one to suit her exactly. So she lay down upon it, and said her prayers like a good child, and fell fast asleep.

When it got quite dark the masters of the little house returned. They were seven dwarfs who worked in the mines, right down deep in the heart of the mountain. They lighted their seven little lamps, and as soon as their eyes got accustomed to the glare they saw that someone had been in the room, for all was not in the same order as they had left it.

The first said:

'Who's been sitting on my little chair?'

The second said:

'Who's been eating my little loaf?'

The third said:

'Who's been tasting my porridge?'

The fourth said:

'Who's been eating out of my little plate?'

The fifth said:

'Who's been using my little fork?'

The sixth said:

'Who's been cutting with my little knife?'

The seventh said:

'Who's been drinking out of my little tumbler?'

Then the first dwarf looked round and saw a little hollow in his bed, and he asked again:

'Who's been lying on my bed?'

The others came running round, and cried out when they saw their beds:

'Somebody has lain on ours too.'

But when the seventh came to his bed, he started back in amazement, for there he beheld Snowdrop fast asleep. Then he called the others, who turned their little lamps full on the bed, and when they saw Snowdrop lying there they nearly fell down with surprise.

'Goodness gracious!' they cried, 'what a beautiful child!'

And they were so enchanted by her beauty that they did not wake her, but let her sleep on in the little bed. But the seventh dwarf slept one hour with each of his companions in turn, and in this way he managed to pass the night.

In the morning Snowdrop awoke, but when she saw the seven little dwarfs she felt very frightened. But they were so friendly, and asked her what her name was in such a kind way, that she replied, 'I am Snowdrop.'

'Why did you come to our house?' continued the dwarfs.

Then she told them how her step-mother had wished her put to death, and how the huntsman had spared her life, and how she had run the whole day till she had come to their little house. The dwarfs, when they had heard her sad story, asked her, 'Will you stay and keep house for us, cook, make the beds, do the washing, sew and knit? If you give satisfaction and keep everything neat and clean, you shall want for nothing.'

'Yes,' answered Snowdrop, 'I will gladly do all you ask.'

And so she took up her abode with them. Every morning the dwarfs went into the mountain to dig for gold, and in the evening when they returned home, Snowdrop always had their supper ready for them. But during the day the girl was left quite alone, so the good dwarfs warned her, saying, 'Beware of your step-mother. She will soon find out you are here, and whatever you do don't let anyone into the house.'

Now the Queen, after she thought she had eaten Snowdrop's heart, never dreamed but that she was once more the most beautiful woman in the world; so stepping before her mirror one day she said:

'Mirror, mirror, hanging there,
Who in all the land's most fair?'

and the mirror replied:

'My Lady Queen, you are fair, 'tis true,
But Snowdrop is fairer far than you.
Snowdrop, who dwells with the seven little men,
Is as fair as you, as fair again.'

When the Queen heard these words she was nearly struck dumb with horror, for the mirror always spoke the truth, and she knew now that the huntsman must have deceived her, and that Snowdrop was still alive. She pondered day and night how she might destroy her, for as long as she felt she had a rival in the land her jealous heart left her no rest. At last she hit upon a plan. She stained her face and dressed herself up as an old pedlar woman, so that she was quite unrecognisable. In this guise she went over the seven hills till she came to the house of the seven dwarfs. There she knocked at the door, calling out at the same time, 'Fine wares to sell, fine wares to sell!'

Snowdrop peeped out of the window, and called out:

'Good-day, mother, what have you to sell?'

'Good wares, fine wares,' she answered; 'laces of every shade and description,' and she held one up that was made of some gay coloured silk.

'Surely I can let the honest woman in,' thought Snowdrop; so she unbarred the door and bought the pretty lace.

'Good gracious! child,' said the old woman, 'what a figure you've got. Come! I'll lace you up properly for once.'

Snowdrop, suspecting no evil, stood before her and let her lace her bodice up, but the old woman laced her so quickly and so tightly that it took Snowdrop's breath away, and she fell down dead.

'Now you are no longer the fairest,' said the wicked old woman and then she hastened away.

In the evening the seven dwarfs came home, and you may think what a fright they got when they saw their dear Snowdrop lying on the floor, as still and motionless as a dead person. They lifted her up tenderly, and when they saw how tightly laced she was they cut the lace in two, and she began to breathe a little and gradually came back to life. When the dwarfs heard what had happened, they said, 'Depend upon it, the old pedlar woman was none other than the old Queen. In future you must be sure to let no one in, if we are not at home.'

As soon as the wicked old Queen got home she went straight to her mirror, and said:

> 'Mirror, mirror, hanging there,
> Who in all the land's most fair?'

and the mirror answered as before:

> 'My Lady Queen, you are fair, 'tis true,
> But Snowdrop is fairer far than you.
> Snowdrop, who dwells with the seven little men,
> Is as fair as you, as fair again.'

When she heard this she became as pale as death, because she saw at once that Snowdrop must be alive again.

'This time,' she said to herself, 'I will think of something that will make an end of her once and for all.'

And by the witchcraft which she understood so well she made a poisonous comb; then she dressed herself up and assumed the form of another old woman. So she went over the seven hills till she reached the house of the seven dwarfs, and knocking at the door she called out, 'Fine wares for sale.'

Snowdrop looked out of the window and said, 'You must go away, for I may not let anyone in.'

'But surely you are not forbidden to look out?' said the old woman, and she held up the poisonous comb for her to see.

It pleased the girl so much that she let herself be persuaded, and opened the door. When they had settled their bargain the old woman said, 'Now I'll comb your hair properly for you, for once in a way.'

Poor Snowdrop thought no evil, but hardly had the comb touched her hair than the poison worked and she fell down unconscious.

'Now, my fine lady, you're really done for this time,' said the wicked woman, and she made her way home as fast as she could.

Fortunately it was now near evening, and the seven dwarfs returned home. When they saw Snowdrop lying dead on the ground, they at once suspected that her wicked step-mother had been at work again; so they searched till they found the poisonous comb, and the moment they pulled it out of her head Snowdrop came to herself again, and told them what had happened. Then they warned her once more to be on her guard, and to open the door to no one.

As soon as the Queen got home she went straight to her mirror, and asked:

> 'Mirror, mirror, hanging there,
> Who in all the land's most fair?'

and it replied as before:

> 'My Lady Queen, you are fair, 'tis true,
> But Snowdrop is fairer far than you.
> Snowdrop, who dwells with the seven little men
> Is as fair as you, as fair again.'

When she heard these words the Queen literally trembled and shook with rage.

'Snowdrop shall die,' she cried; 'yes, though it cost me my own life.'

Then she went to a little secret chamber, which no one knew of but herself, and there she made a poisonous apple. Outwardly it looked beautiful, with white and red cheeks, and everyone who saw it longed to eat it, but anyone who might do so would certainly die on the spot. When the apple was quite finished she stained her face and dressed herself up as a peasant, and so she went over the seven hills to the seven dwarfs' house. She knocked at the door, as usual, but Snowdrop put her head out of the window and called out, 'I may not let anyone in, the seven dwarfs have forbidden me to do so.'

'Are you afraid of being poisoned?' asked the old woman. 'See, I will cut this apple in half. I'll eat the white cheek and you can eat the red.'

But the apple was so cunningly made that only the red cheek was poisonous. Snowdrop longed to eat the tempting fruit, and when she saw that the peasant woman was eating it herself, she couldn't resist the temptation any longer, and stretching out her hand she took the poisonous half. But hardly had the first bite passed her lips than she fell down dead on the ground. Then the eyes of the cruel Queen sparkled with glee, and laughing aloud she cried:

'As white as snow, as red as blood, and as black as ebony, this time the dwarfs won't be able to bring you back to life.'

When she got home she asked the mirror:

> 'Mirror, mirror, hanging there,
> Who in all the land's most fair?'

and this time it replied:

> 'You are most fair, my Lady Queen,
> None fairer in the land, I ween.'

Then her jealous heart was at rest – at least, as much at rest as a jealous heart can ever be.

When the little dwarfs came home in the evening they found Snowdrop lying on the ground, and she neither breathed nor stirred.

They lifted her up, and looked round everywhere to see if they could find anything poisonous about. They unlaced her bodice, combed her hair, washed her with water and wine, but all in vain; the child was dead and remained dead. Then they placed her on a bier, and all the seven dwarfs sat round it, weeping and sobbing for three whole days. At last they made up their minds to bury her, but she looked as blooming as a living being, and her cheeks were still such a lovely colour, that they said, 'We can't hide her away in the black ground.'

So they had a coffin made of transparent glass, and they laid her in it, and wrote on the lid in golden letters that she was a royal princess. Then they put the coffin on the top of the mountain, and one of the dwarfs always remained beside it and kept watch over it. And the very birds of the air came and bewailed Snowdrop's death, first an owl, and then a raven, and last of all a little dove.

Snowdrop lay a long time in the coffin, and she always looked the same, just as if she were fast asleep, and she remained as white as snow, as red as blood, and her hair as black as ebony.

Now it happened one day that a prince came to the wood and passed by the dwarfs' house. He saw the coffin on the hill, with the beautiful Snowdrop inside it, and when he had read what was written on it in golden letters, he said to one of the dwarfs, 'Give me the coffin. I'll give you whatever you like for it.'

But the dwarf said, 'No; we wouldn't part with it for all the gold in the world.'

'Well, then,' he replied, '*give* it to me, because I can't live without Snowdrop. I will cherish and love it as my dearest possession.'

He spoke so sadly that the good dwarfs had pity on him, and gave him the coffin, and the Prince bade his servants bear it away on their shoulders. Now it happened that as they were going down the hill they stumbled over a bush, and jolted the coffin so violently that the poisonous bit of apple Snowdrop had swallowed fell out of her throat. She gradually opened her eyes, lifted up the lid of the coffin, and sat up alive and well.

'Oh! dear me, where am I?' she cried.

The Prince answered joyfully, 'You are with me,' and he told her all that had happened, adding, 'I love you better than anyone in the whole wide world. Will you come with me to my father's palace and be my wife?'

Snowdrop consented, and went with him, and the marriage was celebrated with great pomp and splendour.

Now Snowdrop's wicked step-mother was one of the guests invited to the wedding feast. When she had dressed herself very gorgeously for the occasion, she went to the mirror, and said:

> 'Mirror, mirror, hanging there,
> Who in all the land's most fair?'

and the mirror answered:

> 'My Lady Queen, you are fair, 'tis true,
> But Snowdrop is fairer far than you.'

When the wicked woman heard these words she uttered a curse, and was beside herself with rage and mortification. At first she didn't want to go to the wedding at all, but at the same time she felt she would never be happy till she had seen the young Queen. As she entered Snowdrop recognised her, and nearly fainted with fear; but red-hot iron shoes had been prepared for the wicked old Queen, and she was made to get into them and dance till she fell down dead.

Snow-White and Rose-Red

A POOR widow once lived in a little cottage with a garden in front of it, in which grew two rose trees, one bearing white roses and the other red. She had two children, who were just like the two rose trees; one was called Snow-white and the other Rose-red, and they were the sweetest and best children in the world, always diligent and always cheerful; but Snow-white was quieter and more gentle than Rose-red. Rose-red loved to run about the fields and meadows, and to pick flowers and catch butterflies; but Snow-white sat at home with her mother and helped her in the household, or read aloud to her when there was no work to do.

The two children loved each other so dearly that they always walked about hand in hand whenever they went out together, and when Snow-white said, 'We will never desert each other,' Rose-red answered, 'No, not as long as we live;' and the mother added, 'Whatever one gets she shall share with the other.' They often roamed about in the woods gathering berries and no beast hurt them; on the contrary, they came up to them in the most confiding manner; the little hare would eat a cabbage leaf from their hands, the deer grazed beside them, the stag would bound past them merrily, and the birds remained on the branches and sang to them with all their might. No evil ever befell them; if they tarried late in the wood and night overtook them, they lay down together on the moss and slept till morning, and their mother knew they were quite safe, and never felt anxious about them.

Once, when they had slept the night in the wood and had been wakened by the morning sun, they perceived a beautiful child in a shining white robe sitting close to their resting-place. The figure got up, looked at them kindly, but said nothing, and vanished into the wood. And when they looked round about them they became aware that they had slept quite close to a precipice, over which they would certainly have fallen had they gone on a few steps further in the darkness. And when they told their mother of their adventure, she said what they had seen must have been the angel that guards good children.

Snow-white and Rose-red kept their mother's cottage so beautifully clean and neat that it was a pleasure to go into it. In summer Rose-red looked after the house, and every morning before her mother awoke she placed a bunch of flowers before the bed, from each tree a rose. In winter Snow-white lit the fire and put on the kettle, which was made of brass, but so beautifully polished that it shone like gold. In the evening when the snowflakes fell their mother said, 'Snow-white, go and close the shutters;' and then they drew round the fire, while the mother put on her spectacles and read aloud from a big book, and the two girls listened and sat and span. Beside them on the ground lay a little lamb, and behind them perched a little white dove with its head tucked under its wings.

One evening as they sat thus cosily together someone knocked at the door as though he desired admittance. The mother said, 'Rose-red, open the door quickly; it must be some traveller seeking shelter.' Rose-red hastened to unbar the door, and thought she saw a poor man standing in the darkness outside; but it was no such thing, only a bear, who poked his thick black head through the door. Rose-red screamed aloud and sprang back in terror, the lamb began to bleat, the dove flapped its wings, and Snow-white ran and hid behind her mother's bed. But the bear began to speak, and said, 'Don't be afraid: I won't hurt you. I am half frozen, and only wish to warm myself a little.'

'My poor bear,' said the mother, 'lie down by the fire, only take care you don't burn your fur.'

Then she called out, 'Snow-white and Rose-red, come out; the bear will do you no harm: he is a good, honest creature.'

So they both came out of their hiding-places, and gradually the lamb and the dove drew near too, and they all forgot their fear. The bear asked the children to beat the snow a little out of his fur, and they fetched a brush and scrubbed him till he was dry. Then the beast stretched himself in front of the fire, and growled quite happily and comfortably. The children soon grew quite at their ease with him, and led their helpless guest a fearful life. They tugged at his fur with their hands, put their small feet on his back, and rolled him about here and there, or took a hazel wand and beat him with it; and if he growled they only laughed. The bear submitted to everything with the best possible good-nature, only when they went too far he cried, 'Oh! children, spare my life!

> 'Snow-white and Rose-red,
> Don't beat your lover dead.'

When it was time to retire for the night, and the others went to bed, the mother said to the bear, 'You can lie there on the hearth, in heaven's name; it will be shelter for you from the cold and wet.'

As soon as the day dawned the children let him out, and he trotted over the snow into the wood. From this time on the bear came every evening at the same hour, and lay down by the hearth and let the children play what pranks they liked with him; and they got so

accustomed to him that the door was never shut till their black friend
had made his appearance.

When spring came, and all outside was green, the bear said one
morning to Snow-white, 'Now I must go away, and not return again
the whole summer.'

'Where are you going to, dear bear?' asked Snow-white.

'I must go to the wood and protect my treasure from the wicked
dwarfs. In winter, when the earth is frozen hard, they are obliged to
remain underground, for they can't work their way through; but
now, when the sun has thawed and warmed the ground, they break
through and come up above to spy out the land and steal what they
can; what once falls into their hands and into their caves is not easily
brought back to light.'

Snow-white was quite sad over their friend's departure, and when
she unbarred the door for him, the bear, stepping out, caught a piece
of his fur in the door-knocker, and Snow-white thought she caught
sight of glittering gold beneath it, but she couldn't be certain of it;
and the bear ran hastily away, and soon disappeared behind the
trees.

A short time after this the mother sent the children into the wood to
collect faggots. They came in their wanderings upon a big tree which
lay felled on the ground, and on the trunk among the long grass they
noticed something jumping up and down, but what it was they
couldn't distinguish. When they approached nearer they perceived
a dwarf with a wizened face and a beard a yard long. The end of his
beard was jammed into a cleft of the tree, and the little man sprang
about like a dog on a chain, and didn't seem to know what he was to
do. He glared at the girls with his fiery red eyes, and screamed out,
'What are you standing there for? Can't you come and help me?'

'What were you doing, little man?' asked Rose-red.

'You stupid, inquisitive goose!' replied the dwarf; 'I wanted to
split the tree, in order to get little chips of wood for our kitchen fire;
those thick logs that serve to make fires for coarse, greedy people like
yourselves quite burn up all the little food we need. I had successfully driven in the wedge, and all was going well, but the cursed
wood was so slippery that it suddenly sprang out, and the tree closed
up so rapidly that I had no time to take my beautiful white beard out,

so here I am stuck fast, and I can't get away; and you silly, smooth-faced, milk-and-water girls just stand and laugh! Ugh! what wretches you are!'

The children did all in their power, but they couldn't get the beard out; it was wedged in far too firmly.

'I will run and fetch somebody,' said Rose-red.

'Crazy blockheads!' snapped the dwarf; 'what's the good of calling anyone else? You're already two too many for me. Does nothing better occur to you than that?'

'Don't be so impatient,' said Snow-white, 'I'll see you get help;' and taking her scissors out of her pocket she cut the end off his beard.

As soon as the dwarf felt himself free he seized a bag full of gold which was hidden among the roots of the tree, lifted it up, and muttered aloud, 'Curse these rude wretches, cutting off a piece of my splendid beard!' With these words he swung the bag over his back, and disappeared without as much as looking at the children again.

Shortly after this Snow-white and Rose-red went out to get a dish of fish. As they approached the stream they saw something which looked like an enormous grasshopper, springing towards the water as if it were going to jump in. They ran forward and recognised their old friend the dwarf.

'Where are you going to?' asked Rose-red; 'you're surely not going to jump into the water?'

'I'm not such a fool,' screamed the dwarf. 'Don't you see that cursed fish is trying to drag me in?'

The little man had been sitting on the bank fishing, when unfortunately the wind had entangled his beard in the line; and when immediately afterwards a big fish bit, the feeble little creature had no strength to pull it out; the fish had the best of it, and was dragging the dwarf towards him. He clung on with all his might to every rush and blade of grass, but it didn't help him much; he had to follow every movement of the fish, and was in great danger of being drawn into the water. The girls came up just at the right moment, held him firm, and did all they could to disentangle his beard from the line; but in vain, beard and line were in a hopeless muddle. Nothing remained but to produce the scissors and cut the beard, by which a small part of it was sacrificed.

When the dwarf perceived what they were about he yelled to them, 'Do you call that manners, you toadstools! to disfigure a fellow's face? It wasn't enough that you shortened my beard before, but you must now needs cut off the best bit of it. I can't appear like this before my own people. I wish you'd been at Jericho first.' Then he fetched a sack of pearls that lay among the rushes and without saying another word he dragged it away and disappeared behind a stone.

It happened that soon after this the mother sent the two girls to the town to buy needles, thread, laces and ribbons. Their road led over a heath where huge boulders of rock lay scattered here and there. While trudging along they saw a big bird hovering in the air, circling slowly above them, but always descending lower, till at last it settled on a rock not far from them. Immediately afterwards they heard a sharp, piercing cry. They ran forward, and saw with horror that the eagle had pounced on their old friend the dwarf, and was about to carry him off. The tender-hearted girls seized a hold of the little man, and struggled so long with the bird that at last he let go his prey.

When the dwarf had recovered from the first shock he screamed in his screeching voice, 'Couldn't you have treated me more carefully? You have torn my thin little coat all to shreds, useless, awkward hussies that you are!' Then he took a bag of precious stones and vanished under the rocks into his cave. The girls were accustomed to his ingratitude, and went on their way, and did their business in town. On their way home, as they were again passing the heath, they surprised the dwarf pouring out his precious stones on an open space, for he had thought no one would pass by at so late an hour. The evening sun shone on the glittering stones, and they sparkled and gleamed so beautifully that the girls stood still and gazed on them.

'What are you standing there gaping for?' screamed the dwarf, and his ashen-grey face became scarlet with rage. He was about to go off with these angry words when a sudden growl was heard, and a black bear trotted out of the wood. The dwarf jumped up in a great fright, but he hadn't time to reach his place of retreat, for the bear was already close to him. Then he cried in terror, 'Dear Mr Bear, spare me! I'll give you all my treasure. Look at those beautiful precious stones lying there. Spare my life! What pleasure would you get from a poor feeble little fellow like me! You won't feel me between your teeth. There, lay hold of these two wicked girls, they will be a tender morsel for you, as fat as young quails; eat them up, for heaven's sake.' But the bear, paying no attention to his words, gave the evil little creature one blow with his paw, and he never moved again.

The girls had run away, but the bear called after them, 'Snow-white and Rose-red, don't be afraid; wait, and I'll come with you.'

Then they recognised his voice and stood still, and when the bear was quite close to them his skin suddenly fell off, and a beautiful man stood beside them, all dressed in gold.

'I am a king's son,' he said, 'and have been doomed by that unholy little dwarf, who had stolen my treasure, to roam about the woods as a wild bear till his death should set me free. Now he has got his well-merited punishment.'

Snow-white married him, and Rose-red his brother, and they divided the great treasure the dwarf had collected in his cave between them. The old mother lived for many years peacefully with her children; and she carried the two rose trees with her, and they stood in front of her window, and every year they bore the finest red and white roses.

Spindle, Shuttle, and Needle

ONCE UPON a time there was a girl who lost her father and mother when she was quite a tiny child. Her godmother lived all alone in a little cottage at the far end of the village, and there she earned her living by spinning, weaving, and sewing. The old woman took the little orphan home with her, taught her to work, and brought her up to be both industrious and virtuous.

When the girl was fifteen years old, her godmother fell ill, and, calling the child to her bedside, she said, 'My dear daughter, I feel that my end is near. I leave you my cottage, which will, at least, shelter you, and also my spindle, my weaver's shuttle, and my needle, with which to earn your bread.'

Then she laid her hands on the girl's head, blessed her, and added, 'Be good, and then all will go well with you.' With that she closed her eyes for the last time, and when she was carried to her grave the girl walked behind her coffin weeping bitterly, and paid her all the last honours.

After this the girl lived all alone in the little cottage. She worked hard, spinning, weaving, and sewing, and her old godmother's blessing seemed to prosper all she did. The flax seemed to spread and increase; and when she wove a carpet or a piece of linen, or made a shirt, she was sure to find a customer who paid her well, so that not only did she feel no want herself, but she was able to help those who did.

Now, it happened that about this time the King's son was making a tour through the entire country in search of a bride. He could not marry a poor woman, and he did not wish for a rich one.

'She shall be my wife,' said he, 'who is at once the poorest and the richest.'

When he reached the village where the girl lived, he asked who was the richest and who the poorest woman in it. The richest was named first; the poorest, he was told, was a young girl who lived alone in a little cottage at the far end of the village.

The rich girl sat at her door dressed out in all her best clothes, and when the King's son came near she got up, and went to meet him, and made him a low curtsy. He looked well at her, said nothing, but rode on further.

When he reached the poor girl's house he did not find her at her door, for she was at work in her room. The Prince reined in his horse, looked in at the window through which the sun was shining brightly, and saw the girl sitting at her wheel busily spinning away.

She looked up, and when she saw the King's son gazing in at her, she blushed red all over, cast down her eyes and worked on. Whether the thread was quite as even as usual I really cannot say, but she went on spinning till the King's son had ridden off. Then she stepped to the window and opened the lattice, saying, 'The room is so hot,' but she looked after him as long as she could see the white plumes in his hat.

Then she sat down to her work once more and span on, and as she did so an old saying, which she had often heard her godmother repeat whilst at work, came into her head, and she began to sing:

> 'Spindle, spindle, go and see,
> If my love will come to me!'

Lo, and behold! the spindle leapt from her hand and rushed out of the room, and when she had sufficiently recovered from her surprise to look after it she saw it dancing merrily through the fields, dragging a long golden thread after it, and soon it was lost to sight.

The girl, having lost her spindle, took up the shuttle and, seating herself at her loom, began to weave. Meantime the spindle danced on and on, and just as it had come to the end of the golden thread, it reached the King's son.

'What do I see?' he cried; 'this spindle seems to wish to point out the way to me.' So he turned his horse's head and rode back beside the golden thread.

Meantime the girl sat weaving, and sang:

> 'Shuttle, weave both web and woof,
> Bring my love beneath my roof!'

The shuttle instantly escaped from her hand, and with one bound was out at the door. On the threshold it began weaving the loveliest

carpet that was ever seen. Roses and lilies in full bloom bordered both sides, and in the centre a thicket seemed to grow with rabbits and hares running through it, stags and fawns peeping through the branches, whilst on the topmost boughs sat birds of brilliant plumage and so life-like one almost expected to hear them sing. The shuttle flew from side to side and the carpet seemed almost to grow of itself.

As the shuttle had run away the girl sat down to sew. She took her needle and sang:

> 'Needle, needle, stitch away,
> Make my chamber bright and gay!'

and the needle promptly slipped from her fingers and flew about the room like lightning. You would have thought invisible spirits were at work, for in next to no time the table and benches were covered with green cloth, the chairs with velvet, and elegant silk curtains hung before the windows. The needle had barely put in its last stitch when the girl, glancing at the window, spied the white plumed hat of the King's son who was being led back by the spindle with the golden thread.

He dismounted and walked over the carpet into the house, and when he entered the room there stood the girl blushing like any rose. 'You are the poorest and yet the richest,' said he. 'Come with me, you shall be my bride.'

She said nothing, but she held out her hand. Then he kissed her, led her out, lifted her on his horse and took her to his royal palace, where the wedding was celebrated with great rejoicings.

The spindle, the shuttle, and the needle were carefully placed in the treasury, and were always held in the very highest honour.

Stan Bolovan

ONCE UPON a time what happened did happen, and if it had not happened this story would never have been told. On the outskirts of a village, just where the oxen were turned out to pasture, and the pigs roamed about, burrowing with their noses among the roots of the trees, there stood a small house. In the house lived a man who had a wife, and the wife was sad all day long.

'Dear wife, what is wrong with you that you hang your head like a drooping rosebud?' asked her husband one morning. 'You have everything you want; why cannot you be merry like other women?'

'Leave me alone and do not seek to know the reason,' replied his wife, bursting into tears, and the man thought it was no time to question her and went away to his work.

He could not, however, forget all about it, and a few days later he asked again the reason of her sadness, only to be given the same reply. At length he felt he could bear it no longer and tried a third time, and then his wife answered him.

'Good gracious!' cried she. 'Why cannot you let things be as they are? If I were to tell you, you would become just as wretched as myself. If you would only believe it, it is far better for you to know nothing.'

But no man yet was ever content with such an answer. The more you beg him not to inquire, the greater is his curiosity to learn the whole.

'Well, if you must know,' said the wife at last, 'I will tell you. There is no luck in this house – no luck at all!'

'Is not your cow the best milker in all the village? Are not your trees as full of fruit as your hives are full of bees? Has anyone corn-fields like ours? Really, you talk nonsense when you say things like that!'

'Yes, all that you say is true, but we have no children.'

Then Stan understood, and, when a man once understands and has his eyes opened, it is no longer well with him. From that day the little house on the outskirts contained an unhappy man as well as an unhappy woman. And at the sight of her husband's misery the woman became more wretched than ever.

And so matters went on for some time.

Weeks passed, and Stan thought he would consult a wise man who lived a day's journey from his own house. The wise man was sitting before his door when he came up and Stan fell on his knees before him.

'Give me children, my lord, give me children.'

'Take care what you are asking,' replied the wise man. 'Will not children be a burden to you? Are you rich enough to feed and clothe them?'

'Only give them to me, my lord, and I will manage somehow!' And at a sign from the wise man Stan went his way.

He reached home that evening tired and dusty but with hope in his heart. As he drew near his house a sound of voices struck upon his ear and he looked up to see the whole place full of children. Children in the garden, children in the yard, children looking out of every window – it seemed to the man as if all the children in the world must be gathered there. And none was bigger than the other, but each was smaller than the other, and every one was more noisy and more impudent and more daring than the rest. Stan gazed and grew cold with horror as he realised that they all belonged to him.

'Good gracious! How many there are! How many!' he muttered to himself.

'Oh, but not one too many.' His wife smiled, coming up with a crowd of more children clinging to her skirts.

But even she found that it was not so easy to look after a hundred children. And when a few days had passed and they had eaten up all the food there was in the house, they began to cry, 'Father! I am hungry – I am hungry,' till Stan scratched his head and wondered what he was to do next.

It was not that he thought there were too many children, for his life had seemed more full of joy since they appeared, but now it came to the point he did not know how he was to feed them. The cow had ceased to give milk and it was too early for the fruit trees to ripen.

'Do you know, old woman,' said he one day to his wife, 'I must go out into the world and try to bring back food somehow, though I cannot tell where it is to come from.'

To the hungry man any road is long, and then there was always the thought that he had to satisfy a hundred greedy children as well as himself.

Stan wandered and wandered and wandered, till he reached the end of the world, where that which is, is mingled with that which is not. There he saw, a little way off, a sheepfold, with seven sheep in it. In the shadow of some trees lay the rest of the flock.

Stan crept into hiding, hoping that at nightfall he might manage to decoy some of the sheep away and drive them home for food for his family. But he found this could not be done. For at midnight there was a rushing noise, and through the air flew a dragon who drove away a ram, a sheep and a lamb and three fine cattle that were lying down close by. And besides these he took the milk of seventy-seven sheep and carried it home to his old mother that she might bathe in it and grow young again. And this happened every night.

The shepherd of the flock bewailed his loss in vain; the dragon only laughed, and Stan saw that this was not the place to get food for his family. But though he quite understood that it was almost hopeless to fight against such a powerful monster, yet the thought of the hungry children at home clung to him like a burr and would not be shaken off.

At last he said to the shepherd, 'What will you give me if I rid you of the dragon?'

'One of every three rams, one of every three sheep, one of every three lambs,' answered the herdsman.

'It is a bargain,' replied Stan, though at the moment he did not know how, supposing he did come off the victor, he would ever be able to drive so large a flock home. However, that matter could be settled later. At present night was not far off and he must consider how best to fight with the dragon.

Just at midnight, a horrible feeling that was new and strange to him came over Stan – a feeling that he could not put into words even to himself, but which almost forced him to give up the battle and take the shortest road home again. He started; then he remembered the children and turned back.

'You or I,' said Stan to himself, and took up his position on the edge of the flock.

'Stop!' he suddenly cried, as the air was filled with a rushing noise and the dragon came dashing past.

'Dear me!' exclaimed the dragon, looking round. 'Who are you, and where do you come from?'

'I am Stan Bolovan, who eats rocks all night and in the day feeds on the flowers of the mountain. If you meddle with those sheep I will carve a cross on your back.'

When the dragon heard these words he stood quite still in the middle of the road, for he knew he had met his match.

'But you will have to fight me first,' he said in a trembling voice, for when you faced him properly the dragon was not brave at all.

'I fight you?' replied Stan. 'Why, I could slay you with one breath!' Then, stooping to pick up a large cheese which lay at his feet, he added, 'Go and get a stone like this out of the river so we may lose no time in seeing who is the better man.'

The dragon did as Stan bade him and brought back a stone out of the brook.

'Can you get buttermilk out of your stone?' asked Stan.

The dragon picked up his stone with one hand and squeezed it till it fell into powder, but no buttermilk flowed from it. 'Of course I can't!' he said angrily.

'Well, if you can't, I can,' answered Stan, and he pressed the cheese till buttermilk flowed through his fingers.

When the dragon saw that, he thought it was time he made the best of his way home again, but Stan stood in his path.

'We have still some accounts to settle,' said he, 'about what you have been doing here.' And the poor dragon was too frightened to stir, lest Stan should slay him at one breath and bury him among the flowers in the mountain pastures.

'Listen to me,' he said at last. 'I see you are a very useful person and my mother has need of a fellow like you. Suppose you enter her service for three days, which are as long as one of your years, and she will pay you each day seven sacks full of ducats.'

Three times seven sacks full of ducats! The offer was very tempting, and Stan could not resist it. He did not waste words, but nodded to the dragon, and they started along the road.

It was a long, long way, but when they came to the end they found the dragon's mother, who was as old as time itself, expecting them. Stan saw her eyes shining like lamps from afar, and when they entered the house they beheld a huge kettle standing on the fire, filled with milk. When the old mother found that her son had arrived empty-handed she grew very angry, and fire and flame darted from her nostrils, but before she could speak the dragon turned to Stan.

'Stay here,' said he, 'and wait for me. I am going to explain things to my mother.'

Stan was already repenting bitterly that he had ever come to such a place, but since he was there, there was nothing for it but to take everything quietly and not show that he was afraid.

'Listen, mother,' said the dragon as soon as they were alone. 'I have brought this man in order to get rid of him. He is a terrific fellow who eats rocks and can press buttermilk out of a stone.' And he told her all that had happened the night before.

'Oh, just leave him to me!' said the dragon's mother. 'I have never yet let a man slip through my fingers.' So Stan had to stay and do her service.

The next day she told him that he and her son should try which

was the stronger, and she took down a huge club, bound seven times
with iron.

The dragon picked it up as if it had been a feather, and after
whirling it round his head, flung it lightly three miles away, telling
Stan to beat that if he could.

They walked to the spot where the club lay. Stan stooped and felt
it; then a great fear came over him, for he knew that he and all his
children together would never lift that club from the ground.

'What are you doing?' asked the dragon.

'I was thinking what a beautiful club it was and what a pity it is
that it should cause your death.'

'How do you mean – my death?' asked the dragon.

'Only that I am afraid that if I throw it you will never see another
dawn. You don't know how strong I am!'

'Oh, never mind that; be quick and throw.'

'If you are really in earnest, let us go and feast for three days:
that will at any rate give you three extra days of life.'

Stan spoke so calmly that this time the dragon began to be a little
frightened, though he did not quite believe that things could be as
bad as Stan said.

They returned to the house, took all the food that could be found
in the old mother's larder, and carried it back to the place where the
club was lying. Then Stan seated himself on the sack of provisions and
remained quietly watching the setting moon.

'What are you doing?' asked the dragon.

'Waiting till the moon gets out of my way.'

'What do you mean? I don't understand.'

'Don't you see that the moon is exactly in my way? But, of course,
if you like, I will throw the club into the moon.'

At these words the dragon grew uncomfortable for the second time.
He prized the club, which had been left him by his grandfather, very
highly, and had no desire that it should be lost in the moon.

'I'll tell you what,' he said, after thinking a little. 'Don't throw the
club at all. I will throw it a second time and that will do just as well.'

'No, certainly not!' replied Stan. 'Just wait till the moon
sets.'

But the dragon, in dread lest Stan should fulfil his threats, tried what bribes could do, and in the end had to promise Stan seven sacks of ducats before he was suffered to throw back the club himself.

'Oh, dear me, that is indeed a strong man,' said the dragon, turning to his mother. 'Would you believe that I have had the greatest difficulty in preventing him from throwing the club into the moon?'

Then the old woman grew afraid too. Only to think of it! It was no joke to throw things into the moon! So no more was heard of the club, and the next day they had all something else to think about.

'Go and fetch me water!' said the mother, when the morning broke, and gave them twelve buffalo skins with the order to keep filling them till night.

They set out at once for the brook, and in the twinkling of an eye the dragon had filled the whole twelve, carried them into the house, and brought them back to Stan. Stan was tired; he could scarcely lift the buckets when they were empty and he shuddered to think of what would happen when they were full. But he only took an old knife out of his pocket and began to scratch up the earth near the brook.

'What are you doing there? How are you going to carry the water into the house?' asked the dragon.

'How? Dear me, that is easy enough! I shall just take the brook!'

At these words the dragon's jaw dropped. This was the last thing that had ever entered his head, for the brook had been as it was since the days of his grandfather.

'I'll tell you what,' he said. 'Let me carry your skins for you.'

'Most certainly not,' answered Stan, going on with his digging. The dragon, in dread lest he should fulfil his threat, tried what bribes would do, and in the end had again to promise seven sacks of ducats before Stan would agree to leave the brook alone and let the dragon carry the water into the house.

On the third day the old mother sent Stan into the forest for wood and, as usual, the dragon went with him. Before you could count three he had pulled up more trees than Stan could have cut down in a lifetime, and had arranged them neatly in rows. When the dragon had finished, Stan began to look about him and, choosing the biggest tree, he climbed up it and, breaking off a long rope of wild vine, bound the top of the tree to the one next it. And so he did to a whole line of trees.

'What are you doing there?' asked the dragon.

'You can see for yourself,' answered Stan, going quietly on with his work.

'Why are you tying the trees together?'

'Not to give myself unnecessary work; when I pull up one, all the others will come up too.'

'But how will you carry them home?'

'Dear me! Don't you understand that I am going to take the whole forest back with me?' said Stan, tying two other trees as he spoke.

'I'll tell you what,' cried the dragon, trembling with fear at the thought of such a thing, 'let me carry the wood for you and you shall have seven times seven sacks full of ducats.'

'You are a good fellow and I agree to your proposal,' answered Stan, and the dragon carried the wood.

Now the three days' service, which were to be reckoned as a year, were over, and the only thing that disturbed Stan was how to get all those ducats back to his home.

In the evening the dragon and his mother had a long talk, but Stan heard every word through a crack in the ceiling.

'Woe be to us, mother,' said the dragon. 'This man will soon get us into his power. Give him his money, and let us be rid of him.'

But the old mother was fond of money, and did not like this. 'Listen to me,' said she, 'you must kill him this very night.'

'I am afraid,' answered the dragon.

'There is nothing to fear,' replied the old mother. 'When he is asleep take the club and hit him on the head with it. It is easily done.'

And so it would have been, had not Stan heard all about it. When the dragon and his mother had put out their lights, he took the pigs' trough and filled it with earth, placed it in his bed, and covered it with clothes. Then he hid himself underneath, and began to snore loudly.

Very soon the dragon stole softly into the room and gave a tremendous blow on the spot where Stan's head should have been. Stan groaned loudly from under the bed, and the dragon went away as softly as he had come. Directly he had closed the door, Stan lifted out the trough and lay down himself, after making everything clean and tidy, but he was wise enough not to shut his eyes that night.

The next morning he came into the room where the dragon and his mother were having breakfast.

'Good morning,' said he.

'Good morning. How did you sleep?'

'Oh, very well, but I dreamed that a flea had bitten me and I seem to feel it still.'

The dragon and his mother looked at each other. 'Do you hear that?' whispered he. 'He talks of a flea. I broke my club on his head.'

This time the mother was as frightened as her son. There was nothing to be done with a man like this, and she made all haste to fill the sacks with ducats, to be rid of Stan as soon as possible. But on his side Stan was trembling like an aspen, for he could not lift even one sack from the ground. So he stood still and looked at them.

'What are you standing there for?' asked the dragon.

'Oh, I was standing here because it has just occurred to me that I should like to stay in your service for another year. I am ashamed that when I get home they should see I have brought back so little. I know that they will cry out, "Just look at Stan Bolovan, who in one year has grown as weak as a dragon".'

Here a shriek of dismay was heard from both the dragon and his mother, who declared they would give him seven or even seven times seven the number of sacks if he would only go away.

'I'll tell you what,' said Stan at last. 'I see you don't want me to stay and I should be very sorry to make myself disagreeable. I will go at once, but only on condition that you shall carry the money home yourself that I may not be put to shame before my friends.'

The words were hardly out of his mouth before the dragon had snatched up the sacks and piled them on his back. Then he and Stan set forth.

The way, though really not far, was yet too long for Stan, but at length he heard his children's voices, and stopped short. He did not wish the dragon to know where he lived, lest some day he should come to take back his treasure. Was there nothing he could say to get rid of the monster? Suddenly an idea came into Stan's head, and he turned round.

'I hardly know what to do,' said he. 'I have a hundred children and I am afraid they may do you harm, for they are always ready for a fight. However, I will do my best to protect you.'

A hundred children! That was indeed no joke! The dragon let fall the sacks from terror and then picked them up again. But the children, who had had nothing to eat since their father had left them, came rushing towards him, waving knives in their right hands and forks in their left, and crying, 'Give us dragon's flesh! We will have dragon's flesh!'

At this dreadful sight the dragon waited no longer. He flung down his sacks where he stood and took flight as fast as he could, so terrified at the fate that awaited him that from that day he has never dared to show his face in the world again.

The Stone-Cutter

ONCE UPON a time there lived a stone-cutter, who went every day to a great rock in the side of a big mountain and cut out slabs of stone for gravestones or for houses. He understood very well the kinds of stones wanted for the different purposes, and as he was a careful workman he had plenty of customers. For a long time he was quite happy and contented, and asked for nothing better than what he had.

Now in the mountain dwelt a spirit which appeared to men now and then, and helped them in many ways to become rich and prosperous. The stone-cutter, however, had never seen this spirit, and only shook his head, with an unbelieving air, when anyone spoke of it. But a time was coming when he learned to change his opinion.

One day the stone-cutter carried a gravestone to the house of a rich man, and saw there all sorts of beautiful things, of which he had never even dreamed. Suddenly his daily work seemed to grow harder and heavier, and he said to himself, 'Oh, if only I were a rich man, and could sleep in a bed with silken curtains and golden tassels, how happy I should be!'

And a voice answered him, 'Your wish is heard; a rich man you shall be!'

At the sound of the voice the stone-cutter looked round, but could see nobody. He thought it was all his fancy, and picked up his tools and went home, for he did not feel inclined to do any more work that day. But when he reached the little house where he lived, he stood still with amazement, for instead of his wooden hut was a stately mansion filled with splendid furniture, and most splendid of all was the bed, in every respect like the one he had envied. He was nearly beside himself with joy, and in his new life the old one was soon forgotten.

It was now the beginning of summer, and each day the sun blazed more fiercely. One morning the heat was so great that the stone-cutter could scarcely breathe, and he determined he would stop at home till the evening. He was rather dull, for he had never learned how to amuse himself, and was peeping through the closed blinds to see what was going on in the street, when a little carriage passed by, drawn by servants dressed in blue and silver. In the carriage sat a prince, and over his head a golden umbrella was held, to protect him from the sun's rays.

'Oh, if I were only a prince!' said the stone-cutter to himself, as the carriage vanished round the corner. 'Oh, if I were only a prince, and could go in such a carriage and have a golden umbrella held over me, how happy I should be!'

And the voice of the mountain spirit answered, 'Your wish is heard; a prince you shall be.'

And a prince he was. Before his carriage rode one company of men and another behind it; servants dressed in scarlet and gold bore him along, the coveted umbrella was held over his head, everything heart could desire was his. But yet it was not enough. He looked round still for something to wish for, and when he saw that in spite of the water he poured on his grass the rays of the sun scorched it, and that in spite of the umbrella held over his head each day his face grew browner and browner, he cried in his anger, 'The sun is mightier than I; oh, if I were only the sun!'

And the mountain spirit answered, 'Your wish is heard; the sun you shall be.'

And the sun he was, and felt himself proud in his power. He directed his beams above and below, on earth and in heaven; he burnt up the grass in the fields and scorched the faces of princes as well as of poorer folk. But in a short time he began to grow tired of his might, for there seemed nothing left for him to do. Discontent once more filled his soul, and when a cloud covered his face and hid the earth from him, he cried in his anger, 'Does the cloud hold captive my rays, and is it mightier than I? Oh, that I were a cloud, and mightier than any!'

And the mountain spirit answered, 'Your wish is heard; a cloud you shall be!'

And a cloud he was, and lay between the sun and the earth. He caught the sun's beams and held them, and to his joy the earth grew green again and flowers blossomed. But that was not enough for him, and for days and weeks he poured forth rain till the rivers overflowed their banks, and the crops of rice stood in water. Towns and villages were destroyed by the power of the rain, only the great rock on the mountain-side remained unmoved. The cloud was amazed at the sight and cried in wonder, 'Is the rock, then, mightier than I? Oh, if I were only the rock!'

And the mountain spirit answered, 'Your wish is heard; the rock you shall be!'

And the rock he was, and gloried in his power. Proudly he stood, and neither the heat of the sun nor the force of the rain could move him. 'This is better than all!' he said to himself. But one day he heard a strange noise at his feet, and when he looked down to see what it could be, he saw a stone-cutter driving tools into his surface. Even while he looked a trembling feeling ran all through him, and a great block broke off and fell upon the ground. Then he cried in his wrath, 'Is a mere child of earth mightier than a rock? Oh, if I were only a man!'

And the mountain spirit answered, 'Your wish is heard. A man once more you shall be!'

And a man he was, and in the sweat of his brow he toiled again at his trade of stone-cutting. His bed was hard and his food scanty, but he had learned to be satisfied with it, and did not long to be something or somebody else. And as he never asked for things he had not got, or desired to be greater and mightier than other people, he was happy at last, and heard the voice of the mountain spirit no more.

The Story of the Fisherman and his Wife

THERE WAS once a fisherman and his wife who lived together in a little hut close to the sea, and the fisherman used to go down every day to fish; and he would fish and fish. So he used to sit with his rod and gaze into the shining water; and he would gaze and gaze.

Now, once the line was pulled deep under the water, and when he hauled it up he hauled a large flounder with it. The flounder said to him, 'Listen, fisherman. I pray you to let me go; I am not a real flounder, I am an enchanted prince. What good will it do you if you kill me? I shall not taste nice. Put me back into the water and let me swim away.'

'Well,' said the man, 'you need not make so much noise about it; I am sure I had much better let a flounder that can talk swim away.' With these words he put him back again into the shining water, and the flounder sank to the bottom, leaving a long streak of blood behind. Then the fisherman got up, and went home to his wife in the hut.

'Husband,' said his wife, 'have you caught nothing to-day?'

'No,' said the man. 'I caught a flounder who said he was an enchanted prince, so I let him swim away again.'

'Did you wish nothing from him?' said his wife.

'No,' said the man. 'What should I have wished from him?'

'Oh!' said the woman, 'it's dreadful to have to live all one's life in this hut that is so small and dirty; you ought to have wished for a cottage. Go now and call him; say to him that we choose to have a cottage, and he will certainly give it you.'

'Alas!' said the man, 'why should I go down there again?'

'Why,' said his wife, 'you caught him, and then let him go again, so he is sure to give you what you ask. Go down quickly.'

The man did not like going at all, but as his wife was not to be persuaded, he went down to the sea.

When he came there the sea was quite green and yellow, and was no longer shining. So he stood on the shore and said:

> 'Once a prince, but changed you be
> Into a flounder in the sea.
> Come! for my wife, Isabel,
> Wishes what I dare not tell.'

Then the flounder came swimming up and said, 'Well, what does she want?'

'Alas!' said the man, 'my wife says I ought to have kept you and wished something from you. She does not want to live any longer in the hut; she would like a cottage.'

'Go home, then,' said the flounder; 'she has it.'

So the man went home, and there was his wife no longer in the hut, but in its place was a beautiful cottage, and his wife was sitting in front of the door on a bench. She took him by the hand and said to him, 'Come inside, and see if this is not much better.' They went in, and inside the cottage was a tiny hall, and a beautiful sitting-room, and a bedroom in which stood a bed, a kitchen and a dining-room all furnished with the best of everything, and fitted up with every kind of tin and copper utensil. And outside was a little yard in which were chickens and ducks, and also a little garden with vegetables and fruit trees.

'See,' said the wife, 'isn't this nice?'

'Yes,' answered her husband; 'here we shall remain and live very happily.'

'We will think about that,' said his wife.

With these words they had their supper and went to bed. All went well for a week or a fortnight, then the wife said, 'Listen, husband; the cottage is much too small, and so is the yard and the garden; the flounder might just as well have sent us a larger house. I should like to live in a great stone castle. Go down to the flounder, and tell him to send us a castle.'

'Ah, wife!' said the fisherman, 'the cottage is quite good enough; why should we live in a castle?'

'I want to,' said the wife. 'You go down; the flounder can quite well do it.'

'No, wife,' said the man; 'the flounder gave us the cottage. I do not like to go to him again so soon; he might take it amiss.'

'Go,' said his wife. 'He can certainly give it to us, and ought to do so willingly. Go at once.'

The fisherman's heart was very heavy, and he did not like going. He said to himself, 'It is not right.' Still, he went.

When he came down to the sea, the water was all violet and dark-blue, and dull and thick, and no longer green and yellow, but it was still smooth.

So he stood there and said:

> 'Once a prince, but changed you be
> Into a flounder in the sea.
> Come! for my wife, Isabel,
> Wishes what I dare not tell.'

'What does she want now?' said the flounder.

'Oh!' said the fisherman, half-ashamed, 'she wants to live in a great stone castle.'

'Go home; she is standing before the door,' said the flounder.

The fisherman went home and found his wife standing on the steps of a great stone castle, about to enter. She took him by the hand and said, 'Come inside.'

Then he went with her, and inside the castle was a large hall with a marble floor, and there were many servants who threw open the great doors, and the walls were covered with beautiful tapestry, and in the apartments were gilded chairs and tables, and crystal chandeliers hung from the ceiling, and all the rooms were beautifully carpeted. The best of food and drink also was set before them when they wished to dine. And outside the house was a large courtyard with horse and cow stables and a coach-house – all fine buildings; and a splendid garden with most beautiful flowers and fruit, and in a park quite a league long were stags and deer and hares, and everything one could wish for.

'Now,' said the wife, 'isn't this beautiful?'

'Yes, indeed,' said the fisherman. 'Now we will stay here and live in this beautiful castle, and be very happy.'

'We will consider the matter,' said his wife, and they went to bed.

The next morning the wife woke up first at daybreak, and looked out of the bed at the beautiful country stretched before her. Her husband was still sleeping, so she dug her elbows into his side and said, 'Husband, get up and look out of the window. Could we not become king of all this land? Go down to the flounder and tell him we choose to be king.'

'Oh, wife!' replied her husband, 'why should we be king? I don't want to be king.'

'Well,' said his wife, 'if you don't want to be king, *I* will be king. Go down to the flounder; I will be king.'

'Alas! wife,' said the fisherman, 'why do you want to be king? I can't ask him that.'

'And why not?' said his wife. 'Go down at once. I must be king.'

So the fisherman went, though much vexed that his wife wanted to be king. 'It is not right! It is not right,' he thought. He did not wish to go, yet he went.

When he came to the sea, the water was a dark-grey colour, and it was heaving against the shore. So he stood and said:

> 'Once a prince, but changed you be
> Into a flounder in the sea.
> Come! for my wife, Isabel,
> Wishes what I dare not tell.'

'What does she want now?' asked the flounder.

'Alas!' said the fisherman, 'she wants to be king.'

'Go home; she is that already,' said the flounder.

The fisherman went home, and when he came near the castle he saw that it had become much larger, and that it had great towers and splendid ornamental carving on it. A sentinel was standing before the gate, and there were numbers of soldiers with kettledrums and trumpets. And when he went into the palace, he found everything was of pure marble and gold, and the curtains of damask with tassels of gold. Then the doors of the hall flew open, and there stood the whole Court round his wife, who was sitting on a high throne of gold and diamonds; she wore a great golden crown, and had a sceptre of gold and precious stones in her hand, and on either side stood six pages in a row, each one a head taller than the other. Then he went before her and said, 'Oh, wife! are you king now?'

'Yes,' said his wife. 'Now I am king.'

He stood looking at her, and when he had looked for some time, he said, 'Let that be enough, wife, now that you are king! Now we have nothing more to wish for.'

'Nay, husband,' said his wife restlessly, 'my wishing powers are boundless; I cannot restrain them any longer. Go down to the flounder; king I am, now I must be emperor.'

'Alas! wife,' said the fisherman, 'why do you want to be emperor?'

'Husband,' said she, 'go to the flounder; I *will* be emperor.'

'Oh, wife,' he said, 'he cannot make you emperor; I don't like to ask him that. There is only one emperor in the land. Indeed and indeed he cannot make you emperor.'

'What!' said his wife. 'I am king, and you are my husband. Will you go at once? Go! If he can make king he can make emperor, and emperor I must and will be. Go!'

So he had to go. But as he went, he felt quite frightened, and he thought to himself, 'This can't be right; to be emperor is too ambitious; the flounder will be tired out at last.'

Thinking this he came to the shore. The sea was quite black and thick, and it was breaking high on the beach; the foam was flying about, and the wind was blowing; everything looked bleak. The fisherman was chilled with fear. He stood and said:

> 'Once a prince, but changed you be
> Into a flounder in the sea.
> Come! for my wife, Isabel,
> Wishes what I dare not tell.'

'What does she want now?' asked the flounder.

'Alas! flounder,' he said, 'my wife wants to be emperor.'

'Go home,' said the flounder; 'she is that already.'

So the fisherman went home, and when he came there he saw the whole castle was made of polished marble, ornamented with alabaster statues and gold. Before the gate soldiers were marching, blowing trumpets and beating drums. Inside the palace barons, counts, and dukes were acting as servants; they opened the door, which was of beaten gold. And when he entered, he saw his wife upon a throne which was made out of a single block of gold, and which was quite six cubits high. She had on a great golden crown which was three yards high and set with brilliants and sparkling gems. In one hand she held a sceptre, and in the other the imperial globe, and on either side of her stood two rows of halberdiers, each smaller than the other, from a seven-foot giant to the tiniest little dwarf no higher than my little finger. Many princes and dukes were standing before her. The fisherman went up to her quietly and said, 'Wife, are you emperor now?'

'Yes,' she said, 'I am emperor.'

He stood looking at her magnificence, and when he had watched her for some time, said, 'Oh, wife, let that be enough, now that you are emperor.'

'Husband,' said she, 'why are you standing there? I am emperor now, and I want to be pope too; go down to the flounder.'

'Alas! wife,' said the fisherman, 'what more do you want? You cannot be pope; there is only one pope in Christendom, and the flounder cannot make you that.'

'Husband,' she said, 'I *will* be pope. Go down quickly; I must be pope to-day.'

'No, wife,' said the fisherman; 'I can't ask him that. It is not right; it is too much. The flounder cannot make you pope.'

'Husband, what nonsense!' said his wife. 'If he can make emperor, he can make pope too. Go down this instant; I am emperor and you are my husband. Will you be off at once?'

So he was frightened and went out; but he felt quite faint, and trembled and shook, and his knees and legs began to give way under him. The wind was blowing fiercely across the land, and the clouds flying across the sky looked as black as night; the leaves were being blown from the trees; the water was foaming and seething and dashing upon the shore, and in the distance he saw the ships in great distress, dancing and tossing on the waves. Still the sky was very blue in the middle, although at the sides it was an angry red as in a great storm. So he stood shuddering in fear, and cried:

> 'Once a prince, but changed you be
> Into a flounder in the sea.
> Come! for my wife, Isabel,
> Wishes what I dare not tell.'

'Well, what does she want now?' asked the flounder.

'Alas!' said the fisherman, 'she wants to be pope.'

'Go home, then; she is that already,' said the flounder.

Then he went home, and when he came there he saw, as it were, a large church surrounded by palaces. He pushed his way through the people. The interior was lit up with thousands and thousands of candles, and his wife was dressed in cloth of gold and was sitting on a much higher throne, and she wore three great golden crowns.

Round her stood many Church dignitaries, and on either side were two rows of tapers, the largest of them as tall as a steeple, and the smallest as tiny as a Christmas-tree candle. All the emperors and kings were on their knees before her, and were kissing her foot.

'Wife,' said the fisherman, looking at her, 'are you pope now?'

'Yes,' said she; 'I am pope.'

So he stood staring at her, and it was as if he were looking at the bright sun. When he had watched her for some time he said, 'Oh, wife, let it be enough now that you are pope.'

But she sat up stiff and straight, and did not move or speak. He said again, 'Wife, be content now that you are pope. You cannot become anything more.'

'We will think about that,' said his wife.

With these words they went to bed. But the woman was not content; her greed would not allow her to sleep, and she kept on thinking and thinking what she could still become. The fisherman slept well and soundly, for he had done a great deal that day, but his wife could not sleep at all, and turned from one side to another the whole night long, and thought, till she could think no longer, what more she could become. Then the sun began to rise, and when she saw the red dawn she went to the window and looked out of it, and as she was watching the sun rise, she thought, 'Ha! could I not make the sun and moon rise?'

'Husband,' said she, poking him in the ribs with her elbows, 'wake up. Go down to the flounder; I will be a god.'

The fisherman was still half asleep, yet he was so frightened that he fell out of bed. He thought he had not heard aright, and opened his eyes wide and said, 'What did you say, wife?'

'Husband,' she said, 'if I cannot make the sun and moon rise when I wish I cannot rest. I shall never have a quiet moment till I can make the sun and moon rise.'

He looked at her in horror, and a shudder ran over him.

'Go down at once; I will be a god.'

'Alas! wife,' said the fisherman, falling on his knees before her, 'the flounder cannot do that. Emperor and pope he can make you. I implore you, be content and remain pope.'

Then she flew into a passion, her hair hung wildly about her face, she kicked him with her foot and screamed, 'I am not contented, and I shall not be contented! Will you go?'

So he hurried on his clothes as fast as possible, and ran away as if he were mad.

But the storm was raging so fiercely that he could scarcely stand. Houses and trees were being blown down, the mountains were being shaken, and pieces of rock were rolling in the sea. The sky was as black as ink, it was thundering and lightening, and the sea was tossing in great waves as high as church towers and mountains, and each had a white crest of foam.

So he shouted, not able to hear his own voice:

> 'Once a prince, but changed you be
> Into a flounder in the sea.
> Come! for my wife, Isabel,
> Wishes what I dare not tell.'

'Well, what does she want now?' asked the flounder.
'Alas!' said he, 'she wants to be a god.'
'Go home, then; she is sitting again in the hut.'
And there they are sitting to this day.

The Story of the Seven Simons

FAR, FAR away, beyond all sorts of countries, seas and rivers, there stood a splendid city where lived King Archidej, who was as good as he was rich and handsome. His great army was made up of men ready to obey his slightest wish; he owned forty times forty cities, and in each city he had ten palaces with silver doors, golden roofs, and crystal windows. His council consisted of the twelve wisest men in the country, whose long beards flowed down over their breasts, each of whom was as learned as a whole college. This council always told the King the exact truth.

Now the King had everything to make him happy, but he did not enjoy anything because he could not find a bride to his mind.

One day, as he sat in his palace looking out to sea, a great ship sailed into the harbour and several merchants came on shore. Said the King to himself, 'These people have travelled far and beheld many lands. I will ask them if they have seen any princess who is as clever and as handsome as I am.'

So he ordered the merchants to be brought before him, and when they came he said, 'You have travelled much and visited many wonders. I wish to ask you a question, and I beg you to answer truthfully.

'Have you anywhere seen or heard of the daughter of an emperor, king, or prince, who is as clever and as handsome as I am, and who would be worthy to be my wife and queen of my country?'

The merchants considered for some time. At last the eldest of them said, 'I have heard that across many seas, in the island of Busan, there is a mighty king, whose daughter, the Princess Helena, is so lovely that she can certainly not be plainer than your Majesty, and so clever that the wisest greybeard cannot guess her riddles.'

'Is the island far off, and which is the way to it?'

'It is not near,' was the answer. 'The journey would take ten years,' and we do not know the way. And even if we did, what use would that be? The Princess is no bride for you.'

'How dare you say so?' cried the King angrily.

'Your Majesty must pardon us; but just think for a moment. Should you send an envoy to the island he will take ten years to get there and ten more to return – twenty years in all. Will not the Princess have grown old in that time and have lost all her beauty?'

The King reflected gravely. Then he thanked the merchants, gave them leave to trade in his country without paying any duties, and dismissed them.

After they were gone the King remained deep in thought. He felt puzzled and anxious; so he decided to ride into the country to distract his mind, and sent for his huntsmen and falconers. The huntsmen blew their horns, the falconers took their hawks on their wrists, and off they all set out across country till they came to a green hedge. On the other side of the hedge stretched a great field of maize as far as the eye could reach, and the yellow ears swayed to and fro in the gentle breeze like a rippling sea of gold.

The King drew rein and admired the field. 'Upon my word,' said he, 'whoever dug and planted it must be good workmen. If all the fields in my kingdom were as well cared for as this, there would be more bread than my people could eat.' And he wished to know to whom the field belonged.

Off rushed all his followers at once to do his bidding, and found a nice, tidy farmhouse, in front of which sat seven peasants, eating rye bread and drinking water. They wore red shirts bound with gold braid, and were so much alike that one could hardly tell one from another.

The messengers asked, 'Who owns this field of golden maize?' And the seven brothers answered, 'The field is ours.'

'And who are you?'

'We are King Archidej's labourers.'

These answers were repeated to the King, who ordered the brothers to be brought before him at once. On being asked who they were, the eldest said, bowing low, 'We, King Archidej, are your labourers, children of one father and mother, and we all have the same name, for each of us is called Simon. Our father taught us to be true to our king, and to till the ground, and to be kind to our neighbours. He also taught each of us a different trade which he thought might be useful to us, and he bade us not neglect mother earth, who would be sure amply to repay our labour.'

The King was pleased with the honest peasant, and said, 'You have done well, good people, in planting your field, and now you have a golden harvest. But I should like each of you to tell me what special trades your father taught you.'

'My trade, O King!' said the first Simon, 'is not an easy one. If you will give me some workmen and materials, I will build you a great white pillar that shall reach far above the clouds.'

'Very good,' replied the King. 'And you, Simon the second, what is your trade?'

'Mine, your Majesty, needs no great cleverness. When my brother has built the pillar I can mount it, and from the top, far above the clouds, I can see what is happening in every country under the sun.'

'Good,' said the King. 'And Simon the third?'

'My work is very simple, sire. You have many ships built by

learned men, with all sorts of new and clever improvements. If you wish it I will build you quite a simple boat – one, two, three, and it's done! But my plain little home-made ship is not grand enough for a king. Where other ships take a year, mine makes the voyage in a day, and where they would require ten years mine will do the distance in a week.'

'Good,' said the King again. 'And what has Simon the fourth learnt?'

'My trade, O King, is really of no importance. Should my brother build you a ship, then let me embark in it. If we should be pursued by an enemy I can seize our boat by the prow and sink it to the bottom of the sea. When the enemy has sailed off, I can draw it up to the top again.'

'That is very clever of you,' answered the King. 'And what does Simon the fifth do?'

'My work, your Majesty, is mere smith's work. Order me to build a smithy and I will make you a cross-bow, but from which neither the eagle in the sky nor the wild beast in the forest is safe. The bolt hits whatever the eye sees.'

'That sounds very useful,' said the King. 'And now, Simon the sixth, tell me your trade.'

'Sire, it is so simple I am almost ashamed to mention it. If my brother hits any creature I catch it quicker than any dog can. If it falls into the water I pick it up out of the greatest depths, and if it is in a dark forest I can find it even at midnight.'

The King was much pleased with the trades and speech of the six brothers, and said, 'Thank you, good people; your father did well to teach you all these things. Now follow me to the town, as I want to see what you can do. I need such people as you about me; but when harvest time comes I will send you home with royal presents.'

The brothers bowed and said, 'As the King wills.' Suddenly the King remembered that he had not questioned the seventh Simon, so he turned to him and said, 'Why are you silent? What is your handicraft?'

And the seventh Simon answered, 'I have no handicraft, O King; I have learnt nothing. I could not manage it. And if I *do* know how to do anything it is not what might properly be called a trade – it is rather a sort of performance; but it is one which no one – not the King himself – must watch me doing, and I doubt whether this performance of mine would please your Majesty.'

'Come, come,' cried the King. 'I will have no excuses, what is this trade?'

'First, sire, give me your royal word that you will not kill me when I have told you. Then you shall hear.'

'So be it, then; I give you my royal word.'

Then the seventh Simon stepped back a little, cleared his throat, and said, 'My trade, King Archidej, is of such a kind that the man who follows it in your kingdom generally loses his life and has no hopes of pardon. There is only one thing I can do really well, and that is – to steal, and to hide the smallest scrap of anything I have stolen. Not the deepest vault, even if its lock were enchanted, could prevent my stealing from it anything that I wished to have.'

When the King heard this he fell into a passion. 'I will *not* pardon you, you rascal,' he cried; 'I will shut you up in my deepest dungeon on bread and water till you have forgotten such a trade. Indeed, it would be better to put you to death at once, and I've a good mind to do so.'

'Don't kill me, O King! I am really not as bad as you think. Why, had I chosen, I could have robbed the royal treasury, have bribed your judges to let me off, and built a white marble palace with what was left. But though I know how to steal I don't do it. You yourself asked me my trade. If you kill me you will break your royal word.'

'Very well,' said the King. 'I will not kill you. I pardon you. But from this hour you shall be shut up in a dark dungeon. Here, guards! Away with him to the prison. But you six Simons follow me and be assured of my royal favour.'

So the six Simons followed the King. The seventh Simon was seized by the guards, who put him in chains, and threw him in prison with only bread and water for food. Next day the King gave the first Simon carpenters, masons, smiths and labourers, with great stores of iron, mortar, and the like, and Simon began to build. And he built his great white pillar far, far up into the clouds, as high as the nearest stars; but the other stars were higher still.

Then the second Simon climbed up the pillar and saw and heard

all that was going on through the whole world. When he came down
he had all sorts of wonderful things to tell. How one king was
marching in battle against another, and which was likely to be the
victor. How, in another place, great rejoicings were going on, while
in a third people were dying of famine. In fact there was not the
smallest event going on over the earth that was hidden from him.

Next the third Simon began. He stretched out his arms, once, twice,
thrice, and the wonder-ship was ready. At a sign from the King it
was launched, and floated proudly and safely like a bird on the waves.
Instead of ropes it had wires for rigging, and musicians played on
them with fiddle bows and made lovely music. As the ship swam
about, the fourth Simon seized the prow with his strong hand, and
in a moment it was gone – sunk to the bottom of the sea. An hour
passed, and then the ship floated again, drawn up by Simon's left
hand, while in his right he brought a gigantic fish from the depth of
the ocean for the royal table.

Whilst this was going on the fifth Simon had built his forge and
hammered out his iron, and when the King returned from the harbour
the magic cross-bow was made.

His Majesty went out into an open field at once, looked up into
the' sky and saw, far, far away, an eagle flying up towards the sun and
looking like a little speck.

'Now,' said the King, 'if you can shoot that bird I will reward you.'

Simon only smiled; he lifted his cross-bow, took aim, fired, and
the eagle fell. As it was falling the sixth Simon ran with a dish, caught
the bird before it fell to earth and brought it to the King.

'Many thanks, my brave lads,' said the King; 'I see that each of
you is indeed a master of his trade. You shall be richly rewarded.
But now rest and have your dinner.'

The six Simons bowed and went to dinner. But they had hardly
begun before a messenger came to say that the King wanted to see
them. They obeyed at once and found him surrounded by all his
court and men of state.

'Listen, my good fellows,' cried the King, as soon as he saw them.
'Hear what my wise councillors have thought of. As you, Simon the
second, can see the whole world from the top of the great pillar, I
want you to climb up and to see and hear. For I am told that, far

away, across many seas, is the great kingdom of the island of Busan, and that the daughter of the King is the beautiful Princess Helena.'

Off ran the second Simon and clambered quickly up the pillar. He gazed around, listened on all sides, and then slid down to report to the King.

'Sire, I have obeyed your orders. Far away I saw the island of Busan. The King is a mighty monarch, but full of pride, and harsh and cruel. He sits on his throne and declares that no prince or king on earth is good enough for his lovely daughter, that he will give her to none, and that if any king asks for her hand he will declare war against him and destroy his kingdom.'

'Has the King of Busan a great army?' asked King Archidej. 'Is his country far off?'

'As far as I could judge,' replied Simon, 'it would take you nearly ten years in fair weather to sail there. But if the weather were stormy we might say twelve. I saw the army being reviewed. It is not so *very* large – a hundred thousand men at arms and a hundred thousand knights. Besides these, he has a strong bodyguard and a good many cross-bowmen. Altogether you may say another hundred thousand, and there is a picked body of heroes who reserve themselves for great occasions requiring particular courage.'

The King sat for some time lost in thought. At last he said to the nobles and courtiers standing round, 'I am determined to marry the Princess Helena, but how shall I do it?'

The nobles, courtiers and councillors said nothing, but tried to hide behind each other. Then the third Simon said, 'Pardon me, your Majesty, if I offer my advice. You wish to go to the island of Busan? What can be easier? In my ship you will get there in a week instead of in ten years. But ask your council to advise you what to do when you arrive – in one word, whether you will try to win the Princess peacefully or by war?'

But the wise men were as silent as ever.

The King frowned, and was about to say something sharp, when the Court Fool pushed his way to the front and said, 'Dear me, what are all you clever people so puzzled about? The matter is quite clear. As it seems it will not take long to reach the island why not send the seventh Simon? He will steal the fair maiden fast enough, and then the King, her father, may consider how he is going to bring his army over here – it will take him ten years to do it! – no less! What do you think of my plan?'

'What do I think? Why, that your idea is capital, and you shall be rewarded for it. Come, guards, hurry as fast as you can and bring the seventh Simon before me.'

Not many minutes later, Simon the seventh stood before the King, who explained to him what he wished done, and also that to steal for the benefit of his king and country was by no means a wrong thing, though it was very wrong to steal for his own advantage.

The youngest Simon, who looked very pale and hungry, only nodded his head.

'Come,' said the King, 'tell me truly. Do you think you could steal the Princess Helena?'

'Why should I not steal her, sire? The thing is easy enough. Let my brother's ship be laden with rich stuffs, brocades, Persian carpets, pearls and jewels. Send me in the ship. Give me my four middle brothers as companions, and keep the two others as hostages.'

When the King heard these words his heart became filled with longing, and he ordered all to be done as Simon wished. Everyone ran about to do his bidding; and in next to no time the wonder-ship was laden and ready to start.

The five Simons took leave of the King, went on board, and had no sooner set sail than they were almost out of sight. The ship cut through the waters like a falcon through the air, and just a week after starting they sighted the island of Busan. The coast appeared to be strongly guarded, and from afar the watchman on a high tower called out, 'Halt and anchor! Who are you? Where do you come from, and what do you want?'

The seventh Simon answered from the ship, 'We are peaceful people. We come from the country of the great and good King Archidej, and we bring foreign wares — rich brocades, carpets, and costly jewels, which we wish to show to your king and the Princess. We desire to trade – to sell, to buy, and to exchange.'

The brothers launched a small boat, took some of their valuable goods with them, rowed to shore and went up to the palace. The Princess sat in a rose-red room, and when she saw the brothers coming near she called her nurse and other women, and told them to inquire who and what these people were, and what they wanted.

The seventh Simon answered the nurse. 'We come from the country of the wise and good King Archidej,' he said, 'and we have brought all sorts of goods for sale. We trust the king of this country may condescend to welcome us, and to let his servants take charge of our wares. If he considers them worthy to adorn his followers we shall be content.'

This speech was repeated to the Princess, who ordered the brothers to be brought to the red room at once. They bowed respectfully to her and displayed some splendid velvets and brocades, and opened cases of pearls and precious stones. Such beautiful things had never been seen in the island, and the nurse and waiting women stood bewildered by all the magnificence. They whispered together that they had never beheld anything like it. The Princess too saw and wondered, and her eyes could not weary of looking at the lovely things, or her fingers of stroking the rich soft stuffs, and of holding up the sparkling jewels to the light.

'Fairest of princesses,' said Simon. 'Be pleased to order your waiting-maids to accept the silks and velvets, and let your women trim their head-dresses with the jewels. These are no special treasures, they are as nothing to the many coloured tapestries, the gorgeous stones and ropes of pearls in our ship. We did not like to bring more with us, not knowing what your royal taste might be; but if it seems good to you to honour our ship with a visit, you might condescend to choose such things as were pleasing in your eyes.'

This polite speech pleased the Princess very much. She went to the King and said, 'Dear father, some merchants have arrived with the most splendid wares. Pray allow me to go to their ship and choose out what I like.'

The King thought and thought, frowned hard and rubbed his ear. At last he gave consent, and ordered out his royal yacht, with a hundred cross-bows, a hundred knights, and a thousand soldiers, to escort the Princess Helena.

Off sailed the yacht with the Princess and her escort. The brothers Simon came on board to conduct the Princess to their ship, and, led by the brothers and followed by her nurse and other women, she crossed the crystal plank from one vessel to another.

The seventh Simon spread out his goods, and had so many curious and interesting tales to tell about them, that the Princess forgot everything else in looking and listening, so that she did not know that the fourth Simon had seized the prow of the ship, and that all of a sudden it had vanished from sight, and was racing along in the depths of the sea.

The crew of the royal yacht shouted aloud, the knights stood still with terror, the soldiers were struck dumb and hung their heads. There was nothing to be done but to sail back and tell the King of his loss.

How he wept and stormed! 'Oh, light of my eyes,' he sobbed; 'I am indeed punished for my pride. I thought no one good enough to be your husband, and now you are lost in the depths of the sea, and have left me alone! As for all of them who saw this thing – away with them! Let them be put in irons and lock them up in prison, whilst I think how I can best put them to death!'

Whilst the King of Busan was raging and lamenting in this fashion, Simon's ship was swimming like any fish under the sea, and when the island was well out of sight he brought it up to the surface again. At that moment the Princess recollected herself. 'Nurse,' said she, 'we have been gazing at these wonders only too long. I hope my father won't be vexed at our delay.'

She tore herself away and stepped on deck. Neither the yacht nor the island was in sight! The Princess Helena wrung her hands and beat her breast. Then she changed herself into a white swan and flew off. But the fifth Simon seized his bow and shot the swan, and the sixth Simon did not let it fall into the water but caught it in the ship, and the swan turned into a silver fish, but Simon lost no time and caught the fish when, quick as thought, the fish turned into a black mouse and ran about the ship. It darted towards a hole, but before it could reach it Simon sprang upon it more swiftly than any cat, and then the little mouse turned once more into the beautiful Princess Helena.

Early one morning King Archidej sat thoughtfully at his window gazing out to sea. His heart was sad and he would neither eat nor drink. His thoughts were full of the Princess Helena, who was as lovely as a dream. Is that a white gull he sees flying towards the shore, or is it a sail? No, it is no gull, it is the wonder-ship flying along with billowing sails. Its flags wave, the fiddlers play on the wire rigging, the anchor is thrown out and the crystal plank laid from the ship to the pier. The lovely Helena steps across the plank. She shines like the sun, and the stars of heaven seem to sparkle in her eyes.

Up sprang King Archidej in haste. 'Hurry, hurry,' he cried. 'Let us hasten to meet her! Let the bugles sound and the joy bells be rung!'

And the whole court swarmed with courtiers and servants. Golden carpets were laid down and the great gates thrown open to welcome the Princess.

King Archidej went out himself, took her by the hand and led her into the royal apartments.

'Madam,' said he, 'the fame of your beauty had reached me, but I had not dared to expect such loveliness. Still I will not keep you here against your will. If you wish it, the wonder-ship shall take you back to your father and your own country; but if you will consent to stay here, then reign over me and my country as our queen.'

What more is there to tell? It is not hard to guess that the Princess listened to the King's wooing, and their betrothal took place with great pomp and rejoicings.

The brothers Simon were sent again to the island of Busan with a letter to the King from his daughter to invite him to their wedding, and the wonder-ship arrived at the island of Busan just as all the knights and soldiers who had escorted the Princess were being led out to execution.

Then the seventh Simon cried out from the ship, 'Stop! stop! I bring a letter from the Princess Helena!'

The King of Busan read the letter over and over again, and ordered the knights and soldiers to be set free. He entertained King Archidej's ambassadors hospitably, and sent his blessing to his daughter, but he could not be brought to attend the wedding.

When the wonder-ship got home King Archidej and Princess Helena were enchanted with the news it brought.

The King sent for the seven Simons. 'A thousand thanks to you, my brave fellows,' he cried. 'Take what gold, silver, and precious stones you will out of my treasury. Tell me if there is anything else you wish for and I will give it to you, my good friends. Do you wish to be made nobles, or to govern towns? Only speak.'

Then the eldest Simon bowed and said, 'We are plain folk, your Majesty, and understand simple things best. What figures should we cut as nobles or governors? Nor do we desire gold. We have our fields which give us food, and as much money as we need. If you wish to reward us then grant that our land may be free of taxes, and of your goodness pardon the seventh Simon. He is not the first who has been a thief by trade and he will certainly not be the last.'

'So be it,' said the King; 'your land shall be free of all taxes, and Simon the seventh is pardoned.'

Then the King gave each brother a goblet of wine and invited them to the wedding feast. And *what* a feast that was!

The Swineherd

THERE WAS once a poor prince. He possessed a kingdom which, though small, was yet large enough for him to marry on, and married he wished to be.

Now it was certainly a little audacious of him to venture to say to the Emperor's daughter, 'Will you marry me?' But he did venture to say so, for his name was known far and wide. There were hundreds of princesses who would gladly have said 'Yes', but would she say the same?

Well, we shall see.

On the grave of the Prince's father grew a rose-tree, a very beautiful rose-tree. It only bloomed every five years, and then bore but a single rose, but oh, such a rose! Its scent was so sweet that when you smelt it you forgot all your cares and troubles. And he had also a nightingale which could sing as if all the beautiful melodies in the world were shut up in its little throat. This rose and this nightingale the Princess was to have, and so they were both put into silver caskets and sent to her.

The Emperor had them brought to him in the great hall, where the Princess was playing 'Here comes a duke a-riding' with her ladies-in-waiting. And when she caught sight of the big caskets which contained the presents, she clapped her hands for joy.

'If only it were a little pussy-cat!' she said. But the rose-tree with the beautiful rose came out.

'But how prettily it is made!' said all the ladies-in-waiting.

'It is more than pretty,' said the Emperor, 'it is charming!'

But the Princess felt it, and then she almost began to cry.

'Ugh! Papa,' she said, 'it is not artificial, it is *real*!'

'Ugh!' said all the ladies-in-waiting, 'it is real!'

'Let us see first what is in the other casket before we begin to be angry,' said the Emperor, and then out came the nightingale. It sang so beautifully that no one could utter a cross word against it.

'*Superbe! charmant!*' said the ladies-in-waiting, for they all chattered French, each one worse than the other.

'How much the bird reminds me of the musical snuff-box of the late Empress!' said an old courtier. 'Ah, yes, it is the same tone, the same execution!'

'Yes,' said the Emperor; and then he wept like a little child.

'I hope that this, at least, is not real?' asked the Princess.

'Yes, it is a real bird,' said those who had brought it.

'Then let the bird fly away,' said the Princess, and she would not on any account allow the Prince to come.

But he was nothing daunted. He painted his face brown and black, drew his cap well over his face, and knocked at the door. 'Good-day, Emperor,' he said. 'Can I get a place here as servant in the castle?'

'Well,' said the Emperor, 'there are so many who ask for a place that I don't know whether there will be one for you; but, still, let me think. Yes, it has just occurred to me that I want someone to look after the pigs, for I have so very many of them.'

And the Prince got the situation of Imperial Swineherd. He had a

wretched little room close to the pigsties; here he had to live, but the
whole day he sat working, and when evening was come he had made a
pretty little pot. All round it were bells, and when the pot boiled they
jingled most beautifully and played the old tune:

> 'Where is Augustus dear?
> Alas! he's not here, here, here!'

But the wonderful thing was, that when one held one's finger in the
steam of the pot, then at once one could smell what dinner was ready
in any fire-place in the town. That was indeed something quite
different from the rose and the nightingale.

Now the Princess came walking past with all her ladies-in-waiting,
and when she heard the tune she stood still and her face beamed with
joy, for she also could play 'Where is Augustus dear?'

It was the only tune she knew, and she could play it with one
finger.

'Why, that is what I play!' she said. 'He must be a most accomplished swineherd! Listen! Go down and ask him what the instrument
costs.'

And one of the ladies-in-waiting had to go down; but she first
put on wooden clogs. 'What will you take for the pot?' asked the
lady-in-waiting.

'I will have ten kisses from the Princess,' answered the swineherd.

'Heaven forbid!' said the lady-in-waiting.

'Yes, I will sell it for nothing less,' replied the swineherd.

'Well, what does he say?' asked the Princess.

'I really hardly like to tell you,' answered the lady-in-waiting.

'Oh, then you can whisper it to me. . . .'

'He is disobliging!' said the Princess, and went away. But she
had only gone a few steps when the bells rang out so prettily:

> 'Where is Augustus dear?
> Alas! he's not here, here, here.'

'Listen!' said the Princess. 'Ask him whether he will take ten
kisses from my ladies-in-waiting.'

'No, thank you,' said the swineherd. 'Ten kisses from the Princess,
or else I keep my pot.'

'That is very tiresome!' said the Princess. 'But you must put yourselves in front of me, so that no one can see.'

And the ladies-in-waiting placed themselves in front and then spread out their dresses; so the swineherd got his ten kisses, and she got the pot.

What happiness that was! The whole night and the whole day the pot was made to boil; there was not a kitchen in the whole town where they did not know what was being cooked, whether it was at the chancellor's or at the shoemaker's.

The ladies-in-waiting danced and clapped their hands.

'We know who is going to have soup and pancakes; we know who is going to have porridge and sausages – isn't it interesting?'

'Yes, very interesting!' said the first lady-in-waiting.

'But don't say anything about it, for I am the Emperor's daughter.'

'Oh, no, of course we won't!' said everyone.

The swineherd – that is to say, the Prince (though they did not know he was anything but a true swineherd) – let no day pass without making something, and one day he made a rattle which, when it was turned round, played all the waltzes, galops, and polkas which had ever been known since the world began.

'But that is *superbe*!' said the Princess as she passed by. 'I have never heard a more beautiful composition. Listen! Go down and ask him what this instrument costs; but I won't kiss him again.'

'He wants a hundred kisses from the Princess,' said the lady-in-waiting who had gone down to ask him.

'I believe he is mad!' said the Princess, and she went on; but she had only gone a few steps when she stopped.

'One ought to encourage art,' she said, 'and I am the Emperor's daughter! Tell him he shall have, as before, ten kisses; the rest he can take from my ladies-in-waiting.'

'But we wouldn't at all like being kissed by him,' said the ladies-in-waiting.

'That's nonsense,' said the Princess. 'If I can kiss him, you can too. Besides, remember that I give you board and lodging.'

So the ladies-in-waiting had to go down to him again.

'A hundred kisses from the Princess,' said he, 'or each keeps his own.'

'Put yourself in front of us,' she said then; and so all the ladies-in-waiting put themselves in front, and he began to kiss the Princess.

'What can that commotion be by the pigsties?' said the Emperor, who was standing on the balcony. He rubbed his eyes and put on his spectacles. 'Why those are the ladies-in-waiting up to some of their games; I'd better go down to them.'

So he pulled up the back of his slippers, which were shoes that he had trodden down at heel. What a hurry he was in, to be sure!

As soon as he came into the yard he walked very softly, and the ladies-in-waiting were so busy counting the kisses and seeing fair play that they never noticed the Emperor. He stood on tiptoe.

'What's all this?' he said, when he saw the kissing; and then he struck them over the head with his slipper just as the swineherd was taking his eighty-sixth kiss.

'Be off with you!' said the Emperor, for he was very angry. And the Princess and the swineherd were driven out of his kingdom.

Then she stood still and wept while the swineherd was scolded, and the rain came streaming down.

'Oh, what a miserable creature I am!' sobbed the Princess. 'If only I had taken the beautiful Prince! Alas, how unhappy I am!'

And the swineherd went behind a tree, washed the black and brown off his face, threw away his old clothes, and then stepped forward in splendid dress, looking so handsome that the Princess felt obliged to curtsy.

'I have come to this,' he said. 'I despise you! You would have nothing to do with a noble prince; you did not appreciate the rose or the nightingale, but you could kiss the swineherd for the sake of a toy. Now you have your reward!' And he went into his kingdom and shut the door in her face, and she had to stay outside singing:

> 'Where's my Augustus dear?
> Alas! he's not here, here, here!'

To Your Good Health!

LONG, LONG ago there lived a king who was such a mighty monarch that whenever he sneezed everyone in the whole country had to say 'To your good health!' Everyone said it except the shepherd with the bright blue eyes, and he would not say it.

The King heard of this and was very angry, and sent for the shepherd to appear before him.

The shepherd came and stood before the throne, where the King sat looking very grand and powerful. But however grand or powerful he might be the shepherd did not feel a bit afraid of him.

'Say at once, "To my good health!"' cried the King.

'To my good health!' replied the shepherd.

'To mine – to *mine*, you rascal, you vagabond!' stormed the King.

'To mine, to *mine*, your Majesty,' was the answer.

'But to *mine* – to my own,' roared the King, and beat on his breast in a rage.

'Well, yes; to mine, of course, to my own,' cried the shepherd, and gently tapped his breast.

The King was beside himself with fury and did not know what to do, when the Lord Chamberlain interfered.

'Say at once – say this very moment, "To your health, your Majesty"; for if you don't say it you'll lose your life,' whispered he.

'No, I won't say it till I get the Princess for my wife,' was the shepherd's answer. Now the Princess was sitting on a little throne beside the King, her father, and she looked as sweet and lovely as a

322

little golden dove. When she heard what the shepherd said she could
not help laughing, for there is no denying the fact that this young
shepherd with the staring eyes pleased her very much; indeed he
pleased her better than any king's son she had yet seen.

But the King was not as pleasant as his daughter, and he gave
orders to throw the shepherd into the white bear's pit.

The guards led him away and thrust him into the pit with the
white bear, who had had nothing to eat for two days and was very
hungry. The door of the pit was hardly closed when the bear rushed
at the shepherd; but when it saw his eyes it was so frightened that it
was ready to eat itself. It shrank away into a corner and gazed at him
from there, and, in spite of being so famished, did not dare to touch
him, but sucked its own paws from sheer hunger. The shepherd felt
that if he once removed his eyes from the beast he was a dead man,
and in order to keep himself awake he made songs and sang them, and
so the night went by.

Next morning the Lord Chamberlain came to see the shepherd's
bones, and was amazed to find him alive and well. He led him to the
King, who fell into a furious passion, and said, 'Well, you have
learned what it is to be very near death, and *now* will you say "To
my good health"?'

But the shepherd answered, 'I am not afraid of ten deaths! I will
only say it if I may have the Princess for my wife.'

'Then go to your death,' cried the King; and ordered him to be
thrown into the den with the wild boars. The wild boars had not been
fed for a week, and when the shepherd was thrust into their den they
rushed at him to tear him to pieces. But the shepherd took a little
flute out of the sleeve of his jacket and began to play a merry tune,
on which the wild boars first of all shrank shyly away, and then got
up on their hind legs and danced gaily. The shepherd would have
given anything to be able to laugh, they looked so funny; but he
dared not stop playing, for he knew well enough that the moment he
stopped they would fall upon him and tear him to pieces. His eyes
were of no use to him here, for he could not have stared ten wild
boars in the face at once; so he kept on playing, and the wild boars
danced very slowly, as if in a minuet, then by degrees he played
faster and faster till they could hardly twist and turn quickly enough,

and ended by all falling over each other in a heap, quite exhausted and out of breath.

Then the shepherd ventured to laugh at last; and he laughed so long and so loud that when the Lord Chamberlain came early in the morning, expecting to find only his bones, the tears were still running down his cheeks from laughter.

As soon as the King was dressed the shepherd was again brought before him; but he was more angry than ever to think the wild boars had not torn the man to bits, so he said, 'Well, you have learned what it feels to be near ten deaths, *now* say "To my good health!"'

But the shepherd broke in with, 'I do not fear a hundred deaths, and I will only say it if I may have the Princess for my wife.'

'Then go to a hundred deaths!' roared the King and ordered the shepherd to be thrown down the deep vault of scythes.

The guards dragged him away to a dark dungeon, in the middle of which was a deep well with sharp scythes all round it. At the bottom of the well was a little light by which one could see if anyone was thrown in whether he had fallen to the bottom.

When the shepherd was dragged to the dungeons he begged the guards to leave him alone a little while that he might look down into the pit of scythes; perhaps he might after all make up his mind to say 'To your good health' to the King. So the guards left him alone and he stuck up his long stick near the well, hung his cloak round the stick and put his hat on the top. He also hung his knapsack up inside the cloak so that it might seem to have some body within it. When this was done he called out to the guards and said that he had considered the matter but after all he could not make up his mind to say what the King wished. The guards came in, threw the hat and cloak, knapsack and stick all down the well together, watched to see how they put out the light at the bottom and came away, thinking that now there really was an end of the shepherd. But he had hidden in a dark corner and was laughing to himself all the time.

Quite early next morning came the Lord Chamberlain carrying a lamp, and he nearly fell backwards with surprise when he saw the shepherd alive and well. He brought him to the King, whose fury was greater than ever, but who cried, 'Well, now you have been near a hundred deaths; will you say, "To your good health"?'

But the shepherd only gave the same answer, 'I won't say it till the Princess is my wife.'

'Perhaps after all you may do it for less,' said the King, who saw that there was no chance of making away with the shepherd; and he ordered the state coach to be got ready, then he made the shepherd get in with him and sit beside him, and ordered the coachman to drive to the silver wood. When they reached it he said, 'Do you see this silver wood? Well, if you will say, "To your good health", I will give it to you.'

The shepherd turned hot and cold by turns, but he still persisted, 'I will not say it till the Princess is my wife.'

The King was much vexed; he drove further on till they came to a splendid castle, all of gold, and then he said, 'Do you see this golden castle? Well, I will give you that too, the silver wood and the golden castle, if only you will say that one thing to me: "To your good health".'

The shepherd gaped and wondered and was quite dazzled, but he still said, 'No; I will *not* say it till I have the Princess for my wife.'

This time the King was overwhelmed with grief, and gave orders to drive on to the diamond pond, and there he tried once more.

'Do you see this diamond pond? I will give you that too, the silver wood and the golden castle and the diamond pond. You shall have them all – all – if you will but say, "To your good health!"'

The shepherd had to shut his staring eyes tight not to be dazzled with the brilliant pond, but still he said, 'No, no; I will not say it till I have the Princess for my wife.'

Then the King saw that all his efforts were useless, and that he might as well give in, so he said, 'Well, well, it's all the same to me – I will give you my daughter to wife; but, then, you really and truly must say to me, "To your good health".'

'Of course I'll say it; why should I not say it? It stands to reason that I shall say it then.'

At this the King was more delighted than anyone could have believed. He made it known all through the country that there were to be great rejoicings, as the Princess was going to be married. And everyone rejoiced to think that the Princess, who had refused so many royal suitors, should have ended by falling in love with the blue-eyed shepherd.

There was such a wedding as had never been seen. Everyone ate and drank and danced. Even the sick were feasted, and quite tiny new-born children had presents given them.

But the greatest merry-making was in the King's palace; there the best bands played and the best food was cooked; a crowd of people sat down to table, and all was fun and merrymaking.

And when the groomsman, according to custom, brought in the great boar's head on a big dish and placed it before the King so that he might carve it and give everyone a share, the savoury smell was so strong that the King began to sneeze with all his might.

'To your very good health,' cried the shepherd before anyone else, and the King was so delighted that he did not regret having given him his daughter.

In time, when the old King died, the shepherd succeeded him. He made a very good king and never expected his people to wish him well against their wills; but, all the same, everyone did wish him well, for they all loved him.

The Troll's Daughter

THERE WAS once a lad who went to look for a place. As he went along he met a man who asked him where he was going. He told him his errand, and the stranger said, 'Then you can serve me; I am just in want of a lad like you, and I will give you good wages – a bushel of money the first year, two the second year, and three the third year, for you must serve me three years, and obey me in everything, however strange it seems to you. You need not be afraid of taking service with me, for there is no danger in it if you only know how to obey.'

The bargain was made, and the lad went home with the man to whom he had engaged himself. It was a strange place indeed, for he lived in a bank in the middle of the wild forest, and the lad saw there no other person than his master. Now his master was a great troll, and had marvellous power over both men and beasts.

Next day the lad had to begin his service. The first thing that the troll set him to was to feed all the wild animals from the forest. These the troll had tied up, and there were wild birds, wolves and bears, deer and hares, which the troll had gathered into stalls in his stable down beneath the ground, and that stable was a mile long. The boy, however, accomplished all this work on that day, and the troll praised him and said that it was very well done.

Next morning the troll said to him, 'To-day the animals are not to be fed; they don't get the like of that every day. You have leave to play about for a little, until they are to be fed again.'

Then the troll spoke some words to him which he did not understand, and with that the lad turned into a hare, and ran out into the wood. He had plenty to run for, too, for all the hunters aimed at him, and tried to shoot him, and the dogs barked and ran after him wherever they got wind of him. He was the only animal that was left in the wood now, for the troll had tied up all the others, and every hunter in the whole country was eager to knock him over. But in this they met with no success; there was no dog that could overtake him, and no marksman that could hit him. They shot and shot at him, and he ran and ran. It was an unquiet life, but in the long run

327

he got used to it, when he saw that there was no danger in it, and it even amused him to befool all the hunters and dogs that were so eager after him.

Thus a whole year passed, and when it was over the troll called him home, for he was now in his power like all the other animals. The troll then spoke some words to him which he did not understand, and the hare immediately became a human being again. 'Well, how do you like serving me?' said the troll, 'and how do you like being a hare?'

The lad replied that he liked it very well; he had never been able to go over the ground so quickly before. The troll then showed him the bushel of money that he had already earned, and the lad was well pleased to serve him for another year.

The first day of the second year the boy had the same work to do as on the previous one – namely, to feed all the wild animals in the troll's stable. When he had done this the troll again spoke some words to him, and with that he became a raven, and flew high up into the air. This was delightful, the lad thought; he could go even faster now than when he was a hare, and the dogs could not come after him. This was a great delight to him, but he soon found out that he was not to be left quite at peace, for all the marksmen and hunters who saw him aimed at him and fired away, for they had no other birds to shoot at, as the troll had tied up all the others.

This, however, he also got used to, when he saw that they could never hit him, and in this way he flew about all that year, until the troll called him home again, spoke some strange words to him, and gave him his human shape again. 'Well, how did you like being a raven?' said the troll.

'I liked it very well,' said the lad, 'for never in all my days have I been able to rise so high.' The troll then showed him the two bushels of money which he had earned that year, and the lad was well content to remain in his service for another year.

Next day he got his old task of feeding all the wild beasts. When this was done the troll again spoke some words to him, and at these he turned into a fish, and sprang into the river. He swam up and he swam down, and thought it was pleasant to let himself drift with the stream. In this way he came right out into the sea, and swam further and further out. At last he came to a glass palace, which stood at the bottom of the sea. He could see into all the rooms and halls, where everything was very grand; all the furniture was of white ivory, inlaid with gold and pearl. There were soft rugs and cushions of all the colours of the rainbow, and beautiful carpets that looked like the finest moss, and flowers and trees with curiously crooked branches, both green and yellow, white and red, and there were also little fountains which sprang up from the most beautiful snail-shells, and fell into bright mussel-shells, and at the same time made a most delightful music, which filled the whole palace.

The most beautiful thing of all, however, was a young girl. She was all alone, and she went about from one room to another, but did not seem to be happy with all the grandeur she had about her. She walked in solitude and melancholy, and never even thought of looking at her own image in the polished glass walls that were on every side of her, although she was the prettiest creature anyone could wish to see. The lad thought so too while he swam round the palace and peeped in from every side.

'Here, indeed, it would be better to be a man than such a poor dumb fish as I am now,' said he to himself; 'if I could only remember the words that the troll says when he changes my shape, then perhaps I could help myself to become a man again.' He swam and he pondered and he thought over this until he remembered the sound of what the troll said, and then he tried to say it himself. In a moment he stood in human form at the bottom of the sea.

He made haste then to enter the glass palace, and went up to the young girl and spoke to her.

At first he nearly frightened the life out of her, but he talked to her so kindly and explained how he had come down there that she soon recovered from her alarm, and was very pleased to have some company to relieve the terrible solitude that she lived in. Time passed so quickly for both of them that the youth (for now he was quite a young man, and no more a lad) forgot altogether how long he had been there.

One day the girl said to him that now it was close on the time when he must become a fish again – the troll would soon call him home, and he would have to go, but before that he must put on the shape of the fish, otherwise he could not pass through the sea alive. Before this, while he was staying down there, she had told him that she was a daughter of the same troll whom the youth served, and he had shut her up there to keep her away from everyone. She had now devised a plan by which they could perhaps succeed in coming together again, and so spend the rest of their lives together. But there was much to attend to, and he must give careful heed to all that she told him.

She told him then that all the kings in the country round about were in debt to her father the troll, and the King of a certain kingdom was the first who had to pay, and if he could not do so at the time appointed he would lose his head. 'And he cannot pay,' said she; 'I know that for certain. Now you must, first of all, give up your service with my father; the three years are past, and you are at liberty to go. You will go off, with your six bushels of money, to the kingdom that I have told you of, and there enter the service of the King. When the time comes near for his debt to become due you will notice that he is ill at ease. You shall then say to him that you know well enough what it is that is weighing upon him – that it is the debt which he owes to the troll, and cannot pay, but that you can lend him the money. The amount is six bushels – just what you have. You shall, however, only lend this to him on condition that you may accompany him when he goes to make the payment, and run before him dressed as a fool. When you arrive at the troll's abode, you must perform all kinds of foolish tricks, and see that you break a whole lot of his windows, and do what other damage that you can.

'The troll will then get very angry, and as the King must answer for what his fool does he will sentence him, even although he has paid his debt, either to answer three questions or to lose his life. The first question the troll will ask will be, "Where is my daughter?" Then you shall step forward and answer, "She is at the bottom of the sea." He will then ask you whether you can recognise her, and to this you will answer "Yes". Then he will bring forward a whole troop of women, and cause them to pass before you, in order that you may pick out the one that you take for his daughter. You will not be able to recognise me at all, and therefore I will catch hold of you as I go past, and you must then make haste to catch me and hold me fast. You have then answered his first question.

'His next question will be, "Where is my heart?" You shall then step forward again and answer, "It is in a fish". "Do you know that fish?" he will say, and you will again answer "Yes". He will then cause all kinds of fish to come before you, for you to choose between them. I shall take good care to keep by your side, and when the right fish comes I will give you a little push, and with that you will seize the fish and cut it up. Then all will be over with the troll; he will ask no more questions, and we shall be free to wed.'

When the youth had got all these directions as to what he had to do when he got ashore again, the next thing was to remember the words which the troll said when he changed him from a human being to an animal; but these he had forgotten, and the girl did not know them either. He went about all day in despair, and thought and thought, but he could not remember what they sounded like. During the night he could not sleep, until towards morning he fell into a slumber, and all at once it flashed upon him what the troll used to say. He made haste to repeat the words, and at the same moment he became a fish again and slipped out into the sea. Immediately after this he was called back, and swam through the sea up the river to where the troll stood on the bank and restored him to human shape with the same words as before.

'Well, how do you like to be a fish?' asked the troll.

It was what he had liked best of all, said the youth, and that was no lie, as everybody can guess.

The troll then showed him the three bushels of money which he had earned during the past year; they stood beside the other three, and all six now belonged to him.

'Perhaps you will serve me for another year yet,' said the troll, 'and you will get six bushels of money for it; that makes twelve in all, and that is a pretty penny.'

'No,' said the youth; he thought he had done enough, and was anxious to go to some other place to serve, and learn other people's ways; but he would, perhaps, come back to the troll some other time.

The troll said that he would always be welcome; he had served him faithfully for the three years they had agreed upon, and he could make no objections to his leaving now.

The youth then got his six bushels of money, and with these he betook himself straight to the kingdom which his sweetheart had told him of. He buried his money in a lonely spot close to the King's palace, and then went in there and asked to be taken into service. He obtained his request, and was taken on as stableman, to tend the King's horses.

Some time passed, and he noticed how the King always went about sorrowing and grieving, and was never glad or happy. One day the King came into the stable, where there was no one present except the youth, who said straight out to him that, with his Majesty's permission, he wished to ask him why he was so sorrowful.

'It's of no use speaking about that,' said the King; 'for you cannot help me.'

'You don't know about that,' said the youth. 'I know well enough what it is that lies so heavy on your mind, and I know also of a plan to get the money paid.'

This was quite another case, and the King had more talk with the stableman, who said that he could easily lend the King the six bushels of money, but would only do it on condition that he should be allowed to accompany the King when he went to pay the debt, and that he should then be dressed like the King's court fool, and run before him. He would cause some trouble, for which the King would be severely spoken to, but he would answer for it that no harm would befall him.

The King gladly agreed to all that the youth proposed, and it was now high time for them to set out.

When they came to the troll's dwelling it was no longer in the bank, but on the top of this bank stood a large castle which the youth had never seen before. The troll could, in fact, make it visible or invisible, just as he pleased, and, knowing as much as he did of the troll's magic arts, the youth was not at all surprised at this.

When they came near to this castle, which looked as if it was of pure glass, the youth ran on in front as the King's fool. He ran sometimes facing forwards, sometimes backwards, stood sometimes on his head, and sometimes on his feet, and he broke so many of the troll's big glass windows and doors that it was something awful to see, and overturned everything he could, and made a fearful disturbance.

The troll came rushing out in anger and abused the King with all his might for bringing such a wretched fool with him, as he was sure that he could not pay the least bit of all the damage that had been done when he could not even pay off his old debt.

The fool, however, spoke up, and said that he could do so quite easily, and the King then came forward with the six bushels of money which the youth had lent him. They were measured and found to be correct. This the troll had not reckoned on, but he could make no objection. The old debt was honestly paid, and the King got his bond back again.

But there still remained all the damage that had been done that day, and the King had nothing with which to pay for this. The troll, therefore, sentenced the King either to answer three questions that he would put to him, or lose his head, as was agreed in the old bond.

There was nothing to be done but to try to answer the troll's riddles. The fool then stationed himself just by the King's side while the troll came forward with his questions. He first asked, 'Where is my daughter?'

The fool spoke up and said, 'She is at the bottom of the sea.'

'How do you know that?' said the troll.

'The little fish saw it,' said the fool.

'Would you know her?' said the troll.

'Yes, bring her forward,' said the fool.

The troll made a whole crowd of women go past them, one after the other, but all these were nothing but shadows and deceptions. Amongst the very last was the troll's real daughter, who pinched the fool as she went past him to make him aware of her presence. He thereupon caught her round the waist and held her fast, and the troll had to admit that his first riddle was solved.

Then the troll asked again, 'Where is my heart?'

'It is in a fish,' said the fool.

'Would you know that fish?' said the troll.

'Yes, bring it forward,' said the fool.

Then all the fishes came swimming past them, and meanwhile the troll's daughter stood just by the youth's side. When at last the right fish came swimming along she gave him a nudge, and he seized it at once, drove his knife into it, and split it up, took the heart out of it, and cut it through the middle.

At the same moment the troll fell dead and turned into pieces of flint. With that all the bonds that the troll had bound were broken; all the wild beasts and birds which he had caught and hid under the ground were free, and dispersed themselves in the woods and in the air.

The youth and his sweetheart entered the castle, which was now theirs, and held their wedding; and all the kings roundabout, who had been in the troll's debt, and were now out of it, came to the wedding, and saluted the youth as their emperor, and he ruled over them all, and kept peace between them, and lived in the castle with his beautiful empress in great joy and magnificence. And if they have not died since they are living there to this day.

The Twelve Brothers

THERE WERE once upon a time a king and a queen who lived happily together, and they had twelve children, all of whom were boys. One day the King said to his wife, 'If our thirteenth child is a girl, all her twelve brothers must die, so that she may be very rich and the kingdom hers alone.'

Then he ordered twelve coffins to be made, and filled them with shavings, and placed a little pillow in each. These he put away in an empty room, and, giving the key to his wife, he bade her tell no one of it.

The Queen grieved over the sad fate of her sons and refused to be comforted, so much so that the youngest boy, who was always with her, and whom she had christened Benjamin, said to her one day, 'Dear mother, why are you so sad?'

'My child,' she answered, 'I may not tell you the reason.'

But he left her no peace, till she went and unlocked the room and showed him the twelve coffins filled with shavings, and with the little pillow laid in each.

Then she said, 'My dearest Benjamin, your father has had these coffins made for you and your eleven brothers, because if I bring a girl into the world you are all to be killed and buried in them.'

She wept bitterly as she spoke, but her son comforted her and said, 'Don't cry, dear mother; we'll manage to escape somehow, and will fly for our lives.'

'Yes,' replied his mother, 'that is what you must do – go with your eleven brothers out into the wood, and let one of you always sit on the highest tree you can find, keeping watch on the tower of the castle. If I give birth to a little son I will wave a white flag, and then you may safely return; but if I give birth to a little daughter I will wave a red flag, which will warn you to flee as quickly as you can, and may kind Heaven have pity on you. Every night I will get up and pray for you, in winter that you may always have a fire to warm yourselves by, and in summer that you may not languish in the heat.'

Then she blessed her sons and they went off into the wood. They

335

found a very high oak tree, and there they sat, turn about, keeping their eyes always fixed on the castle tower. On the twelfth day, when the turn came to Benjamin, he saw a flag waving in the air, but alas! it was not white, but blood red, the warning which told that they were doomed to die. When the brothers heard this they were very angry, and said, 'Shall we forsooth suffer death for the sake of a wretched girl? Let us all swear vengeance, and vow that wherever and whenever we shall meet one of her sex, she shall die at our hands.'

Then they went their way deeper into the wood, and in the middle of it, where it was thickest and darkest, they came upon a little enchanted house which stood empty.

'Here,' they said, 'let us take up our abode, and you, Benjamin, you are the youngest and weakest, you shall stay at home and keep house for us; we others will go out and hunt for food.'

So they went forth into the wood, and shot hares and roe-deer, birds and wood-pigeons, and any other game they came across. They always brought their spoils home to Benjamin, who soon learned to make them into tasty dishes. So they lived for ten years in this little house, and the time slipped merrily away.

In the meantime their little sister at home was growing up. She was kind-hearted and of a fair countenance, and she had a gold star right in the middle of her forehead. One day a big washing was going on at the palace, and the girl looking down from her window saw twelve little shirts hanging up to dry, and asked her mother, 'Who in the world do these shirts belong to? Surely they are far too small for my father?'

And the Queen answered sadly, 'Dear child, they belong to your twelve brothers.'

'But where are my twelve brothers?' said the girl. 'I have never even heard of them.'

'Heaven alone knows in what part of the wide world they are wandering,' replied her mother.

Then she took the child and opened the locked-up room; she showed her the twelve coffins filled with shavings, and with the little pillow laid in each.

'These coffins,' she said, 'were intended for your brothers, but they stole secretly away before you were born.'

Then she proceeded to tell her all that had happened, and when she had finished her daughter said, 'Do not cry, dearest mother; I will go and seek for my brothers till I find them.'

So she took the twelve shirts and went out straight into the big wood. She walked all day long, and came in the evening to the little enchanted house. She stepped in and found a youth who, marvelling at her beauty, at the royal robes she wore, and at the golden star on her forehead, asked her where she came from and whither she was going.

'I am a princess,' she answered, 'and am seeking for my twelve brothers. I mean to wander as far as the blue sky stretches over the earth till I find them.'

Then she showed him the twelve shirts and Benjamin knew that it must be his sister, and said, 'I am Benjamin, your youngest brother.'

So they wept for joy, and kissed and hugged each other again and again. After a time Benjamin said, 'Dear sister, there is still a little difficulty, for we had all agreed that any girl we met should die at our hands, because it was for the sake of a girl that we had to leave our kingdom.'

'But,' she replied, 'I will gladly die if by that means I can restore my twelve brothers to their own.'

'No,' he answered, 'there is no need for that; only go and hide under that tub till our eleven brothers come in, and I'll soon make matters right with them.'

She did as she was bid, and soon the others came home from the chase and sat down to supper.

'Well, Benjamin, what's the news?' they asked.

But he replied, 'I like that; have you nothing to tell me?'

'No,' they answered.

Then he said, 'Well, now, you've been out in the wood all day and I've stayed quietly at home, and all the same I know more than you do.'

'Then tell us,' they cried.

But he answered, 'Only on condition that you promise faithfully that the first girl we meet shall not be killed.'

'She shall be spared,' they promised, 'only tell us the news.'

Then Benjamin said, 'Our sister is here!' and he lifted up the tub and the Princess stepped forward, with her royal robes and with the golden star on her forehead, looking so lovely and sweet and charming that they all loved her on the spot.

They arranged that she should stay at home with Benjamin and help him in the housework, while the rest of the brothers went out into the wood and shot hares and roe-deer, birds and wood-pigeons. And Benjamin and his sister cooked their meals for them. She gathered herbs to cook the vegetables in, fetched the wood, and watched the pots on the fire, and always when her eleven brothers returned she had their supper ready for them. Besides this, she kept the house in order, tidied all the rooms, and made herself so generally useful that her brothers were delighted, and they all lived happily together.

One day the two at home prepared a fine feast, and when they were all assembled they sat down and ate and drank and made merry.

Now there was a little garden round the enchanted house, in which grew twelve tall lilies. The girl, wishing to please her brothers, plucked the twelve flowers, meaning to present one to each of them as they sat at supper. But hardly had she plucked the flowers when her brothers were turned into twelve ravens, who flew croaking over the wood, and the house and garden vanished also.

So the poor girl found herself left all alone in the wood, and as she looked round her she noticed an old woman standing close beside her, who said, 'My child, what have you done? Why didn't you leave the flowers alone? They were your twelve brothers. Now they are changed for ever into ravens.'

The girl asked, sobbing, 'Is there no means of setting them free?'

'No,' said the old woman, 'there is only one way in the whole world to free them, and that is too difficult a task for you to perform, for you would have to be dumb for seven years, not speaking or laughing, and if you uttered a single word, though but an hour were wanting to the time, your silence would all have been in vain, and that one word would slay your brothers.'

Then the girl said to herself, 'If that is all I am quite sure I can free my brothers.' So she searched for a high tree, and when she had found one she climbed up it and spun all day long, never laughing or speaking one word.

Now it happened one day that a king was hunting in the wood. He was accompanied by a large greyhound, who ran sniffing to the tree on which the girl sat, and jumped round it, yelping and barking furiously. The King's attention was attracted, and when he looked up and beheld the beautiful Princess with the golden star on her forehead, he was so enchanted by her beauty that he asked her on the spot to be his wife. She gave no answer, but nodded slightly with her head. Then he climbed up the tree himself, lifted her down, put her on his horse and bore her home to his palace.

The marriage was celebrated with much pomp and ceremony, but the bride neither spoke nor laughed.

When they had lived for a few years happily together, the King's mother, who was a wicked old woman, began to slander the young Queen, and said to the King, 'She is only a low-born beggar maid that you have married; who knows what mischief she is up to? If she is deaf and can't speak, she might at least laugh; depend upon it, those who don't laugh have a bad conscience.'

At first the King paid no heed to her words, but the old woman harped so long on the subject, and accused the young Queen of so many bad things, that at last he let himself be talked over, and condemned his beautiful wife to death.

So a great fire was lit in the courtyard of the palace, where she was to be burnt, and the King watched the proceedings from an upper window, weeping bitterly the while, for he still loved his wife dearly. But just as she had been bound to the stake, and the flames were licking her garments with their red tongues, the very last moment of the seven years had come. Then a sudden rushing sound was heard in the air, and twelve ravens were seen flying overhead. They swooped downwards, and as soon as they touched the ground they turned into her twelve brothers, and she knew that she had freed them.

They quenched the flames and put out the fire, and, unbinding their dear sister from the stake, they kissed and hugged her again and again. And now that she was able to open her mouth and speak, she told the King why she had been dumb and not able to laugh.

The King rejoiced greatly when he heard she was innocent, and they all lived happily ever afterwards.

The Twelve Huntsmen

THERE WAS once a king's son who became betrothed to a princess whom he dearly loved. One day as he sat by her side feeling very happy, he received news that his father was lying at the point of death, and desired to see him before his end. So he said to his love, 'Alas! I must leave you, but take this ring and wear it as a remembrance of me, and when I am king I will return and fetch you home.'

Then he rode off, and when he reached his father he found him mortally ill and very near death.

The King said, 'Dearest son, I have desired to see you again before my end. Promise me, I beg of you, that you will marry according to my wishes;' and he then named the daughter of a neighbouring king who he was anxious should be his son's wife. The Prince was so overwhelmed with grief that he could think of nothing but his father, and exclaimed, 'Yes, yes, dear father, whatever you desire shall be done.' Thereupon the King closed his eyes and died.

After the Prince had been proclaimed king, and the usual time of mourning had elapsed, he felt that he must keep the promise he had made to his father, so he sent to ask for the hand of the King's daughter, which was granted to him at once.

Now, his first love heard of this, and the thought of her lover's desertion grieved her so sadly that she pined away and nearly died. Her father said to her, 'My dearest child, why are you so unhappy? If there is anything you wish for, say so, and you shall have it.'

His daughter reflected for a moment, and then said, 'Dear father, I wish for eleven girls as nearly as possible of the same height, age and appearance as myself.'

Said the King, 'If the thing is possible your wish shall be fulfilled;' and he had his kingdom searched till he found eleven maidens of the same height, size, and appearance as his daughter.

The Princess desired twelve complete huntsmen's suits to be made, all exactly alike, and the eleven maidens had to dress themselves in eleven of the suits, while she herself put on the twelfth. After this she took leave of her father, and rode off with her girls to the court of her former lover.

Here she inquired whether the King was in need of huntsmen, and if he would not take them all into his service. The King saw her but did not recognise her, and as he thought them fine-looking young men, he said, yes, he would gladly engage them all. So they became the twelve royal huntsmen.

Now, the King had a most remarkable lion, for it knew every hidden or secret thing.

One evening the lion said to the King, 'So you think you have got twelve huntsmen, do you?'

'Yes, certainly,' said the King, 'they *are* twelve huntsmen.'

'There you are mistaken,' said the lion; 'they are twelve maidens.'

'That is not possible,' replied the King; 'how can you prove it?'

'Just have some dried peas strewed over the floor of your ante-chamber,' said the lion, 'and you will soon see. Men have a strong, firm tread, so that if they happen to walk over peas not one will stir, but girls trip, and slip, and slide, so that the peas roll about.'

The King was pleased with the lion's advice, and ordered the peas to be strewn in his ante-room.

Fortunately one of the King's servants had become very attached to the young huntsmen, and hearing of the trial they were to be put to, he went to them and said, 'The lion wants to persuade the King that you are only girls;' and then told them all the plot.

The Princess thanked him for the hint, and after he was gone she said to her maidens, 'Now make every effort to tread firmly on the peas.'

Next morning, when the King sent for his twelve huntsmen, and they passed through the ante-room which was plentifully strewn with peas, they trod so firmly and walked with such a steady, strong step that not a single pea rolled away or even so much as stirred. After they were gone the King said to the lion, 'There now – you have been telling lies – you see yourself they walk like men.'

'Because they knew they were being put to the test,' answered the lion; 'and so they made an effort; but just have twelve spinning-wheels placed in the ante-room. When they pass through you'll see how pleased they will be, quite unlike any man.'

The King was pleased with the advice, and desired twelve spinning-wheels to be placed in his ante-chamber.

But the good-natured servant went to the huntsmen and told them all about this fresh plot. Then, as soon as the Princess was alone with her maidens, she exclaimed, 'Now, pray make a great effort and don't even *look* at those spinning-wheels.'

When the King sent for his twelve huntsmen next morning they walked through the ante-room without even casting a glance at the spinning-wheels.

Then the King said once more to the lion, 'You have deceived me again; they *are* men, for they never once looked at the spinning-wheels.'

The lion replied, 'They knew they were being tried, and they did violence to their feelings.' But the King declined to believe in the lion any longer.

So the twelve huntsmen continued to follow the King, and he grew daily fonder of them. One day whilst they were all out hunting, it so happened that news was brought that the King's intended bride was on her way and might soon be expected. When the true bride heard of this she felt as though a knife had pierced her heart, and she fell fainting to the ground. The King, fearing something had happened to his dear huntsman, ran up to help, and began drawing off his gloves. Then he saw the ring which he had given to his first love, and as he gazed into her face he knew her again, and his heart was so touched that he kissed her, and as she opened her eyes, he cried, 'I am thine and thou art mine, and no power on earth can alter that.'

To the other Princess he despatched a messenger to beg her to return to her own kingdom with all speed. 'For,' said he, 'I have got a wife, and he who finds an old key again does not require a new one.'

Thereupon the wedding was celebrated with great pomp, and the lion was restored to the royal favour, for after all he had told the truth.

Wali Dad the Simple-Hearted

ONCE UPON a time there lived a poor old man whose name was Wali Dad Gunjay, or Wali Dad the Bald. He had no relations, but lived all by himself in a little mud hut some distance from any town, and made his living by cutting grass in the jungle, and selling it as fodder for horses. He only earned by this five halfpence a day; but he was a simple old man, and needed so little out of it, that he saved up one halfpenny daily, and spent the rest upon such food and clothing as he required.

In this way he lived for many years until, one night, he thought that he would count the money he had hidden away in the great earthen pot under the floor of his hut. So he set to work, and with much trouble he pulled the bag out on to the floor, and sat gazing in astonishment at the heap of coins which tumbled out of it. What should he do with them all? he wondered. But he never thought of spending the money on himself, because he was content to pass the rest of his days as he had been doing for ever so long, and he really had no desire for any greater comfort or luxury.

At last he threw all the money into an old sack, which he pushed under his bed, and then, rolled in his ragged old blanket, he went off to sleep.

Early next morning he staggered off with his sack of money to the shop of a jeweller, whom he knew in the town, and bargained with him for a beautiful little gold bracelet. With this carefully wrapped up in his cotton waistband he went to the house of a rich friend, who was a travelling merchant, and used to wander about with his camels and merchandise through many countries. Wali Dad was lucky enough to find him at home, so he sat down, and after a little talk he asked the merchant who was the most virtuous and beautiful lady he had ever met with. The merchant replied that the Princess of Khaistan was renowned everywhere as well for the beauty of her person as for the kindness and generosity of her disposition.

'Then,' said Wali Dad, 'next time you go that way, give her this little bracelet, with the respectful compliments of one who admires virtue far more than he desires wealth.'

With that he pulled the bracelet from his waistband, and handed it to his friend. The merchant was naturally much astonished, but said nothing, and made no objection to carrying out his friend's plan.

Time passed by, and at length the merchant arrived in the course of his travels at the capital of Khaistan. As soon as he had opportunity he presented himself at the palace, and sent in the bracelet, neatly packed in a little perfumed box provided by himself, giving at the same time the message entrusted to him by Wali Dad.

The Princess could not think who could have bestowed this present on her, but she bade her servant to tell the merchant that if he would return, after he had finished his business in the city, she would give him her reply. In a few days, therefore, the merchant came back, and received from the Princess a return present in the shape of a camel-load of rich silks, besides a present of money for himself. With these he set out on his journey.

Some months later when he got home again he proceeded to take Wali Dad the Princess's present. Great was the perplexity of the good man to find a camel-load of silks tumbled at his door! What was he to do with these costly things ? But, presently, after much thought, he begged the merchant to consider whether he did not know of some young prince to whom such treasures might be useful.

'Of course,' cried the merchant, greatly amused; 'from Delhi to Baghdad, and from Constantinople to Lucknow, I know them all; and there lives none worthier than the gallant and wealthy young Prince of Nekabad.'

'Very well, then, take the silks to him, with the blessing of an old man,' said Wali Dad, much relieved to be rid of them.

So, the next time that the merchant journeyed that way he carried the silks with him, and in due course arrived at Nekabad, and sought an audience of the Prince. When he was shown into his presence he produced the beautiful gift of silks that Wali Dad had sent, and begged the young man to accept them as a humble tribute to his worth and greatness. The Prince was much touched by the generosity of the giver, and ordered, as a return present, twelve of the finest breed of horses for which his country was famous to be delivered over to the merchant, to whom also, before he took his leave, he gave a munificent reward for his services.

As before, the merchant at last arrived at home; and next day, he set out for Wali Dad's house with the twelve horses. When the old man saw them coming in the distance he said to himself, 'Here's luck! A troop of horses coming! They are sure to want quantities of grass, and I shall sell all I have without having to drag it to market.' Thereupon he rushed off and cut grass as fast as he could. When he got back, with as much grass as he could possibly carry, he was greatly discomfited to find that the horses were all for himself. At first he could not think what to do with them, but, after a little, a brilliant idea struck him! He gave two to the merchant, and begged him to take the rest to the Princess of Khaistan, who was clearly the fittest person to possess such beautiful animals.

The merchant departed, laughing. But, true to his old friend's request, he took the horses with him on his next journey, and eventually presented them safely to the Princess. This time the Princess sent for the merchant, and questioned him about the giver. Now, the merchant was usually a most honest man, but he did not quite like to describe Wali Dad in his true light as an old man whose income was five halfpence a day, and who had hardly clothes to cover him. So he told her that his friend had heard stories of her beauty and goodness, and had longed to lay the best he had at her feet. The Princess then took her father into her confidence, and begged him to advise her what courtesy she might return to one who persisted in making her such presents.

'Well,' said the King, 'you cannot refuse them; so the best thing you can do is to send this unknown friend at once a present so magnificent that he is not likely to be able to send you anything better, and so will be ashamed to send anything at all!' Then he ordered that, in place of each of the ten horses, two mules laden with silver should be returned by her.

Thus, in a few hours, the merchant found himself in charge of a splendid caravan; and he had to hire a number of armed men to defend it on the road against robbers, and he was glad indeed to find himself back again in Wali Dad's hut.

'Well, now,' cried Wali Dad, as he viewed all the wealth laid at his door, 'I can well repay that kind prince for his magnificent present of horses; but to be sure you have been put to great expense! Still, if you will accept six mules and their loads, and will take the rest straight to Nekabad, I shall thank you heartily.'

The merchant felt handsomely repaid for his trouble, and wondered greatly how the matter would turn out. So he made no difficulty about it; and as soon as he could get things ready, he set out for Nekabad with this new and princely gift.

This time the Prince, too, was embarrassed, and questioned the merchant closely. The merchant felt that his credit was at stake, and whilst inwardly determining that he would not carry the joke any further, could not help describing Wali Dad in such glowing terms that the old man would never have known himself had he heard them. The Prince, like the King of Khaistan, determined that he would send in return a gift that would be truly royal, and which would perhaps prevent the unknown giver sending him anything more. So he made up a caravan of twenty splendid horses caparisoned in gold embroidered cloths, with fine morocco saddles and silver bridles and stirrups, also twenty camels of the best breed, which had the speed of race-horses, and could swing along at a trot all day without getting tired; and, lastly, twenty elephants, with magnificent silver howdahs and coverings of silk embroidered with pearls. To take care of these animals the merchant hired a little army of men; and the troop made a great show as they travelled along.

When Wali Dad from a distance saw the cloud of dust which the caravan made, and the glitter of its appointments, he said to himself, 'By Allah! here's a grand crowd coming! Elephants, too! Grass will be selling well to-day!' And with that he hurried off to the jungle and cut grass as fast as he could. As soon as he got back he found the caravan had stopped at his door, and the merchant was waiting, a little anxiously, to tell him the news and to congratulate him upon his riches.

'Riches!' cried Wali Dad. 'What has an old man like me with one foot in the grave to do with riches? That beautiful young Princess, now! She'd be the one to enjoy all these fine things! Do you take for yourself two horses, two camels, and two elephants, with all their trappings, and present the rest to her.'

The merchant at first objected to this, and pointed out to Wali Dad that he was beginning to feel these embassies a little awkward. Of course he was himself richly repaid, so far as expenses went; but still he did not like going so often, and he was getting nervous. At length, however, he consented to go once more, but he promised himself never to embark on another such enterprise.

So, after a few days' rest, the caravan started off once more for Khaistan.

The moment the King of Khaistan saw the gorgeous train of men and beasts entering his palace courtyard, he was so amazed that he hurried down in person to inquire about it, and became dumb when he heard that these also were a present from the princely Wali Dad, and were for the Princess, his daughter. He went hastily off to her apartments, and said to her, 'I tell you what it is, my dear, this man wants to marry you; that is the meaning of all these presents! There is nothing for it but that we go and pay him a visit in person. He must be a man of immense wealth, and as he is so devoted to you, perhaps you might do worse than marry him!'

The Princess agreed with all that her father said, and orders were issued for vast numbers of elephants and camels, and gorgeous tents

and flags, and litters for the ladies, and horses for the men, to be
prepared without delay, as the King and Princess were going to pay
a visit to the great and munificent Prince Wali Dad. The merchant,
the King declared, was to guide the party.

The feelings of the poor merchant in this sore dilemma can hardly
be imagined. Willingly would he have run away, but he was treated
with so much hospitality as Wali Dad's representative, that he was
hardly alone for an instant, and had no opportunity of slipping
away. In fact, after a few days, despair possessed him to such a degree
that he made up his mind that all that happened was fate, and that
escape was impossible; but he hoped devoutly some turn of fortune
would reveal to him a way out of the difficulties which he had, with
the best of intentions, drawn upon himself.

On the seventh day they all started, amidst thunderous salutes
from the ramparts of the city, and much dust, and cheering, and
blaring of trumpets.

Day after day they moved on, and every day the poor merchant
felt more ill and miserable. He wondered what kind of death the
King would invent for him, and went through almost as much torture,
as he lay awake nearly the whole of every night thinking over the
situation, as he would have suffered if the King's executioners were
already setting to work upon his neck.

At last they were only one day's march from Wali Dad's little
mud home. Here a great encampment was made, and the merchant
was sent on to tell Wali Dad that the King and Princess of Khaistan
had arrived and were seeking an interview. When the merchant
arrived he found the poor old man eating his evening meal of onions
and dry bread, and when he told him of all that had happened he
had not the heart to proceed to load him with the reproaches which
rose to his tongue. For Wali Dad was overwhelmed with grief and
shame for himself, for his friend, and for the name and honour of
the Princess; and he wept and plucked at his beard, and groaned
most piteously. With tears he begged the merchant to detain them for
one day by any kind of excuse he could think of, and to come in the
morning to discuss what they should do.

As soon as the merchant was gone Wali Dad made up his mind that
there was only one honourable way out of the shame and distress that

he had created by his foolishness, and that was – to kill himself. So, without stopping to ask anyone's advice, he went off in the middle of the night to a place where the river wound along at the base of steep rocky cliffs of great height, and determined to throw himself down and put an end to his life. When he got to the place he drew back a few paces, took a little run, and at the very edge of that dreadful black gulf he stopped short! He *could* not do it!

From below, unseen in the blackness of the deep night shadows, the water roared and boiled round the jagged rocks – he could picture the place as he knew it, only ten times more pitiless and forbidding in the visionless darkness; the wind soughed through the gorge with fearsome sighs, and rustlings and whisperings, and the bushes and grasses that grew in the ledges of the cliffs seemed to him like living creatures that danced and beckoned, shadowy and indistinct. An owl laughed 'Hoo! hoo!' almost in his face, as he peered over the edge of the gulf, and the old man threw himself back in a perspiration of horror. He was afraid! He drew back shuddering, and covering his face in his hands he wept aloud.

Presently he was aware of a gentle radiance that shed itself before him. Surely morning was not already coming to hasten and reveal his disgrace! He took his hands from before his face, and saw before him two lovely beings whom his instinct told him were not mortal, but were peris from Paradise.

'Why do you weep, old man?' said one, in a voice as clear and musical as that of the bulbul.

'I weep for shame,' replied he.

'What do you here?' questioned the other.

'I came here to die,' said Wali Dad. And as they questioned him, he confessed all his story.

Then the first stepped forward and laid a hand upon his shoulder, and Wali Dad began to feel that something strange – what, he did not know – was happening to him. His old cotton rags of clothes were changed to beautiful linen and embroidered cloth; on his hard, bare feet were warm, soft shoes, and on his head a great jewelled turban. Round his neck there lay a heavy golden chain, and the little old bent sickle, which he cut grass with, and which hung in his waistband, had turned into a gorgeous scimitar, whose ivory hilt gleamed in the pale light like snow in moonlight. As he stood wondering, like a man in a dream, the other peri waved her hand and bade him turn and see; and, lo! before him a noble gateway stood open. And up an avenue of giant plane trees the peris led him, dumb with amazement. At the end of the avenue, on the very spot where his hut had stood, a gorgeous palace appeared, ablaze with myriads of lights. Its great porticoes and verandahs were occupied by hurrying servants, and guards paced to and fro and saluted him respectfully as he drew near, along mossy walks and through sweeping grassy lawns where fountains were playing and flowers scented the air. Wali Dad stood stunned and helpless.

'Fear not,' said one of the peris; 'go to your house, and learn that God rewards the simple-hearted.'

With these words they both disappeared and left him. He walked on, thinking still that he must be dreaming. Very soon he retired to rest in a splendid room, far grander than anything he had ever dreamed of.

When morning dawned he woke, and found that the palace, and himself, and his servants were all real, and that he was not dreaming after all!

If he was dumbfounded, the merchant, who was ushered into his presence soon after sunrise, was much more so. He told Wali Dad that he had not slept all night, and by the first streak of daylight had started to seek out his friend. And what a search he had had! A great stretch of wild jungle country had, in the night, been changed into parks and gardens; and if it had not been for some of Wali Dad's new servants, who found him and brought him to the palace, he would have fled away under the impression that his trouble had sent him crazy, and that all he saw was only imagination.

Then Wali Dad told the merchant all that had happened. By his advice he sent an invitation to the King and Princess of Khaistan to come and be his guests, together with all their retinue and servants, down to the very humblest in the camp.

For three nights and days a great feast was held in honour of the royal guests. Every evening the King and his nobles were served on golden plates and from golden cups; and the smaller people on silver plates and from silver cups; and each evening each guest was requested to keep the plates and cups that they had used as a remembrance of the occasion. Never had anything so splendid been seen. Besides the great dinners, there were sports and hunting, and dances, and amusements of all sorts.

On the fourth day the King of Khaistan took his host aside, and asked him whether it was true, as he had suspected, that he wished to marry his daughter. But Wali Dad, after thanking him very much for the compliment, said that he had never dreamed of so great an honour, and that he was far too old and ugly for so fair a lady; but he begged the King to stay with him until he could send for the Prince of Nekabad, who was a most excellent, brave, and honourable young man, and would surely be delighted to try to win the hand of the beautiful Princess.

To this the King agreed, and Wali Dad sent the merchant to Nekabad, with a number of attendants, and with such handsome presents that the Prince came at once. He fell head over ears in love with the Princess, and married her at Wali Dad's palace amidst a fresh outburst of rejoicings.

And now the King of Khaistan and the Prince and Princess of Nekabad each went back to their own country; and Wali Dad lived to a good old age, befriending all who were in trouble, and preserving, in his prosperity, the simple-hearted and generous nature that he had when he was only Wali Dad Gunjay, the grass-cutter.

The Wounded Lion

THERE WAS once a girl so poor that she had nothing to live on, and wandered about the world asking for charity. One day she arrived at a thatched cottage, and inquired if they could give her any work. The farmer said he wanted a cowherd, as his own had left him, and if the girl liked the place she might take it. So she became a cowherd.

One morning she was driving her cows through the meadows when she heard near by a loud groan that sounded almost human. She hastened to the spot from which the noise came, and found it proceeded from a lion who lay stretched upon the ground.

You can guess how frightened she was! But the lion seemed in such pain that she was sorry for him, and drew nearer and nearer till she saw he had a large thorn in one foot. She pulled out the thorn and bound up the place, and the lion was grateful, and licked her hand by way of thanks with his big rough tongue.

When the girl had finished she went back to find the cows, but they had gone, and though she hunted everywhere she never found them; and she had to return home and confess to her master, who scolded her harshly, and afterwards beat her. Then he said, 'Now you will have to look after the asses.'

So every day she had to take the asses to the woods to feed, until one morning, exactly a year after she had found the lion, she heard a groan which sounded quite human. She went straight to the place from which the noise came, and, to her great surprise, beheld the same lion stretched on the ground with a deep wound across his face.

This time she was not afraid at all, and ran towards him, washing the wound and laying soothing herbs upon it; and when she had bound it up the lion thanked her in the same manner as before.

After that she returned to her flock, but they were nowhere to be seen. She searched here and she searched there, but they had vanished completely!

Then she had to go home and confess to her master, who first scolded her and afterwards beat her. 'Now go,' he said, 'and look after the pigs!'

So the next day she took out the pigs, and found them such good feeding grounds that they grew fatter every day.

Another year passed by, and one morning when the maiden was out with her pigs she heard a groan which sounded quite human. She ran to see what it was, and found her old friend the lion, wounded through and through, fast dying under a tree.

She fell on her knees before him and washed his wounds one by one, and laid healing herbs upon them. And the lion licked her hands and thanked her, and asked if she would not stay and sit by him. But the girl said she had her pigs to watch, and she must go and see after them.

So she ran to the place where she had left them, but they had vanished as if the earth had swallowed them up. She whistled and called, but only the birds answered her.

Then she sank down on the ground and wept bitterly, not daring to return home until some hours had passed away.

And when she had had her cry out she got up and searched all up and down the wood. But it was no use; there was not a sign of the pigs.

At last she thought that perhaps if she climbed a tree she might see further. But no sooner was she seated on the highest branch than something happened which put the pigs quite out of her head. This was a handsome young man who was coming down the path; and when he had almost reached the tree he pulled aside a rock and disappeared behind it.

The maiden rubbed her eyes and wondered if she had been dreaming. Next she thought, 'I will not stir from here till I see him come out, and discover who he is.' Accordingly she waited, and at dawn the next morning the rock moved to one side and a lion came out.

When he had gone quite out of sight the girl climbed down from the tree and went to the rock, which she pushed aside, and entered the opening before her. The path led to a beautiful house. She went in, swept and dusted the furniture, and put everything tidy. Then she ate a very good dinner, which was on a shelf in the corner, and once more clambered up to the top of her tree.

As the sun set she saw the same young man walking gaily down the path, and, as before, he pushed aside the rock and disappeared behind it.

Next morning out came the lion. He looked sharply about him on all sides, but saw no one, and then vanished into the forest.

The maiden then came down from the tree and did exactly as she had done the day before. Thus three days went by, and every day she went and tidied up the house. At length, when the girl found she was no nearer to discovering the secret, she resolved to ask the young man, and in the evening when she caught sight of him coming through the wood she came down from the tree and begged him to tell her his name.

The young man looked very pleased to see her, and said he thought it must be she who had secretly kept his house for so many days. And he added that he was a prince enchanted by a powerful giant, but was only allowed to take his own shape at night, for all day he was forced to appear as the lion whom she had so often helped; and, more than this, it was the giant who had stolen the oxen and the asses and the pigs in revenge for her kindness.

And the girl asked him, 'What can I do to disenchant you?'

But he said he was afraid it was very difficult, because the only way was to get a lock of hair from the head of a king's daughter, to spin it, and to make from it a cloak for the giant, who lived up on the top of a high mountain.

'Very well,' answered the girl, 'I will go to the city and knock at the door of the King's palace, and ask the Princess to take me as a servant.'

So they parted, and when she arrived at the city she walked about the streets crying, 'Who will hire me for a servant? Who will hire me for a servant?' But, though many people liked her looks, for she was clean and neat, the maiden would listen to none, and still continued crying, 'Who will hire me for a servant? Who will hire me for a servant?'

At last there came the waiting-maid of the Princess.

'What can you do?' she said; and the girl was forced to confess that she could do very little.

'Then you will have to do scullion's work, and wash up dishes,' said she; and they went straight back to the palace.

Then the maiden dressed her hair afresh, and made herself look very neat and smart, and everyone admired and praised her, till by and by it came to the ears of the Princess. And she sent for the girl, and when she saw her, and how beautifully she had dressed her hair, the Princess told her she was to come and comb out hers.

Now the hair of the Princess was very thick and long, and shone like the sun. And the girl combed it and combed it till it was brighter than ever. And the Princess was pleased, and bade her come every day and comb her hair, till at length the girl took courage, and begged leave to cut off one of the long, thick locks.

The Princess, who was very proud of her hair, did not like the idea of parting with any of it, so she said no. But the girl could not give up hope, and each day she entreated to be allowed to cut off just one tress. At length the Princess lost patience, and exclaimed, 'You may have it, then, on condition that you shall find the handsomest prince in the world to be my bridegroom!'

And the girl answered that she would, and cut off the lock, and wove it into a coat that glittered like silk, and brought it to the young man, who told her to carry it straight to the giant. But that she must be careful to cry out a long way off what she had with her, or else he would spring upon her and run her through with his sword.

So the maiden departed and climbed up the mountain, but before she reached the top the giant heard her footsteps, and rushed out breathing fire and flame, having a sword in one hand and a club in the other. But she cried loudly that she had brought him the coat, and then he grew quiet, and invited her to come into his house.

He tried on the coat, but it was too short, and he threw it off, and declared it was no use. And the girl picked it up sadly, and returned quite in despair to the King's palace.

The next morning, when she was combing the Princess's hair, she begged leave to cut off another lock. At first the Princess said no, but the girl begged so hard that at length she gave in on condition that she should find her a prince as bridegroom.

The maiden told her that she had already found him, and spun the lock into shining stuff, and fastened it on to the end of the coat. And when it was finished she carried it to the giant.

This time it fitted him, and he was quite pleased, and asked her what he could give her in return. And she said that the only reward he could give her was to take the spell off the lion and bring him back to his own shape.

For a long time the giant would not hear of it, but in the end he gave in, and told her exactly how it must all be done. She was to kill the lion herself and cut him up very small; then she must burn him, and cast his ashes into the water, and out of the water the Prince would come free from enchantment for ever.

But the maiden went away weeping, lest the giant should have deceived her, and that after she had killed the lion she would find she had also slain the Prince.

Weeping she came down the mountain, and weeping she joined the Prince, who was awaiting her at the bottom; and when he had heard her story he comforted her, and bade her be of good courage, and to do the bidding of the giant.

And the maiden believed what the Prince told her; and in the morning when he put on his lion's form she took a knife and slew him, and cut him up very small, and burnt him, and cast his ashes into the water, and out of the water came the Prince, beautiful as the day, and as welcome as the sun himself.

Then the young man thanked the maiden for all she had done for him, and said she should be his wife and none other. But the maiden only wept sore, and answered that she could never be, for she had given her promise to the Princess when she cut off her hair that the Prince should wed her and her only.

But the Prince replied, 'If it is the Princess, we must go quickly. Come with me.'

So they went together to the King's palace. And when the King and Queen and Princess saw the young man a great joy filled their hearts, for they knew him for the eldest son, who had long ago been enchanted by a giant and lost to them.

And he asked his parents' consent that he might marry the girl who had saved him, and a great feast was made, and the maiden became a princess, and in due time a queen, and she richly deserved all the honours showered upon her.

THE END

About this book and its origins

The stories in this book come from the original editions of the fairy-tale collections edited by Andrew Lang (1844–1912) and published during the years 1889 to 1910. There were twelve books in all, named and bound according to colour; *The Blue Fairy Book* was the first and *The Lilac Fairy Book* the last.

In 1889, the year *The Blue Fairy Book* appeared, Lang was an active and respected member of London's literary circle; he was recognised as poet, critic and essayist, and known as the translator (with Butcher, Leaf and Myers) of the *Odyssey of Homer* and the *Iliad of Homer*. His life-long interest in anthropology was also widely known for he had written articles on various aspects of folklore and his important two-volume work, *Myth, Ritual and Religion*, had been published in 1887.

Although Lang had written three original fairy stories for children, what prompted him to make *The Blue Fairy Book* we shall now probably never know. It is clear, however, both from the selection of stories in this volume (it is more of a mixture than the later books) and from his own forewords to *The Red Fairy Book* and *The Green Fairy Book* that a succession of fairy-tale books had not been planned (even if the initial undertaking with his publishers had been for some kind of series for the young). *The Blue Poetry Book* followed the second volume of fairy tales and *The True Story Book* was published in 1893, a year after *The Green Fairy Book*, which Lang said was 'the third, and probably the last, of the Fairy Books of many colours.'

It would seem, then, that most of the twelve were issued to satisfy public demand. Lang, of course, was well equipped for this work – his own knowledge of fairy tales and folklore must have been unique. But it was not as the professional anthropologist nor as a literary man that he approached his work for children – he says that *The Blue Fairy Book* was 'made for the pleasure of children and without scientific purpose' – but rather as the boy he had been in Scotland, who had listened to old stories of local tradition told aloud, and who read avidly from an early age all the fairy tales he could find. What Lang heard and read as a little boy he never forgot. In maturity when reviewing some Japanese 'bogie books' in *Books and Bookmen* he wrote: 'Perhaps even Nelson would have found out "what fear was" or the lad in the Norse tale would have "learned to shiver" if he'd been left alone to peruse *Jane Eyre* and "The Black Cat" and "The Fall of the House of Usher" ... Between these and "The Yellow Dwarf" I personally had as bad a time of it in the night watches as any happy British child has survived.' It was to the children's great good fortune that he could still see fairy tales with the 'eye of a child' and his only stipulation was that all should be good stories.

But by 1894 an annual collection for children must have been an accepted undertaking, and Lang produced a book every year for the rest of his life. The fairy books came at irregular intervals interspersed with varied collections from literature and history and there were twenty-five in all. In this undertaking Lang depended on a band of helpers. Mrs Lang was the chief of these – frequently in prefaces to the fairy books occur the words '... stories have been adapted or translated by Mrs Lang,' and several young ladies are also mentioned by name as translators.

Lang's fame as editor of the 'colour' fairy books was widespread even in his lifetime. More than this, he was even supposed by many to have 'made up' the stories – a charge he had constantly to deny. In *The Orange Fairy Book* (1906) he said, 'These Fairy Books are not written by the Editor, as he has often explained, "out of his own head".' And still later, in the last book, he is reiterating, 'I find out where the stories are, and advise, and, in short, superintend. *I do not write the stories out of my own head*. The reputation of having written all the Fairy Books ... is "the burden of an honour unto which I was not born".'

Lang kept his enthusiasm for 'good stories only' throughout the whole of the series, and retained what might be called the amateur's point of view. The scholar never obtrudes on the children's book editor – Lang could even be accused of casualness, for he does not appear always to have been particular about what version was used, nor is he consistent about giving the sources of the stories and the names of the translators.

There are great differences in style; many of the stories could hardly be improved, and have not been improved in more recent collections, but some, as for example those of Hans Andersen (always a difficult subject for the English translator), Asbjornsen and some of Grimm, are ragged. In such instances in this book I have not attempted to re-write but I have tried to make the narrative less rough. Some stories which should be in any collection labelled 'favourite' I have not included because the version used by Lang is not as good as that now available elsewhere, and regretfully I have left out some fine Scottish folk tales because the dialect is difficult to read, and all of Perrault because these – given by Lang in the first English translation – seemed too dated to combine well with the rest.

It is not surprising that there should be this unevenness in style when one remembers the speed with which the books were published, the great variety of sources and the number of stories included. Each book contained well over thirty stories, and they came from all over the world. Even these *Fifty Favourite Fairy Tales*, although not chosen to emphasise the point, give some indication of how widely Lang ranged in his choice. Leaving out the more familiar stories from Grimm and elsewhere, we find 'Wali Dad' from India, 'Stan Bolovan' from Rumania, 'Jesper who herded the Hares' from Scandinavia, 'The Boy who found Fear at last' from Turkey, 'He wins who waits' from Armenia, 'The Stone-Cutter' from Japan, 'Drakestail' from France and 'Shepherd Paul' from Hungary.

When one considers the whole of Lang's output for children, which includes, as well as the twelve fairy books, *The Book of Romance*, *The Arabian Nights* and *Tales of Troy and Greece* as well as volumes of stories from legend and history, it is clearly seen what a valuable 'library' he provided and in particular what a world of imaginative literature he revealed to the children of his day. The recently re-designed Fairy Books and the present revival of his re-tellings from Homer are evidence that Lang's influence and the debt owing to him by children have extended long past his own time.

This selection of *Fifty Favourite Fairy Tales* is a tribute from two of Lang's 'children' to whom his books spelt enchantment, and from Margery Gill, who in sharing the stories with her young daughter has rediscovered their magic fifty years after Lang's death.

December 1962   KATHLEEN LINES